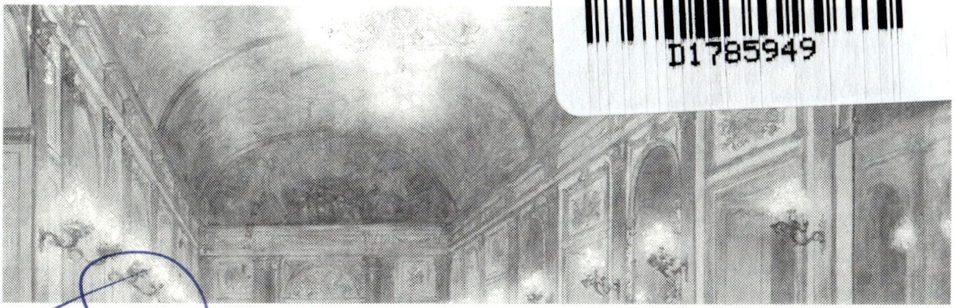

To Diana,

Forever Gentleman

May you remain forever happy, healthy & young at heart.

ROLAND COLTON

Roland Colton

ANAPHORA LITERARY PRESS

AUGUSTA, GEORGIA

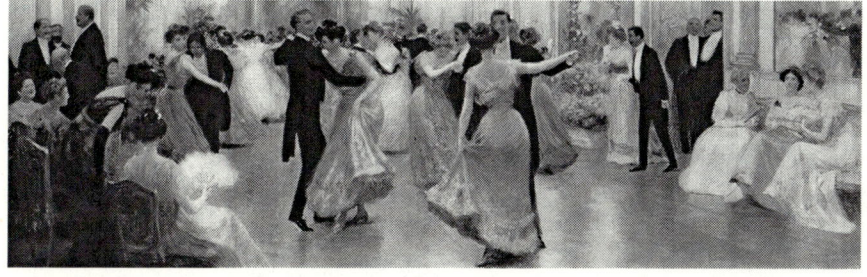

Anaphora Literary Press
2419 Southdale Drive
Hephzibah, GA 30815
http://anaphoraliterary.com

Book design by Anna Faktorovich, Ph.D.

Copyright © 2016 by Roland Colton

All rights reserved. No part of this book may be reproduced in any form or by any electronic or mechanical means, including information storage and retrieval systems, without permission in writing from Roland Colton. Writers are welcome to quote brief passages in their critical studies, as American copyright law dictates.

Printed in the United States of America, United Kingdom and in Australia on acid-free paper.

Images: "Homeless" by Thomas Kennington, 1890, oil on canvas, 166.6×151.7 cm. Bendigo Art Gallery.
"Scène de Bal" by Victor Gabriel Gilbert. The Athenaeum.
"London Innere Stadt" or "London Inner City" by Joseph Meyer. Leipzig, Bibilographisches.
Back Cover: "1867 Steinway Grand Piano" used with Permission from: Mark Slotkin, Antiquarian Traders, Los Angeles, California, Antiquariantraders.com.

Edited by: Erin Willard.

Published in 2016 by Anaphora Literary Press

Forever Gentleman
Roland Colton—1st edition.

Library of Congress Control Number: 2016900567

Library Cataloging Information
Colton, Roland, 1951-, author.
　Forever gentleman / Roland Colton
　480 p. ; 9 in.
　ISBN 978-1-68114-280-7 (softcover : alk. paper)
　ISBN 978-1-68114-229-6 (hardcover : alk. paper)
　ISBN 978-1-68114-261-6 (e-book)
1. Fiction—Historical—General. 2. Fiction—Literary.
3. Fiction—Urban Life. I. Title.
PN3427-3448: Prose fiction: Fiction genres
813: American fiction in English

Forever Gentleman

ROLAND COLTON

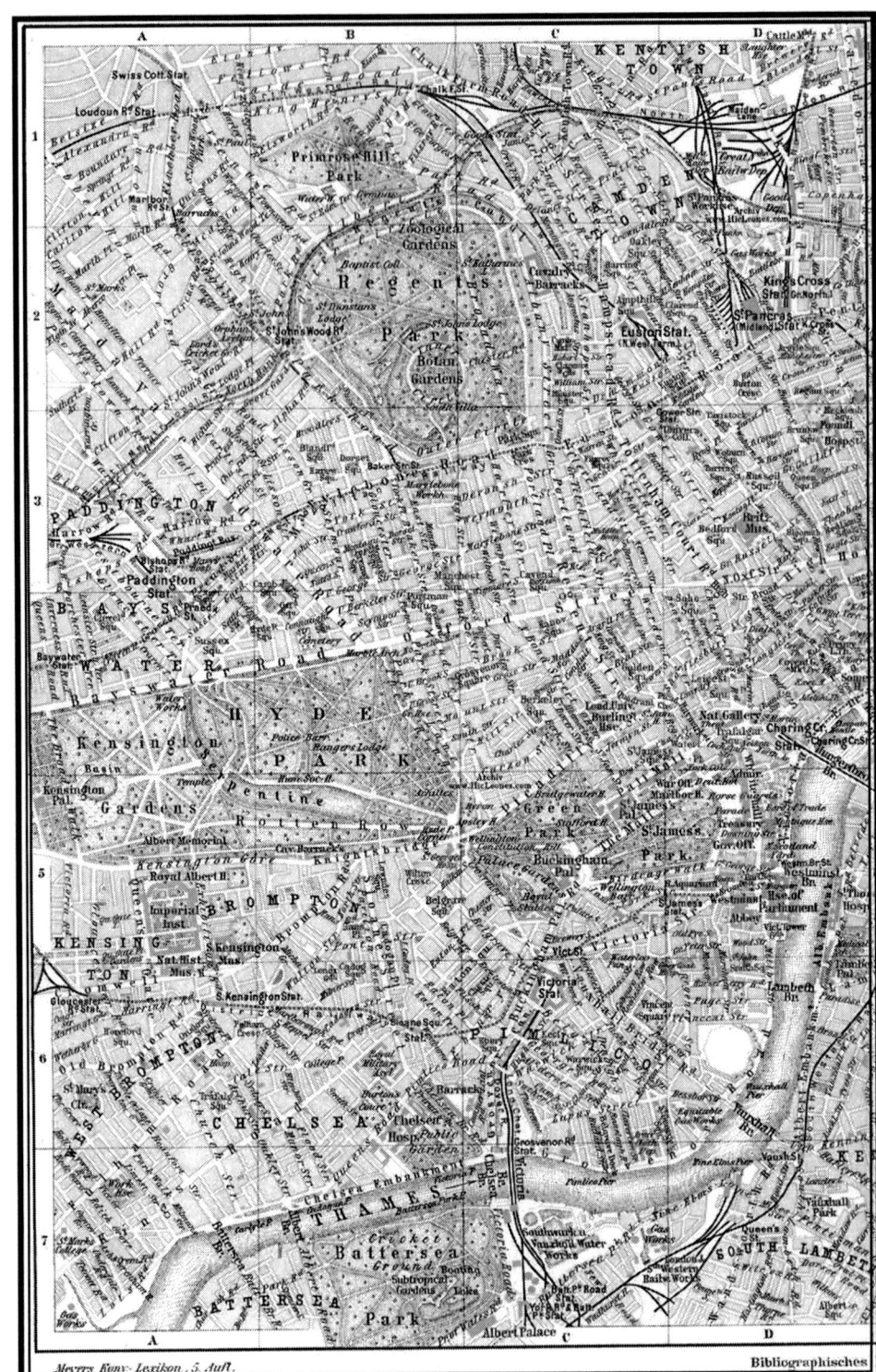

To my dear mother, Alice Mae, my first piano teacher, who still plays beautifully in her 96th year, and to my late father, Glade, who instilled a love for classical music.

and

To my lovely wife, Nahid, the most beautiful woman I have ever known.

Prologue

> Beauty abounds, but is subjective to the beholder. Few would disagree, however, that some beauty transcends subjectivity and is universal: a crimson cloud-layered setting of the sun, a fragrant rose in full bloom, the prism of colors in a rainbow at inclemency's end, winter's first-fallen snow in the light of a bright moon, and the human form and perfection of Miss Jocelyn Charlesworth.
> —Society Page, *Sunday Times*, June 6, 1869

The *Sunday Times* author had heard rumors of Miss Charlesworth's unsurpassed beauty before composing his piece. The reports had been so extraordinary that he endeavored to observe her appearance firsthand and dispel the myths once and forever. He subsequently described his personal encounter with Miss Charlesworth at a society fundraiser as follows:

> I was suspicious, assuming that my eyes would fall upon simply a pretty face, such as exist throughout our fair city. Convinced that the coronation placed upon her was unwarranted, I approached her from afar, notably impressed with her golden hair and her figure, but certain that a closer inspection of her facial features would expunge the hyperbole.
>
> I was mistaken, for once you gaze upon her countenance, it is impossible to resist staring. You cast convention aside and ache for another look, again, again and again. Each time, you blink your eyes, disbelieving that a face could be so radiant, desirable, youthful, and flawless. And if your eyes are fortunate enough to meet hers, your knees will weaken, your tongue will tie, and you will know that no man is worthy of such perfection.

Miss Charlesworth's aura was further enhanced by her family's vast fortune; their land holdings and wealth rivaled Queen Victoria's. Not yet nineteen, she had burst into London society after four years of study at the elite Académie Royale d'Écouen in Paris, an establishment reserved for the offspring of kings, presidents, and potentates.

The *Sunday Times* article ignited a frenzy among a multitude of eligible men, young and old, who clambered for an introduction. Soon after, Miss Charlesworth was receiving a dozen letters a day from wealthy men of high rank and station. Nearly every letter claimed a familial connection or a professional attachment to her father, the powerful and influential Lord Charlesworth, and sought an introduction, or even proffered a proposal of marriage. The would-be suitor's family and rank occasionally required a reception, and into the third month of her return from Paris, Jocelyn had already been compelled to make the acquaintance of fifteen well-connected bachelors, in addition to the countless others foisted upon her at social gatherings.

Chapter 1

The powerful Welsh cobs galloped in the dusk, splashing sewage and waste in their wake, as they pulled the lavishly appointed landau carriage toward Palace Garden. Their pounding hooves were muted by the thick layer of muddy grime blanketing the cobbled road, the muck a by-product of rotting pipes, backed-up drains, and sewage overflow from the Thames. Pristine lavender an hour before, filth had now blackened the bottom of the coach's exterior. The carriage's interior was all burgundy damask, except for the patent leather seats and paneled floor. Its passengers inhaled through scented handkerchiefs, masking the foul odor that permeated the tiny crevasses of the conveyance. Rain had all but disappeared during this suffocating summer, and Londoners feared a repeat of the "Big Stink," which had paralyzed the city ten years before.

It was now the middle of July and the sun had just set, and while the silhouettes of the wigged driver and footmen perched atop the coach were barely visible in the growing darkness, the Charlesworth gilded-peregrine crest was still discernible in the reflected light from boulevard lanterns.

***

A great crowd had gathered at Fairfield Park, which bordered Belgrave Square. Scented geraniums perfumed the mansion's many parlors, giving the London elite temporary refuge from the city's massive sewer failures. The dwelling was plentifully adorned with sculptures by Jean Goujon, Barthélemy Prieur, and Antonio Canova, while masterpieces from Jacob More, William Collins, and William Parrott graced its walls. Panels of grisaille-stained glass in clerestories and ceilings illuminated the home's lavish furnishings, tapestries, and frescoes. Accompanying the ostentatious display of wealth was a serenade by violin, cello, and pianoforte.

Nathan Sinclair stood alone in a far corner of the cavernous ballroom of the opulent residence and felt his stomach growl. He calculated with precision the passage of thirty-two hours since his last meal, if one could call it that: stale bread and gruel. A waiter passed nearby with a silver tray containing an array of triangular-shaped toast with pâté de foie gras. Nathan edged closer and discreetly lifted one, savoring the delicate flavor on his palette. The hors d'oeuvres would provide a welcome meal tonight.

Nathan was clean-shaven, with thickly cropped dark hair. He had a light complexion and handsome features enhanced by a naturally sanguine countenance. He was lean and taller than most men, and like most present, Nathan displayed a confident and impressive air. He was consuming his sixth hors d'oeuvre when reports reverberated that Lord Charlesworth's carriage had arrived, fueling speculation that his celebrated daughter might soon appear. The crowd's excitement surged, and Nathan felt a rush of anticipation to view a beauty that the *Sunday Times* said could not be described with mere words.

Moments later the celebrity guests were announced, creating a furor among the expectant crowd. All heads turned toward the entrance, as guests strained for their first view of Jocelyn Charlesworth. Those nearest the entrance broke into spontaneous applause as their eyes beheld the beauty. Other less-fortunate guests pressed toward the entrance, creating near pandemonium among the throng. Order was soon restored, and the crowd parted as Lord Charlesworth and his daughter navigated toward the center of the room.

His chin slightly elevated, the grandiloquent Lord Charlesworth treated onlookers with subtle nods of his head as he slowly migrated through the crowd. Reaction remained at a fever pitch as spectators pushed and peered through cracks in the crowd to glimpse the hair, profile, and face of the elegant Jocelyn. They were not disappointed. Those who caught even a reflection of Jocelyn's face could hardly contain themselves, producing involuntary gasps of breath or ardent exclamations of praise.

The bachelor public collectively straightened their posture, elevated their bearing, and plotted the contrivance and form of an introduction. Infected with the crowd's excitement, Nathan also followed Jocelyn's procession across the floor, though the throng obscured his view. While he had no expectation of an introduction, he was sufficiently intrigued to desire a view of her face. Nathan pressed forward in Jocelyn's direction, but was turned away time and again by the jostling crowd. One observer took note of Nathan's efforts and approached.

"Why Mr. Sinclair, I'm surprised to see that you also are in pursuit of Miss Charlesworth."

Nathan turned and found himself facing the mistress of the estate, Lady Sommersby. She had tastefully camouflaged the many wrinkles on her face with a pink foundation and powder, creating an illusion of youthfulness from a distance. Close up, her six decades of existence were manifest, as was evidence of her weakness for superb cuisine. For this evening's event, she gloried in exhibiting her prize hyacinth necklace, hair clip, and earrings, which matched her orange chiffon dress and elbow gloves. She wore a perpetual smile, tacitly acknowledging the privileged class who had graciously accepted her invitation to attend.

Embarrassed, Nathan smiled and nodded. "I shamelessly confess that you are quite right."

"She *is* positively radiant. However, I suspect her beauty is having the opposite effect on the women. They are instantly jealous and wish to avoid being observed within too close a proximity, fearful their own appearance, by comparison, will diminish."

"I have not yet had the privilege of making that 'comparison,' but she must truly be a great beauty, judging from her admiring throng," Nathan responded.

Lady Sommersby smiled. "Do you wish to make her acquaintance?"

"Thank you, my lady, that is so very kind of you, but I am quite content to observe her fairness from afar."

"Without an introduction, your eyes may never pierce the surrounding horde to glimpse her face."

"Quite true. But, perhaps the crowd will dissipate in time, and I shall be blessed with that brief glimpse," Nathan's responded with a smile. "That will suffice."

"Please allow me the pleasure," Lady Sommersby persisted. "I have known the family for years and Miss Charlesworth in particular, though I have not seen her since she departed to France. As a young girl she was a rare beauty and has apparently now blossomed into perfection. I would be doing her a great service to introduce her to one of the finest young men in London."

Nathan blushed at the compliment, but experienced a flush of nervousness at the prospect of an introduction. He continued to politely protest, but Lady Sommersby settled things by taking his arm and leading him in Jocelyn's direction. With Nathan in tow, Lady Sommersby plowed through the crowd, lightly tapping shoulders and barking her apologies. A few moments later, the final layer of guests parted, and they found themselves standing directly behind

Miss Charlesworth.

Nathan's eyes opened wide in wonder. The view of Jocelyn from the rear was far beyond anything he had imagined. Taller than he had expected, the top of Jocelyn's golden hair was lifted high with a resplendent diamond-inlaid barrette, while the rest was gathered in exquisitely twisted plaits cascading down her back to her waist. Her provocative evening dress with multi-shaded folds and overskirts exhibited the latest Parisian fashions and revealed the perfection of her statuesque hourglass figure. The sight ignited an unprecedented passion within Nathan, and he yearned to see if the front view of Miss Charlesworth could possibly match the back.

Jocelyn was conversing with two young women when Lady Sommersby approached her from the side and released Nathan. Lady Sommersby took Jocelyn's gloved hands in hers, welcoming her back from Paris and inquiring about her health, her family, and her experience abroad. Not wanting to appear complicit in the forced introduction, Nathan shyly looked away, feeling intensely conspicuous standing alone. As the two women conversed, Nathan felt his heart beating rapidly and his confidence beginning to wane, and he considered losing himself back into the crowd. Before he could act on his impulse, Lady Sommersby turned to her left and again took hold of Nathan's arm, gently maneuvering him in front of Jocelyn.

"Miss Charlesworth, may I present Nathan Sinclair."

Suddenly Nathan was standing directly in front of Jocelyn. As he took in the vision, an intoxication of senses swept over him. Jocelyn's hair sloped upward from her forehead with another diamond clasp fully exposing the freshness of her face. Her features were astonishing: the gentle curve of her cheekbones, the setting of her large azure-blue eyes, the delicate nose, and gracefully-sculpted chin. Draping her elegantly long neck was a three-layered diamond necklace, with matching earrings adorning her lobes. Front and back views of the exquisite young woman merged into perfection. Never had Nathan's gaze fallen upon a portrait of such unimaginable beauty.

He caught his breath and nodded politely.

"Mr. Sinclair, it is my pleasure to present to you Miss Jocelyn Charlesworth, newly arrived from Paris."

While Jocelyn curtsied, Lady Sommersby's attention was diverted by a loud greeting from a distinguished magistrate and dear friend whom she felt compelled to engage. With the introduction interrupted, Nathan held his breath as Jocelyn's eyes returned their focus to his, and he felt a pang in his stomach and weakness in his knees. His eyes were not worthy of the vision, yet he could not look away.

Dare I open my mouth?

At a loss for words, Nathan sensed impatience and boredom in Jocelyn's expression at the paralysis of his tongue—she had undoubtedly endured the star-struck look from other men innumerable times before. Struggling to speak, he finally expelled the first words that entered his mind.

"A great pleasure to make the acquaintance of the young lady about whom all of London is talking." He instantly regretted his prosaic remarks. Jocelyn dispensed a phlegmatic smile and looked away as a bystander brushed her arm.

Obsessed with regaining her attention, Nathan inquired further: "How did you find Paris, my lady?"

"Why with a sextant and compass, of course," Jocelyn responded whimsically.

Nathan was taken aback by her retort. "Pardon me. I know you not at all and was merely venturing to make polite conversation."

Jocelyn coquettishly raised her eyebrows as if the true meaning of Nathan's inquiry had finally dawned upon her. "I 'found' Paris far more interesting than this punctilious metropolis. If you've never been there, you wouldn't understand. Paris is alive, uninhibited, teeming with excitement, ideas, art, and music." Briefly animated as she spoke, her look of boredom quickly returned.

"Is London truly so wearisome?" Nathan tilted his head.

"As different as night and day."

Nathan offered a nervous smirk, unable to provide a witty retort. Another awkward pause passed between them as neither spoke.

"Mr. Sinclair, is it?" Jocelyn inquired.

"Yes, my lady."

"So, you shall soon inform me that you descend from a Scottish king... or hail from a noble clan?"

"No, my lady." Nathan felt a tinge of embarrassment and cast his eyes shyly downward.

"I didn't know there were any *other* Sinclairs," Jocelyn lowered her voice with a bemused look, truly scrutinizing Nathan for the first time.

"There are others," Nathan's said defensively.

"Then you *must* enlighten me, please."

Nathan was unsure how to respond, but sensed his brief audience with Jocelyn was coming to an abrupt end. There was no need to be ambiguous; the truth would suffice. "I am blissfully unsure of my paternal heritage, my lady. I know of no particular connection of my family name, only that its origin is most likely *infinitely* more humble."

As Nathan spoke, Jocelyn's expression changed to one of irritation. In an icily pitched tone, she slowly enunciated: "I thought this gala was restricted to the elite families of London."

"I must confess that I have no membership in that fraternity."

"Yet, you are here!" Jocelyn's face displayed controlled impatience.

"I have been asked to perform a humble service tonight," Nathan said meekly.

"Oh, indeed!" The beauty in her face disintegrated into an exasperated scowl, as she raised one eyebrow. "And yet you presume to make my acquaintance?"

Looking Nathan up and down, Jocelyn glared imperiously. "I should have known from your attire. You are twenty years out of fashion."

Nathan froze.

Turning to a female companion nearby, Jocelyn raised her chin and elevated her voice in a scathing rebuke overheard by nearby guests: "I didn't know the servants were allowed to mingle with the guests! How dare he entreat me?!"

Foregoing all decorum, Jocelyn turned her back on Nathan. "I wonder what subterfuge he employed to gain my introduction..." were the last words Nathan heard as her voice and presence faded into the crowd.

Nathan's face turned red as he sensed scolding eyes and shaking heads from nearby guests. Head down, he sulked away, losing himself in the crowd.

***

As the first plaintive chords of Chopin's Quatrième Ballade echoed in the Sommersby ballroom, the lady in the lavender dress shivered. It was a composition rarely played. Because of its complexity, few pianists could master it. Nevertheless, it was one of her favorites. To her further delight, it was being performed by a masterful artist.

Thrilled at the prospect of hearing the rarely performed work, she separated from friends and glided in the direction of its source.

She was astonished at the tender expression of the Slavonic melody followed by the thunder of octaves rising in a furious crescendo. So moved was she by the melancholy theme that she felt her eyes welling up, as she marveled at the pianist's precision. The pianoforte was now in her view, though the open clavier obscured the artist. The musical instrument was located at the rear of the room, a short distance from long velvet drapes, which cloaked the view of the magnificent grounds outside. She maneuvered breathlessly yet gracefully side to side, in order to catch a glimpse of the talented musician. Now coming into view, she observed hands sprinting up and down the keyboard in a frenetic pace, as the turbulent coda came near its close. The pianist's head turned slightly in her direction as his hands thundered down the keyboard to the bass keys, signaling the end of the ballade. As she saw his face, she let out a gasp of recognition.

The applause erupted as the pianist completed the composition. As the final chord echoed in the room, Nathan Sinclair lifted his hands from the keyboard with dramatic flair. He rose from the bench and turned to his left, bowing in acknowledgment of the rousing reception. As the applause crescendoed, his eyes spanned the appreciative crowd and his eyes fixed, for an instant, on a young lady whose stare was in turn riveted upon him. During their split-second connection, he sensed a distant familiarity in her deep brown eyes and had a profound impression of tenderness and innocence; he instantly wanted to know her. But his shame at the hands of Miss Charlesworth had extinguished any confidence he had in making a second introduction to the London elite, and he quickly cast his eyes downward.

As the applause faded away, Lady Sommersby approached.

"What a captivating performance, Nathan. You were positively masterful tonight. Thank you for performing for us."

Acknowledging her thanks, Nathan bowed. "Your pianoforte is magnificent. It was an exquisite pleasure to have the honor to perform on it." He returned her regard, but wished to scan the audience again, in search of the eyes that had impressed him so deeply. As the chamber orchestra resumed its play and Lady Sommersby mingled with her guests, Nathan discreetly surveyed the crowd. He remembered her olive skin, and her brown hair gathered attractively on top of her head. What inner beauty and tenderness had shone through her eyes, though her features had not seemed so remarkable.

Nathan attempted to navigate his way through the crowd, hoping to catch another glimpse of the lovely eyes, but a grateful crowd repeatedly impeded his progress, intent on sharing their enthusiasm for his performance. Nathan came upon several dark-haired ladies, but none with the expressive eyes. Abandoning his quest after making a second tour of the ballroom, Nathan left the estate much sooner than he had intended.

As he proceeded homeward in a horse-drawn cab, Nathan felt insecurity and shame such as he had never known before.

Why should the offense of one woman affect me so? She knows me not at all. Nor would I have any interest in a woman so devoid of inner beauty. She may be externally the most beautiful of all women, but she has a prideful and withered soul. Let her trouble my mind no longer.

Miss Charlesworth's affront was mollified in part by the honorarium Nathan had received from Lady Sommersby. When he had bid her farewell, she had inserted a folded note into his coat pocket. He had protested, as on previous occasions, but she was insistent, as always. The five-pound notes were always appreciated far more than Lady Sommersby could ever know.

The cab came to a stop on Dockhead Road in the borough of Bermondsey, a busy industrial district in east London and a short distance south of the Thames. Nathan hesitated for several seconds, peering out the window up and down the boulevard. He then fastened his scarf tightly around his neck and lower face, exiting the cab sixty feet distant from the four-story brick commercial building where both his residence and office were located. The stench of sewage from the nearby Thames invaded his olfactory nerves as he stepped into the mire that covered the cobblestone street. The road was nearly empty this late hour and Nathan scraped the grime from his boots on the edge of the sidewalk. Kerosene from the gaslamp overhead had been exhausted weeks before, but not the lamp fifty feet away; it provided just enough light for Nathan to navigate around the random clumps of manure, which had been cast upon the sidewalk by the steady onslaught of livestock earlier that day.

Standing on the sidewalk some distance from the building's front door in the faint artificial light, Nathan strained to see if there was anyone lurking near the entrance before he committed to his destination. He lowered his hat and lifted his scarf above his nose, so that only his eyes were visible. He walked past the front door, keeping his eyes forward as he continued down the sidewalk to the end of the corner. He fingered the keychain in his pocket and selected, by touch, the thick long metal key that matched the entry lock. Taking a deep breath, he retraced his steps to the building's entrance and quickly inserted the key into the lock.

As the door opened, he heard the sound of rapid footsteps approaching on the sidewalk.

"Mr. Sinclair!"

Nathan ignored the petition, hurried inside, and slammed the door behind. He heard the frantic pounding on the door as he climbed up the stairs and heard his name called again. His heart was racing. That had been a narrow escape!

Nathan walked down the long hallway and opened the door to his apartment. It was pitch black inside. He bent down and extended his hand as he shuffled to the right, in search of the crate near the open door. His finger sensed the wooden object and he slid the palm of his hand along the top, locating the candlestick and box of matches. Nathan pulled a match out and lit the wick. The ignited candle cast light on the cracks in the drab walls and ceiling and on the blackened wooden floors. The room was bare except for the piano that stood next to the opposite wall, the one keepsake that remained from his mother's musical legacy. He closed the front door and placed an old newspaper on the floor, and with a knife, he scraped the remaining mud and grime from his boots.

In his stocking feet, Nathan entered his bedroom and changed into his nightclothes. He sat on the edge of his bed, staring straight ahead, as he reflected on the evening's bittersweet events. On the same evening of his public humiliation, he had encountered the mesmerizing eyes of a woman in whom he sensed a powerful connection. He wondered who she was and if he would ever see her again. If he did, would she react that same way Miss Charlesworth did, when she learned of his common background and lack of wealth? The tenderness in her eyes gave him confidence that she would not. Though he doubted their paths would cross again, even the possibility of another encounter, however remote, promised a pleasant mental escape from the long day as he sought slumber—until he remembered the man in pursuit. Discomfiture descended forcefully upon him. He couldn't be certain, but who else would have been calling his name at the late hour?

Nathan stood up from the bed and walked into the front room of his apartment. He sat down on a bench in front of the piano and stared at the keyboard. It was an old box piano designed by Guillaume-Lebrecht Petzold, rectangular with curved corners, featuring a full complement of keys. The piano's light-brown stain had largely faded, and the ornate carvings on the exterior displayed the erosion of wear. Inside the piano case, the wires were cross-strung in acute angles above the hammers, with a crank escapement and individual hammer flanges. The instrument was more than thirty years old, but Nathan tended the strings and keys with care, ensuring it was always in tune.

He closed his eyes as he readied to play, trying to free his mind from the cares of the day. In the distance, he heard the peal of church bells and then the chime announcing the hour.

It was midnight.

As the last chime echoed in the distance, Nathan raised his hands to the keyboard and began playing Schubert's Impromptu in G-flat Major. The peaceful flow of the harp-like accompaniment soothed Nathan's troubled mind as the painfully beautiful melody emerged in the treble register, modulated by bass trills. Immersing himself in music renewed his spirit, graced his mind with peace, and instilled optimism for the future. From Schubert, Nathan moved onto Chopin's Etude no. 4 from Opus 25 in A Minor, losing himself in the brilliance of the composer's artistry, and imagining, as he often did, that he was performing in the grandest orchestral halls of Europe. Music had been his first love. He remembered fondly his mother's touch as she explained the wonder of notes, keys, and harmony. It had come so easily to him. His mother's dream had been for Nathan to become a concert pianist—a dream that she once had for herself; instead, she had found her calling in the opera.

An hour later, Nathan returned to his bedroom. He lay on the bed, failing miserably in his attempt to find sleep. Disquietude from the nocturnal visitor continued to invade his peace.

Has my time finally run out?

Chapter 2

When he finally slumbered, Nathan dreamt he was in the bedroom of his childhood home in Moret-et-Loing, France, lying in bed. Seated next to him as she tucked him in, Nathan's mother began singing his favorite lullaby, Mozart's "Ruhe Sanft":

> *Ruhe sanft, mein holdes Leben,*
> *Schlafe, bis dein Glück erwacht;*
> *Aa, mein Bild will ich dir geben,*
> *Schau, wie freundlich es dir lacht,*
> *Ihr süßen Träume, wiegt ihn ein,*
> *Und lasset sienen Wunsch am Ende*
> *Aie wollustreiechen Gegenstände*
> *Zu reifer Wirklichkeit gedeihn*[1]

Nathan stared into her eyes and melancholy smile as his mother sang. He imagined her handing him her portrait. He knew that when he awakened, happiness would find him, as it did every morning.

When the light of the early morning sun filtered into Nathan's bedroom, he slowly roused with a feeling of contentment from the lovely dream. What an extraordinary blessing to have had an operatic mother perform nightly for him alone. With eyes still closed, he wondered when she had stopped singing him lullabies; he tried to remember how old he had been.

The temporary serenity was soon shattered by thoughts of the anonymous visitor from the night before. Nathan tried to reassure

---

1   Gently rest, my dearest love,
Sleep until your happiness awakes;
Here, I will give you my portrait,
See how kindly it smiles at you.

You gentle dreams, rock him to sleep,
And may the imaginings
Of his dreams of love
Become at last reality.

himself that it was nothing, but he knew in the back of his mind that the visitor's appearance was a confirmation of his worst fears. Fears on which he would not allow his mind to dwell.

Forcing his thoughts on to more pleasant matters, Nathan reflected upon Lady Sommersby's generosity, which would enable him to eat well for the first time in weeks. He had been skimping on breakfast, spending only a penny or two on an occasional currant cake or bowl of gruel and a cup of coffee adulterated with chicory from the corner coffee stall. But today he could afford to indulge his voracious appetite. The thought of freshly fried bread with butter, honey-cured back bacon and a cup of pure coffee spurred him out of bed, and he was soon dressed.

After grabbing his top hat and coat, Nathan walked to the front door of his apartment, which led to the hallway, and listened carefully. Hearing no sound of footsteps, he opened the door a sliver and peered down the hallway in the direction of the stairway. There was no sign of life. Opening the door a few inches more, he extended his head outward beyond the door and looked back down the opposite side. Not a soul was present.

Nathan quietly walked into the hallway, locking the door behind him, and hurried down the hallway to the back stairway. Before exiting the rear of the building, he pulled his coat up around his neck and lowered his hat down over his forehead, though the morning temperature was pleasant. The rancid smell of sewage overflowing onto the alleyway assaulted Nathan's nostrils when he opened the door. With the Thames at high tide, river water had seeped into the subterranean sewer pipes and drains, forcing the muddy mire to spill into the streets.

It's surprisingly similar in smell and appearance to the gruel I had for breakfast the other day, Nathan snickered to himself as he surveyed the deep brown filth on the ground.

He negotiated his boots gingerly through the mire, not wanting it to splash onto his trousers. Reaching the side street, he stepped up to the sidewalk (which was thankfully several inches higher than the polluted road) where street vendors were busy calling out their wares over the din of bleating sheep and grunting pigs. People stood at street stalls eating breakfast, while carriage wheels splattered mire onto street sweepers seeking to carve clean pathways for their clients. Thick steam rose from the street, left by trampling cattle on their way to a nearby slaughterhouse.

Nathan looked up and down the street. From his height, he could see up above the sea of pedestrians who were unwilling to step aside into the muck as they struggled to maintain purchase with the sidewalk. Impeded by the crowds, Nathan navigated slowly up the sidewalk, turning his head frequently to glance behind. He passed several women holding nosegays close to their nostrils to obscure the pungent odor of sewage. As he turned left onto Abbey Street, he suddenly felt a hand clamp onto his wrist. His face creased in dread as he recognized the man standing to his side.

Winston Sedgwick.

Sedgwick had a corpulent face and figure and a balding head, which he failed to camouflage with stray strands of hair. In the morning sun, the beads of perspiration on his face facilitated the migration of his spectacles down his thick red nose. He wore a black suit with a grey waistcoat two sizes too small, though six months ago, it had been a perfect fit—he had "lost a cartful and found a wagon." He was eight inches shorter than Nathan and more than double his age.

"Mr. Sinclair. How nice of you to pay me a visit this lovely morning. I was just on my way to see you." Sedgwick's high-pitched voice dripped with sarcasm, as he tilted his head back to stare up into Nathan's eyes.

Nathan tried his best to maintain a calm demeanor, though his heart was racing.

"And you are prepared to hand over the sixty pounds you owe?" Sedgwick's lips curled up into a sly smile as he held out his free hand, palm up. The debt had only been thirty-eight pounds nine months before, when Nathan had borrowed the money; the rest was accrued interest.

"I am on my way, just now, to call on Mr. Allenby for the debt *he* owes." Nathan did his best to make the lie sound casual. "Once collected, you shall be paid in full."

Sedgwick's forced smile turned into a scowl and his voice lowered. "Mr. Allenby. Good dear Mr. Allenby. I have been hearing his name for some time now." Sedgwick's forced smile returned. "But I could swear you told me Mr. Allenby's residence lies in west London, not to the east."

Nathan's averting eyes gave himself away.

"You have been promising to collect that debt for months. Your time is up!" Sedgwick tightened his grip on Nathan's arm and extracted a document from his coat with his free hand. In a loud tone he declared, "This is a judgment from the Court of Common Pleas *and* a warrant of execution for your arrest."

The blood drained from Nathan's face. He had feared this moment since a friend, who worked in the court clerk's office, had informed him that an arrest warrant had been issued several days before. Three months earlier, he had been served with a plaint and summons requiring his attendance in court. The day had come and gone and Nathan had failed to appear. Why bother? What defense did he have? He owed the money. Six weeks later, he had been served with a Judgment Summons. He had taken note of the July court date on the summons, and he knew that he was obliged to attend in order to explain why he hadn't paid the judgment as directed. He had planned to appear, hoping to gain the judge's sympathy and a modest repayment plan, but his friend advised otherwise, informing him that he would certainly be arrested on the spot. Once again, Nathan had seen the date come and go and had done nothing. During the same time, he had waited daily for the check from Mr. Allenby that would clear the debt in full. Each day, the postman disappointed him. Now it was too late. He would be sent to debtors' prison, his freedom would be forfeited, and his good name and reputation would be forever tarnished!

While tightly grasping Nathan's arm, Sedgwick's head moved quickly back and forth, scanning the crowd from his tiptoes. His head stopped abruptly and he yelled out, "Constable!"

That instant, Nathan forcefully chopped down on Sedgwick's inner elbow joint with his free hand, releasing the grip. Nathan jumped from the sidewalk into the filth of the crowded street, spraying mud in all directions and inciting curses as he ran down the opposite direction, dodging pedestrians, horses, and carriages.

"Stop that man!" Sedgwick cried out.

Nathan sprinted to the street corner and glanced back at Sedgwick, who was frantically waving the papers in his hand above the crest of heads and top hats. With no constable in sight, Nathan turned down Neckinger Road behind a Paddington–City omnibus. A short distance later, he turned right into a narrow alley, through a swath of tenement housing with clothes drying on makeshift wires; Nathan nearly retched from the foul discharge of water closets into the alley mixing with the sewage overflow. Wide-eyed young children with dirty faces and grime-stained shirts stared as Nathan speedily stomped through the liquid filth, splashing black splotches onto hanging clothes and triggering a cascade of threats and oaths from irritated dwellers. He exited the alley and turned right onto Grange Road, a busy thoroughfare bustling with traffic.

Nathan continued running, then slowed to a walk when the crowd thickened. He forced his way through the sweaty mass of flesh, but welcomed the horde of humanity that would further impede his pursuers. When the path opened again, he resumed running full speed until he reached Bermondsey New Road, a less crowded street, and jogged through random alleys and side streets until arriving at Walworth Road.

The boulevard was teeming with commerce and traffic, hosting a cacophony of beggars' petitions, vendors' cries, and mad shouts in the midst of noxious fat-boilers, glue-renderers, tripe-scrapers, and livestock. Confident he had evaded his pursuer, Nathan slumped on his haunches, gasping for breath and perspiring heavily, his trousers, boots, and coat covered with grime. He was disgusted with himself—a common criminal, trying to evade the law.

He had been warned about Sedgwick before seeking the loan. Sedgwick had a reputation for showing no mercy to defaulting clients—inmates at Coldbath Fields Prison in North London would attest to that. At the time, Nathan felt he had no alternative, as his many debts had mounted. Sedgwick himself had warned Nathan there would be no extensions, and that dire consequences would ensue if the debt was not timely repaid. When Nathan defaulted, Sedgwick threatened him with arrest and debtors' prison. Nathan knew it would take time to get a judgment, and he had been certain that he would be able to coerce Allenby into paying the eighty pounds he owed for the extensive renovation project Nathan had designed, managed, and completed before year's end. Allenby inveterately promised, but never paid. Since the project's completion, Nathan had collected just a miserly five pounds.

The day of reckoning had finally come, a day that Nathan had never imagined. He shook his head in disgust.

How did I ever get myself into this accursed mess?

Never before had the clarity of vision of his financial affairs descended upon him so forcefully. He had been blessed with an abundant serving of optimism—too much, perhaps—which had always carried him through difficult times. In a painful bolt of reality, he viewed his career in a far more pessimistic manner than ever before.

What dreams he had envisioned when he was a student at École Spéciale de Lausanne. His mother had sacrificed greatly to pay Nathan's costly tuition and boarding expenses during the four years he studied in Switzerland. Thereafter, Nathan had apprenticed for a time at Calemby & Co., where he had learned the practical trade and had participated in the design of several prominent properties. Anxious to pursue his lofty dreams, Nathan had left Calemby

& Co. shortly after receiving his architectural credential. When he embarked on his own eighteen months ago, he believed that he had secured sufficient funds to finance the bold undertaking.

He had located a low-rent office in a barely respectable commercial area on the east side of London. The office had shown signs of neglect: cracked exterior glass, stains on the ceiling from past water leaks, peeling wallpaper. The fireplace was too small, but that mattered little since the cost of wood was an extravagance avoided until the temperature plummeted during late fall and winter. When he had first let the property, the disrepair hadn't bothered him much. He had planned to promptly make renovations. Unfortunately, as it turned out, even the modest amount necessary to improve the cosmetics of his office demanded too large a sum from his meager funds, so he kept putting it off. The well-worn furniture he had inherited from the landlord he had also vowed to replace; now, a year and a half later, the same ponderous and drab desk and threadbare chairs remained. However, the real setback had occurred when he had been forced to give up his residence and had surreptitiously taken up dwelling in the two unused rooms of his office.

Nathan reflected on his predicament. He needed to come up with sixty pounds in a hurry. Nine months before, when he had borrowed the money to pay off past-due debts, he had accepted a rate of interest of 25 percent for six months without a second thought, so relieved was he to have found a willing lender. That had added nine and a half pounds to his debt, making the total forty-seven and a half pounds. The interest rate doubled upon the default. He did a quick calculation. Sedgwick was right; it had ballooned to sixty pounds.

Allenby remained his only hope. But Allenby had gone heavily into debt renovating his home in the expectation that he would be able to sell it for a handsome profit. Could Nathan reasonably expect repayment from Allenby when Allenby had prevailed upon Nathan to lend him twenty pounds to finish the project? At the time, Nathan had been pleased to come to the aid of his client. In hindsight, it had been an utterly foolish act, since the residence had been on the market for six months without a buyer. Nathan had already been left with no alternative but to sell prize pieces of his mother's furniture and much of her jewelry, at a fraction of their value, to remain afloat. The only meaningful asset that remained, other than her silver locket and wedding band, was the antique piano he had inherited from her, and he doubted it would fetch much in its worn condition. It was Allenby who was responsible for his present dire circumstances, and it was Allenby who would need to come to his aid.

After a short rest, Nathan continued walking a good distance before stopping at the fruit market on Trafalgar Street. Wagons had arrived in the early morning and set up shop in their habitual locations. The finest of delicate soft fruit—strawberries, peaches, bananas, and pears—filled the center spring-vans. On either side, wagons filled with apples, greengages, carrots, cabbage, radishes, tomatoes, turnips, potatoes, and onions beckoned. Customers milled around the wagons, examining each species of fruit or vegetable as if it were the last item they would ever consume.

The sight of fresh fruit made Nathan ravenous. He pulled out the paper note that Lady Sommersby had inserted in his coat pocket the night before—and quickly looked again. It wasn't five pounds. It was ten! Nathan hadn't even bothered to retrieve it until now. The unexpected windfall gave him a giddy feeling.

Lady Sommersby! What a delightful woman you are. Now, if only I can perform for you every other evening for a fortnight, that should take care of Sedgwick.

Ten pounds was a far cry from the debt he owed, and even if he paid it all to Sedgwick, it would make little difference. Sedgwick would still have him arrested and thrown in prison. Nevertheless, ten pounds could make all the difference in Nathan's world during the ensuing days and weeks. His optimism returned.

Fearing that Sedgwick might reappear at any moment, there was no time to waste, but first Nathan needed to get something to eat and drink. Desperately dehydrated from his flight in the warm sun, he dug out the only remaining coin in his pocket, a penny, and walked over to a street-seller who had a fountain of "Persian Sherbet"—lemonade made with spring water, essence of lemon, sugar, raspberries, and cream of tartar. The wooden boards at the end of the stall bore a painting of a Persian princess decked in jewelry, wearing flowing white robes, and holding a glass of the rose-colored drink. Nathan handed over the penny and received a tall glass. He drained the tart liquid in no time, then looked at his options for food.

Nathan's meals invariably came from street vendors, because he, like the vast majority of the laboring class, had no equipment or facility for cooking meals; that option was lost to him since moving his residence inside the commercial building. Even before the move, Nathan rarely took advantage of the kitchen, not interested in cooking for just himself. Besides, street food was inexpensive, varied, and often quite tasty; the only risk was in not knowing all the food's ingredients or the length of time since its preparation.

Nathan walked up to a coffee stall made up of a spring barrow with two wheels and a trestle, topped by a board. On top of the board were three five-gallon cans, each with a small iron firepot beneath, perforated like a rushlight shade. Charcoal burned inside the pots, keeping the cans of coffee and tea hot. The vendor also offered a number of food items. Nathan ordered some warm bread and butter, bacon, a boiled egg, and a cup of coffee for three pence. The keeper looked at Nathan's ten-pound note and scowled; he clearly had no change for it, and motioned to a seller of fruit and vegetables a short distance away.

"She kin 'elp you thar, but you best buy somethin'."

Although Nathan didn't cook meals, fresh fruit and vegetables were always welcome. He picked up a bag and filled it with bananas, apples, oranges, carrots, potatoes, and radishes. Displaying the note triggered another frown from the frumpy lady behind the counter, but she grabbed it and gave Nathan change. Nathan returned to the coffee stall, paid the stall keeper, and proceeded to devour his breakfast. After purchasing fresh bread, nuts, and a tart, he was ready to return home.

On his way, Nathan had hoarded the large bag of food with both hands and covered his face with a scarf and hat, feeling as though all eyes were upon him—any one of the multitude of people he saw could be a surrogate for Sedgwick. He charted his journey home by arcing eastward a good distance before turning northwest, circumnavigating through a labyrinth of streets and alleys until he reached the back alley of his building. By this time, though it had been several hours since his encounter with his creditor, it was barely noon. Unlocking the back door of the building, he crept up the steps and surveyed the hallway. All clear. He entered his apartment, placed the food in the bare cupboards, and went into his bedroom.

Nathan's bedroom had a second door—a hidden portal with no handle, merely a latch—leading directly into his business office. At the time he had leased the four-room unit, he had intended that it all serve as his place of establishment for his architect business, with enough space to add two draftsmen and a junior architect as business grew. Shortly after moving in, the landlord had opened up the wall to make the second half of the unit accessible to the other two rooms, but it had never been finished. Once Nathan began dwelling in the unused rooms, he re-plastered the wall, added a door and latch, and installed some carefully placed molding, causing the door to blend into the wall. To his knowledge, he was the only *dweller* in the office building. Certainly, no one resided near his space, since he was able to play his midnight overtures without complaints from nearby occupants.

At least I don't have to worry about being evicted, Nathan thought. The landlord had required rent be paid once a year in advance. Eleven pounds from the Sedgwick loan had been used to pay for the second year's prepayment on his lease—he had six months of paid rent remaining.

Nathan unlocked the latch and entered his private office. His office and dwelling each consisted of two rooms, identical in size and shape, both with separate access from the hallway. The office room adjacent to the hallway served as his reception, and the interior room behind it was his work area where he composed his architectural drawings and sketches. Numerous sheets of large drafting paper littered his desk, giving the appearance of a practice far busier than it was. Nathan removed the cardboard sign that leaned against the window, which bore his name and profession, not wanting to make things too easy for Sedgwick and the constable.

Nathan walked to the reception area, grateful that his clerk was not in today. He placed his ear to the outer door, listening for footsteps. Opening the door, he found a vacant hallway. He removed the wooden placard nailed on the door that bore his name and profession; the outer hallway door would be just one of many unmarked doors in the interior of the building.

Nathan knew he had to be exceedingly vigilant. He had kept his dwelling in the office building secret—it was a source of embarrassment, after all. But Nathan wondered if Sedgwick had discovered he was living in the building. Why else would he have been accosted the evening before, late at night? Sedgwick had undoubtedly checked with his former landlord and discovered that Nathan had moved out.

Horrific stories of debtors languishing in prison for years filled Nathan's mind with dread. He could hardly imagine finding himself on the brink of such a catastrophe. Miss Charlesworth had been painfully on point. What right did he have to mingle with London's elite—especially now that he was an outlaw, literally running from the law? He felt a melancholy humor at the thought of pursuing the woman with the mesmerizing eyes.

Maybe I can invite her to dine with me at Coldbath Fields. I must check first with the chef, to see how they are preparing the rats and dumplings.

It was imperative that he find another place to live and work. And soon.

Chapter 3

The morning mail contained an envelope addressed to Randolph Travers, senior partner in the law firm of Amory, Tillinghast & Travers. Their three-story building was located on Bennett's Hill in the heart of Birmingham's prestigious business district. Amory and Tillinghast were both deceased, making Mr. Travers, at the age of 74, the sole survivor of the firm's founding partners, though of the abundance of younger lawyers and clerks employed by the firm, each hoped to see his name engraved someday on the granite slab set above the building's entrance.

It was a melancholy time for Mr. Travers. Just two years before, he had lost his beloved wife of fifty years to a long illness. After her death, he had taken a lengthy sabbatical from the firm—there were plenty of lawyers and clerks to take up the slack—and the firm had continued to prosper in his absence. Months later and with reluctance, he had resumed the mantle of the firm's leadership and management, though he rarely performed legal work himself. Nevertheless, because his name held such prestige and appeal, he rarely went a day without meeting at least one of the firm's many clients, always providing assurances that he would personally take an interest in the case. On rare occasions since his wife's passing, he actually *had* taken an interest; one was a sensational acquittal in a heavily publicized murder case. He intended that trial to be his last, a fitting climax to his illustrious long career.

Mr. Travers strode through the front door of his law firm in early afternoon after lunching with two members of Parliament, acknowledging greetings from his staff with subtle nods of the head as he passed by. He had a full set of hair, which, along with his thick sideburns and mustache, had long since turned white. His deep bass voice could still resonate with fury, if occasion required; that, along with his imposing height, had consistently been an aid in the courtroom. Always impeccably dressed, Mr. Travers provided the quintessential personification of a senior partner from a prominent London law firm—the immaculately tailored suit, waistcoat, winged-collar shirt, and silk ties adorning a man whose demeanor exuded vast experience, expertise, and success.

Mr. Travers entered his private office, tossing his hat on the nearby rack. The mahogany-appointed ceilings, walls, and bookshelves were stained two shades lighter than those in the still-vacant offices of his two deceased partners. He walked over to the centerpiece of his sanctum: a large regency ornamental desk, also in mahogany, imported from Italy. The desktop contained three sections of inlaid full-grain leather dyed black, separated by inch-wide wood borders. Perched upon the desk, squarely in the middle section, was one solitary envelope—his only correspondence for the day.

I should be home in time for tea, Mr. Travers smiled sarcastically as he settled into the deeply cushioned black leather chair behind the desk. He opened the envelope and withdrew the letter, glancing at the author's signature before reading the contents. He recognized the name, though he had never met the author.

The first sentence stressed the utmost necessity of maintaining the confidentiality of the author. The prospective client then explained the assignment: a request for a thorough investigation into the background of one particular individual. Mr. Travers was surprised that the surname of that individual was unfamiliar to him, in light of the author's identity; he would have expected the inquiry to pertain to a recognizable name of the English gentry. It was also peculiar that there was no indication in the letter as to the purpose or motive for the investigation.

Mr. Travers's first instinct was to assign the task to one of the firm's junior attorneys. After further reflection, however, he decided to take the assignment himself, intrigued at the prospect of making the personal acquaintance of his new client.

As he stared out the window, Mr. Travers had one thought on his mind.

Who the devil is Nathan Sinclair?

***

Nathan stayed indoors the remainder of the day. There was nowhere to turn for help, no one with whom to share his financial misery. Nathan had been an only child and his parents were both deceased—his father had died before his birth and his mother had passed on during the final year of his studies at École Spéciale de Lausanne. Nathan had moved with his mother to England when he was a young boy, after she retired from the opera. Thereafter, communications with her family in France had grown less frequent, until they had all but disappeared before he departed for Switzerland to begin his studies. He had made many friends during the four years he studied at École Spéciale, but none resided in London. Although Nathan had inherited friends of his mother's, his association with them was based more upon a love of his musical talent than any intimate attachment. As to his father, Nathan knew nothing of any family members or relatives. Although he had casual friends and acquaintances, Nathan had no close friends or affections nearby. He was alone in the world.

If I disappear, there will not be a soul who cares. No one will pay the slightest heed if I languish the rest of my life in prison. I matter not at all to any man or woman.

Nathan opened the hidden door to his office and sat down behind the desk. He stared at the papers in front of him, but the encounter with Sedgwick had left him with such anxiety and gloom that he had little desire to work. He wandered over to the second-story window, surveying the street below, wondering if Sedgwick was watching and waiting for him to exit. Smoke and dust rose from the street in the late-afternoon's endless stream of carriages, interspersed with the occasional omnibus; the office's walls and windows muted the cries from vendors and beggars, the squeal of pigs, and the whine of livestock. From inside the building it was difficult to see the exterior entrance to the building without opening the window and extending his head outward—but such an act would be too conspicuous. Since there were no curtains on the window, he stood discreetly to the side and peered at the bustling throng. In the haze, the silhouette of Sedgwick should not have been too difficult to pick up, if he were anywhere on the street.

After searching and finding no one, Nathan returned to his desk and began re-sketching a preliminary design for a small backyard landscaping project that he had recently received from a relative of an acquaintance. The pay was meager, but at least it was work. He willed his mind to focus on the specifications the client had requested, but every ten or fifteen minutes he wandered back to the window. After his fifth trip with no sighting of Sedgwick, Nathan relaxed a bit. Hopefully Sedgwick had more important things to do than to conduct round-the-clock surveillance on him.

As night descended, Nathan dared not leave the premises, so he lit a fire in his bedroom fireplace, baking potatoes and other vegetables. After eating, he walked into the inner room and sat at the bench of the box piano where a score of Liszt's Second Hungarian Rhapsody was perched above the keys. It was a flamboyant and ostentatious piece he had been working on during the past few weeks, and he had nearly committed it to memory. He placed his fingers on the keys, getting ready to begin, seeking refuge in the music. He paused, then dropped his fingers from the keyboard before making a sound, and walked away. He didn't have the energy or interest tonight. He imagined the disappointment his mother would feel, if she knew what had become of him. All the sacrifices she had made for him had been in vain.

***

Sedgwick sat at his desk fuming. No one of consequence had escaped his clutches before. He cursed himself for letting Sinclair get away. He had more than enough deadbeats languishing in Coldbath for a few guineas' debt. He needed a respectable man like Sinclair to be incarcerated as a deterrent to his other large debtors. If word ever spread that Sinclair was at liberty while in severe delinquency, other clients might follow Sinclair's path.

Sedgwick earned most of his money by making loans to street vendors. He routinely charged them 20 percent interest for a week's loan—a five-shillings' loan netted a shilling profit. When adding the volume of peddlers who borrowed small sums, his monthly take was nearly a hundred pounds from them alone. Larger debtors were charged much less interest, negotiated by risk and collateral.

Sinclair had been a high-risk borrower since he had no collateral or steady wages. Sedgwick well remembered how convincing Sinclair had been in his promise to repay. He also recalled how emphatically he had advised Sinclair of the consequences of nonpayment, including debtors' prison. Since the loan had been made, Sinclair hadn't paid a single shilling! Sedgwick's blood was boiling, and he was not about to stand for the loss without prosecuting Sinclair to the fullest extent of the law. He would spare no expense to find Sinclair and have him arrested.

Within hours of the failed encounter with Sinclair, Sedgwick recruited two ruffians at a guinea each for a week's work. If necessary, he would hire more. He would keep Sinclair's building under surveillance, scouring the neighborhood until he surfaced again.

The young architect would pay with his freedom.

Chapter 4

Nathan experienced another restless night, not succumbing to sleep until the early hours of the morning. When he arose in the middle of the morning, he fixed himself a quick breakfast and got dressed. It was time to have a chat with his clerk, Percy Stumbolt. Nathan had never informed his clerk that he had *moved in* next door to the office—it was too shameful. So, as was his custom, he entered his office from the front door, instead of passing through the connecting hidden door of his bedroom.

Stumbolt had been a "gift" from the landlord, who couldn't wait to pawn the distant relative off on the unsuspecting Sinclair. Stumbolt was past middle age, short and plump, with balding hair and mustache. He always wore a finely pressed suit and waistcoat with a perfectly tied cravat. As a much younger man, Stumbolt had tasted society through the benevolence of another distant relative, a fact that Stumbolt frequently wove into conversations with Nathan. That brief baptism had endowed him with the accoutrements and pretense of English gentry, which he wore with excessive pride and condescension. A self-professed expert on most topics, including architecture, Nathan soon learned that Stumbolt's knowledge was superficial. Between master and servant, it became apparent to Nathan that Stumbolt felt their roles should be reversed.

On full alert, Nathan walked out the front door of his living quarters, turned left, and walked ten paces to the front door of his office. He turned the handle on the door—it was unlocked.

Nathan froze.

Somebody *other than* Stumbolt must be inside, since he had given Stumbolt specific instructions to keep the front door locked at all times, after learning that the arrest warrant had been issued the prior week. Nathan slowly pushed the door open. The room was empty.

Where in tarnation is Stumbolt?

The door to his inner office was ajar. Who was inside? Nathan took a deep breath, creeping forward to see who had penetrated the sanctity of his inner office. Peering in, he first saw the soles of boots perched on top of his desk.

Nathan jerked back, as though he had seen a ghost.

He looked again. Clearly, someone was making himself welcome. As his field of vision expanded, he recognized the contour of Stumbolt reading the newspaper. Shaking his head in disgust, Nathan reminded himself for the hundredth time that he needed to replace his clerk.

Nathan stepped loudly into his office, wearing a frown. Surprised by the unwelcome intrusion, Stumbolt rose from the chair, pretending to rearrange the three lone items on Nathan's desk.

Clearing his voice, he spoke: "Everything is in order, sir." Nathan nodded irritatedly and stood at the opened doorway until Stumbolt exited the room.

"Please, it is *imperative* that the front door remain locked at all times, unless we are expecting a client's visit," Nathan commanded.

"I did lock it, sir."

"Well, it was unlocked when I entered."

"Someone else must have unlocked it," Stumbolt protested.

Nathan shook his head in disbelief.

Maybe it was the butcher, baker, or candlestick maker!

Nathan sank down into his office chair with a feeling of hopelessness. If he did nothing, as he had recklessly done before in failing to appear in court, the inevitable would occur and he would end up in prison; it was just a matter of time. That thought propelled him from his chair and he walked to the window. Taking care not to be noticed from below, he gazed from the window's edge. His eyes fastened on a street sweeper who seemed bent on cutting a path through the wretched mud, using a stump of an old broom to build up a dam on either side, only to have his barricade trampled by horses or carriages. When a distinguished-looking gentleman attempted to cross the street, the sweep tried unsuccessfully to halt traffic to allow the man an unimpeded mudless path to the other side. Nathan admired the young sweep's ambition, but chuckled at the utter futility of it all.

Easier to stem the tide of the Thames than to halt the unbroken chain of carriages and horses on Dockhead Road.

Nathan followed the progress of the distinguished-looking man toward the opposite side of the street—the man had advanced halfway across the boulevard, unsullied under the street sweeper's care, when the dam broke and freed oozing watery mud into his path and onto his shiny black boots—until Nathan's eyes fell upon a sight that caused him to brace backward against the wall, away from the window.

Damn! I hope they didn't see me.

Standing on the opposite side of the road, fifty feet west of Nathan's building, the corpulent silhouette of Sedgwick was visible. Sedgwick was talking with two large men, and Nathan immediately surmised that their task was to restrain him until a constable arrived. The taller of the two men had short black hair, with thick bushy eyebrows and a prominent forehead that protruded noticeably from his face. The other man had a pockmarked face, with mustache and sideburns extending down to his beard. Both men exuded an intimidating presence.

Nathan's focus remained riveted on the three men. Sedgwick pointed to the front entrance of Nathan's building as he spoke to the men. Nathan assumed they were waiting for him to exit at the noon hour and eat lunch with his customary street vendor. He wondered if a fourth accomplice stood guard at the rear of the building. Unfortunately, he couldn't observe the back door from the building's interior. There was no time to delay. He needed to get out. Now!

Nathan hurriedly walked into Stumbolt's office and asked him for the spare key to the inner office, explaining that he had misplaced his own. He didn't want to make things too easy for the Metropolitan Police. If he heard someone trying to open the door, or for that matter, breaking the door down, he'd at least have enough time to escape to the other side.

"I don't wish to be disturbed," Nathan instructed him. He shut the door and locked it behind him.

Nathan returned to the window to ensure that Sedgwick and his henchmen were still in sight. They were. He quickly formulated a plan. He would wait until nightfall to depart. In the meantime, he would pack some bare necessities and the working drawings for the few projects he had. For his plan to work, it was imperative that Sedgwick continued to believe that he was conducting business from his office; that way Sedgwick would not actively search for him in other boroughs.

Nathan's heart beat rapidly as he pored over the stack of drawings on his desk, trying to determine which to take with him. Suddenly, he heard a knock on his office door; startled, Nathan rose from his chair and moved quietly toward the hidden door, ready to escape to his bedroom.

"The post, sir." He heard Stumbolt's voice and relaxed.

Damn it! I told him I didn't want to be disturbed.

Nathan unlocked the door and Stumbolt entered Nathan's office with the day's mail.

"I believe you are being summoned to perform again," Stumbolt announced sanctimoniously, as he carefully positioned the lone envelope on the edge of Nathan's desk with an exaggerated importance of the mundane task.

"Perhaps it would be better for you to close your office and become a full-time musician, since your musical commissions are far more frequent than your architectural ones."

"You may kindly keep your opinions to yourself," Nathan muttered under his breath, locking the door again once Stumbolt exited. He examined the seal of one of his benefactors: Countess von Brandt. She kindly solicited a recital at her home two weeks hence for a social affair. It had been nearly a year since he had performed at her opulent residence. She had an unusually beautiful pianoforte—a Viennese piano with opposite coloring of the keyboard, the natural keys were black and the accidental keys white—in a sitting room with excellent acoustics. Nathan smiled at the invitation, knowing that he would receive another much-needed monetary reward for performing.

He returned to his task of choosing which drawings to take with him. He then located the drafting equipment he would need and placed the papers and equipment into a large briefcase. He looked out the window again. It was nearly noon. Sedgwick and his men hadn't moved from their place across the street. He breathed a sigh of relief.

Nathan left his office through the hidden door into his bedroom, locking the latch behind him. He grabbed another bag and started filling it with clothes, food, and other essentials. It took him a half hour to organize and pack. Everything was in place for a rapid departure. It might be difficult to find a cab late at night, so Nathan expected to walk a good distance. His plan called for going to Chelsea, the west side of London, not far from where he had lived as a youth. He remembered an old inn near King's Road and Church Street—Craven's Inn. Nathan expected that the cost of boarding there would be modest; it would also provide him inconspicuous shelter for a few days until he found something more permanent. Unfortunately, his beloved piano would have to remain behind; it was far too heavy and cumbersome to be transported without the aid of another man and a cart.

It was half past noon and the streets were teeming with people. After packing, Nathan looked out the window of his bedroom, which provided the same view as his office, except twenty feet to the east. To his chagrin, Sedgwick and his cohorts had disappeared.

He felt a lump in his throat. Where had they gone? What were they up to?

Nathan opened the latch to his office to look out the window and see further west of where Sedgwick and his men had been standing. Against his better judgment, he opened the window halfway to extend his head outward and view the sidewalk directly below. Still no sign of Sedgwick.

Agitated, Nathan neglected to close the window but returned in haste to his bedroom, again locking the latch on the hidden door behind him. He walked rapidly to the front room of his living area and considered opening the door to spy on the hallway, but thought the better of it. Moments later, he heard the sound of footsteps coming down the hallway, and he stiffened. The footsteps stopped and there was a pounding on a door close to him—to his left. It was the door to his office's reception. Then he heard a shout.

"Open up! Police!"

Panic seized Nathan's breast. His heart started beating madly and he realized the next decision he made would dictate his future.

Nathan heard more voices and the sound of heavy steps entering the adjacent room.

There was no more time. He must do something. Opening the door a crack, he peered down the hallway. There he saw a man just outside his office reception, his back turned.

Too risky!

Nathan considered his options. Carrying his briefcase and bag, he wouldn't be able to outrun anyone. Was he prepared to drop everything and run?

He heard more commotion inside the room next door. Keeping his eye on the man standing in the hallway, Nathan was unable to decide whether to stay put or make a run for it.

Suddenly he heard a voice shouting: "Harrison, come in here! On the double! We need to break the door down!"

That was Nathan's cue.

He pushed the door open further and walked stealthily into the hallway, locking the door behind him; he quickly made his way in the opposite direction to the back staircase. He turned at the top of the stairs and looked back. No one was following him—yet. He descended the stairs with his briefcase and bag in tow, but paused at the bottom of the stairs in front of the exit door. He couldn't afford to be careless. He quietly turned the knob on the door and opened it an inch. Ten feet away to his right, a large man with a protruding forehead was standing, looking up and down the alley with his arms folded, his back against the wall. Nathan immediately recognized him as one of the two men he had seen earlier with Sedgwick. He allowed the door to close without the lock engaging, fearful the sound might reach the man's ears. Where to go now?

Nathan crept along the ground-floor hallway, trying to open each door he passed. The fifth door attempted was unlocked, and Nathan found himself looking into a large dark storage closet. Light from the hallway allowed him to see inside to a table littered with tools, and three large barrels underneath it. Nathan stepped inside and pulled on one of the barrels, but it didn't budge. Mustering all his strength, he yanked hard a second time and was able to drag the barrel outward a couple of inches. He squatted down, put his arms around the container, and pulled as hard as he could, gradually maneuvering it a couple of feet away from the wall. After repeating the process with the other two barrels, he closed the door and crouched into the vacant space he had created. Nathan placed his bag and briefcase next to him and pulled hard on the far barrel, so the three barrels together fully concealed his presence. With the door shut, it was pitch black.

Nathan did his best to control his rapid breathing and tried to get comfortable in the cramped quarters; he sat with his legs tightly bent, the back of his feet touching his derriere. He placed the bag of clothes behind his head, against the wall, and the briefcase in front of his feet. In the confined area, he shuddered as he recalled accounts of men who had been incarcerated for debts as little as three pounds, never able to emerge because they had no means of earning enough money in prison to pay even such a paltry debt.

His thoughts then turned to the events of recent days. The gloss and thrill of the Fairfield Park gathering two nights before had largely faded from his mind in the stress of his exigent circumstances; that experience now seemed part of another world. How silly that Miss Charlesworth's rebuke had upset him. How ludicrous to envision encountering the other woman, the one with the mesmerizing eyes. It seemed altogether preposterous to imagine another evening among London's society, when he was fleeing for his freedom.

In truth, Nathan had spent much of his youth in opulent surroundings, mingling with high society, a product of his mother's fame and talent. A soloist of great renown in France, she had retired from the stage early in her career to care for her son after moving to London. There, she had been frequently asked to perform among the gentry class, with Nathan a spectator. Their own dwelling had been far more modest than the many homes they frequented. When his mother had passed on, Nathan continued to mingle with London's elite from time to time, but only as a performer, a *servant* of sorts. Were it not for his musical talent, he would never have partaken of their company. He had no noble heritage and now was nothing more than a common criminal, frantically attempting to evade the law.

As he sat huddled in the dark, amid the suffocating stink of grease, Nathan tried to calm his anxiety by replaying musical compositions in his mind. He rehearsed pieces he had recently mastered, and imagined performing them in the grand halls of Europe. It was his mother he had to thank for that wondrous gift. It was she who had taught him the magic of music. His earliest memory was of her placing his tiny fingers on the keyboard—an expanse of white extending far in either direction. She showed him the correct technique in depressing a key to make a sound. Back then, his universe of notes encompassed only the middle of the keyboard—beyond that small world of ivory, the sounds mysteriously increased in much higher or lower tones. Occasionally he would venture further up or down the keyboard, and he could still recall the wonder he felt when he discovered that the same sounds repeated themselves again, but in lower or higher pitch, with half or double frequency.

Eventually, the fear and anxiousness evaporated into the dark, and Nathan's consciousness faded.

Sometime later, Nathan woke with a start. He was no longer in darkness. Shafts of light filtered into his cramped quarters, and he heard footsteps *inside the room*. Nathan held his breath, desperate to slow his pounding heart. He heard a dull thud—it sounded like the kick of a boot against the barrel.

Nathan closed his eyes, hoping he hadn't been seen. To his horror, he heard the grating scrape of one of the barrels moving on the wooden floor. It had only moved an inch or two, but Nathan knew he would soon be exposed. He was trapped.

Next came a loud grunt as the barrel moved again. Nathan sat petrified, waiting to be discovered. There was nothing he could do.

A man cursed.

More footsteps.

The light dimmed.

The door clicked shut. It was pitch black once more.

Had he been discovered? Was the man going for help? Nathan waited in the darkness, expecting the worst, but praying he hadn't been seen. The seconds marched into minutes. After the passage of half an hour, Nathan's fears began to recede, and he became acutely aware of numbness in his legs. The air was stale and he felt the soak of sweat under his arms and on his back. He wondered how long he had been hiding, but it was too dark to see the hands of his pocket watch. Nathan listened intently for any outward noises. Hearing none, he braced his back against the wall and pushed hard against the barrel in front of his feet until he had enough room to fully extend his legs. He felt the blood flow freely to his lower extremities and exercised his legs. After a few minutes, he tugged the barrel back and hunkered down for another indeterminate stay under the table.

In the quiet blackness, Nathan's thoughts turned to the day, four years earlier, when he had been summoned home from Switzerland. A letter informed him that his mother was deathly ill and desperate to see him before passing on; it also stated that she had important information to share concerning his father.

On the long desperate journey home, Nathan feared he wouldn't reach his mother in time. As the train traveled deep into France, he remembered the sound of the conductor's voice calling out "Nemours!" a small town ten miles from Moret-sur-Loing, the city of his birth. It brought back another early memory; Nathan sitting on the bank of the Loing River alongside his mother, painting the medieval homes, ruins, flowers, and trees on the opposite side of the water. At seven years of age, Nathan and his mother moved away from Moret, never to return, forever enshrining the magical memory of the ancient fortified town in his mind.

Nathan closed his eyes and recalled the train trudging into Paris's Gare du Midi. He remembered the chaos when he exited the train in a swarm of travelers—everyone in a hurry, heading in different directions. In the confusion, he had missed the next train to Calais, delaying his trip two hours, an occurrence he had profoundly regretted ever since. By the time he reached Calais, it was mid-afternoon. He had walked through the town in a daze, waiting for the evening ferry to Dover. There, he had booked a cheap motel, anxiously awaiting the morning train to London.

The train arrived in London before noon during a heavy downpour. When he entered his mother's bedroom, soaked and chilled, Nathan sensed he was too late. She lay motionless on her bed and the expression on the face of the doctor, seated nearby, confirmed the worst. Then he heard a cough and Nathan realized that his mother was yet alive. He rushed to her side and took her right hand in his; he felt the light pressure of her fingers on his hand. She opened her eyes and smiled, recognizing his face. Her left hand moved toward him, revealing a gold wedding band that Nathan had never seen before.

She opened her mouth in a whisper. *"N'oublie jamais combien... je t'aime... mon cher fils. "*[2] She coughed again and tried to whisper again, with greater difficulty: *"Ton père... français... il ma... maq..."*[3] She spoke the "q" forcefully, exhaling hard. It was her last breath. Her open eyes stared vacantly, and Nathan knew she was gone.

Nathan collapsed onto his knees at the side of his mother's bed; he could restrain his tears no longer and they fell plentifully upon his mother's sleeve. Through misted eyes, he took her wedding band and stared at it in the dim light. He noticed an engraving inside the ring. There were two sets of initials, largely faded: "E.S. & A.M." A.M. stood for his mother, of course: Allysandra Mercier. But E.S.? His father's name was Stephen Sinclair. He brought the band closer to his eyes and studied it again. The letters had nearly worn away; it must have originally read "S.S." He placed the ring in his coat pocket—the only memento he had from his father.

Many times since, Nathan had pondered the words his mother had intended to convey about his father. So few clues. "Your father... French." Had his father been French? Nathan disregarded such a notion, since his mother had always told him his father was an Englishman. What had she meant to say, then? Nathan wondered. Was she speaking of her French relatives? Her final syllables had been nearly undecipherable: "*Il ma... maq*" probably had meant "*Il me manque*"—I miss him.

After her death, Nathan had searched his mother's possessions, hoping for more clues. There had been nothing; no letters or other belongings that shed light upon her dying words. Whatever message she had intended for him she had carried to her grave. A quiet funeral followed, with friends and neighbors attending, honoring the memory of a woman who had graced their lives with her peaceful, sweet presence and charity. Two weeks later, Nathan was back in Lausanne, completing his studies; his mother would have wanted that.

As the memory of his mother's final minutes faded, Nathan felt enveloped in loneliness and dread. He couldn't remain sequestered under the table forever. Would he be able to escape Sedgwick's

---

2   Never forget how much... I love you... my dearest son.
3   Your father... French... he—.

clutches again and flee to a distant corner of London? Or would he be apprehended once he left the safety of the closet? He guessed it was early evening and resigned himself, with anxious foreboding, to stay put until after midnight. The hours slowly plodded on until Nathan dozed off again.

When he awoke a second time, Nathan felt disoriented. He knew he had been asleep for a considerable length of time, as his stomach was cramping. He had no feeling in his legs, and his shoulders and coccyx were aching. He tried to estimate how much time had elapsed. He pushed away the barrel and crawled out from behind the table, stood up, and extended his limbs. After the feeling returned in his legs, Nathan opened the closet door and peered into the hallway. The hallway was dark, but a window at the end of the hall provided slight visibility. Nathan pulled out his watch and studied the barely discernible hour and minute hands. He couldn't tell for sure, but the watch appeared to register a quarter to three. Nathan was astounded that so much time had passed. He had spent nearly fourteen hours confined in the closet.

There would never be a better time for him to attempt his escape.

His first instinct was to return to the second floor to see if his living quarters had been breached. As he considered climbing the steps to the second floor, he wondered if Sedgwick had left a man behind, inside his office, waiting for his return. It was too dangerous. The next dilemma was deciding which way to exit. Even at the late hour, Nathan wondered if the building was being watched.

Paranoid that both the front entrance and rear door remained under surveillance, Nathan decided that the better option would be to exit via the rear door. He grabbed his belongings and walked down the hallway to the door. As before, he quietly opened the door a crack and strained to see images in the dark. A few inches more expanded his angle of vision and he suddenly paused. Seated several feet away, leaning against the brick wall on the back porch, he saw the outline of the same large man with thick eyebrows and protruding forehead that he had noticed in the early afternoon. The man's head angled backward against the wall and he was snoring.

Nathan felt unbridled joy, anticipating an opportunity to leave the building undetected. He opened the door slowly, stopping for a few seconds each time the door made a sound. When he had opened it enough, he crept out, holding bag and briefcase, slowly shutting the door until the lock engaged. He winced at the sound, but the sleeping man did not stir. Gingerly, taking care with each step, he walked painstakingly past the seated man, the muddy grime on the cobbled stones silencing his footsteps. Nathan did not begin his normal pace until he left the dark alley. He was still a free man!

Chapter 5

In the dark of a moonless night, Nathan breathed a sigh of relief after he had reached Long Lane, a half-mile west of his office. He did his best to remain on larger boulevards, wanting to avoid night thieves and gangs. On Borough Road, just two hours before dawn, a pale young woman came up to Nathan out of the shadows, covered in heavy makeup, the top of her breasts exposed. She licked her bright red lips and urged Nathan to follow her with the promise of a warm bed for just ten shillings. Nathan ignored her, but she kept following for half a block before giving up.

It seemed as though the briefcase and bag gained weight with each step, and by the time he reached Westminster Bridge, his shoulders and biceps were aching. He sat down at the bridge's entrance, resting his weary limbs. He had traveled the distance of two miles and had three more to go.

The bridge looked like an apparition in the dark sky, with extending arches surmounted by a lofty balustrade with semi-circular octangular recesses and half domes. In the stillness of the night, the sound of a man snoring from the opposite side echoed the length of the bridge. Nathan gathered his things and began walking across the twelve-hundred-foot-long bridge. He was surprised at the number of people slumbering on the bridge; many appeared to be beggars waiting for the morning traffic. Nathan heard the sound of a water cart off in the distance coming his way across the bridge, long before it appeared in view, bringing spring water to replenish the vendors of cool drinks.

Nathan completed the crossing without incident, reaching Victoria Street, when suddenly a teenaged boy with a dirty broom appeared and began sweeping the mud from Nathan's path, using short rapid strokes. Nathan was amused by the boy's efforts, but both Nathan's hands were fully employed carrying his heavy load and he didn't want to risk putting anything on the ground, fearing that a concealed companion of the boy's might appear and grab his bag as he searched for a copper. At the end of the block, the boy gave a slight bow and took off his hat, holding it in front, hoping for a reward.

"Sorry, young chap, but I cannot help you today. Another time."

The boy gave a disappointed look and disappeared into the shadows. A few moments later, Nathan heard the sound of footsteps approaching rapidly from behind. Two young boys, the cross-sweeper and his companion, were closing in on him. Nathan turned and began brandishing both briefcase and bag in a windmill motion, challenging them to try. The sweeper dove for Nathan's right leg while the other grabbed onto the bag in his left arm. Nathan kicked the sweeper hard in the chest and slammed his heavy briefcase on the back of the other assailant, causing him to drop to the ground. The sweeper groaned in pain as the other boy cursed at Nathan. Nathan hurried down the road, knowing he could fend off two youngsters, but not many more. Soon reaching Eaton Square, Nathan was relieved to see the early morning street vendors setting up shop. Daylight would be soon arriving, and the threat of attack would diminish as the sun rose.

Where Eaton Square turned into King's Road, the first filter of morning light came from the east, and by the time Nathan reached Craven's Inn, the sun was just becoming visible on the east horizon. The tide had lowered during his trek and much of the muck from sewers had receded back into the street pipes and gutters. Earlier in the morning, King's Road had been swept by professional sweepers, creating a mirage of cleanliness upon the cobbled stones in the light of early dawn, but Nathan knew that it would soon be dirtied again by the daily procession of vendors, horses, and livestock. Exhausted from the nocturnal trek, his arms and shoulders felt as if they were going to burst. He was also famished, not having eaten since noon the day before.

Nathan entered a corner restaurant near the inn, installed himself at a table against the wall where he could keep his possessions out of sight, and ordered a breakfast of bacon, sausage, cheese, and fried bread. As he sat, he considered his options. Would it be best to flee London and start over somewhere else? It seemed drastic, but the thought held great appeal. A fresh start, far away from Sedgwick's clutches. France was a natural choice, since it was his first language and he had lived there as a young boy. Unfortunately, he didn't know a soul in France. He would be starting over again as an architect; he would have to find work with a firm since he had no resources to open up his own shop.

The other option was to stay put and try to find a way out of his desperate plight. London was, after all, his home. He did have a few clients and a responsibility to complete their projects. To give up was repugnant to Nathan, and contrary to all of his principles and pride. Everything depended on Allenby. If he could get Allenby to pay his debt, he could take care of Sedgwick and continue his life in London. Either way, he needed to find some discreet living quarters, which would give him time to make a reasoned decision.

What dreams Nathan had once had! Eighteen months earlier, he had left Calemby & Co. with visions of designing and creating opulent dwellings of unparalleled beauty, elegance, and grace. During the past year, in his free time—of which he had altogether too much—Nathan had sketched designs which, if built, would be destined to become architectural masterpieces. Unfortunately, there were no qualified clients with whom to share his brilliant handiwork. Such lofty architectural visions could only be fulfilled by the few elite firms that had resumes featuring other similarly grand projects. Gaining a commission for such a landmark structure would surely catapult him to fame and fortune, but it was a dream that had completely faded from Nathan's mind. He was convinced it would never happen.

Nathan deeply regretted the fateful day he decided to leave Calemby & Co. Although it would have taken him many years of hard work and dedication there to participate in grand projects, he wouldn't be in the disastrous financial predicament that now confronted him, nor be facing an indeterminate confinement in prison. It had been the boredom and tedium of low-level drafting that had caused him to resign.

God, give me that boredom now.

As he voraciously consumed his breakfast, Nathan vacantly stared out the window, overlooking the busy traffic on an unusually windy summer morning. When he had first opened his practice, he had fantasized that his first commission would come from a wealthy merchant wishing for a magnificent estate in the London suburbs. To date, the closest he had come to such an ambitious undertaking were the extension of a manor house, a face-lift of a London dwelling, and a backyard landscape the size of a sitting room.

Nathan's goal had been to generate the ambitious sum of five hundred pounds in his first year of practice. He soon realized how unrealistic that goal was. Instead, he had accrued an income of a less than a quarter of that sum in eighteen months' time. Disappointing but not disastrous, were it not that the majority of his income remained unpaid and the balance had been used to pay rent for his office, clerk's wages, living quarters, and other expenses. He had been fortunate to supplement his architect income with gratuities received for his random piano performances.

***

After he finished breakfast, Nathan walked the short distance to Craven's Inn. The five-story structure had seen better years and was acutely in need of paint. As he entered, Nathan saw that the ground floor housed a large tavern. Though the chairs were perched on the tables and the floor was being swept as Nathan glanced at the rectangular room, he assumed a boisterous throng would arrive later in the day, staying until the wee hours of the morning, and he wanted a room as far removed from the noise as possible. He walked to the reception desk and asked for a room on the top floor. He signed in under an assumed name and booked a room for a week, hoping that would be long enough to find something more permanent and inconspicuous nearby. He walked up four flights of stairs to his room and dropped his briefcase and bag onto the floor. The room's ceiling followed the pitch of the roof, imposing a cramped feeling on the tall architect. But the bed beckoned and Nathan collapsed on the mattress. He felt secure in his anonymity for the present. Minutes later, he succumbed to his fatigue.

Chapter 6

The cab stopped at the edge of Belgrave Square. Mr. Travers exited the conveyance and walked leisurely to the front of the elegant mansion. He paused and gazed at the high arched stone entryway and etched-glass door with wrought iron railing, before engaging the knocker. In the letter, his client had recommended that the investigation start here. Through the glass, the silhouette of the butler shortly appeared and the door opened. Mr. Travers handed him his card and the butler retreated with it; moments later the butler invited Mr. Travers in and escorted him to the main parlor.

As he waited for the mistress of the residence, Mr. Travers's eyes were drawn to Barthélemy Prieur's marble sculpture of the goddess Justice in the far corner of the parlor. *That can't possibly be the original,* Mr. Travers marveled. *It would be far more fitting in my office than here.* He imagined the magnificent piece perched on a marble slab in his private office.

Suddenly, he heard footsteps approaching. It was time to stop coveting the damn sculpture and play his role. Mr. Travers's demeanor was instantly adaptable to the circumstances—if required, he could rage like a lion, exude excessive humility, or portray any shade of emotion between. Now, his role called for gentility and politeness.

The mistress of the house appeared. She was only ten years younger than Mr. Travers, and seemed to have put on ten extra pounds since their last encounter.

"How nice to see you again, Randolph."

"The pleasure is all mine, Ophelia," Mr. Travers responded.

"And what brings you here to my home today?" the mistress inquired.

Mr. Travers wasted no time getting to the point. "I have been retained by a client who prefers to remain nameless. My client has a special interest in a guest who was present at your gathering a few days ago."

"Truly? I was hoping you may have had other intentions on your mind," she responded with a sly smile.

Mr. Travers had never been attracted to the woman seated before him, although her wealth certainly held an enticement. Politely, he responded, "Ophelia, shame on you. I am much too old for you."

"We are not so far apart in age." She took the compliment with a smile.

"Rubbish. I am old enough to be your father," Mr. Travers lied.

Ophelia laughed. "So, of which guest is your client inquiring?"

"Before I respond, may I have your solemn promise that you will keep our conversation strictly confidential?" Mr. Travers gave a serious look, but cloaked his question in a polite tone.

"How can I make such a promise without knowing the object and purpose of the inquiry?"

"I can't make that disclosure until I have your promise, but I assure you that there is no illicit motive. My client is a wealthy, well-respected member of the community, who has taken a singular interest in a certain young man."

"Lawyers are always asking for favors, but rarely granting them. I think it would be a breach of etiquette to divulge private information about one of my guests."

"I can assure you it would be in the young man's interest, if you do." Mr. Travers didn't know if his statement was true or not, since no motive or purpose had been provided in the letter. Nevertheless, certain liberties had to be taken from time to time, in the legal profession.

"All right, my lips shall remain sealed. Who, pray tell, has the interest of your esteemed client?"

Mr. Travers paused and then spoke the name slowly, waiting for any facial indication the name might provoke. "Mr. Nathan Sinclair."

The facial indication on Ophelia Sommersby was one of wholesome delight. "Oh, indeed! What an exceptional young man he is. So, am I to assume Mr. Sinclair has a female admirer among the English gentry?"

Fifty years of experience in dealing with client confidences had prepared Mr. Travers to maintain a stoic expression; there was not even the slightest hint offered in response.

Thirty minutes later, quite satisfied with the interview, Mr. Travers left the residence.

***

It was mid-afternoon when Nathan awoke. Before opening his eyes, he believed he was in his bedroom on Dockhead Street, until the scent and feeling of the coarse bed cover reminded him he was a temporary guest in the inn and a man with no longer a home. He was confident that he had not been followed during the long trek but knew that he needed to continue to take precautions. The building had a single staircase, and Nathan was concerned about his escape options if he ever needed to make a hasty exit. A single large dormer window in the middle of the room opened onto a small ledge. Nathan opened the window and felt a strong breeze against his face. He crawled onto the ledge, looking down onto the boulevard sixty feet below. The street traffic was heavy in the afternoon sun and he could hear the cries of vendors and curses from angry drivers.

With the wind howling, Nathan cautiously stood up from the ledge, surveying for a viable exit route should he ever find himself forced to flee. The pitch of the roof was steep, but if he climbed up from the window ledge, he could reach the crown of the roof where it would be possible to walk on a relatively stable platform to the adjacent building's roof. Taking care to balance himself against the gusting wind, Nathan determined that he needed to essay his mount at roughly a forty-five degree angle. He carefully took a couple of steps upward, secure that he could catch the lintel that capped the dormer wall if his feet gave way. But his feet held on the steep grade as he continued slowly up the roof, temporarily leaving the safety of the dormer's lintel. As he neared the crown, though, Nathan felt his right foot begin to slide downward and he quickly grabbed onto the transom at the rooftop and steadied himself until he was perched on top.

Once there, the strength of the wind nearly caused Nathan to lose his balance. Crouching low, he continued to the edge of the neighboring building, whose flat roof was about two feet lower than the inn's; the gap of three feet between the buildings was a distance Nathan could safely negotiate. If he was forced to flee in haste, the only risk would be the initial climb to the roof's crest.

Nathan retraced his steps along the roof's ridge and realized that descending would be far more treacherous than his upward climb. He continued until he reached the roof's crown directly above the dormer and slid down the roof, stopping at the lintel at the top of window. There, he carefully lowered himself past the pediment and onto the window's ledge. He reentered his room through the open window. Although he had an exit route, it was not without significant risk. He also knew that since he could be forced to flee on a moment's notice, it would be important to keep his possessions packed at all times.

No one knows I'm here, Nathan thought to himself. *I must maintain a low profile and stay indoors during the day. I always wanted to be a hermit,* he laughed inwardly. *Now, if I can outlive Sedgwick, I shall be free to roam once more—in just twenty or thirty years' time.*

Nathan's first order of business was to break the rule he had just enacted, the rule to remain indoors. It was imperative that he confront Mr. Allenby and tell him of his dire predicament. Nathan was furious at himself for not having insisted on an advance retainer before starting work on his project, although Allenby had seemed a reasonable risk at the time. He would also remind Allenby how he had come to his aid, advancing twenty pounds to his client to help complete the project. Nathan had pestered him many times before, but this time he would accept none of Allenby's excuses. Nathan washed his face, changed his shirt, and readied himself for a spirited encounter with his former client. With renewed determination and vigor, he felt there might yet be a way out of his living nightmare.

Nathan descended the four flights of stairs to the ground floor. Opening the front door of the inn onto the street, he was pleasantly surprised that the air smelled less foul than usual. A strong smell of manure from the livestock continued, but the putrid smell of sewage was largely absent. The massive intercepting aqueduct flanking the north side of the Thames had recently been completed, while the south-side system was still in construction; the aqueducts were intended to divert sewers and drains into treatment plants where deodorized water was discharged into the river. The enormous undertaking had involved eighty-two miles of brick intercepting sewers built beneath London's streets, channeling all waste eastward by gravity. These connected to over four hundred and fifty miles of main sewers, themselves receiving the contents of thirteen thousand miles of small local sewers, dealing daily with a half-million gallons of waste. It was certainly working better here on the west side of London than in the east side, south of the Thames, where Nathan had been dwelling. Farther down the Thames, as more sewage collected, sewage congestion posed much more of a problem.

Before venturing into the street, Nathan remained in the frame of the open door for several moments, carefully scanning the street up and down for any sign of Sedgwick or his cohorts. He studied idle men standing near a vendor of cold drinks. Every face, every man could be a surrogate of Sedgwick's. At a large stand on the corner of the street, women and men were examining produce and fruit. Across the street, Nathan observed young children playing in front of a dilapidated building, supervised by a stern-looking older man. The children were being taunted by young street urchins with dirty faces, whom Nathan surmised were homeless. Random congregations of men in small groups were conversing, some laughing, others in serious discussion. Nathan was oblivious to the sound of neighing horses, grunting pigs, and other livestock, sounds to which he had long grown accustomed, as he watched the mass of carriages fighting for space.

Surveying the scene before him, his attention was diverted by a young lady hailing a cab, her scarf flailing in the wind; she was standing in front of the building where the children were playing. There was something familiar about her. Then he stared in disbelief. Could it be? Improbable, but it appeared to be. Yes, she was the possessor of the eyes that had transfixed him a few nights before at the Sommersby residence! The vivid recollection of that brief encounter electrified him, and all thoughts of his dire circumstances instantly faded, as he immediately set chase on foot after the horse-drawn cab.

With traffic congested, the cab plied slowly up King's Road. Nathan was able to keep up with a fast-paced walk and occasional jog. After several blocks, the traffic eased and Nathan found himself sprinting to keep the cab in sight in the heavy dusky air. The cab turned left on Sloan Street, and the congestion and noise of commercial streets soon gave way to a more tranquil residential neighborhood, whose homes grew in size and stature as the distance from the business district increased. Running out of breath and strength, Nathan fell far behind and had abandoned hope of keeping the cab in sight, when, to his surprise and delight, the conveyance came to a stop a short distance from Belgrave Square. From afar, Nathan observed the young lady exit the cab and enter a residence. Catching his breath, Nathan swiftly walked to the residence and made a mental note of its street and number: 34 *Faubourg Lane*.

It was an impressive home, indeed, as were all of the structures on either side of the avenue. The detached homes were large, many three or four levels high, with well-manicured yards in front and spacious gardens in back. There were mansions with steeply pitched roofs with turrets, eaves, and gables, and others possessing verandas with porch posts and spindles.

I need the name of the occupants, Nathan surmised. He stood on the sidewalk near the front of the elegant residence, trying to appear as nonchalant as possible. After a few uncomfortable and conspicuous minutes, Nathan saw a maid appear outside the adjoining residence and begin sweeping the front porch. Seizing the opportunity, Nathan casually walked up to the porch.

"Excuse me, miss," he politely inquired. "Might you tell me the name of the family who dwells next door?"

The maid looked up and suspiciously eyed the stranger. "Ah'm tow'd to keep ta missef, sir. Wee neighbors 'spect thea pree-vacy."

Nathan smiled at her. "I am on love's errand. I saw the young lady next door at Fairfield Park a few days ago, but was unable to gain an introduction before she slipped out."

The maid gasped in astonishment. "Yer 'av bin ter Fairfield Park, sir?"

"I am a friend of Lady Sommersby," Nathan offered, hoping that information might do the trick.

"Oh, Ah ain't 'ed t' pleasure a-makin' thea acquaint'ess, but mah mistress... shi 'as bin theear." Examining Nathan up and down and considering him a handsome and harmless chap, she volunteered. "Ah guess it worn't 'arm none if ah tell yer tha's t'Lancastah 'ome. But yer dint 'ear it from me."

"And the young lady's name?"

"Why, 'at's Sir Lancastah's niece, right... Miss Regina."

Delighted to now have a name to associate with the splendid eyes, Nathan heartily thanked the maid, assuring her that he would keep her assistance confidential.

Sauntering back down the street, Nathan felt lighter and in excellent spirits. His happy affect, however, soon became dampened by a vivid reminder of his imminent arrest, his financial poverty, and his inferior rank in the presence of such magnificent and expensive homes. He also recalled with great clarity the degrading episode with Miss Charlesworth. He fretted that if he could somehow clear his debt with Sedgwick, an introduction with Regina might result in another episode of degradation. But he took comfort in the tenderness in her eyes; she would never offend him the way Miss Charlesworth had. He was certain of that. There had been a shared moment, however brief, of mutual respect and interest. He now had a name to match the face. Surely, there would be an opportunity to meet her again. He felt renewed optimism as he retraced his steps back to the inn, momentarily distracted from his task to visit Mr. Allenby.

***

Sedgwick was sitting at his desk when he heard the knock on the door he'd been expecting. The two men he had hired to track down Sinclair walked in, neither looking pleased.

"I take it you've had no luck finding him?"

Both men shook their heads.

"He is a sneaky one. You have got to use your heads. Think how he thinks. Outsmart him." As he looked at the two men, he wondered if these hulks had brains at all.

"I copied down the names and addresses of Sinclair's clients, when we barged into his office yesterday. There are only five listed. The key one is Theodore Allenby, who lives in Paddington. He owes Sinclair a great deal of money, although the man's mortgaged to the hilt and couldn't rub two coppers together. I am bloody certain that Sinclair will be paying him a visit."

Sedgwick turned to the man with the mustache and sideburns. "I want you over there. Now! Keep out of sight. You find him... cuff your wrist to his. Do not let him get away—he's a slippery bastard!" Sedgwick pushed over the handcuffs he'd purchased earlier in the day.

"Then what do I do?" The man had a puzzled look on his face.

"You put him in a cab and bring him back to my office, imbecile. I shall personally escort him to the police station." Sedgwick gave him the street address.

"An extra sovereign to whoever catches him. On your way!"

Chapter 7

Nathan had an early dinner at a restaurant several blocks from the inn. Having a name and address to go with the possessor of the beautiful eyes had buoyed his spirits.

If I hadn't been forced to flee, I might never have seen her again, he thought to himself—a silver lining to his misery.

"Regina Lancaster," he whispered softly. He loved the sound of her name and imagined being introduced to her in society. No sooner did he visualize the encounter than he laughed to himself.

I must be mad, to think she or anyone from her background could ever have interest in a man as pathetic as I.

Having finished dinner, it was time to return to the task at hand. Nathan hailed a cab and reached Allenby's residence on Westbourne Terrace a half hour later. The summer's sun still hung in the heavens, casting long shadows on the ground, as Nathan exited the cab in front of Allenby's residence. Nathan dispensed a few shillings to the cab driver and walked onto the sidewalk.

Nathan looked at the impressive structure and felt a touch of pride at the contribution he had made to its striking appearance. Suddenly, he heard a twig break behind him. Nathan turned abruptly, looking at the large trees nearby, studying the shadows.

It is just the wind.

Nathan tried the gate. It was shut, but unlocked. He opened the gate, walked to the front porch, and rang the bell.

***

The large man with bushy sideburns and mustache barked the address to the cab driver. From Sedgwick's office in Whitechapel, it took forty-five minutes to reach west London. He told the driver to stop a couple of blocks west of Allenby's residence, wanting to canvass the neighborhood before approaching the residence. He moved methodically down the boulevard, looking in all directions. As he approached the block where Allenby's home was located, he took in the view of the street and the large trees on either side of the road. There was no one in sight.

He looked for a place to hide where he would have full view of Allenby's residence. He found a spot sixty feet east, where there were several poplar trees heavily laden with leaves. He sat down behind the trees and watched as random leaves blew gently down the cleanly swept cobbled road. It was as fine a neighborhood as he had ever seen.

He had only been waiting a short time when he saw a hansom cab approaching from the west. The large man stood up and watched as the conveyance came to a stop directly in front of Allenby's manor home. From behind the trees he spied a tall man in a black suit emerge. He was sure it was Sinclair and took a step forward, crushing a dead tree root that branched onto the sidewalk. It made a crack-splitting sound and he instantly retreated behind the poplars.

Holding his breath, the man stayed put for ten more seconds and then peered again from behind the trees. Sinclair had advanced through the front gate, and the man heard the door chime.

***

Nathan heard footsteps coming from inside. The door opened and an elderly man appeared.

"May I help you, sir?"

"Is Mr. Allenby home?" Nathan contrived a friendly expression.

"Who may I ask is calling?"

"Nathan Sinclair."

"One moment, please." The elderly man closed the door. A few minutes later, he returned.

"I am sorry. Mr. Allenby is indisposed."

Nathan frowned. "Indisposed? Tell him it is a matter of great urgency."

"He cannot be disturbed."

"Tell him that if he does not see me now, I shall be hiring an attorney and filing a lis pendens against his residence." Nathan's clerk friend had suggested the choice of words.

The elderly man hesitated, pondering whether to convey the message. With just a nod, he closed the door once more.

***

The large man observed the door open for a few seconds, then close, with Sinclair still standing outside. He scratched his head, wondering why Sinclair hadn't been ushered inside. If Allenby wasn't home, why was Sinclair still at the door? Now was the perfect time to advance, while Sinclair's back was facing him. He planned his approach, excited by the thought of collecting the extra sovereign. He needed to get as close to Sinclair as possible, before Sinclair realized who he was; otherwise, he might not be able to catch him in a chase. Tentatively, he stepped onto the boulevard, taking care to keep as quiet as possible.

With deliberation, he took a second step, then a third, and continued his silent advance. He felt his heart beating madly, aware that the prey was nearly in his grasp.

Just a few steps now, and he would be at the front gate. Sinclair would have nowhere to run.

Suddenly, the door to Allenby's residence opened and the large man froze in his tracks.

***

The front door opened a third time, and Mr. Allenby appeared.

Allenby was in his mid-forties and nearly the same height as Nathan, although not nearly as lean. He had light curly hair and wore a perpetual dimpled smile on his face, even when he was not smiling inside. He had on a dinner jacket and it was evident that Nathan had arrived during his meal.

"How nice to see you, Nathan. I was just finishing dinner. Sorry to keep you waiting. Please come in."

Nathan followed him in and the door closed behind them.

***

The large man stood petrified for a moment, hoping his presence wouldn't register on the face of the man who had appeared at the open door. He resumed walking on the sidewalk past the residence, trying to appear as nonchalant as possible. He saw Sinclair enter and the door shut behind him. He cursed at himself, knowing he had been too slow to react. If he hadn't hesitated so long behind the tree, he would have captured Sinclair. At least he had Sinclair cornered now. It was just a matter of time before he exited; the man would be ready to pounce on him when he did.

There was a large oak tree in front of Allenby's gated residence. If he stood carefully behind the tree, it would shield his frame from

Sinclair when he left the dwelling. Relaxing a bit, not expecting detection while Sinclair was inside, he retraced his steps to the tree and positioned himself so that he could not be observed from the front porch of Allenby's home. He was less than fifteen feet from the gate's entrance. Sinclair wouldn't be able to react in time.

Ten minutes went by and the large man continued standing behind the tree, occasionally poking his head from behind the tree and looking at the porch. His heart continued to beat rapidly as he anticipated his next move. He would wait until Sinclair opened the gate and then catch him by surprise. He took the handcuffs out of his coat pocket and made ready for his prey.

***

"So, what brings you my way tonight?" Allenby's jovial expression displayed genuine curiosity.

There was no joy in Nathan's expression, and he wasted no time with pleasantries. "You owe me seventy-five pounds. It has been six months since your project was finished. Because of you, a warrant has been issued for my arrest, *based on money I borrowed to finish your home*. But for the grace of God, I should be in prison this very evening!"

"Oh. What a pity! I am so sorry." Allenby's pleasant demeanor changed instantly into abject empathy.

"I need full payment tonight. I have been running for my life, forced to abandon my home and office because of the warrant. I must have full payment tonight. I must!"

"Oh, dear me. I don't know how I can possibly do that. I am deeply in debt myself and have been living off the generosity of my many creditors, including you." Allenby's lips curled up in a smile that conveyed his utmost gratitude.

Nathan's stomach churned.

"Mr. Allenby. I can wait no longer."

"When my house sells, you shall be paid." Allenby's smile had vanished.

"It has been on the market for six months now," Nathan demurred.

"Yes I know, but a willing buyer may show up tomorrow."

"That is not good enough. My situation is desperate. I must be paid tonight."

Allenby only shook his head.

Nathan squirmed in his seat. "You are forcing me to take drastic action."

Allenby gave Nathan a helpless look.

"I shall have my solicitor file a plaint and a lis pendens against your residence."

Allenby raised one eyebrow and Nathan sensed Allenby's doubt that he had the ability to hire a lawyer.

"If you choose to take legal action, you will have to wait in line with the others." There was no more softness in Allenby's regard. He stood up, a signal that Nathan was being excused.

Nathan refused to take the cue and remained seated. A feeling of gloom came over him as he spoke quietly. "I don't understand why you insist on treating me so shabbily, after all the work, time, and money I spent to help beautify your home."

Allenby went over to Nathan and patted him on his back. "There, there. I am sure things will work out for both of us."

Nathan looked ashamed and embarrassed. "I have nowhere to go."

Allenby hesitated, but once the words were spoken, he couldn't retrieve them. "Let me see if I can find something to help."

Nathan waited with his head down.

Ten minutes later, Allenby entered the room and handed Nathan a small pouch containing coins.

"This is the best I can do." Nathan stood up and took the pouch, opening it. It was full of shillings and pence. It couldn't be more than five pounds altogether. Nathan thrust it back at Allenby in anger. "I can do nothing with that!"

Allenby seemed relieved to possess the pouch once more.

"I am sorry. If you cannot accept my extreme generosity in these difficult times, then there is nothing more I can do."

On principle and pride, the right thing to do was to storm out, without the pouch. But desperate men do desperate things. Pride be damned! Nathan grabbed the pouch from Allenby's grasp, and stormed toward the entry.

"Nathan," Allenby called after him before Nathan could open the front door.

Nathan turned around, removing his hand from the doorknob.

Allenby stood and stared at him for a few moments. His pride still smarting, Nathan gave a reluctant smile and nod. Try as he might, he couldn't stay angry with the man. Nathan turned back to the door to exit.

"Nathan, don't go."

A ray of hope entered Nathan's mind. Maybe he had more to

offer.

Allenby walked up to him.

"My butler noticed a man lurking in front of the house," Allenby spoke gravely.

Nathan's eyes opened wide in horror. It dawned on him how foolish he had been to visit Allenby, when Sedgwick was certainly aware of where he lived.

"Come with me, I will show you. You can look discreetly through the window and see if you recognize him." Nathan followed him to the library, which had a window facing the boulevard.

Standing at the corner of the window, Allenby first peered out. "Tall man standing behind a tree. He has something shiny in his hands. You must see this."

Allenby retreated and Nathan approached. With the window twenty feet east of the front porch, the man was clearly visible, and Nathan recognized him instantly. He also saw the handcuffs dangling from the man's right hand.

"I need to exit by the rear, at once," he said to Allenby.

Allenby nodded and escorted Nathan to the back of the house. "Let me check, first," Allenby said as he walked into the backyard and looked around.

He reentered the house seconds later. "Coast is clear. You'd better leave now. Climb over the fence and you can easily get to the next street through my neighbor's yard."

Nathan thanked him, but remembered Allenby's initial hesitation and wondered if Allenby had nearly opted to let him be thrown to the wolves—one less creditor to deal with.

Nathan jumped over the fence and was soon on another tree-lined boulevard. He walked several blocks before spying a cab and continuing on his journey back to Craven's Inn. Relieved to have escaped Sedgwick's clutches again, Nathan also knew that Allenby would not be able to bail him out of the debt he owed. There were no other options, and the stifling feeling of hopelessness returned.

***

The large man waited patiently. Fortunately, the boulevard had been quiet during dinnertime; no one had passed by since he had positioned himself near the front gate. He checked his watch. It had been an over an hour since Sinclair had gone inside. The large man assumed Sinclair had been invited to dine. The sun was setting and the man wondered how much longer he would have to remain before he saw his prey.

Another hour passed. It was nearly dark. His legs were aching from standing in one place. He was also getting hungry. It was taking too long.

Yet another hour passed, and the lights inside the residence turned off. The large man readied himself for the capture. Surely, Sinclair would be leaving now! He waited for the front door to open, but the house remained motionless. He saw a light in an upper story chamber. Twenty minutes later, the house was totally dark.

Confused, the large man finally sat down behind the tree in the dark and continued to wait until he heard bells from a distant church, followed by twelve chimes. It was midnight. Where the bloody hell was Sinclair? Had Allenby invited him to stay the evening? There was no point staying any longer tonight. His throat was parched, so he stood up and began walking in the direction of a tavern he had noticed on his way to Allenby's. He would return in the morning before the sun rose to continue his surveillance.

Chapter 8

He hadn't been to Bermondsey in years—and it would be years again before he returned, if he had anything to do with it. Through the cab window he surveyed, with disgust, the open cesspool on Grange Road and instantly pulled a scented handkerchief from his coat, placing it under his nostrils. Construction work on the sewers had caused traffic to jam the arteries pouring into Dockhead Road, forcing Mr. Travers to endure an extra fifteen minutes of suffocating, sweltering heat and toxic fumes. When the cab finally came to a stop, he waited patiently for a street sweeper to cut a path through the frothing grime. He wondered if the vast sewage project would ever be completed.

Mr. Travers walked up to the brick building and shook his head. He couldn't begin to imagine what possible interest his client had in this Sinclair fellow. Certainly, no member of the English gentry in their right mind would employ an architect who conducted business in such a blighted neighborhood. Mr. Travers examined the building's small rectangular marquee situated in the front door's alcove, searching for Sinclair's name. Plenty of names, but nothing resembling Sinclair. He then stepped back onto the sidewalk and looked up at the windows, wondering if there might be a sign for the architect there. There was nothing. Could Lady Sommersby have been mistaken about Sinclair's address? He needed to find out.

I would like to get a good look at him, Mr. Travers thought, but realized that he didn't dare venture inside the building, for fear that his mission might be compromised. Engaging the services of another sweep, he walked across the squalid road to a vendor who was preparing for the noonday crowd.

"Excuse me. I want to confirm whether I have arrived at the correct address. Do you know if a Mr. Nathan Sinclair has offices in the building over there?" Mr. Travers motioned to the building directly across the street.

"Oh, Mista' Sin-clah. Yessir. I know 'im well. E's a regulah 'ere, 'though I ain't seen 'im for a week o' so. E's real keen on mah smoked ham—care to sample a morsel?"

Mr. Travers shook his head.

Interesting riddle, Mr. Travers thought. *Sinclair, hobnobbing with London's elite, all the while living like a pauper.*

***

The following day, Nathan dared not venture outdoors after the narrow escape at Allenby's. He still had some fruit and vegetables from his purchase the day before. Inside the cramped room with slanting walls and low ceiling, Nathan felt claustrophobic and restless. Sedgwick was not about to give up, and he was sly. It was just a matter of time before he tracked Nathan down again, and Nathan knew he might not be so lucky next time.

Reflecting on the police trespass into his office, Nathan realized that Sedgwick might well have the names and addresses of all of his clients.

I will need to avoid visiting them for the time being. For the moment, though, he felt secure.

He forced himself to get his mind off Sedgwick by extracting some drafting papers from his briefcase and reviewing the sketches he had made for the backyard landscape.

I may never have a chance to see this project come together.

It was hard to stay focused on such a mundane task, when his whole future was at risk. After three hours, he had little more than erasure marks to show for his work.

He walked over to the bed and slumped against the headboard. Amid his misery and despair, there was thankfully one pleasant thought on his mind—Regina Lancaster. He relived the instant when he had stood up from the piano and discovered her mesmerizing eyes staring back at him. Why did they seem so familiar? The two of them had shared a special moment, he was certain of it.

Has she ever thought of me since that day? Nathan wondered to himself. *Did I make a singular impression on her, as well? Or have I been forgotten altogether?*

I must see her again. God, allow me to remain a free man long enough to see her eyes once more.

He let his mind wander and imagined their next encounter. He imagined being introduced to her, conversing with her, and hearing the voice that matched the eyes. Yet the more he reflected on her, the more the notion seemed preposterous.

Suddenly an utterly insane thought entered his mind.

Maybe there is a way to see her again, Nathan thought. But just as quickly, he discarded the bold notion. It wouldn't leave his mind, however, and as he continued to mull it over, he started to believe that the idea didn't seem quite so ridiculous. Countess von Brandt's home was just half a mile from Faubourg Lane and the Lancaster home. He would pay his respects and personally accept the Countess's recent invitation to perform. Then he would make his own request of her. Unfortunately, it would necessitate another trip outside the inn and another breach of his inviolate rule to remain inside until dark.

***

An hour later, the butler escorted Nathan into the von Brandt residence. The Countess appeared soon after, clearly immensely delighted to be receiving Nathan. A patron of the arts, she particularly loved the piano and had even studied for several years when she was a girl, although she had never played as an adult. She looked younger than her seventy years, due in part to her excellent figure and the hair she took care to dye much darker than its natural color.

The Countess had been a widow for fifteen years. Despite the passage of time, she always wore black in perpetual mourning of her deceased husband. Nathan had heard that the two had never gotten along in marriage, arguing incessantly and demeaning each another openly and often. However, once her husband was buried, the Countess only spoke in the most loving and glowing terms of her late companion, such that one would have thought that their life together had been pure bliss. Her homage may have been a result of the vast fortune he had bequeathed to her, despite his frequent threats during their marriage to leave her penniless.

"What a pleasure to see you again, Nathan." The Countess put forth her hand. "I hope your visit today is in confirmation of your acceptance of my invitation."

Nathan smiled gallantly. "It would do me the greatest honor to perform." After further polite exchanges, Nathan inquired about the topic for which he had arrived personally.

"Dear Countess, I wonder if you are acquainted with Sir Lancaster on Faubourg Lane?"

"Why, of course. A fine man, respected by all."

"And do you know his niece?" Nathan inquired timorously.

"Regina? A lovely girl of extraordinary sagacity. Orphaned at an early age, but treated like his own daughter. Do *you* know them?"

"Not precisely. They were present at a gathering at Fairfield Park a short time ago, where I performed a Chopin ballade. I observed her from afar following my performance..." Nathan averted his gaze, searching for words, embarrassed at the confession he was about to make.

The Countess eased his task. "And you would like an introduction?"

"I would like that very much." Nathan's face lit up.

"You are wondering if they are on the guest list?" The Countess gave a knowing smile. "I think we have room for more. I will send out an invitation today."

"Only if you are certain it would not be an imposition."

"Not at all. It will be my exquisite pleasure to make the introduction."

Nathan left the von Brandt residence in great anticipation, intent on developing a repertoire fashioned especially for Regina's ears. For that, he would need access to a piano and his sheet music.

I am certainly mad! Nathan thought to himself. *Inviting Miss Lancaster to the Countess von Brandt's so that she can make an introduction. How humiliating it would be for the Countess if I should be cast in prison before the dinner party.*

Well, it shan't be too expensive for her to transport her lovely pianoforte to Coldbath Fields Prison, and her guests will surely follow. I will give them all a concert they'll never forget.

As he thought of performing for the Countess *and particularly for Regina*, he was reminded of Miss Charlesworth's words: "You are twenty years out of fashion." Nathan decided *that* would not be the case if he was still a free man when the day of the gathering arrived. He would go to a tailor today and have a suit made. After all, he had most of the ten pounds remaining from Lady Sommersby's generosity, plus the pouch of coins from Allenby containing another five. That should be enough for a well-tailored suit.

Later that afternoon, Nathan visited a well-respected tailor, seeking the latest and best in men's fashions. The tailor's quoted price of thirteen pounds, eight shillings seemed excessive and distressed Nathan. He offered seven pounds. After further negotiations, a price of ten pounds was agreed. That would leave Nathan with a little over three pounds upon which to survive.

Thank God for Allenby's miserly donation, Nathan thought. *I'm glad I didn't let pride stand in my way of snaring the pouch. Without it, I wouldn't be able to afford the suit.*

Buying the new suit had nothing to do with Miss Charlesworth's biting remarks, or so Nathan told himself. It was simply time for new formalwear. For Regina's sake, he should be attired with the latest London fashions, so she didn't feel awkward in his presence. He wanted to make a good first impression. Nevertheless, Nathan couldn't help wondering if Regina would reject him once she learned of his lowly station and desperate circumstances. But hadn't she been touched by his performance at Lady Sommersby's? Imprinted in his mind was the vivid memory of the moment when their eyes had met.

The tailor went over the latest cuts and men's fashions with Nathan. He proposed a dark tailcoat with wide lapels, a collarless waistcoat, and matching trousers. He showed Nathan materials in black and in dark shades of grey; there really wasn't too much in the way of color choices. Black it was, of course, for evening attire. The tailor took the measurements and promised the suit would be ready the evening before the party.

One problem vexed Nathan. He had no pianoforte on which to rehearse his program for Miss Lancaster. He could get by without it, but he didn't want to just *get by*. He wanted to astound her. He had an extensive supply of sheet music back at his flat, which would aid him in selecting the right compositions and perfecting them. He needed to return to his living quarters, and Nathan knew that doing so would be a considerable risk. After all, it had only been four days since the police had burst into his office. Sedgwick's men were likely still scouting the area, waiting for him to reappear. He reflected on the best time to return. Late at night or in the wee hours of the morning remained his best option.

His mandate to remain inside his room was all but forgotten as Nathan hailed the first cab that came his way before the sun set. As the cab trundled back over Westminster Bridge and entered east London, the strong sewage smell returned, getting particularly foul as he approached Abbey Road. He instructed his driver to stop four blocks from his office. Nathan scanned the proximity through the glass before exiting. He didn't recognize a soul. He slowly made his way back to his building, stopping at each turn in the road, studying the landscape, searching for signs of his creditor. When he reached Dockhead Road, Nathan hid behind a corner building and carefully examined the surrounding area. There was no sign of Sedgwick or his men, nor did it appear as though anyone else was staking out his building, as far as he could tell. Nathan retraced his steps a couple of blocks and tucked into a local tavern, hiding himself at a dark corner table, where he would remain until the time was right.

Just after midnight, Nathan emerged and carefully walked back to Dockhead Road. He feared entering from the main thoroughfare and opted to go down the alley again. He looked up and down the narrow passage, unable to discern in the dark anyone in the rear of the building. He walked slowly up the alley, still muddy from sewage overflow, although significantly less so than before, the tide having lowered.

Twenty feet into the alleyway, Nathan heard a sound behind him. He stopped in his tracks. There was silence. He took another step forward and stopped, wondering if it was his imagination. He turned around, trying to determine if anyone had followed him.

Suddenly, a large man came lunging toward him. Nathan had just enough time to back up a half step and raise his arms defensively before the force from the man knocked him onto the ground and into the mud. Both men slid a couple of feet in the mire. His attacker was on top and the attacker's hands were trying to find purchase on secure ground, but slipping in the mud. Nathan exerted all the strength he had to push the man's torso until they were side by side. As they wrestled in the filth, Nathan managed to connect a hard blow to the man's face. It stunned the man and Nathan took advantage, climbing on top of his assailant. Nathan forcefully dug his knee into the chest of his attacker and placed his hands around his throat, squeezing tightly. The man flailed at him, struggling for breath. When the man stopped moving, Nathan released his grip on the man's neck. The assailant gasped for breath, his lungs finally filling. In the dark, it was evident to Nathan that the man was not one of the two men he had previously seen with Sedgwick.

Still kneeling on top of the coughing man, Nathan asked in a menacing voice, "How much is Sedgwick paying you?"

The man gave a confused look.

"Winston Sedgwick!" Nathan raised his voice. He tightened his grip again.

The man grunted and shook his head.

Could he be just a random thief?

He looked down at him. "You ever try that again, and you shall have hell to pay! Do you understand?" The man was silent. Nathan stood up and kicked him hard in the mid-section, and the man grunted in acknowledgment.

Covered in filth, Nathan wiped the grime from his face as best he could with his moist hands. He continued down the alley, took out his key, and unlocked the back door. With one eye on his assailant, who still lay groaning on the ground, Nathan scraped the mud from the bottom of his boots on the porch step and walked inside, shutting the door behind. He was not yet in the clear and wondered if Sedgwick had left someone inside his office, or worse yet, in his living area. He quietly walked up the steps, bracing himself for the sound of a pursuer. He finally reached his living quarters, unlocked the door, and opened it a crack. It was pitch black inside. Nathan inched to the crate where the candle and matches lay, and light soon appeared. He rejoiced when he saw his box piano still ensconced against the wall. He checked the cupboards—they were still full of food. With new confidence, he walked into his bedroom. Everything was as he had left it. The room hadn't been breached; the hidden door was still locked.

Nathan breathed a sigh of relief. Fortunately, he had left some clothes behind. He removed the clothes covered in grime and washed the dirt off his face. He put on clean underwear and a new set of clothes.

My God! I should have stayed put, he thought. *They probably think I jumped out the window.* He remembered forgetting to shut his office window in his haste. What a lucky break!

Nathan yearned to sit down and play his beloved piano, but he didn't dare do so unless he was certain that no one was waiting for him inside the office next door. Nathan assumed Sedgwick knew that he was a pianist.

The only way to find out if someone was lying in wait was to peer inside the office. It was half past midnight, and Nathan assumed anyone lurking in the office might have nodded off by now. He went to the hidden door in his bedroom, and quietly lifted the latch and opened the door a few inches. There was some light from the kerosene lamp on the street that filtered into the room through the window. He waited for his eyes to adjust to the dark. There was no one there. On the table against the wall was a stack of random drawings that he had left in the office; they didn't appear to have been disturbed. Nor had the shelf above, which still contained his drafting texts from Lausanne.

Nathan noticed that the door between the office and reception was ajar. There was a large crack where the door bulged outward from the doorknob to the middle of the door—undoubtedly a result of the police trespass from before. The window was now shut.

Nathan grabbed the lit candle, walked quietly into the office, and then continued into the reception room. The drawers of the desk were closed; there was no sign that papers had been disturbed in the reception area. Nathan found it curious that both the reception and office were neat and tidy. He checked the front door and was pleased to find it locked.

How strange, thought Nathan. *Everything is in order. The only sign of the intrusion is the damage to the interior door.* He had expected to see strewn papers, open drawers, and books littering the floor.

Quietly and confidently, he returned back to his adjacent dwelling, closing and locking the hidden door. He placed the candle near the piano. He had already decided on the opening composition he would perform at Countess von Brandt's: Beethoven's *Pastoral* Sonata. He closed his eyes and imagined that he was seated at the Countess's pianoforte, with Regina Lancaster standing nearby. Tentatively and quietly, he began playing the sonata's first movement. After playing the opening stanzas he stopped, listening for footsteps or a voice. He waited a couple of minutes, but heard nothing. He resumed the composition, his ears attentive, but there was only the sound of Beethoven's musical genius.

After completing the sonata, Nathan went through the sheet music stacked on the piano, contemplating what other pieces to perform. He wondered if he should limit the concert to one composer, or mix in several artists. Should the music be optimistic or melancholy? His vivid recollection of Regina's eyes caused him to opt for themes with a serious, contemplative mood. He narrowed down his remaining selections to a Chopin mazurka and etude, a Muller scherzo, and selections from Onslow's *Six Pièces pour Piano*.

Nathan continued playing the instrument until the morning sun filtered through the bedroom window and into the interior room through the open door. He was surprised he had been seated at the keyboard for five hours without a break. Fatigue enveloped him, spurred by the onset of a new day. Secure in the certainty that his hidden dwelling hadn't been detected, Nathan lay down on his bed and went to sleep.

Nathan was dreaming peaceably when suddenly he heard the sound of the hardwood floor creaking. He opened his eyes and to his shock saw Mr. Sedgwick standing at the foot of his bed with a maniacal smile, accompanied by a member of the Metropolitan Police.

The men rustled him from bed and stood watch while he changed into his clothes. Nathan felt overpowering dread. His life was over. He would never see Regina again.

"Please, is there no other solution?" Nathan pleaded.

Sedgwick laughed lustily. "You shall be there 'til the day you die. No one will come to your rescue—not to the tune of sixty pounds. You will rot with the maggots and mice." Sedgwick had a look of exquisite satisfaction.

The policeman clasped his hand on Nathan. "Don't try anything, young man. You will just make matters worse."

The constable directed Nathan out the door into the hallway. Strangely, there were people in the hallway, applauding. To his horror, Nathan saw the Countess von Brandt, Regina Lancaster, and other members of the aristocracy standing and staring at him. In humiliation, Nathan turned away and looked back, but the policeman and Sedgwick had disappeared. The hallway had inexplicably transformed into a large ballroom, where London's elite were celebrating.

Nathan woke with a start from his dream. It had been so vivid, so real. As he gained full control over his faculties, he became aware of sounds coming from next door. A door shutting. Footsteps. A chair moving. His heart beating rapidly, Nathan got up and went to the wall, trying to listen. There was no sound of voices.

Sedgwick had undoubtedly placed one of his men inside the office, hoping that Nathan would return. The security he had felt earlier in his living quarters had been breached. He felt frighteningly vulnerable and knew he was at great risk if he stayed. It was just a matter of time before Sedgwick contacted his landlord and learned that there were two additional rooms leased to him.

Nathan looked out the window of his bedroom onto the street below. Traffic was heavy at midday, and from his window he could hear the cries from street vendors and the random sounds of animals and carriages below. He looked up and down the street, searching for Sedgwick and his men. Scanning the road for several minutes, there was no one who looked familiar, nor was there any constable in sight. He carefully examined the masses, scouring for someone who might be studying the building's entrance from afar, but found no one. Nathan wondered if he could exit the building's entrance and disappear in the sea of pedestrians.

He carefully pondered which way to exit the building. The rear entrance concerned him; he feared that his singular presence in the alley might be more visible in broad daylight than mixing with the morning foot traffic in front. He listened carefully for sounds from his office. A man coughed and later cleared his throat. There was no question that someone was installed in his office. Nathan prepared to leave, still debating which route to take. He grabbed the sheet music for the compositions he planned to play at Countess von Brandt's, opened his door into the hallway, and looked left toward his office entrance. The door to his office was shut. He walked quietly past the door and continued to the front staircase, still uncertain as to which way to proceed. While he hesitated, he heard footsteps above and he saw the legs of two men descending the stairs from the floor above. Nathan retreated a few feet into the shelter of the hallway and observed the men as they continued down the stairs. He didn't recognize either man, so he fell into step behind them as they descended to the ground floor. One of the men opened the entrance door, and Nathan followed the two men out the door, pretending to be in their party. The two men turned left, continuing along the sidewalk, and Nathan caught up with them, walking stride-by-stride on their left. Nathan kept himself between the building and the two strangers as he walked, just one among the currents of humanity, walking with purpose and in a hurry. After a few blocks, Nathan hailed a cab, and an hour later he reached Craven's Inn without further incident.

Chapter 9

Normally, Mr. Travers dictated letters to his secretary. But this matter needed to be kept confidential even from his staff. He dipped his quill into the recessed inkwell on his desktop and began composing a letter on stationery with the firm's masthead.

To whom it may concern.

It had taken little effort to locate the address of École Spéciale in Lausanne, Switzerland. The school was well respected.

> *My firm represents a client who seeks a reference for one of your former students. The client has an interest in retaining his services on a substantial architectural undertaking and wants assurances as to his matriculation and academic standing. The former student's name is Mr. Nathan Sinclair, currently residing in London.*

Had Mr. Sinclair actually attended the school? Mr. Travers wondered. It was hard to imagine, given his present humble surroundings. Had he graduated? How had he performed as a student? Those were all questions that interested him and, he felt, would be of interest to his client, although he had no idea if his client intended to retain Sinclair for architectural work. Mr. Travers completed the letter, inserted it into the envelope he had earlier addressed, and sealed it. On his way home, he personally posted the letter.

Mr. Travers was anxious for the response. There were a few pieces left to fill in, but a portrait of the young man was beginning to emerge.

***

During the succeeding days, Nathan remained alone in his room at the inn, studying the sheet music for Onslow's *Six Pièces pour Piano*, the one selected piece which he had not yet memorized, and rehearsing the others. The unusually hot summer's sun continued to blister the city of London, providing no relief from the putrid odor of the nearby Thames. Thankfully, it wasn't as severe on the west side, north of the Thames, where Nathan was currently hiding. Still, inside his room, Nathan had to choose between suffocating heat or, when the windows were open, the ventilating stink from outdoors.

Nathan sat on the chair next to the small table, his fingers tapping the pieces on the wooden table, recreating in his mind the sound of the imaginary keys he struck. For several hours a day, he perfected his phrasing and committed each note and dynamic to memory. He left the inn only at night or in the early hours of the morning to gain nourishment. Music was his refuge, if only in his mind. He reflected little on his dire financial circumstances, preferring to dwell rather on the upcoming encounter with Miss Lancaster, as he continued to tap out the notes on the tabletop.

He envisioned hearing Miss Lancaster's voice for the first time, wondering what melody accompanied her beautiful eyes.

***

The day before the von Brandt gathering, it finally began to rain. The city celebrated the change in weather; it was London's first rain in more than forty days. For the first time in weeks, the ponderous foul odor began to dissipate. The rain continued to pelt the city so heavily that Nathan felt sufficiently secure in venturing outdoors in the misty torrent to pick up his new suit. The tailor was a short distance away and Nathan walked with umbrella in hand, staying on sidewalks to avoid the water that began flooding the streets. Inside the tailor's store, Nathan tried the suit on. He was delighted with the fit and felt a new confidence. Soon after, he was back in his room, again rehearsing the compositions he would be performing the following day.

***

The rain continued unabated as the next day came, not stopping until early afternoon. By then, the street water was overflowing onto the sidewalks. Over the next few hours the water began to recede; by evening, Chelsea appeared to have been washed clean, and odor from the sewage had altogether disappeared. Nathan perceived the clean air as a good omen as he boarded the cab to the von Brandt residence. He was impatient for the evening to unfold, and Sedgwick's arrest warrant lay buried deeply in his mind.

***

Arriving at the residence of Countess von Brandt in the early evening, Nathan felt confidence and optimism, aided by his newly tailored suit and the well-rehearsed repertoire he would soon be performing. He rejoiced that he remained a free man and looked forward with great anticipation to the coming encounter with Miss Lancaster.

At least no one will observe that I am out of fashion. Jocelyn Charlesworth's affront had been fully neutralized.

Nathan arrived early, before the guests, anxious to finally rehearse his repertoire on a live instrument. He went through the compositions in the order he intended to perform them, luxuriating in the music the pianoforte made, no longer needing to rely on his imagination. When the task was completed, he absented to the back gardens, composing in his mind the words he would say to Regina when the introduction was made. When at length he reentered the residence, carriages were beginning to arrive. His heart thrilled when he observed Regina's entrance from afar, accompanied by an older gentleman whom he presumed to be her uncle. Soon after, dinner was served.

Nathan sat at the far end of the massive dining table, which accommodated more than forty people. Before the first course was served, the Countess stood and welcomed her guests. She looked down the table where Nathan was seated and asked him to stand. Surprised by the request, Nathan smiled shyly as he rose to his feet.

"Some of you have previously heard the musical genius of this young man," the Countess began. "He is a treasure we hold dear. One of the best-kept secrets in London. I remember first meeting him in Paris, where his mother was singing in the title role of La Juive at the Salle Le Peletier. Afterward, my dear deceased husband and I went to pay our respects for her enthralling performance and were introduced to this young man. You could not have been more than six years old then, Nathan." The Countess looked tenderly at Nathan and he gave a modest nod.

"Yet, your mother was already remarking that you would be a concert pianist one day. He has graciously consented to share his talents with us tonight following dinner." The crowd applauded lustily.

I wonder if anyone knows that I am running from the law? Nathan speculated as his eyes scanned the crowd. *Well, if the constable is called, I shall be at least well dressed for my new home. Perhaps I may be allowed to finish the Beethoven sonata before they chain me up.*

His eyes then fell upon Regina. As their eyes briefly met, she gave him a sweet smile. Nathan felt a rush of happiness and couldn't wait for his opportunity to impress.

When dinner ended, the crowd withdrew into the large parlor room where the von Brandt pianoforte was located. Discreetly, he surveyed the crowd and noticed Regina and her uncle talking to other guests in close proximity to the pianoforte. Several minutes later, the Countess nodded to Nathan and he walked over to the bench and sat down. He stared at the keyboard, composing his mind and reflecting on the first composition he would play. It was always odd performing on the von Brandt piano, with its reverse coloring of keys.

The eyes of the crowd were upon him as he paused before playing. He sensed Regina's presence a short distance away and a surge of excitement flowed over him that he had never felt before. Inspired by the presence of Miss Lancaster, Nathan took his time with the luminous opening movement of Beethoven's *Pastoral* Sonata in D Major. Gradually building the intensity, his fingers introduced the second melody in F-sharp minor with its constant quavers gathering more angst and drama as the sound crescendoed powerfully, then gradually faded away into a recapitulation of the elegant opening theme. Nathan felt as if he were peering through the eyes of Regina, observing his fingers moving on their own as the musicality elevated to a level beyond his own lofty standards. When the sonata came to end, the crowd shouted and applauded, knowing they had witnessed a performance equal to any in the finest concert halls of London. Nathan continued to perform the other pieces he had rehearsed, finally ending with the vitality of the Muller Scherzo. He withdrew his hands and remained seated in the thunder of the crowd's acclaim, then stood up and bowed as the grateful audience came rushing over to praise and thank him. He acknowledged their compliments with modesty and a pleasant smile, but his mind remained preoccupied with the impending encounter with Regina.

In the periphery of his view, Nathan was aware that Sir Lancaster and his niece were walking toward him, accompanied by the Countess. His attention was soon directed their way. Time seemed to slow to a snail's pace as he beheld Regina as she approached. She was wearing a light orange dress with a tight bodice, high neck, and buttoned front. The dress was adorned with white lace on the collar and cuffs, while the skirt was flat fronted with emphasis in the back.

Nathan's attention was diverted away from Regina's form when the Countess spoke.

"My, Nathan. You took my breath away tonight. What a performance! May I have the pleasure of introducing you to two members of your grateful audience?"

The Countess turned to the gentleman standing next to her. He was in his early sixties, with white hair, sideburns, and mustache with no beard, and stood several inches shorter than Nathan, attired in a single-breasted black jacket, high starched white collar, and black cravat. "Sir Lancaster. May I present Nathan Sinclair."

Nathan bowed his head and Sir Lancaster nodded.

The Countess then took Regina by hand. "And this is Sir Lancaster's niece, Miss Regina Lancaster." Nathan bowed again and Regina offered a curtsy and a pleasant smile.

Sir Lancaster looked at Nathan. "My niece explained that she has now twice been blessed with hearing you perform. I am astonished you are not affiliated with the Philharmonic Society."

Nathan felt pride and looked Regina's way. Their eyes met again, longer this time, as Nathan relived the special connection they had shared at Lady Sommersby's.

"You are much too kind, sir. Music is one of my great passions, and I particularly enjoy sharing that passion with others."

Nathan studied Regina from close range for the first time. She was no great beauty. Her nose was too long for her face, though that was only apparent when she turned her head side to side. She had dark hair, which she wore in a chignon with a closely curled fringe bordering her olive complexion. She was of average height with slender figure. The allure was her large eyes. Once you looked into her eyes, it was impossible not to be intrigued. Close up, her deep dark brown eyes opened the windows of her soul, conveying the impression that she had suffered some unspeakable tragedy in her life, had known indescribable grief. She appeared in all respects in her early twenties, her true age, but her face communicated maturity and poise far beyond her years. Along with this reflection was the recognition that Regina had come through the other side of sorrow, with an unparalleled depth of character and deep appreciation for the gift of life. There was no bitterness or anger in her eyes, but rather a profound and aching tenderness; nor was there any façade or false air in her manner. Purity, innocence, and virtue shined forth in her countenance.

"I believe my niece shares your passion."

For the first time, Nathan was on the verge of hearing the sound of her voice. He had already imagined it a hundred times before. When the first words flowed from her breath, Nathan was struck by their sweetness and tenderness.

"I have always been partial to Mozart. But you have caused me to quite reconsider my partiality. Your performances of Chopin and Beethoven were marvelous." The soothing sound reminded him of his mother's voice. Nathan imagined that Regina could have been an opera singer like his mother, if she had received the training. Her voice perfectly matched her unforgettable eyes. Her manner was genteel and elegant.

"Do you have a favorite sonata of Mozart's?" Nathan inquired, and suddenly felt they were the only two people in the room.

Regina maintained Nathan's stare as they spoke. "I am quite certain that I do not know them all," she responded modestly. "But I do so love his Sonata in C Major."

Nathan knew the piece well. "It would give me great pleasure to perform it for you the next time we meet."

"You are too kind," Regina said quietly. "I have never been offered such a rare opportunity to influence a musician's selection of music."

"I hope you may influence me often in the future."

Regina turned shyly away, breaking the trance, causing Nathan to wonder if he had been too bold in his reply.

"With your voice, you must be a singer. I would love to accompany you some time."

Regina blushed. "Mr. Sinclair, I assure you, you do not want to hear me sing."

Nathan laughed. He marveled at how modest and refreshing her disposition was in comparison to the haughty dialogue that had quickly deteriorated with Miss Charlesworth a couple of weeks before.

"Well, if it is really so abhorrent, I shall play *fortississimo* and be sure to drown it out."

Regina pretended offense. "I may not be as bad as that!"

"We shall see. May I accompany you on a few arias my mother used to sing?" Nathan raised his eyebrows, while pointing to the piano.

Regina had temporarily forgotten the Countess's remarks that Nathan's mother was an opera singer and, now reminded, responded with a horrified look. "You shall *never* hear me sing!"

Their conversation continued and Nathan felt no inferiority of position or rank. She had no pretension of superiority nor lofty pride, despite her elevated heritage as the niece of Sir Lancaster. Modest in her dress, manner, and language, she could not cloak the light of her wholesome goodness and inner beauty. Every gesture, every movement was conveyed with grace and understated elegance. Her words and tone betrayed an unfathomable well of purity and virtue. The longer Nathan conversed, the more beautiful she appeared. When he stared into her compelling eyes, he felt his soul exposed and drawn into her being.

Their conversation had gone superbly, but Nathan's insecurity as to his rank and circumstances inhibited his taking the next step, until finally he threw caution to the wind, hoping for the best but expecting the worst. "May I call upon you, sometime soon?"

Regina looked down, hesitating.

I was too impetuous, Nathan instantly regretted his bold request. *She hardly knows me.*

Her large dark eyes returned to Nathan's. Nathan observed a distant look of sadness in her eyes, but just for an instant. "It would do me pleasure to see you again, sir."

Nathan's face brightened, as he bid her farewell, but her hesitation made him wonder if she was interested in another man.

***

When he reached the inn later that night, Nathan's mind remained in a world vastly removed from his present surroundings. Entering the building, the sound of lusty laughing, curses, and oaths assaulted his ears from the nearby smoke-filled tavern, reminding him that it was time to return to the real world.

Nathan walked past the reception desk without a glance.

"'Scuse me, Mist'a Sin-clah," the clerk spoke.

Nathan stopped cold, surprised that his name had been called. After all, he had been using an alias at the inn.

"You be Mist'a Sin-clah, right?" Nathan's reaction had given him away. "Ah wornt worry. Your secret be safe w'me. A man came by hearlier this evenin' askin' about a Mist'a Sin-clah, wonderin' if 'e be a-stayin' at the inn. 'E described yer to a *T*. But, 'e wornt seem the friendly sort and 'ah told him 'ah didn't know no one by tha' name."

"Thank you," Nathan responded and felt his heart beating quickly. *My God, they've found me!* "Can you tell me what he looked like?"

The clerk described, in words and mannerisms, a man of large stature, with dark hair, thick eyebrows, and protruding forehead. Nathan immediately recognized the description of one of Sedgwick's men.

"You shall tell me if you see him again?" Nathan reached into his pocket and handed the clerk a half crown.

The clerk accepted the gratuity with a smile. "Certain, sir. If I was yer, Ah be mighty cer'ful. I feared he was a-conversin' a' others, on the street corner. 'Twas earlier t'day."

Nathan nodded. His feeble efforts to erect a wall around his feelings of doom and hopelessness had been shattered again. Sedgwick was closing in. Nathan had created a fragile illusion that he was beyond Sedgwick's grasp, five miles away on the far west side of London, but it was clear that there was no safe haven. He needed to move again, and soon.

***

As he lay in bed, Nathan's mind was in turmoil. Only after he forced his mind to concentrate on Regina's eyes and voice was he able to find some small island of calm. Thoughts of her brought peace and the hint of a world where he was no longer Sedgwick's pawn; a world where he felt no fear; a world where Regina was at his side.

Nathan believed in first impressions. He allowed his heart to imagine that he had found the woman with whom he could share his life's journey. He had met some women during his twenty-five years who had interested him, but never to this degree. None possessed the compelling inner beauty, modesty, grace, and depth of character that he observed in Regina. These qualities were intimately associated with his mother, but he had never encountered them in another woman—until now. He longed to comprehend Regina's past. He longed to salve the sorrow and suffering that her eyes conveyed. He longed for the next encounter.

Would there ever be another encounter?

Chapter 10

Nathan knew he had been fortunate. The inn clerk could just as well have turned him in for half a crown. Certainly, there had been others who had noticed him, from the nearby street vendors to the employees of the restaurant. He got dressed, ate some of the food he had purchased the day before, and made sure his bags were all packed; he would plan his departure for the evening.

Nathan sat at the desk in his room pondering his future, when his senses became aware of commotion below. He heard the sound of voices and then pounding on a door. Loud voices. A door slamming shut. More pounding. More voices. Nathan opened the door to the hallway, near the stairway. From the proximity of the noise, he could tell they were on the floor below. This time the words were clear: "Police! Open the door!"

Nathan quickly shut and locked the door behind him, grabbing his briefcase and bag of clothes. He opened the window and climbed out of the room, taking care to shut the window tightly behind him. Standing on the small level platform outside the dormer window, Nathan heaved first the briefcase, then his clothes bag, onto the roof's crown. His heart raced as he studied the deeply pitched roof; it seemed far more daunting than he remembered. He had mounted it with great care before, but he didn't have the luxury of time now.

Taking a deep breath, Nathan stepped onto the roof's wooden shingles and began his ascent, angling toward the top, taking small steps upward as rapidly as he dared.

Suddenly, his right boot started to slide—and he was too far removed from the lintel above the window's side wall to secure his safety. In panic, he pressed his foot down hard on the shingles, trying to regain traction, but it only accelerated the slide, causing his legs to split and his left boot to also lose its grip on the roof. He collapsed onto his hands and knees, unable to stop his downward momentum. Frantically, his hands searched for something to grab onto, but there was nothing within reach. In desperation, he thrust his palms hard against the shingles, trying to slacken his descent.

Nathan's downward slide continued, and to his horror, his feet and then his knees lost contact with the roof, going over the edge. Paralyzed with fear, Nathan knew there was nothing to stop his plunge off the roof and onto the ground far beneath. A fraction of a second later, his stomach and chest cleared the roof and then his chin scraped the metal gutter at the roof's edge, the weight of his body pulling him downward with great force.

He had one desperate chance. In a last-gasp effort, Nathan flung out both arms, hoping to grasp the gutter with his hands, just as his head disappeared over the roof's edge. His fingers felt the gap between the last row of shingles and the drain, and he clamped hard on the protruding metal edge. His fall came to an abrupt stop, as his lower extremities and torso slammed hard against the brick siding, then ricocheted outward, his body swinging back and forth.

Nathan had just seconds to act, knowing his grip on the gutter was tenuous. Stifling a scream, he angled his head awkwardly downward, looking at the building's brick exterior as his body's swinging slowed. Dangling a foot from the building's side, he searched for something to gain a foothold on. Terror seized his breast as he saw the traffic far below and instantly imagined falling to his death.

My God! Is this how my life shall end?

With imminent death staring him in the face, Nathan felt all hope vanish. His grip was weakening; in seconds he would be plummeting to his doom. Nathan closed his eyes and he envisioned his mother waiting for him on the other side. He imagined the look of disappointment in her eyes at his pathetic end; all her years of sacrifice had been for naught.

The thought of the coming encounter spurred Nathan to action. He willed his eyes open and studied the facade of the building next to where he was hanging. He noticed a protruding brick ledge extending out an inch and a half, just below his left knee. Though his fingers were aching with the weight of his full body, he managed to raise his left foot toward the ledge and then wedged his boot in place. If it could hold his weight sufficiently to enable him to move upward to get his elbows onto the rain gutter, there might be a chance yet.

***

There was pounding on the door to Nathan's hotel room. "Police! Open up!"

A few seconds later, the clerk's master key unlocked the door. Officer Smith and Junior Officer Jenkins entered the room. Smith was short and stout with a mustache, and Jenkins was lean and tall and clean-shaven. They had checked every room on the lower floors; all that remained were the four rooms on the south side of the top floor.

Officer Smith looked around. The room appeared empty. The bed was still made. No sign of a soul.

"Jenkins! Check under the bed."

Jenkins crouched down and took a look.

"Nothing there, sir."

Officer Smith walked over to the closet and motioned for Jenkins to stand on the opposite side of the door. Smith slowly placed his hand onto the doorknob and then quickly opened the door. The closet was empty. As Officer Smith glanced around the room again, he thought he saw movement outside the window from the corner of his eye.

***

Nathan's arms were burning and the strength in his fingers quickly draining away, as he struggled to maintain purchase with the gutter drain. Tentatively, he put pressure on his left boot, hoping the tiny ledge would enable him to lift himself several feet up the building's exterior, the task made more difficult by the inverse angle. His foot held with some pressure and he continued applying more weight, slowly raising himself upward until his head was directly under the gutter, next to the cornice. Exerting full weight on the precipice, his head scraped upward first against the cornice, then the gutter, until his chin was anchored onto the gutter's edge. Balancing himself precariously on the ledge, Nathan slowly moved both of his hands toward his chin and lodged his elbows into the gutter's half-cylinder.

He knew his next act might be his last. In one quick, desperate motion, he thrust his right foot upward with all his might.

God help me!

Miraculously, his right foot caught the rain gutter and he wedged the boot into the gutter's opening. With his delicate hold on the gutter, he pulled his torso up and lodged his right knee into the gutter as well. Gasping for breath, Nathan felt his heart convulsing as he paused to regain his strength. He dragged his left leg up and forced the rest of his body over the gutter and onto the wood shingles, bracing his left leg and elbow against the gutter's opening. Nathan relaxed for a moment, wet with perspiration and breathing heavily. He wasn't safe yet. He began to crawl gingerly toward the small platform next to his room's window. As the window came into view, Nathan peered inside and saw no movement. There was still time to escape.

Nathan crouched on the platform, still heaving, and quickly took off his boots and socks to gain better traction going up the steep shingled roof in his bare feet. As he glanced back at the window, ready to make another essay, Nathan saw, to his dread, the helmet and face of a police officer looking his way.

***

Officer Smith walked toward the window, unsure if he had seen something or not. He lifted the window up and leaned out.

In a loud voice, he cried out: "Mr. Sinclair! Are you out there? You are under arrest. I demand you show yourself!"

Officer Smith considered going onto the exterior platform himself, but then thought the better of it.

"Jenkins! I think I saw something. Get out there. See if our man is on the roof."

"Aye aye, sir." Jenkins climbed out onto the platform, steadied himself, and stood up. He scanned the rooftop from one side to the other.

***

With his feet bare, Nathan made quick progress and was soon at the roof's crest. Suddenly, he heard his name called out and he shivered. Grabbing his briefcase, clothes bag, and boots, Nathan ran recklessly along the rooftop until he reached the end of the building. He thrust the briefcase and bag across the three-foot crevasse separating the buildings, and then jumped over to the adjacent roof, his boots in hand.

Landing on his feet, Nathan glanced back. He spied a police helmet pop up from the platform of his hotel window. Nathan immediately dropped down, hiding under cover of the lower rooftop, praying he hadn't been seen. He listened carefully, fearing that the officer might be in pursuit.

Waiting, Nathan heard nothing and so raised his head to see if anyone was following. The policeman's helmet was no longer visible. Nathan took a deep breath and continued quickly to the end of the building. There was no gap between the current and next buildings, but the next roof was six feet lower.

Nathan dropped down to the adjacent rooftop and continued briskly to the building's end. There he found an unlocked door that opened to an interior staircase. Once inside, he put his boots back on and continued down the service stairs. In a few minutes' time, he was in the rear of the building, where there was a narrow alley leading to Paulton Street. A half hour later, he reached the north pier of the Thames, not far from the Battersea Bridge.

By nightfall, Nathan had crossed the bridge and continued south a good distance, finally locating an inn near Castle and Octavia Streets—St. Clement's Inn—where he booked a room for a week. Though he was staying in a new inn on the opposite side of the Thames, Nathan felt intense anxiety and nervousness. He shuddered at how close he had come to falling to his death. He couldn't expect his good luck to last. It was clear Sedgwick was determined to find him, regardless of the cost and time it took. The only intelligent solution was to leave England.

Chapter 11

Upon arriving at the office, Mr. Travers looked at his calendar. Most of the entries for the coming week involved meetings with clients who wanted to ensure the senior partner was involved in their case. Today, however, one item caused a frown: calendared was a trip to the Registry of Actions for the borough of Bermondsey. He dreaded the task, and would have loved to have delegated it to a junior member of the firm, but this was an assignment he would handle exclusively himself.

It had been years since he had spent time in the public offices that housed the endless rolls of parchment, pleadings, and journals. He remembered well the dark and dreary hallways littered with private chambers on either side, their low ceilings and bleak walls reeking with mold. Little had changed in the intervening years and upon entering, memories swiftly returned of visits made in the distant past when he was a junior attorney.

After all, was it truly worth the effort? What was the likelihood that young Sinclair's name would turn up in any pleadings? Tempting though it was, Mr. Travers was not going to take any shortcuts with *this* client.

He arrived at the public offices shortly after nine o'clock, committing himself to devote the entire day to the task, if necessary. In investigating a young man, Mr. Travers surmised, it would be far more prudent to start from the present and move backward in time, instead of vice versa. The room containing the most recent registries had changed since his last visit. After a couple of inquiries with harried clerks, Mr. Travers entered a small, overcrowded room where more than twenty impatient people were vying for one clerk's attention. Mr. Travers passed the frustrated horde, went to the counter, and produced his card. Minutes later, he had three large journals in tow, going back a year and half. He found an empty table in the corner next to a window, pulled out his reading glasses, and prepared for the tedious task of reviewing thousands of entries.

What a waste of a beautiful day.

Less than twenty minutes into his search, Mr. Travers sat back in astonishment. He blinked hard and studied the writing again.

On the page before him was an entry, of very recent origin, referencing Nathan Sinclair's name.

***

The following day, Nathan walked to the Battersea Railway Station. Back on the south side of the Thames, the odor of refuse and sewage was stronger than it had been on King's Road. With the heavy smoke from the coal fires used to propel locomotive engines, it appeared from a distance that the railway station lay under a black cloud. As he approached the station, he breathed in the polluted air and smelled the strong odor of grease and metal. Entering the station, Nathan observed people everywhere walking in all directions in haste. Throngs were waiting to board trains on various platforms. As each train arrived, swarms of passengers descended from the compartments, swelling the mass of humanity in the station, until they filtered out through the exits. Nathan checked the train schedule and fare to Dover and the ferry to Calais. He then estimated a similar expense from Calais to Paris. With the gratuity from the Countess added to his existing funds, he had more than enough to make the journey.

Nathan stood in line at the ticket counter for fifteen minutes, trying to conceal his height and person. It crossed his mind that Sedgwick might have scouts at train stations throughout London, expecting Nathan to flee. He had made up his mind to leave England, and as his turn came at the ticket window, he pulled out his wallet. The one woman he had met who promised a future of love, hope, and happiness weighed heavily on his mind. This would be his farewell to her. He expected never to see her again. That thought struck him cold, and he hesitated.

"Sir, please. There are others waiting." The irritated clerk gave Nathan a frown.

Nathan put his wallet back in his pocket. "Sorry, my mistake." Nathan left the counter and walked out of the train station. His heart was beating hard.

What am I doing? he chided himself. *I can't possibly have a future with Miss Lancaster. I am a fool not to flee. I may be arrested at any time.*

Nathan stopped half a block from the station's entrance. He felt pulled in both directions. The intelligent decision was to leave England; the foolhardy choice was to remain. He finally reached a compromise within himself. He would call upon Regina, as he had promised to do. The proper way would be to send her a letter, of course, asking if he could visit. Regina would need an address to which she might respond. Since Nathan had checked into the hotel under an alias, she couldn't very well send her response to the hotel. He stopped at a post office near the inn and rented a small box.

Nathan decided the question of whether to stay or leave the British Isles would be in the hands of Regina. He wrote a brief note to her, inquiring if he might stop by her uncle's home the following Sunday afternoon. If she failed to reply by week's end or responded in the negative, he would depart for France. If she responded affirmatively, he would remain at least until their next encounter.

He mailed the letter early Monday morning. That would provide Regina plenty of time to reply.

***

Nathan remained indoors Tuesday, recognizing that there was little chance that a return letter would have yet arrived. On Wednesday he left in early afternoon, walking in the opposite direction of the post office and then circling back. No response. As he made his way back to the inn, he convinced himself it was better if she never responded. After all, he had nothing to offer her. During his brief excursion outdoors, he also picked up bread, fruit, vegetables, and spring water, all of which he consumed in the solitude of his hotel room.

Despite his rational logic that it would be far better if he never received a response, he left for his daily trek on Thursday, navigating yet another route, brimming with optimism. He did an internal calculation. She would have received the letter by Tuesday. A lady would not want to appear too anxious. She would probably wait a day before responding. Most likely, she had mailed her reply on Wednesday, so her letter was certain to be in his box today.

With a skip in his step, he waltzed into the post office. He inserted his key and already had imagined the white envelope containing Regina's response. However, when he opened the small door of his postal box, it was empty, just as it had been the previous days. Nathan had an empty feeling, and once more, felt alone in the world. Apparently, she had no interest in seeing him again. On his way back, there was no bounce in his step, no song in his heart. He trudged sluggishly to the inn, almost hoping that he would be apprehended. At least then the unrelenting anxiety of being caught would come to an end. Nathan resigned himself to wait one more day. If he received nothing by Friday afternoon, he would book passage to Dover and leave England behind forever. The last train for Dover would be leaving the station at a quarter past five.

***

Seated at her desk, the dark-haired lady took out a quill and paper. She dipped the quill into the small glass bottle of black ink and began writing:

Dear Mr. Sinclair,

Thank you for your lovely request. I apologize for my delay in responding.

Regina Lancaster paused as she stared out the window. After several minutes' reflection, she continued writing:

Unfortunately, I must decline your request.

***

By Friday, all optimism had vanished. During the prior evening, Nathan had come to his senses. The only reasonable choice was to start life over in France, without the burden of debt and persistent threat of imprisonment. Nathan packed his bags and set off for the train station. The post office was only a few blocks out of his way, and he arrived there in midafternoon, giving himself plenty of time to get to the station to catch the last train to Dover.

The afternoon mail delivery should have arrived by now. Nathan walked into the busy post office and headed to the corner where his box was located. He heard boxes open and close nearby as others gathered their mail. As he pulled the key chain out of his pocket, he felt the brush of a customer against his elbow and for a second panicked that Sedgwick had found him. Looking around, though, no one showed any interest in his presence, and he took a deep breath.

From his chain, he selected the small key to the box. In his mind, he already knew that the box would be empty, just as it had been each day before. Nevertheless, he held his breath as he inserted the key into the keyhole and turned the key. He hesitated before opening the box, and he felt his heart racing.

God, please be there. Give my life a purpose.

Nathan tugged open the small door.

Empty.

His fears were confirmed.

I mean nothing to her. I shall leave. Tonight.

He stared at the box, disbelieving that this would be his final good-bye to the woman of his dreams. Could she have at least responded to his letter?

Nathan shut and locked the small container. He turned and had started walking down the corridor, when he heard a soft ticking sound emanating from the interior of the mailboxes. His senses went on alert. He recognized the sound; it was the sound of envelopes being cast into boxes. Nathan turned around, suddenly filled with hope. The afternoon mail was being sorted into the various boxes, thirty minutes behind the customary schedule.

He walked back to his box and inserted the key. Was it possible? Would there now be a response? He flung open the little door and expected, this time, the precious envelope from Regina. Once again, he was filled with disappointment. It remained empty. Yet the ticking sound of mail continued, and he kept the box open. Eventually the ticking sound began to slow, the clerk nearing the end of his task.

Nathan stood resolutely by, waiting for the sound to end. He stared vacantly at the empty receptacle, feeling rejected and unappreciated.

She does not care.

Suddenly, the small compartment was no longer empty.

Nathan started in disbelief at the ivory envelope that had suddenly appeared. On the front of the envelope he saw his name written in an elegant hand.

I should have shut the box by now. He shuddered at the thought. *I would have always wondered.*

He had been seconds away from leaving his world, and Regina, behind.

Nathan removed the letter from the mailbox, re-locking it. He walked over to the counter, oblivious to other customers. On the opposite side of the envelope was a red wax seal, with the insignia of a rose. Carefully, Nathan opened the envelope and withdrew a folded piece of fine parchment.

Nervousness arrested his euphoria, as now he wondered what message was contained within. The delay in her reply might presage a negative response. It certainly implied that she had been debating her decision.

What if she declines? If so, then his decision would be an easy one. He read the letter slowly, keeping the lower half of the paper folded over, exposing one line at a time.

Dear Mr. Sinclair,
Thank you for your lovely request. I apologize for my delay in responding.

Nathan paused, knowing her response was next. Slowly, he uncovered the next line.

I would be delighted to receive you Sunday afternoon for tea.
Sincerely yours,
Miss Lancaster

Nathan nearly jumped for joy, so thrilled was he to receive her positive response. *Delighted,* he told himself. *She is delighted to receive me. And I shall be delighted to go.*

Life was beautiful. All thoughts of departing for France instantly vanished. He would risk a thousand days in prison for the chance of hearing her voice again.

But, why such a delay in responding? Nathan wondered. *If she were truly delighted to see me again, wouldn't she have written sooner?* A hundred different thoughts swirled through Nathan's mind as he rationalized logical reasons for the delay. The idea that troubled him the most was that there might be another man in her life.

Certainly, I am equal to any worthy man she may have an eye on. More likely than not, I am a better musician, better artist, and decidedly more modest, too. And besides, my rank and wealth are beyond... beyond reproach. Nathan smiled inwardly at the sarcasm. Despite his stark awareness of financial distress, it mattered little. He *would* see her again!

His face was lit up with a perpetual smile on his short trek back to St. Clement's Inn. He felt the most fortunate of all men. Sedgwick be damned! When he reached his room, he took out the thick book of Mozart sonatas and opened it to the Sonata in C Major. He already knew it by heart, but he reviewed the musical score and tapped his fingers on the desk, recreating in his mind the sound of small hammers hitting strings.

Nathan was unaware that the letter mailed by Regina Lancaster had been her fourth draft.

***

Nathan consumed all day Saturday and Sunday morning pondering what to say and how to behave. It was imperative he make a strong and favorable impression upon Regina, and he selected other compositions that he would perform for her. He practiced for hours in his room, wanting to attain perfection with each selection. He would deliver a concert that Miss Lancaster would never forget. Nathan willed the sun to accelerate its orbit and pleaded with the hours to speed by, longing to hasten the encounter.

In Regina, Nathan sensed a woman of inestimable value. Her manner, her carriage, her voice, her depth of character, were without equal. For an instant, his thoughts turned to Jocelyn Charlesworth, the woman of indescribable physical beauty, and he compared the two.

How ironic. I first saw them both the same night. One, whose outer beauty is unparalleled. The other, whose inner beauty shines brightly above all others.

Regaining his senses, he exclaimed out loud to himself as he paused on his imaginary keyboard, restraining an involuntary smile: "How can I be in such danger with her? I hardly know her. No woman could possibly live up to the perfection and virtue that I already impose upon her."

Despite his best efforts to mute such grandiose expectations, he sensed the afternoon would be a turning point in his life.

Dear God, keep me free long enough to see her once more.

Chapter 12

The seconds marched onward and Sunday afternoon did arrive with Nathan still a free man. Upon his arrival at 34 Faubourg Lane, the butler ushered him into a beautiful, spacious parlor. The walls were patterned with peacock-green damask, from the skirting board up to the dado line, below decorative plaster moldings, intricately patterned friezes, and ceiling medallions. The room's elegant furnishings included butler trays, side tables, and an exquisite chiffonier with inlaid ivory, as well as button-backed chairs, pouffes, and an ottoman whose soft-cushioned upholstery matched the wallpaper. On the far side of the room stood a sideboard with a collection of Staffordshire figurines. In one corner, a faux Grecian statue resided on a pedestal. One wall featured a large mirror with ornately embellished carvings. Tapestries and paintings adorned the other walls, and heavy embroidered dark-green curtains bordered the windows. The hardwood floor was polished and covered with rich decorative rugs. Descending from an elaborately gilded ceiling ornament in the center of the room was a large gold-plated chandelier with gas lights.

Nathan was only vaguely aware of the densely lavish furnishings and appointments. Rather, upon entering, his eyes immediately fixated on Regina, who was seated next to an older lady on the ottoman. Regina's dark hair was parted in the middle, curled, and tied in back into a spiral twist. She wore a light-blue dress with two skirts, the top skirt pulled back to reveal embroidered inner gown lining in a darker shade of blue. When their eyes met, Regina smiled sweetly, and Nathan felt all restraint evaporate.

She truly is everything and more than I have imagined. It is imprinted on her face and in her soul.

Regina introduced him to the older lady, identified as her "dear Aunt Hélène." Aunt Hélène had a quiet elegance in her bearing and movement. She was very thin, and her hair, which was as white as snow, was drawn behind her ears, with curls in the back. Nathan seated himself on a chair nearby, and the three engaged in small talk for several minutes. Nathan then offered to play Regina's favorite sonata.

"I am so sorry, Mr. Sinclair," Aunt Hélène interrupted with surprise. "Can you not see that we have no pianoforte?"

Nathan had been so smitten by Regina, that he had been ignorant of the lack of a musical instrument. He apologized for his neglect.

"Perhaps there will be a future occasion to hear you play," Aunt Hélène responded.

As the light faded in the window, Aunt Hélène discreetly receded to another corner of the room. Regina inquired about Nathan's background. He told her of growing up in a small medieval village near Paris, then moving to London when still a child.

"So, French was your first tongue," Regina commented.

"Yes. That is the only language my mother ever spoke to me."

"But your English is perfect, as well. What a blessing to be completely fluent in both languages."

"I suppose I take it for granted," Nathan responded.

"Those of us who speak only one tongue are green with envy," Regina laughed.

I love the sweet sound of your voice, Nathan thought to himself.

During their conversation, Nathan periodically attempted inquiries of Regina, but she seemed reluctant to talk about herself and continually diverted the dialogue back to Nathan. Happy to oblige, Nathan related how his mother had instilled in him a love for music and art at an early age.

Regina then asked Nathan what had inspired him to become an architect. so he related the story. After performing as a soloist in the city of Blois, France, his mother had arranged a special surprise the following day. A picnic lunch was packed, and they boarded a small carriage on a beautiful summer's morning. Soon, they were traveling along a quiet country road carved in a forest of tall trees. Nathan's mother asked the driver to stop, and they continued on foot with the carriage following closely behind. A majestic tower appeared at the end of the road and grew in height with each approaching step. Their pace quickened, and adjacent spires came into view, until a magical city of towers took form. As they continued on foot, it became evident that the many citadels stood upon a magnificent structure. It was the most incredible edifice young Nathan had ever seen. He asked his mother if they had pierced the veil and found the pathway to heaven.

After a picnic on the grounds of Chateau Chambord, they were graciously allowed inside. The interior was nearly as striking as the exterior. Nathan and his mother walked up the double helix staircase to the roof's terrace, where they found themselves amidst the many towers, which a short time ago had seemed so distant and unattainable. The view of the trees and gardens below was breathtaking. The experience transformed his life forever, and his dream to become an architect was born.

Nathan explained to Regina how Leonardo da Vinci had inspired the chateau's design, although he had died shortly before the foundation was laid. Da Vinci's influence was evident in the dramatic staircase and its placement in the center of the structure, the flat roof terraces, and the centralized Greek-cross plan. Nathan related how da Vinci had been anointed *"premier peintre et ingenieu et architecte du Roy"*—the first painter, engineer, and architect of the king. François I had asked da Vinci to design a chateau at Romorantin, and Nathan commented on the striking similarity between the two structures.

In response to another inquiry, Nathan told Regina he knew little of his father, just that he had been an outstanding artist. He shared his mother's influence in motivating Nathan to learn to draw and paint, wishing Nathan to continue his father's artistic legacy. His mother had presented him with brushes, palette, paint, and canvas at an early age and encouraged his artistic talents first in France and later in England.

"So you are an architect, a pianist, *and an artist*," Regina said with wonder. "A man of so many talents. You must intimidate all the young ladies you meet." Nathan smiled modestly. Inwardly, he was pleased to have made a good impression.

"I have witnessed firsthand your musical gift. What of your artistic talents? If they are on par with your musical ability, then you must be an extraordinary artist. What do you draw?"

"As a child, I used to sketch portraits. Still do, occasionally." Nathan turned to a table nearby, which held several sheets of paper and a pencil. Wishing to impress more, he asked. "May I?"

"Of course. What do you intend to draw?"

"You shall see."

Regina couldn't help but notice Nathan staring at her as he sketched. In horror, she cried, "Not me! I do not give my permission for a portrait."

"Permission is not required for the artist." Nathan responded, showing no emotion.

"You must stop immediately!"

Nathan continued sketching, ignoring her protestations.

"Mr. Sinclair. I insist."

"Just a few minutes more," Nathan calmly responded.

Regina shrugged her shoulders and proceeded to make the most horrid face possible. Nathan laughed. She then put her hands to her cheeks and playfully tugged. "Will that do?"

"One more alteration. I must now add the fingers you have attached to your face."

"Please stop." Regina pleaded in a helpless voice.

"I am almost done."

Regina displayed mock disgust and irritated surrender with Nathan's refusal to stop. "Very well, then. You are very stubborn!"

Nathan finished his sketch and presented it to her.

Regina was astonished at the likeness, but protested, "Mr. Sinclair, you have made me far too beautiful."

"That is the best compliment an artist can receive. Then you like it?"

"You are very gifted. May I keep it?"

"So, you are now content that I sketched your likeness?"

"No. Not at all. But I shall keep it anyway."

"I have not yet told you my price."

"You mercenary man!"

"It is not money I want," Nathan smiled.

"Then what is it?"

"Your consent to dine with me next Saturday night, if you—and your aunt, of course—are otherwise disengaged. May I bring a carriage to your home to gather you, at sunset?"

Nathan astonished himself at his own impertinence. It was spontaneous and wholly unpremeditated. His desire was to take them to one of London's finest restaurants, although he could hardly afford to pay for hors d'oeuvres and a bottle of wine. Nathan suddenly realized the foolishness of his offer, but it was too late to retract it.

"My aunt will never consent to such a steep price." Regina teased.

"In which case, you shall have to go without a chaperone." Nathan responded with a smile.

Regina returned his smile and walked over to where Aunt Hélène was seated.

"Dear Aunt. Mr. Sinclair has insisted that we both dine with him Saturday night if I am to keep this lovely portrait." Regina showed her aunt the sketch and Aunt Hélène raised her eyebrows, then glanced at Nathan, nodding in admiration. "He insists on taking me without a chaperone if you are otherwise engaged."

"Well, we cannot permit that, can we?" Regina's aunt responded with an expressive smile.

Regina nodded respectfully and returned to Nathan. "Are you prepared to dine with two women?"

"*Avec grand plaisir,*" Nathan bowed humbly, rejoicing inwardly. He had less than a week to figure out how to pay for dinner.

Chapter 13

Nathan allocated a portion of his meager funds for another week's rent at the inn and researched London's finest restaurants. He also did a quick accounting of his funds. His entire savings would hardly pay for one fine dinner, let alone three. He shook his head.

It's impossible!

From nowhere, an utterly ridiculous notion crept over him. The more he considered it, the more he wondered if it might possibly work.

***

Monday afternoon, Nathan took a cab to St. James's Hall. It was a concert hall designed by Owen Jones, who had also decorated the interior of the Crystal Palace. Nathan had never attended a concert there, although he had heard of its beauty. The concert hall was empty, but locked. Nathan had hoped for a peek inside, but his mission was to arrange for dinner at one of the two restaurants hidden behind the Piccadilly façade.

When he entered the restaurant, he was struck by the meticulously prepared table settings and the sweet fragrance from the bouquet of lilacs held by a silver epergne in the center of every table. Each epergne accommodated a central basin and branches that supported the lilacs, a candelabra, and other decorations. The place settings included an array of glasses and silverware unlike anything Nathan had ever seen, set on spotless, pure white tablecloths. He felt intimidated by the exquisite decor, yet desperately wanted to dine there, knowing that it would make an inestimable impression on Regina and her aunt. He asked to speak to the restaurant manager. Twenty minutes later, he left dejected. His proposal had been abruptly rebuffed.

Nathan spent several more bob on two more cab rides to other fine establishments. Each time, he was turned away.

Disheartened, Nathan decided to try one more elite locale. It was a restaurant he had originally discarded, because it was widely considered the most expensive eating establishment in all of London.

The cab dropped Nathan off at Verrey's on Regent Street. It was the finest French restaurant in all of England and one of the few venues deserving of aristocracy. Nathan scanned the restaurant's interior. It was adorned with an array of glass tables covered with brilliant white lace cloths and stems of violet flowers set in silver vases. Each table setting was meticulously arranged with polished silver that reflected the light from the candelabra above; each porcelain plate was hand-painted with chinoiserie lavender wreaths.

Why not try for the absolute best? I have nothing to lose.

He asked for the maître d'hôtel and to his delight found him to be French.

Maybe it isn't hopeless after all.

Electing a bolder strategy than he had used with the other restaurants, Nathan began speaking in his native tongue. *"J'aimerais dîner samedi soir avec deux dammes très spéciales. Est-ce que huit heures du soir serait acceptable?"*[4]

The maître d'hôtel appeared pleased to be speaking in French and took out his reservation book. *"Certainement. Puis-je avoir votre nom?"*[5]

"Sinclair."

The maître d'hôtel smiled.

"Oh, Monsieur Saint Claire?" He asked for the spelling.

Nathan corrected him.

"Il nous fera plaisir de vous voir samedi soir."[6]

Nathan thanked him and pretended to notice the pianoforte for the first time, sitting on a platform a few feet above the eating area. No dinner guests had yet arrived.

"J'ai été sans pianoforté depuis plusieurs jours. Pourrais-je essayer le vôtre brièvement?"[7]

The maître d'hôtel gave a surprised look. *"Vous êtes un pianist?"*[8]

"Oui."

"*Eh bien, personne n'est ici. Vous pouvez le faire pendant quelques minutes — mais seulement quelques minutes. Les gens vont bientôt*

---

4   I would love to dine here Saturday night with two very special ladies. Would eight o'clock in the evening be acceptable?
5   Most certainly. May I have your name?
6   It shall be a pleasure to see you Saturday night.
7   I have been without a piano the past few days. Would you mind if tried yours briefly?
8   You are a pianist?

*arriver."*⁹

Nathan thanked him and sat down at the elegant-looking London-made piano with Brazilian rosewood, a maple-veneered key-well, and a black cast-iron frame. It was straight-strung with the double-escapement action pioneered by its maker, Erard. It was among the finest pianos Nathan had ever seen.

Time to stop admiring the instrument. Time to make music.

Nathan began playing Chopin's "Winter Wind" Étude, beginning with a simple phrase that any beginner can perform. But suddenly, his hands erupted in a tumultuous cascade of semiquaver tuplets at a dizzying pace. The frenzied pace continued for three minutes until it concluded with a *fortissimo* coda. By this time, the maître d'hôtel, two servers, and a chef from the kitchen were standing nearby in awe. They applauded heartily, and the maître d'hôtel inquired, *"Peut-être vous auriez la gentillese de jouer à nouveau samedi soir?"*¹⁰

Nathan nodded. *"Avec grand plaisir."*¹¹ Then he walked over to the maître d'hôtel, signaling him away from the others, and took him into his confidence.

*"J'ai un petit problème. Peut-etre, vous pourriez m'aider. Je suis arrivé récemment de Paris et ne peux pas accéder à mons fonds de fudicie pour plusiers semaines. J'ai épuisé mon indemnité voyageant ici et j'ai besoin d'un peu d'aide à payer pour le dîner."*¹²

A frown started forming on the maître d'hôtel's face.

Nathan wasted no time. It was his only chance. *"Je suis sans pianoforté jusqu'à ce que mes meubles arrive dans quelques semaines. Pourrais-je offrir à jouer dans votre restaurant tous les soirs pour, par exemple, deux ou trois semaines en échange pour le pris d'un dîner pour trois—c'est une occasion très spéciale. Je pourrais commencer ce soir, sans aucun risque. Si vous n'êtes pas tout à fait satisfait de ma performance ce soir, nous pouvons nous serrer la main et vous pouvez effacer la réservation du samedi."*¹³

---

9 Well, no one is here. You may try it for a few minutes, but just a few minutes. Guests will be arriving soon.
10 Perhaps you would perform for us Saturday night?
11 With great pleasure.
12 I have a small problem perhaps you can help me with. I recently arrived from Paris and cannot my trust fund for several more weeks. I exhausted my allowance on traveling here and need a little help paying for dinner.
13 I am without a piano, until my furniture arrives in a couple of weeks. Might I offer to perform nightly in your fine restaurant for say two or three weeks, in exchange for the price of dinner for threeit is for

The maître d'hôtel thought for a moment. "*Donc, vous dites qu'il ny a pas d'obligation si je vous permets de jouer ce soir et d'attendre la réaction de mes clients?*"[14]

"*C'est correct.*"

"*Et, vous me promettez de jouer tous les soirs pendant trois semaines si j'accepte?*"[15]

"*Exactement.*"

"*Monsieur Sinclair. Notre pianoforté est à votre disposition ce soir.*"[16]

Thirty minutes later, the first guests arrived. After they were seated, Nathan began playing Mozart's Sonata in C Major, the sonata that he had planned to perform for Regina. He continued with the repertoire that he had planned to perform at the Lancasters', but had been unable to perform since they had no instrument. Nathan received thunderous applause by the appreciative guests and by eleven o'clock that night., the maître d'hôtel smiled and said simply, "*À demain.*"[17]

***

Nathan arrived at Verrey's Tuesday morning and brought sheet music with him. He devoted the entire day to working on one particular piece, which he had been practicing before he was displaced from his home: Liszt's Hungarian Rhapsody no. 2. It did require some digit gymnastics, but Nathan expected to conquer it quickly.

Over the coming days, he spent the majority of his time at Verrey's. Without solicitation, the restaurant provided him with a modest lunch and dinner each day, and the restaurant's patronage grew each evening as word traveled among the dinner guests. The maître d'hôtel was delighted with the increase in business and contemplated hiring Nathan for a longer term.

---

a very special occasion. I can begin tonight, if you wish, with no risk to you. If you are not pleased with my performance, then we will shake hands and you may erase Saturday's reservation.

14   So, you are saying there is no obligation if I allow you to perform tonight and wait for my clients' reaction?

15   And you will promise to perform every evening for three weeks, if I accept?

16   Mr. Sinclair. Our pianoforte is at your disposal this evening.

17   See you tomorrow.

Chapter 14

The investigation was nearing an end. Only the final piece of the puzzle was needed before the report would be complete—the response from Switzerland. It arrived in the day's mail. With great interest, Mr. Travers opened the letter from École Spéciale in Lausanne.

Dear Mr. Travers:

It is our great pleasure to respond to your inquiry. We hereby confirm Mr. Sinclair's attendance at École Spéciale from 1863 to 1867. Mr. Sinclair was an outstanding student, held in the highest esteem by his professors. He graduated at the top of his class and received the acclaimed Couronne d'Or in the annual class competition during his final year. Our most tenured professor, Professor Prud'homme, extends his most favorable compliments and profound approbation for his work. He believes that your client will be very well served by retaining his services and recommends Mr. Sinclair in the most glowing terms.

Respectfully yours,

Chancelier Jean-Claude Deschamps

After reading the letter, Mr. Travers lit his pipe, leaned back in his chair, and pondered. How does one put into words the life and character of this enigmatic young man? Parents deceased, no known family. Living on the edge of poverty. Lady Sommersby praises his musical ability and considers him among the finest men she has ever met; his professors apparently concur. Yet, he has shown complete disregard for his financial obligations, is under arrest, and is likely to be soon cast into prison. He appears to have utterly failed as an architect.

For all I know, he lives on the street—there is no known residence address. Can Sinclair possibly be under consideration for an architectural project? If so, my report may doom any chance he has. Too bad; he appar-

ently is not lacking in talent, and such a project would likely transform his life.

Well thankfully, that would be a decision his client would make, not him. As he reflected on the report he would soon prepare, another thought entered his mind: *Maybe the investigation has nothing to do with architecture at all.*

***

On Saturday night, Nathan arrived at Verrey's wearing once again his newly tailored suit, but with a dark blue cravat. Thankfully, the summer's sewer scourge had diminished considerably in recent weeks with the advent of rain. The mud and mire from the suffocating summer had also receded from most streets on the west side of London, making the trip to the restaurant far less disagreeable.

Nathan assisted Regina and Aunt Hélène in disembarking from the coach, and the three walked toward the restaurant in the cool evening air. Aunt Hélène nodded to Nathan, impressed with his choice of dining. When they first entered, the perfumed scent from yellow-flowered magnolias greeted them, masking the unpleasant street odor. The maître d'hôtel quickly came over and gave Nathan a brief smile, but pretended not to know him at all, as had been previously arranged. To Nathan's delight, the maître d'hôtel led the party of three to the restaurant's finest table.

During dinner, Nathan, Regina, and her aunt feasted on bisque d'écrivisses, crème d'asperges, sole à la Mony, tournedos à la Périgneux and consommé à l'okra. The food was superb. As the meal progressed, Aunt Hélène showed interest in becoming better acquainted with Nathan. Nathan repeated much of what he had related to Regina on his prior visit to the Lancasters, though Regina seemed as eager a listener as before.

"Since you graduated from such an esteemed school and apprenticed at such a fine establishment as Calemby & Co., you must be very successful in your business," Aunt Hélène inquired.

"I have been working hard. It does take time to get a new business established."

"So you have now been working on your own for quite some time?"

"A year and a half."

"Has that been long enough for you to have obtained some measure of financial security?" Aunt Hélène conveyed a dubious look.

Nathan paused, wondering what words to choose in response. He didn't want to mislead Regina's aunt, but he also was not prepared to disclose the desperation of his financial predicament.

As Nathan searched for the precise words that would not implicate him in a lie, nor fully reveal his financial peccadilloes, another restaurant guest came over and interrupted their conversation. It was Mrs. Meriweather, who was among the community of music lovers who had previously heard Nathan play; she was dining with her husband and another couple. Mrs. Meriweather was in her late forties, of slender build and average height, and wore a pink silk evening gown, with delicate lace and ribbon trim. She had an enthusiastic smile on her face at seeing Nathan and inquired if he would consider performing a short composition on the pianoforte located on the far side of the dining room.

Nathan was flattered with the request, but modestly declined. Mrs. Meriweather persisted: "I am certain the maître d'hôtel will have no objection."

Before Nathan could politely turn down the request a second time, Regina interjected: "Mr. Sinclair, my aunt has never heard you play. Would you be so kind as to delight us both?"

Nathan could hardly refuse a request from Regina and welcomed a momentary reprieve from her aunt's interrogation. He smiled at Regina and her aunt, then bowed politely to Mrs. Meriweather and walked to the pianoforte.

There was no hesitation deciding which piece to perform. Nathan had played Liszt's Hungarian Rhapsody several evenings before at Verrey's and the composition was fully polished and committed to memory. It was an ostentatious and effulgent piece that impressed, and this would provide him an opportunity to demonstrate his virtuosity to Regina's aunt. A favorable impression upon her could only be advantageous in courting her niece.

The rhapsody began solemnly yet dramatically, but soon his right hand dashed up and down the keyboard with amazing speed and dexterity. After a dramatic exposition of the melancholy theme, the mood of the piece changed entirely as he began the friska in F-sharp minor. Starting softly and simply, it soon began a trek of ever-increasing pace and pianistic bravura, culminating in a whirlwind of *prestissimo* octaves.

He expected the exposition to be well received, but Nathan was not prepared for the rousing applause and clamor from the restaurant patrons and waiters. He gave an appreciative bow. The maître d'hôtel came up to him, playing his part, and shook his hand vigorously as if it were the first time he had ever heard him perform.

After the applause died down and he bowed once more, Nathan discerned from the astonished look on her face that his status with Aunt Hélène had been augmented considerably, due to the performance. Regina was also beaming. All thoughts of his financial nightmare dissolved.

"How marvelous!" Aunt Hélène gushed. "I was in rapture while you were playing. I had no idea you were such an accomplished pianist. You must tell me how you learned to play so beautifully." Nathan obliged, giving due credit to his mother.

Feeling that far too much focus had been placed on his background, Nathan gently probed Regina: "And how did you come to live with your uncle and aunt?"

Regina turned toward Aunt Hélène with fulsome praise. "Oh, I could never say enough about their charity and support. I am so blessed to be a member of their household."

Rather than respond further, she deftly turned the topic back to Nathan: "And it sounds like you were fortunate to have such a devoted and caring mother." Paying further encomiums to his mother, Nathan didn't realize until later that Regina had never responded to his question.

During the evening, Nathan hoped to converse more intimately with Regina outside her aunt's presence, but the moment never presented itself. He desired to know everything about her—the mystery of her past, whether she had ever been in love, if there was anyone in her life to whom she was presently attached. He wanted desperately to gain the answers to these and other queries, at the same time fearing her responses. Was there a hesitancy on her part for their incipient relationship to transcend mere friendship, or was it just his insecurity?

On the drive home, Regina was seated next to her aunt who was directly across from him, which yielded no opportunities for private discourse. The answers to his questions would have to wait for another day. As the carriage reached its destination, Regina and Aunt Hélène thanked Nathan heartily for the lovely evening, but Nathan observed a momentarily glimpse of sadness on Regina's countenance as they parted.

What is her mystery? Nathan wondered. *What is she suppressing? Could it be her tragedy was so terrible that she can never love again?*

After leaving the carriage and walking up the steps to the porch, Regina looked back longingly as the carriage drove off. A tear dropped from her eye as she entered the house.

***

Nathan relived the evening's events in his mind as his cab wound its way back to the inn. He had never felt happier, despite his tenuous circumstances. He longed to understand the profound sadness that Regina carried within her graceful exterior.

I must unlock the key to her soul before she will open up to me and I shall truly know her. Yet, within his heart, Nathan knew that there could be no real future with Regina until he could find a solution to his financial conundrum.

I cannot be so selfish as to cause her to develop affection for me, when my freedom is at risk at any moment. How can I even contemplate a future with this inestimable angel in my present circumstance?

The cab stopped in front of St. Clement's Inn. Nathan paid the driver and exited the cab. As he approached the entrance, Nathan felt that everything would work out in the end. He entered the hotel, humming the theme from the third movement of Mendelssohn's Fourth Symphony.

He glanced at the reception desk, with a broad smile on his face, his mind lingering on the magic of the evening that had come to end.

The desk clerk looked away. Nathan sensed something was wrong.

From behind a large potted plant, a man appeared. Nathan's face went white. It was Sedgwick. Nathan bolted for the door, but the large man with the protruding forehead stood in his way. From the inn's tavern, a member of the Metropolitan Police advanced. He was cornered.

"So, this is our man?" the constable said to Sedgwick.

"Yes, Sergeant. We have the swindling vagabond at last! Mr. Sinclair, you are under arrest," Sedgwick said with a triumphant air.

Chapter 15

The constable clamped handcuffs onto Nathan's wrists.

"You became quite a sensation at Verrey's." Sedgwick couldn't contain his delight. "That was very sporting of you, to publicize your presence so. I am sure you shall find a lovely pianoforte and most grateful audience in Coldbath Fields."

The policeman escorted Nathan out the door as Sedgwick patted his accomplice on the back.

Minutes later, Nathan was seated opposite the sergeant in a police wagon. He was shattered, numb, in disbelief. This couldn't be happening! It was nearly midnight as the wagon trundled over cobblestone streets to London's north. The vehicle crossed Blackfriars Bridge and finally arrived at Coldbath Fields a few minutes after one o'clock, Sunday morning.

Coldbath Fields derived its name from a cold bath nearby, the best known in London in its day, fed by a spring discovered in 1697. The discoverer claimed the water had power equaling that of St. Magnus and St. Winifred for the treatment of nervous diseases and digestive problems. With the passage of time, the name came to provoke a much different reaction: one of severity, deprivation, and suffering.

The desolate and dreary prison contaminated the neighboring streets, turning them into a silent wasteland where few people conducted business or lived, except the vagabonds and vagrants who inhabited condemned buildings. The prison grounds were massive and contained four large galleries, forming a parallelogram by their junction on the sides.

The constable pulled Nathan out of the wagon and dragged him to the front gate where a night guard was on duty. The policeman handed the guard some papers and asked for a signature. The guard's expression registered surprise at how well dressed the new prisoner was. The gate to the prison opened and the policeman pushed Nathan inside.

"He's all yours," the sergeant noted. "He's been a slippery one, from what I've heard. Best you keep an eye on him." The sergeant took out a key, inserted it in the lock, and removed the handcuffs from Nathan's wrists.

The guard smiled, showing a decayed front tooth. "Oh, we'll take good care of 'im, gov'ner."

The guard lit a candle and pushed Nathan into the vast prison yard; the ground was caked in filth. There was not another soul present. The guard led Nathan past a few large buildings, and there appeared to be no end to the massive property. The guard finally directed Nathan to an entrance on the east side of a long brick building. Nathan was led up two sets of stairs through a stairwell that reeked of urine and had a ceiling so low he had to bend down to avoid scraping his head. He heard the groan and wail of prisoners from near and far away. The guard led Nathan down a dreary hallway and then shoved him into a room with a dirty mattress; the springs were exposed and there was a large tear in the fabric. The smell of human excrement was overpowering and Nathan nearly gagged. Next to the mattress lay a tattered blanket covered in grime. In the light of the guard's candle, Nathan saw a mouse scamper into a crack in the wall.

"Your new 'ome, m' lord." The guard gave Nathan an exaggerated bow. "I 'ope you find the accommodations to yer likin'." The guard left with a chuckle, and his laughter continued to build as he walked down the corridor, taking the light with him. Nathan remained standing in total darkness, repulsed by the filthy and foul environment.

The desperation of his circumstances suffocated him. There was not a soul on earth who would come to his rescue, no one to petition for aid. No father, no mother, no brother, no sister, no uncle, no aunt—not a single family member or close friend. Most certainly, he would never inform Regina of his new home.

My life is over. I shall never write her. In a few days, perhaps a week, will she begin to wonder why I have not contacted her, what has become of me? Will she fear that I suffered some terrible fate, or even death? Or will she even care? Better that she believe me dead.

A man with no tomorrow, no hope, no dreams. An interminable nightmare lay ahead.

Chapter 16

As the next day dawned, heavy clouds hovered over London, and Nathan thought that even the sun had forsaken the desperate doomed locked-up souls. He hadn't slept a wink, although he had finally inched up against a wall and slowly slid to the ground, becoming acquainted with a dark corner of the room.

It would have been far better if I had fallen to my death at Craven's Inn. God, why did you grant me strength to save my life, only to suffer a fate far worse?

In the morning, the prisoners gathered in the yard for breakfast. One of the guards came over to Nathan carrying a folded shirt and trousers in pale blue, made from coarse woolen cloth." Prisoners are known by numbers, 'ere," the guard explained matter-of-factly. "You need to shed your clothes and put these on." The guard shoved the uniform into Nathan's mid-section. Nathan put the clothes under his armpit as he remained in line for his breakfast. He was handed a metal bowl and cup. A few minutes later, one of the inmates poured some gruel into the bowl, another handed him a crust of bread, and a third filled his cup with water.

Nathan didn't have the courage to sample the gruel. He bit down on the bread, but spit it out when it tasted of mold. The water in his cup was grey. Nathan swished the liquid around in the cup, but couldn't see the bottom. He remembered reading about epidemics of cholera and diphtheria, which some had attributed to malignant drinking water. Nathan imagined untold swarms of diseased organisms swimming about inside. He had no temptation to drink the contents, and he emptied it on the ground.

Better to waste away in starvation than eat and drink this filth.

It was a world of unimaginable horror and wretchedness. Nathan expected a leper colony would have been far more pleasant. He had nearly avoided this nightmare when he had prepared to depart for France. Yet, his regret was muted by the magical evening he had spent in Regina's company.

I will replay that evening each night in my mind, for as long as I live.

After breakfast, Nathan was issued a mop and bucket, with orders to wipe down the long hallways on his floor. The guard told him he expected every ounce of grime removed, or there would be no dinner. Nathan was herded back to his cell, with instructions to change into the prison garb and begin working. Once the guard disappeared, Nathan threw the coarse clothes on the dirty mattress. He didn't have any interest in changing, nor did he care what adverse consequences he might face if he failed to do so.

Nathan walked down the hallway carrying the mop and pail, and descended the steps to the ground floor to get water. He pointed to the empty bucket, and a guard motioned him to a trough. He filled it with muddy water and retraced his steps back up to the third floor hallway. The floors were caked with grime and random pieces of hardened mud. Nathan spent an hour sweeping away the loose filth with the dry mop. Nathan then retrieved the trousers he had been issued and placed them on the floor in front of him. He kneeled on the trousers and turned the mop around, using the metal end to try to dislodge the grime. After twenty minutes of sporadic labor, he was able to dislodge enough of the dirt to reach the wooden floor beneath. It was three inches below the surface. Nathan looked at the long hallway, which extended more than a hundred feet to the stairwell. It was evident that he had barely scratched the surface. Complying with the guard's edict could take many weeks, maybe even months.

After a couple more hours of lackluster effort, Nathan realized that the task was altogether hopeless. He threw water onto the floor and mopped the water over the grime the length of the hallway, devoid of feeling, numb to life, unconcerned whether he was punished or not.

When dinner was served, Nathan filed in line behind the other prisoners. He felt an emptiness in his stomach, but stood in line more out of curiosity as to what was being served than any desire to eat. The inmates each helped themselves to one of the tin bowls stacked on a wooden table. When it came Nathan's turn, the prisoner assigned the serving task did a double take as he glanced at Nathan's fine suit.

"You'll find our porridge far tastier than what's served in London's finest."

Nathan ignored the comment and the inmate dumped dark brown slop into Nathan's bowl. On Sundays, the slop was rumored to contain meat. Nathan looked at the watery concoction he'd been given in a bowl, without a spoon. The gristle from a chicken leg bobbed at the top of the murky liquid. He felt his stomach growl, but he had no appetite. No guard seemed to mind that he was still wearing his black suit, which was looking less immaculate as it became more wrinkled and dirty by the hour. He walked by the tables where the inmates were eating, placed the bowl on the end of one table, and continued walking. He found a quiet corner nearby and sat down on a stone bench against the wall.

Nathan's eyes were upon the horde of inmates, but his thoughts were elsewhere. It hadn't yet been twenty-four hours and Nathan couldn't imagine how he would be able to endure another week, let alone months and years. He buried his head in his hands and wondered if the sun would ever set on his first full day of prison.

Following dinner, a few prisoners made an attempt to strike up a conversation with their new inmate—his attire and appearance made him exceedingly conspicuous. Others taunted him with exaggerated bows and their pretentious version of society talk, trying to get him to react. Nathan ignored them all, with a faraway look. He wouldn't be among the living long. There was no reason to eat and drink—that would only prolong his spiteful existence.

***

As darkness finally came, the prisoners were ordered to their rooms. In a near-catatonic state, Nathan took the long walk to his building and climbed up the stairs until he reached his cell. He shoved the mattress next to the wall with his feet and brought the blanket over his torso, slumping against the wall.

His head jerked up repeatedly as he faded in and out of sleep.

***

A rarity for him, Mr. Travers had spent the weekend working on the report, finishing it Sunday afternoon. He read it through a second time and gave a satisfied sigh; he was pleased with the detail, including the summarizing paragraph. Though it was Sunday night, he was impatient to deliver the report in person. While he wanted to ensure that no intermediary had access to the confidential information and his client's identity, he also had strong desire to personally meet his client.

With the summer's sun casting long shadows on the ground, it was still light when Mr. Travers arrived in the evening at half past eight. Before seeing it, he was already aware that the residence of his client was among the finest in all of London. Now witnessing it for the first time, he marveled at its outward beauty as he waited for the door to open.

Mr. Travers was ushered in and told to remain in the entry. After five minutes, the butler returned, indicating that he had been instructed to take possession of the documents. Mr. Travers objected, but to no avail; the butler insisted that his instructions were quite clear, further reassuring him that the package would be immediately delivered to the intended party. Reluctantly, Mr. Travers handed the document over to the intermediary.

Disappointed, Mr. Travers left the residence. He had been consumed with meeting the client; it had been the chief reason he had taken such an interest in the assignment. Now it was over, and he was none the wiser. There was no clue or hint as to the purpose behind the investigation. It left him with a hollow feeling. All the wild speculation he had been harvesting for the past weeks had been for naught. He felt unfulfilled, incomplete. Would he ever learn the answer to the mystery? Would he ever hear the name Nathan Sinclair again?

Chapter 17

The following day was the second Monday of August. Nathan kept to himself, avoiding contact with other prisoners. Most had given up trying to communicate with him; they ignored him just as he did them. Nathan's throat was parched and his lips felt thick; he knew he was becoming increasingly dehydrated. In the morning he refused breakfast, though his stomach was cramping. He welcomed death, not able to bear the thought of living the rest of his days in such a dreary and hopeless confinement.

As the day progressed, Nathan felt increasingly weak and light-headed. In the early afternoon, he dutifully poured water on the third floor hallway and spread it on the floor with the grungy mop. As he shuffled through the task, he reflected with regret that the maître d'hôtel at Verrey's would think that he had welched on his promise to perform nightly after having dined there. It surprised Nathan that such an inconsequential concern could bother him, with his life soon ending. For the first time since arriving, he felt sadness that he would never play the piano again. His last performance had been a triumphant and flawless presentation of a difficult Liszt composition. That would be the legacy he would leave the woman he had fallen in love with.

It had been more than forty hours since his last food and drink.

By next Saturday, I will be in the morgue.

The cramping in his stomach worsened. Instead of discomfort, however, it brought peace. With each passing hour, he came closer to deliverance.

Dear God, take me to a better place.

As the day wore on, Nathan returned to his room listless. It was late afternoon, and he preferred to be alone. He yearned for sleep, having slept little during the two days and nights he had been imprisoned. For the first time he allowed himself to lie down on the mattress; he used the still-folded prison clothes as a pillow. The prospect of ticks and vermin no longer mattered. The filth no longer disgusted him. He embraced it.

Soon enough, my flesh and bones will be lowered into the ground. No reason to avoid the mice and maggots—they shall be my companions in death.

As he lay on the bed, in a dream state or conscious, he knew not, Nathan saw the silhouette of a man standing in his open door.

I must be hallucinating.

The hallucination spoke.

"*Sin*-clair! Warden wishes t' see yer."

In a mindless stupor, Nathan rose to his feet and felt as though he were going to faint. After steadying himself, Nathan followed the guard down the stairs. Word must have traveled that he hadn't eaten or drunk—would he be forced to do so against his will? He felt intensely fatigued and weak; never before had the act of walking required so much effort. The guard led him across the endless prison yard, the buildings casting long shadows on the squalid ground. They continued to march toward the warden's office, located near the front of the prison entrance. Twice, the guard ordered Nathan to increase his pace.

The guard knocked on the warden's door and was instructed to enter.

"Prisoner Sinclair," the guard barked and motioned for Nathan to step inside. Seated behind a large mahogany desk was a heavy-set middle-aged man with thick sideburns, a large nose, and a red complexion. He wore a dark suit, white shirt, and black tie. A bottle of port and two empty crystal glasses sat on his desk.

"*Mister* Nathan Sinclair?"

Nathan nodded.

"They tell me you 'aven't 'ad anythin' to eat or drink since you arrived."

Nathan nodded imperceptibly and continued staring in the direction of the warden with a vacant look.

"Can't say as ah blame yer. Ah wouldn't dar' touch the slop 'ere either. Ah dan't rightly know which way 'un 'ould die faster... eatin' that slop or starvin' yerself to death.

"Offer yer a drink?"

Nathan suddenly became aware of the bottle on the desk and the thought of a drink caused an involuntary swallow.

The warden leaned forward in his chair, took the bottle, and poured into the two glasses, doing his best to make them as equal as possible. He stood up from his chair, picked up both glasses, and walked over to Nathan, surveying him up and down.

"Mighty fine clothes for a prisoner 'ere." He extended a glass to Nathan.

Surprised by the gesture, Nathan took the glass. The warden then toasted Nathan's glass. "To yer 'ealth, sir."

Nathan hesitated, not understanding.

"Go a'ead, drink it up. It's nat poison." The warden began draining the contents of his glass.

Nathan put the glass of port to his nose and smelled the sweet aroma. It had a scent of chrysanthemums. It was tempting, but he had taken a vow to never eat or drink again. He felt his willpower dissolving and his dry tongue and throat yearned to savor the sweet silky smooth taste. One sip wouldn't delay the inevitable much. He raised the cup to his lips. A few drops fell upon his tongue and glided down his throat. It was the first liquid he had imbibed in nearly two days. After one taste, he desperately wanted another. Just one more sip. He put the cup to his lips again and took a longer sip, swishing the delicious ambrosia around his lips before swallowing it. One small glass could hardly make any difference. Nathan emptied the remainder of the glass into his throat.

"That's better, Mr. Sinclair. Sorry we 'aven't 'ad a chance to become better 'quainted."

Nathan's mind was elsewhere.

"Yer a damn lucky fellow, yer are. A lucky fellow, indeed."

Those weren't the words he had expected to leave the warden's lips, and Nathan's eyes and ears perked up.

"Yes. You must 'ave been born under a charmed star."

Nathan had no idea what the warden was talking about.

The warden took Nathan's empty glass and motioned to the door. "Yer free to go."

Nathan turned around, still savoring the taste of the port in his throat, and started walking toward the door. His stomach began to cramp and the warden's strange behavior barely registered in his mind.

The warden raised his voice, seeing that the prisoner didn't understand. "Mr. Sinclair. I mean yer *free to leave Coldbath Fields.*"

Nathan turned again at the open door, facing the warden with a look of astonishment, the words just beginning to sink in.

"I 'ave orders 'ere to release you immediately." The warden held up some papers in his hand.

Nathan gave an incredulous look. It didn't make any sense.

"I swear it's the truth," the warden confirmed with a serious look.

What words had his ears just heard? This was preposterous! This was wonderful! How could it be? It had not yet been forty-eight hours since his arrest.

Nathan stared at the warden with an earnest look, wondering if his ears had deceived him. "Did you say I am free to leave Coldbath?"

"Ah, at last the gentleman 'ath found 'is voice. Yes sir, yer free to go."

Nathan's eyes opened wide in utter shock. Someone had come to his rescue? But who? Who could possibly have paid his debt of sixty pounds? Had Regina found out about his imprisonment? Her uncle must have bailed him out.

My Lord. Can it be true? If so, I will be indebted to him for the rest of my life.

He had to know.

"Who was it?"

"Pardon me?" It was the warden's turn to be confused.

"Who paid my debt?" Nathan expected the warden to respond with, "an anonymous benefactor." He was not prepared for the warden's actual reply.

"Parliament."

"Parliament?"

"Yes. Act of Parliament."

"I don't understand."

"Well. I guess you 'aven't 'eard of the Debtors Act of 1869."

Nathan shook his head.

"Me neither, 'til today. Been told it's been in assembly for years. No one ever thought it would pass. But it did. Earlier today. All imprisoned debtors are 'ereby released by order of the Queen."

"You are telling me that I am free to go." Nathan still couldn't quite grasp the message.

"Abolished. No more prison for debts. Yer a free man."

Nathan remained standing.

"I'm not speakin' in jest." The warden waved the official looking document. "It's all 'ere. Only fittin' you should be the first t' go, the way yer dressed and all. No, I can't say I remember the last time we 'ad a real gentlemen 'ere.

"Some heavy gamblin' debts. Am I right?"

In a trance, Nathan ignored the question. He gave a bow, turned and walked out of the warden's office toward the front gate. Was the warden playing a trick on him?

Nathan stopped a few feet back from the gate. It was shut. Nothing made any sense.

Suddenly, the gate opened and the prison guard standing nearby stared at Nathan.

"Well, sir. Yer goin' 'a leave or not?"

With no more invitation needed, Nathan walked straight away out of the gate and into the street. He heard the gate grind shut behind him.

This must be a dream! It can't be.

He started walking tentatively down the street. Before he turned down the boulevard, he looked back, half expecting Sedgwick and the constable to be in pursuit. He stared in wonder at the prison gate, still in disbelief, alone on the street.

It was a miracle! He looked to the sky and praised God.

His pace quickened and he gulped in air, filling his lungs. His lightheadedness and fatigue disappeared as the realization of his newfound freedom grew with every step. The grime covering the streets no longer repulsed him; he welcomed its color, stench, and texture as an old familiar carpet. The air outside the prison complex smelled infinitely sweeter than the wretched odor behind the prison gates. The heavy burden he had been carrying for weeks lifted from his shoulders as a feather blown upward by the wind.

To anyone he passed on the street, Nathan nodded with a "Good day" or a wide smile.

People must think I have gone mad, he thought, yet he wanted to share his madness with the masses.

He had been given a second chance at life.

He had a future, after all.

Regina.

He *would* see her again.

His stomach gave a loud growl and the thought of a finely cooked meal and bottle of wine was suddenly very appealing.

Chapter 18

An Act for the Abolition of Imprisonment for Debt—enacted by the Queen's most excellent Majesty. It was the talk of the town. The laboring class celebrated as news of the Parliament Act spread, an historic and stunning victory for the legion who lived in constant fear of imprisonment for failure to timely pay their debts. The legislation, which had been germinating for more than forty years in various forms, had passed after an emotional and hasty morning debate and subsequent vote. It was now the law of the British Empire.

Still disbelieving his unexpected freedom, Nathan finished his hearty meal at a restaurant a short distance from the prison. He then took a cab to St. Clement's Inn. When he walked in the door, the desk clerk looked up in astonishment.

"Cheese and crust, Mr. Sinclair! 'Ow'd you 'scape?"

"You haven't heard? Parliament has released all those imprisoned for debt."

The clerk may have been the only one among the working class who hadn't yet heard the news.

"Yer a free man?"

"I am."

"Congratulations, Mr. Sinclair! That's mahvelous news."

Nathan couldn't restrain his wide smile. "Didn't expect to be back quite so soon. Are my things still in the room?"

The clerk nodded. "Didn't clean out yer room yet. After all, yer paid 'til 'morrow noonday."

"I shall be departing now. Going home," Nathan could hardly contain his joy as he delivered the words.

A short time later, Nathan was in a cab on his way home.
No more looking over my shoulder.
Nathan had never felt more alive.

The cab dropped him off in front of his building. Nathan stepped out with his briefcase and heavy bag. He entered the *front door* without fear, climbed up the steps, and walked into his apartment. He had hardly slept during the past forty-eight hours, yet felt no fatigue, so electrified was he with his good fortune. He was thrilled to see his box piano undisturbed. He walked into his business office, removed the papers from his briefcase, and put them on his desk. Nothing was out of place. Even though he had several months remaining on his rent, he had assumed that once imprisoned, every possession of his would have been confiscated.

Perhaps it all would have been, if I had languished much longer in Coldbath Fields.

Nathan glanced at the drawings and sketches and relished the thought of working on them again, in the open. He looked forward to new assignments and new challenges, and felt the same optimism in work that he had felt when he had first opened his office. He visualized courting Regina, successful in his business, and someday asking for her hand in marriage. A few hours passed and soon he heard the chime of the church bells strike twelve. It was midnight, a familiar hour for Nathan and his music. A time he often played, when the night was still and his mind was free of the cares of the passing day.

He sat down at his piano, savoring the wonder of creating music with his fingers—something he had never expected to do again. He flexed his fingers above the keyboard, stretching them as he readied to begin playing. Without any particular composition in mind, he began improvising a melody of triumph and liberation in the key of D major. He imagined the sound of a trumpet heralding to a kingdom a great victory from afar, soldiers singing joyously as they returned home bloodied and wounded, having delivered their people from a great enemy and great oppression. As he replayed the theme a second time, he envisioned violins repeating the triumph an octave above, accompanied by woodwind arpeggios—the news of the great victory carried throughout the land, far and wide. He then switched to the minor harmonic and softly told the story, in music, of the dread and pessimism that had fallen upon the people when the enemies had first surrounded the kingdom. In the bass register, he quietly portrayed the darkest hour, when death and enslavement appeared a certainty. As the people united, the melody gradually progressed into the treble clef. Then as the conflict began, the tempo increased, mimicking the battle that ensued. Mixed within the main theme was another melody in counterpoint, telling the tragic story of fallen heroes, sacrificing their lives for the people they loved. The tempo increased to a fury as the battle raged. In the minor key, he recreated the desperation and hopelessness of the struggle, until very briefly, it changed back into the harmonic major. A ray of hope sprung on the battlefield—a soft theme barely developed in the upper register. But the minor key continued to dominate, evoking despair and heartbreak. A small victory broke through in a major key serenade an octave lower than the first strain of the hopeful theme, this time developed longer than before. Back and forth the two harmonic keys fought, until the major key became dominant, the minor key fading and finally defeated. Then, the theme from the opening measures played as the enemies retreated. Nathan ended his composition as he had started it, but much louder, with many trumpets announcing a great victory and the people cheering.

He heard the chime of the second morning hour, seconds after he had concluded his composition.

My Midnight Concerto, Nathan thought to himself with a smile. *I shall never forget it. Someday when I open my soul and reveal everything, I shall play it for the woman I love.*

Nathan suddenly realized how fatigued he was. He walked to his bedroom, changed into his nightclothes, and collapsed onto bed. For the first time in weeks, he had a peaceful slumber.

***

The following morning, Nathan walked over to his office and unlocked the front door. He would manage to get by without a clerk until he started earning a steady income. Opening the door, Nathan was stunned to see a man seated behind the reception room desk. It was Stumbolt. It wasn't clear who was more shocked to see the other.

"I thought you were gone for good," Nathan said.

Stumbolt gave an embarrassed look, as if he didn't want to confess that coming to work gave him purpose. He cleared his throat and spoke. "No sir. I've been coming daily. Someone must look after the office."

"But, after the police showed up?" Nathan had a perplexed expression.

"I remained in the office after they left and returned the following day. Organized things. Did not want any thieves to ransack the office."

"Very good, *Mister* Stumbolt. Very good." Nathan nodded and gave his servant a smile.

There are such precious possessions and furniture here! A band of thieves would be content sifting through the many valuables here for at least a fortnight.

Maybe there was a redeeming attribute hidden among Stumbolt's many flaws.

Nathan entered his private office.

A second chance at life!

Nathan could pursue Regina openly. But though he was free, he remained heavily in debt and knew that he couldn't continue to ignore his obligation to Sedgwick without consequence; if he did acquire any assets, Sedgwick would still be in a position to levy upon them. To ever have a future with Regina still required a substantial change in fortune.

Nathan had performed little work on his projects during the weeks he had been on the run, despite the fact that he had carried his drawings in his briefcase; his heart had simply not been in it. Now, however, he felt a renewed energy and enthusiasm to complete his projects and go after new work. He returned to his customary spot behind his desk and did his best to catch up on the assignments that had been largely dormant while he had been away. Nathan resolved to begin making payments on his debt to Sedgwick, however small they might be. It had been wrong of him to ignore the obligation entirely, although he told himself it had been more due to his lack of income than neglect. Moreover, there was strong incentive to pay it off quickly, since the default rate of interest was oppressive; if the debt continued for any appreciable length of time, it would become virtually impossible to ever be fully discharged.

***

Early in the evening, Nathan took a cab to Verrey's. He apologized profusely to the maître d'hôtel for having failed to appear the evening before. Since the restaurant was closed on Sundays, he had only missed one night. He explained that an urgent personal matter had prevented his appearance.

That's an understatement, if there ever was one, he thought to himself. *If he only knew.*

Still in ecstasy from his unforeseen freedom, Nathan gave a memorable concert that evening, full of inspiring and triumphant melodies.

***

Sedgwick read the headlines in the Tuesday *Times* and fumed. "Act Abolishes Debt Imprisonment."

"Damn, damn, bloody damn!" It had been bad enough to hear rumors the day before, but to see it in print was a hard pill to swallow. His lawyer had assured him that the legislation would never pass; after all, it had languished in Parliament for years. Parliament had passed barely noticeable reforms in 1831 and 1862, but *this* act compared to those was the Black Plague compared to a common cold.

"Sinclair is undoubtedly out already, along with Skelton, Boswith, Meacham and McReady," Sedgwick said under his breath.

Sedgwick was impatient to obtain a copy of the act. The total legislation, encompassing bankruptcy reform as well, would be several hundred pages long. It could be weeks before a printed version became available.

There must be something in the fine print, Sedgwick said to himself. *Some loophole.* He had heard that imprisonment of fraudulent debtors was still permitted. *H-m-m-m,* he thought to himself. *There may be something there.* He would have his lawyer examine every word, ten times over if necessary.

"I would not get too comfortable, Mr. Sin—clair. It is not over yet. Not at all."

Chapter 19

Nathan's euphoria spurred him to venture a visit to Regina on Wednesday, under pretense that he was in the neighborhood for a client interview. Regina would never know the true cause of his jubilant mood; at least not for a very long time. After engaging the doorknocker, Nathan was invited in by the butler. Sir Lancaster presently appeared and informed Nathan that Regina was away assisting in the placement of an orphan child, but was expected back soon. Nathan offered to return another day, but Sir Lancaster invited Nathan to sit in the parlor and await her arrival.

In past encounters, Sir Lancaster had shown an economy of words. Taking a chair next to Nathan, he clearly had something to say now. Nathan dreaded the inevitable pending scrutiny of his financial affairs, which Sir Lancaster's wife had initiated at the restaurant.

"Our niece is a unique and extraordinary young woman, Mr. Sinclair."

"I am finding that out, most definitely, as I have come to know her better," Nathan responded.

"I doubt there is a man on earth worthy of her."

Nathan nodded respectfully in full agreement.

"So, you will forgive my close inspection of any man who wishes to become acquainted with her," Sir Lancaster leaned closer to Nathan, studying him intently.

Nathan nodded again and felt his stomach tighten as he anticipated the next round of questions.

"I am exceedingly impressed with your pianistic bravura and recall your mother's fame as an opera singer, although I never had the pleasure of hearing her. What can you tell me of your father, your family?"

"Sir Lancaster," Nathan started slowly. "Never have I wished to know the answer more than this very moment. Growing up, my father's identity was largely a mystery. Whenever I inquired about him as a young boy and later as a youth, my mother reacted with profound sadness, and I soon learned to avoid even the mention of his name. I was in my final year of studies in Switzerland when I learned that my mother was seriously ill. In her letter, she entreated me to hurry home, explaining she had something important to tell me about my father. Unfortunately, I arrived too late to learn the answer. All I know is his name was Steven Sinclair and he was an artist."

Nathan knew it was inevitable that the inquiry would soon turn to his finances. In his present circumstances, he could not even afford a single lace cloth on one of the room's side tables. In a moment, he would have to reveal the truth; he would never chance a lie with Sir Lancaster. When he disclosed his circumstances, the Lancasters' favorable impression of him would vanish.

"Regina is not preoccupied with romance or finding a husband. Her life is committed to her work with orphans, and the service she renders is incalculable. There has never been a serious rival to her selfless endeavor..." Sir Lancaster paused. "I would advise you to proceed cautiously in becoming acquainted with her. Take your time."

"As you get to know her better, you may find her reticent to speak of her past." Sir Lancaster continued. "It is a very personal matter and I would advise you to never pry. She has suffered a tragedy of such monumental proportions that few could endure it. Yet endure it she has, and with celestial grace. Reliving the events would cause her great pain. If she is ever to discuss it, let it be at her time and her choosing."

"I shall be vigilant in refraining from further inquiry," Nathan responded, as he felt his heart aching over Regina's tragedy, yet unknown to him, dissipating his own pedestrian financial concerns.

Just then, Regina entered in the sitting room. Her eyes instantly lit up as she spied Nathan.

"Mr. Sinclair." Regina gave an extended curtsy.

"Miss Lancaster," Nathan bowed, doing his best to mask his overpowering joy at seeing her again. Regina blushed at Nathan's glowing face.

"How pleasant to see you again." Regina welcomed him with her eyes.

"Thank you. The pleasure is all mine. I hope you will forgive my impromptu intrusion. I happened to be on business nearby, and wanted to pay my respects." Nathan rejoiced inwardly at hearing the sweetness of her voice; only two days before, he was certain he would never see her again.

Regina looked at her uncle and back at Nathan, her head angled playfully in a suspicious look as one eyebrow lowered. "What have the two of you been talking about?"

"Your uncle has merely told me what an extraordinary prize you are."

Regina shook her head quickly, glancing at Sir Lancaster. "That does not sound like my dear uncle's voice."

Sir Lancaster smiled tenderly at his niece. "I shall excuse myself before any confession leaves my lips." He stood up and left Nathan and Regina alone in the room.

"I am so sorry that I was not here to greet you," Regina responded brightly, but then her expression became more reserved.

Nathan noticed the change and suddenly second-guessed his decision to come by unannounced. "It is I who must apologize for the chance visit. Your uncle told me that you were on an errand of mercy for an orphan child."

Instantly Regina's eyes opened wide with delight. "Oh, Mr. Sinclair. It is such a joy to see two dreams intersect. The young child's dream of finding a true home and gaining a mother and father; and the parents' dream of starting a family."

Regina began opening up to Nathan for the first time about her work. Unlike the vast majority of English gentry, Regina was *actively engaged* in good works, not just speaking of them. Nathan learned that she devoted much of her time to helping orphaned children find loving homes. She frequently visited London orphanages and subtly encouraged better care and facilities. More importantly, she sought quality families willing to add another child to their brood or a childless couple seeking to adopt. She meticulously interviewed parents to effectuate a compatible match.

"Every day is a gift," she continued. "I have learned never to take even a second for granted. Tomorrow may be the last day of our lives, and our ability to soften the burdens of humanity will be over. I live each day as if it were my last. There is so much to do. For so long as I live, I will dedicate my life to serving these poor abandoned children. I was brought up believing that I could make a difference in this world." Regina shared her dreams of creating a network of others, like herself, who would sponsor orphans, taking upon themselves the role of "guardian angel" in seeking to find for each of them a loving home.

"Mr. Sinclair, there are tens of thousands of orphans in London on any given day. Most are living in intolerable conditions. Many are laboring hard in workhouses. Thousands eke out a living on the streets. In a city of over three million souls, imagine the miracle that would occur if an equal number of good families would take in an orphan. Poverty and crime would be drastically reduced. In years to come, industry would receive a great boost from children properly educated and instructed. If money were no object, I would love to see the creation of more establishments that could accommodate the numerous homeless children living on the streets. Can you imagine buildings, with adequate and loving staff, housing them all... providing these children a temporary haven and stepping stone to a new home?"

Nathan was touched by her devotion. "May I accompany you some time on one of your visits?"

Regina smiled with pleasure at his interest. "I would be delighted to introduce you to my work. Perhaps you can join me on a future visit."

Regina's beauty and purity increased as Nathan listened intently to her with an admiring regard.

What an extraordinary woman! How could any man be worthy of her?

He could tell how excited she was to share her passion and dreams. Prior to this evening, it had been only Nathan speaking of *his* dreams. He now perceived her in an even more glorious light. At the same time, Nathan wondered if Regina was more excited about sharing her passion than sharing herself.

Chapter 20

As the summer days gave way to autumn, the suffocating stench of the Thames sewage overflow slackened even on the east side of London, as heavy rainstorms repeatedly cleansed the streets. On a crisp autumn day when a morning fog had descended upon the city of London, Nathan had planned his first excursion with Regina to an orphanage. The Asylum for Fatherless Children, affectionately known as the "Home on the Hill," was located near the trunk line of the Dover and Brighton Railway, in Croydon. To be admitted to the Home on the Hill, a child had to be between the ages of three months and ten years, and orphaned or fatherless because of the father's death or severe handicap. It was home to nearly three hundred orphans.

Nathan took a short train ride to Croydon, unable to see twenty feet beyond the tracks because of the fog. By the time he departed the train, visibility had improved, but only slightly. The orphanage was a short walk from the station, up the hill to a promontory. Not until he was nearly upon it was Nathan able to see the large eclectic building of brick and stone. Standing in front, only a small part of the building was distinguishable in the brume—the entrance was visible, but windows on either side of the double doors gradually disappeared into the mist. Looking up, his eyes could see the faint outline of a roof three levels skyward on either side of a rectangular tower that appeared to rise into the heavens.

Nathan arrived shortly before Regina. As Regina exited the cab in the fog-obscured street, Nathan came forward and extended his arm. She gave him a warm smile, and Nathan felt the glow of her caring heart. For a brief moment, Nathan wondered if the glow was for him or for sharing her passion. *Hopefully both*, he thought.

"The baby's name is Glasgow. He is not yet six months old and he is so charming... you shall instantly fall in love with him."

Entering the orphanage, Nathan felt a pang of sadness in viewing dozens of young children, the vast majority older than Glasgow, looking expectantly, in hopes that Nathan and Regina might make their dream come true and take them home.

"It is more crowded than normal," Regina explained. "Some of the children displaced by the closure of the London Orphan Asylum are lodging here temporarily. I am sure you remember the tragic typhoid epidemic that took the loss of so many helpless children."

Nathan had recalled it being in the news. "A terrible tragedy."

"And that was one of the better-run institutions in London." Regina replied.

Nathan was touched by the reception children gave Regina, coming up to her, hugging her, tugging on her leg. He was cheered to see that the orphanage was clean and without any pungent odor or stench. The children were well dressed and appeared well cared for.

Picking up Glasgow from a member of the orphanage staff, Regina explained, "He was left abandoned at the doorstep; something that happens more often than you might think. Placed in a basket with a small stuffed dog and a letter. The letter gave the child's given name and was signed by a grief-stricken father, who had lost his wife to illness shortly after the child's birth. He had been rendered destitute by her medical expenses and expressed heartbreak that his child would starve and die if left under his care. Other sentiments in the letter were so touching that there is no doubt the child had been deeply loved."

Nathan looked at the child and put out his finger, and the child grabbed it. The auburn-haired child smiled as they made eye contact. "And you have a family for him?"

"I do. We are so excited. They should be coming in thirty minutes to see him for the first time. The couple is childless; they have been married for eight years now and desperately want to start a family. I have met with them twice. They live in a comfortable home in Knightsbridge; the father has a steady job and enough income to ensure that the child is well cared for and educated. Most importantly, they appear to be very much in love. But, I would so appreciate your impressions of them, after you meet them."

Shortly thereafter, Nathan met the couple and observed their rapture at the sight of the young boy. He had to admit, Regina seemed to have made a perfect match for the parents and child. Nathan extended his warmest compliments to the match.

"I have nine other children I am currently working on. I wish I could split myself in two or three—there is so much work to be done. Several are at orphanages with standards far below this one. Unfortunately, the older the children, the more difficulty placing them in a home."

"What makes them more difficult?" Nathan had never given

the subject any thought.

"The older the children, the less malleable they are. Parents uniformly prefer adopting as young a child as possible, to be able to teach and mold the child during the formative years. Some parents prefer their child does not know he or she is adopted, at least not until adulthood."

"Your service is truly extraordinary."

"I believe I am more blessed than the children or the parents, Nathan." Regina beamed. It was the first time that Regina had used Nathan's given name, and it thrilled him that she had done so without an invitation. Regina's face, however, turned red when she realized the faux pas.

"There is such joy in bringing happiness to an abandoned child and parents desperately seeking a family, *Mr. Sinclair*." Regina said, correcting her presumptuous error.

"I prefer Nathan to Mr. Sinclair—from you, especially. We know each other well enough to use our given names, do we not?" There was a pause as Regina's eyes looked downward. "*Regina?*"

Hearing her given name from the young man made her blush. "I am so sorry. I did not mean any disrespect. It was accidental."

"Oh, such an accident. *Regina*, please address me again by my Christian name."

She returned his stare with a polite smile, but merely continued with her train of thought. "Changing one child's life is an expression of such selfless love by the new parents. I have been involved in this effort for nearly four years now and I know of no greater work."

"How many children? How many homes?"

"Two hundred twenty-seven. No, with today's, it will be two hundred twenty-eight."

Nathan was stunned by the number. "Astounding! How have you been able to place so many?"

"It is my life's work. I am the lone remaining emissary from my family... from my brothers and sisters, who have passed on. I wish I could do much, much more." Nathan could tell from her expression that Regina instantly regretted the intimate familial disclosure, and he was circumspect to not follow up.

"Do you keep in touch with the families you have helped?"

"I do. I correspond, or in some cases visit, the families at least once a year."

Nathan tried to imagine the letter-writing task that alone would require. "So many children; it must be difficult to follow them all and remember each one."

Regina gave Nathan a stern look. "I remember each name. They leave a permanent imprint. When you place a child in a loving home, *you never forget.*"

Hoping to redeem his imprudent remark, Nathan inquired, "How are they doing?"

"In all but a few cases, the children and parents are thriving. Occasionally there are some difficulties in adjustment, usually with the older children. Tragically, there have been a few deaths... from natural causes, of course. But otherwise, it has been gratifying to see the results. I look forward to following these children as they grow, and meeting each of them when they become adults, with a hope that some may wish to carry on the work."

What a noble and glorious calling! She is irresistible and radiant in her service. There was little question that Regina would be the crowning jewel of any man lucky enough to be found worthy of her. She was the rare woman who would cause a man to put forth his highest and most noble self.

By the time they left the building, the fog had mysteriously vanished, leaving no trace of its earlier presence.

Chapter 21

The sun rose later in the heavens and set earlier in the afternoon. The trees reluctantly relinquished their hold on nature's singular creations, allowing foliage to fall to the ground unappreciated by the indifferent masses. North winds became more common and frigid as overcast skies, more often than not, turned to rain. The city of London took on its autumn gloom with wood-burning hearths blanketing the sky with thick smoke, obscuring the sun's rays on the rare days the clouds parted. Soot painted a black layer on brick buildings, which had been scrubbed clean during the unusually warm summer. Construction continued on the South Thames aqueduct, interfering with the drainage of sewage and refuse, particularly in neighborhoods near the river where Nathan had the misfortune of working and living.

With renewed vigor and confidence inspired by his growing friendship with Regina, Nathan put forth passion and sweat in striving to build his architect business. He visited merchants and other businesses searching for new work. It was small, but there was perceptible progress. A fifteen-pound retainer on a new project had brightened his mood in mid-October. Using two-thirds of the retainer, he made his first payment on his debt with Sedgwick. He tried to imagine Sedgwick's reaction when he opened the envelope containing the check. Unfortunately, Allenby's home remained on the market amid rumors that the bank had filed a notice of foreclosure. Nathan wondered if he would ever be paid the money he was owed.

During the same time, Nathan continued his gentle pursuit of Regina. As the days passed and November arrived, rarely did a week go by that Nathan did not see her. She was always friendly, showing pleasure in his visits, but remained circumspect with her emotions. He was *taking his time* with her. Nevertheless, there were occasional clues that gave Nathan hope. On a late fall afternoon, she provided one.

They were walking in the spacious backyard of the Lancaster estate, bundled up in the frigid cold. No flowers were in bloom, but the garden still held a nostalgic allure, with reminiscences from the summer months. Neatly trimmed hedges were well preserved, despite the lateness of the season, in front of a small pond on the far side of the yard with a connecting man-made grotto to the rear. Regina sat down in the far quarter of the garden on a bench, embowered with honeysuckles and roses in the summer months, but now containing only their dried vines left behind. Here, the architectural beauty and symmetry of the residence was on full display. Nathan sat down next to her.

"What were you like as a boy?" Regina inquired.

"Too tall, too thin, and unbearably shy." Nathan smiled.

"I can't see you as shy."

"Especially around girls."

"Well, you have certainly overcome that."

"I had some help from a most generous friend," Nathan volunteered.

"A female, undoubtedly, by the way you blush."

Nathan could only nod.

"And was she your first love, as well?" Regina inquired.

A smile broke out on Nathan's face.

"So, you are still in love with her?" Regina teased.

"I think I shall be, forever."

"Tell me of her."

"Where to start," Nathan glanced upward. "I was a gangly boy, with long arms that seemed to drag down to the ground. My mother and I had just recently moved to London and I was having a hard time adjusting to new friends. I used to go to a park nearby and watch other children play, longing to join in. I was seated at a bench one day, when the *love of my life* came toward me and sat on the other end of the bench. I was so shy, I could not even bear to look her way. After a few minutes of torment, I ran away."

Regina laughed. "I have had that happen to me before. Must be my great beauty."

"I came back to the park nearly every day thereafter, hoping to see her again. I had not even looked at her face, I was so timid. I didn't even know what she looked like. I only remembered the braids of her hair."

"Like every other girl, to be sure."

"Day after day, I went to the same bench hoping she would come again. But she never did."

"My heart is breaking," Regina playfully mocked.

"Until one day," Nathan said with suspense. "I heard footsteps coming from behind and turned around. There she was. I stared at her and she stared back. I must have given her a frightful scare, but she just smiled and walked by. But, what a smile it was! Never had a girl smiled at me like that. I was forever smitten."

"And you lived happily ever after?"

Nathan chuckled. "One day, she walked up to me and asked my name. I guess she wanted to place a name with her admirer. I was so petrified and unprepared to speak, that I just mumbled something out. She asked me a second time. When I told her my name—actually my nickname—she started laughing. I put my head down, and she apologized. Then she brushed my arm and we started talking. I don't remember a word that was spoken, but I suddenly felt very comfortable with her. I kept returning to the park, hoping to find her. She would often come. We talked and played together, and I found that I could actually talk to a *girl*."

"What was your nickname? I *promise* not to laugh," Regina gently placed her hand on Nathan's arm.

"Never! Even under penalty of death, my lips are forever sealed. Fortunately, not a soul alive knows it."

"Then I must make it my life's ambition to discover it." Regina smiled as Nathan's heart melted.

After that day, Nathan replayed Regina's words over and over in his mind, at odd times and places, safeguarding in his memory the token clue she had fortuitously sent his way.

***

The two-hundred-fifty-page opus on the Parliament Acts of August 9, 1869 sat on Sedgwick's desk. It had taken nearly three months to obtain a complete copy, and he had been impatient to begin his study of the intricate legislation. Sedgwick took out his spectacles and began reading. Not trained as a lawyer, he often had to read a page several times before making any sense of it. He continued into the night, stopping when he reached a hundred pages. Frustrated as he blew out the candle in his bedroom, he told himself, *There must be something there.*

The following morning, he rose early and continued his study of the legislation. In mid-morning, at the bottom of page 122, he stopped at Clause 5 of the Debtors Act. He re-read it a second time, then a third:

> Subject to the provisions herein-after mentioned, and to the prescribed rules, any court may commit to prison

for a term not exceeding six weeks, or until payment of the sum is due, any person who makes a default in payment of any debt or instalment of any debt due from him in pursuance of any order of judgment of that or any other competent court,

He skipped down to sub-article 2:

That such jurisdiction shall only be exercised where it is proved to the satisfaction of the court that the person making default either has or has had since the date of the order or judgment the means to pay the sum in respect of which he has made default and has refused or neglected, or refuses or neglects to pay the same."

Clause 5 *still allowed imprisonment* of a debtor, if it could be shown that the debtor had the means to pay the debt, but refused to pay it. Sedgwick reflected a moment—could that section be applied to Sinclair? There was another condition for Clause 5—that the debtor owed fifty pounds or less. "Who the bloody hell put in that limitation?!" Sedgwick screamed aloud. *But*, Sinclair had unwittingly paid ten pounds, dropping the judgment amount down to fifty pounds.

Imbecile! Well done, Sinclair!

Sedgwick winced, knowing that he would have to forgive a great deal of interest to make it work.

Sedgwick paused after reading it a fourth time, and a smile began to form on his lips. This might be the loophole he needed. It was time to call his lawyer, Aloysius Baumgarten, Esquire.

Chapter 22

Sedgwick sat in the reception room of Isringhausen & Baumgarten. He had been waiting twenty minutes.

Every time I come here, he makes me wait, Sedgwick fumed. *Lawyers! Drown 'em all.*

Sedgwick stood up and walked over to the receptionist and inquired how much longer it might be. He got the same answer he always did. "He shall come out when he is ready to see you."

Sedgwick shook his head. He wondered if Baumgarten had even returned from the pub yet. On days he didn't have an appointment with him, he had observed Baumgarten having drinks in the middle of the day and wondered which clients were waiting patiently in his reception room, assuming he had important affairs to conduct. Now, *he* was one of those clients. Sedgwick walked over to the front door and looked out the window. He knew that Baumgarten had a door in the rear of his office, with direct access to the alley. Sedgwick was tempted to walk outside and wait for him in the alley. Better yet, why not go to the pub and yank him out by his ear?

As Sedgwick debated whether to actually walk outdoors and sneak up on his lawyer, he heard the door to Baumgarten's office open, and observed him shaking the hand of a distinguished man who looked vaguely familiar. The good-bye lasted another ten minutes, as Sedgwick *outwardly* appeared to wait patiently, while *inwardly* he considered which appendage from Baumgarten's body he would dismember first.

The client left, and Baumgarten turned to Sedgwick. "I hope that you haven't been waiting long."

Long? Forty-three minutes to be exact. Next time, I shall send you a bill for my time in the reception!

Sedgwick grunted something indecipherable under his breath and shook Baumgarten's extended hand. *No reason to get the meeting started on the wrong foot.*

After being seated, Baumgarten gave his client his best lawyer's smile. The clock had started ticking. "Now, how may I be of service to my favorite client?"

On his last statement from Isringhausen & Baumgarten, Sedgwick had been charged four hours for "Study and research of Parliament Acts." Sedgwick wondered how many other clients he had charged for the same *study and research.*

"I see that you have read Parliament's legislation," Sedgwick opened.

Baumgarten crinkled his nose and gave Sedgwick an inquiring look. "Legislation?"

"Debtors Act," *you fool,* he said to himself.

Nodding his head in a rotating manner, Baumgarten replied. "Oh, yes. Dear me, of course. There is always legislation to read."

"Well" Sedgwick also knew that the *clock was ticking.* "What did you find out?"

"Find out?" Baumgarten looked at him peculiarly.

"Damn it!" Sedgwick lost his temper. "How do we imprison these worthless sponging idlers who refuse to pay their lawful debts?"

Baumgarten searched for a thick book on his desk amid the many papers present. "Oh, under the new legislation that is going to be most difficult." He found the book he was looking for and began to thumb through it.

Damn man probably hasn't even read it yet!

Baumgarten stopped somewhere in the middle of the book and appeared to be reading to himself.

Sedgwick imagined the clock on the wall through his lawyer's eyes: the "12" on top replaced with the "£" symbol and an "s" for shilling substituted all the other numbers. Measuring the clock, he figured he had already been charged three shillings and the seat of his chair wasn't yet warm.

"Yes. I am afraid that I have studied every word. There is really nothing that can be done." He turned to the first page: "Imprisonment for debtors has been abolished."

Imbecile! "I know imprisonment has been abolished! Damn you, man! What loopholes have you found? That *is* what I am paying you for."

Baumgarten sighed heavily. "I'm afraid Parliament made it nearly impossible to come up with a loophole."

Exasperated, Sedgwick stood up from his chair. "What about Clause 5?"

Baumgarten flipped through pages of the book, apparently attempting to locate "Clause 5."

"Page 122," Sedgwick leaned over the table and whispered.

"Yes, that is where I was." A few more pages were quietly

flipped.

Another shilling down the drain. Sedgwick frowned, realizing that he had just wasted the shilling he would earn from one street vendor's loan.

"Let me tell you what I think about Clause 5," Baumgarten remarked. Sedgwick assumed that now was the first time Baumgarten was actually reading it.

Sedgwick quietly watched another two shillings pass with the clock's minute hand as Baumgarten studied pages 122 and 123.

"It is truly the only provision that permits imprisonment in the whole act."

No jest!

"Can we use it on Sinclair?!" Sedgwick's facial expression demonstrated he was nearing the end of his rope. It had taken ten shillings to get to this point!

"There is a mighty heavy burden the creditor has here. 'Such jurisdiction shall only be exercised where it is proved to the satisfaction of the court that the person making the default either has or has had since the date of order or judgment the means to pay the sum in respect of which he made the default...'"

At least the man can read.

"'...and has refused or neglected, or refuses or neglects, to pay the same.'" Baumgarten pondered for another shilling, then asked, "Do you have any evidence that Sinclair has the *means* to pay?"

Sedgwick had already given the matter considerable thought. "The night he was arrested, he had just returned from Verrey's, the most expensive restaurant in London. He was also wearing a suit from one of the best tailors in the city." *Well, at least that's I was told.*

Baumgarten puffed up his bottom lip in a reflective pose. "The man owes you sixty pounds! That is a start, but..."

"I assume you noticed that imprisonment only applies if it is fifty pounds or less."

Baumgarten cautiously nodded his head, hoping that Sedgwick was right before committing himself. He glanced discretely down at the page the book was opened to until he noticed (1)(b). "Of course, I knew that..."

Like bloody hell you did!

"So, how do you propose we get around that?" the lawyer asked the client.

Who's the lawyer here?

"As luck would have it, Sinclair recently made a payment of ten pounds."

"But, then there is interest," Baumgarten piped in.

"I assume I can *waive* the interest, can I not?"

"You *should* waive the interest, then there would be no problem..."

Brilliant advice!

"...but, once waived, you shall not be able to collect it in the future."

And this is what I am paying twenty shillings to hear? Sedgwick thought as the session approached the hour mark.

"Damn the interest!" Sedgwick raged. "That scoundrel deserves to be in prison." He remembered vividly Sinclair assuring him that the loan would be repaid on time.

Sedgwick caught Baumgarten staring at the clock. "I shall have to give the matter more thought, do some further research..."

Sedgwick felt his blood boil. *And that will cost me another four pounds.*

Chapter 23

The winter solstice arrived, with temperatures dropping to frigid levels as the impatient sun lowered its orbit and preferred to spend most of its time hidden beneath the horizon. London became blanketed with dark smoke from the endless fires burning inside the blackened homes and buildings. The smoke and soot combined to create a thick smog that lingered heavily over the city, darkening the sun's rays on rare cloudless days. Most often, the skies were overcast and the smog filtered out the light, turning midday into a perpetual twilight. Only when the rains came did the smog dissipate—and then, only for a short time.

For Christmas Eve, Regina had extended an invitation to Nathan to accompany her to a south-side London orphanage. It had been arranged for Nathan to meet Regina and Aunt Hélène at their home and then travel together to the orphanage in the family carriage. When he arrived it was twilight, though the sun was still in the heavens, and there was a chill in the air. As Nathan approached the residence, he observed servants carrying large bags to a carriage brimming with gifts for orphans. He felt embarrassed at the few modest items he had brought, tendering his meager offering to the servants, who added them to the other gifts.

Nathan, Regina, and Aunt Hélène took the thirty-minute ride to the orphanage. When they reached their destination, it was clear that some of the older orphans had been previously informed of their visit. Two dozen children ran out to welcome them, dancing and singing as the carriage entered the grounds. It was late afternoon when they arrived, and there was little light remaining from the short winter day. Despite the cold and dreary weather, the children had wonder and light in their eyes. Seeing their excitement, Nathan experienced a rare mixture of exquisite sadness and happiness.

The director of the orphanage greeted them warmly and ushered them inside to a large room where the children were all gathered around a large Christmas tree. Nathan carried two large bags, as did the two coachmen; Regina and Aunt Hélène each managed one. With a full heart, Nathan took part in handing out the gifts.

There were spinning tops, tin soldiers, skipping ropes, marbles, kites, dolls, and a host of other toys. Included were also mince pies, plum pudding, gingerbread, candy canes, assorted cakes, and other holiday treats.

After the gifts had been dispensed, one young girl with long dark hair, not more than four years old, came over to Nathan, who was seated on a chair next to Regina near the Christmas tree. The girl gave him a sweet smile and climbed up, uninvited, onto his lap. Nathan's heart was breaking as he imagined this beautiful young girl without a mother or father.

"What is your name, young lady?"

The girl batted her dark brown eyes up at Nathan and said, "Marta."

"What a lovely name," Nathan said.

"Do you have any children?"

"No, I do not," Nathan responded with a smile.

"Would you like to have a little girl?" she asked unabashedly.

"Someday. That would be lovely."

"*I* could be your little girl."

"And you would make a wonderful daughter."

"Would you be my daddy?"

Would that I could accept such a beautiful offer.

A tear welled in Nathan's eye as he looked down at her. "I can't be your daddy, but I am sure that there is a daddy searching for a little girl just like you."

"Why can't you be my daddy? I think you are very handsome."

Regina smiled as she watched Nathan conversing with the little girl. She stooped down to Marta's eye level. "Hello, Marta. You are so beautiful and sweet, I am sure there are a mother and father who would love to have you as their daughter." *Such an adorable child,* Regina thought as she made a mental note to herself. *I must find a home for her.*

Marta looked up hopefully. "Truly?"

"I am certain of it. But it takes a little time." Nathan observed hope in Marta's eyes. Regina began caressing the little girl's hair. After a few moments, she separated three strands and began braiding the dark locks. Nathan watched with fascination how naturally Regina showed affection for the child, as she took two strands and wove a third around the other two, repeating the process until the young girl's hair was fully plaited.

After dinner was served to the children and guests, the children began singing Christmas carols. Nathan had never felt a brighter glow of the holiday season, as he watched the children sing in expectation of Christmas Day.

In leaving the orphanage, they were surprised to see that snow had fallen; the winter's first snow. This year, the children would awaken to a white Christmas.

As the evening came to a close, they mounted the homeward-bound carriage. Upon arriving at the Lancaster residence, Nathan accompanied Regina and her aunt to the door. Stopping short of the entrance as Aunt Hélène entered ahead of them, Nathan looked lovingly at Regina and placed a small velvet box in her hands. Regina's eyes lit up as she opened it and saw a beautiful silver locket necklace.

"Oh, Nathan. You shouldn't have." It had been his mother's, but Nathan didn't feel he should confess that yet.

"Forgive me, Regina," Nathan said passionately. "I wanted you to have a token of my devotion."

Holding the box, Regina's hands moved almost imperceptibly toward Nathan, and for an instant Nathan wondered if she wished to return the gift. He wondered if he had moved too quickly.

Rather than returning the gift, Regina's hands expanded outward and forward in the blink of an eye, as she gave Nathan a hug. She then rushed into the house without looking back. It was their first embrace.

I could not have wished for a greater gift, Nathan thought, still smelling Regina's sweet fragrance from the brief embrace. In the frigid night air, Nathan had never felt warmer as he walked away in the newly fallen snow under the light of a bright moon on Christmas Eve.

Chapter 24

The new year dawned with hope of better days for all. To the dissatisfaction of the masses, the weather was not compliant with those hopes, forcing desperate families to exhaust their scant fuel supplies sooner than scheduled. By February, the winter's cold had carried on relentlessly, and the optimism of the new year had given way to anxiety and dread.

During the unusually frigid and dreary winter days and nights, Nathan continued his gradual pursuit of Regina's heart. He found in her a beacon of light and hope in the midst of the endless cold and gloom. His attraction toward Regina and her unique beauty grew with each visit, as he became better acquainted with her mind and heart. Despite his profound delight in her company, his struggling practice and financial uncertainty cast a pallor upon any future he might envision with her. If only he had been blessed with a small legacy from his mother or a relative—even the most modest bequest would have been a godsend. The financial burden fell squarely upon his shoulders and his shoulders alone, to create some measure of financial security if there was ever going to be any meaningful future between Regina and himself. Thus far, he had failed miserably in that effort.

***

As the long bleak winter's numbing cold encroached into spring's beginnings, Nathan's feelings of defeat burgeoned and he began having more serious thoughts about a return to Calemby & Co., fearing he would never be free of his burdensome debts. At least at Calemby's, he could regain a stable, but modest, income. At Calemby's, he wouldn't have the added stress of paying his office and business expenses. However, such a compromise came with a great sacrifice, one that would cause him to play second fiddle to more senior architects and would stifle his creativity. Would they even take him back now?

He returned his focus to the project at hand: a modest dwelling he had recently been asked to design. Unfortunately, the client had made it clear that he could afford little for an architect, due to budgetary constraints. What could truly be achieved on such a paltry budget? Despite the monetary limitations, Nathan knew he would eventually concoct a design to make the home unique and beautiful in its own small way.

Suddenly, Stumbolt invaded his somber reflections, opening and then quickly closing the door to his office. Announcing in muted and respectful tones the arrival of a visitor, he handed Nathan a card: *Roderick Charlesworth.*

The last name on the card stunned him. Was he related to *the* Charlesworths—London's celebrity family? If so, what could such a man possibly want with him? A new and exciting commission? Could it be? With anticipation, Nathan motioned for Stumbolt to invite the visitor in.

A moment later, Roderick Charlesworth burst in. He was wearing a dark blue cutaway coat, with a lavishly embroidered white waistcoat and silk shirt. Around his neck was a scarf with a silver filigree ring with Etruscan carving. He wore lavender-seamed trousers with matching lavender gloves. In his hand, he held an ivory-topped cane with ornate glossy silver handiwork on an ebony background. He had polished calfskin boots with stout soles and low, broad heels. His apparel proclaimed to all that he was a man of immense wealth and pedigree. Roderick surveyed the office with a look of disgust written on his face.

Nathan stood up and nodded, extending his hand: "Nathan Sinclair at your service."

When his hand was rejected, Nathan pointed to a chair nearby, inviting his guest to sit.

Remaining standing, Charlesworth blurted out, "Do you know who I am?"

"I know the Charlesworth name, of course."

"Yes, I am most certain that you do. And I am certain you know why I am here."

"I have no inkling..."

Charlesworth gave him a glare. "It's concerning my sister."

"Your *sister*?" Nathan responded, startled.

"My sister, Jocelyn. *I know* that you have been seeing her privately for some time."

Nathan had scarcely reflected on Jocelyn in months, but the reminiscence of her extraordinary beauty burst into his mind. For a brief instant, he longed for one more look at her face. The man claiming to be her brother did not share her flawless looks. His forehead was too prominent, his eyes were too small and his complexion too ruddy. The only similarity was the color of their hair.

"Seeing *your sister*?" Nathan expressed shock. The vivid recollection of the humiliation she had wreaked upon him returned to his mind forcefully, eclipsing the memory of her beauty.

"Do not trifle with me, Sinclair! I promise you, you shall regret it!" Charlesworth stepped forward in a threatening tone. He was the same height as Nathan.

"You are monstrously mistaken..."

"So you are a coward, too!" Charlesworth fired back, elevating his voice. "I know everything! She has confided to me of your plans to marry," he said with teeth clenched.

Dumbfounded, Nathan protested, "Marry... your sister. I hardly know her."

"Be man enough to admit it, you scoundrel!" Charlesworth advanced menacingly until he was directly in front of Nathan.

"You are *absurdly* mistaken and I insist that you leave at once!" Nathan expostulated back in a loud voice.

The power and conviction in Nathan's voice and words caused Charlesworth to hesitate. Despite the obvious fiction of such a report, Nathan registered fleetingly a pleasant intrigue that the most beautiful woman in London could have expressed an interest in him, especially after deflecting his brief advance in such an abominable manner.

In a less combative tone, Nathan inquired, "What is the source of this *preposterous* report?"

"Jocelyn herself informed me last night that she was... in... love... with you and that the two of you intend to marry." Charlesworth's supercilious contempt was so powerful that he could barely enunciate the words.

Jocelyn. In love with me?

"Impossible," Nathan tightened his eyebrows, dismissing such a ridiculous notion. "You obviously have me confused with another man."

"Are there any other architects in London carrying your name?" came Charlesworth's sardonic reply.

"None of whom I am aware."

"Then it is most assuredly you about whom she is carrying on."

Remembering with great clarity their only meeting, Nathan responded. "I assure *you* that on the single *brief* encounter that I had with your sister, her revulsion toward me was made abundantly clear. I would be *stupefied* if she were even to recall my name."

Frankly, her attitude toward me was much the same as your unwelcome affront today."

A momentary glare flared in Charlesworth's eyes. "You are renouncing any private engagement with my sister?"

"There is nothing to renounce!" Nathan exclaimed, showing increasing exasperation. "I have as little interest in your sister as I'm sure she has in me." Taking the offensive, Nathan offered, "I have no interest in pursuing a woman with such a conceited opinion of her *lofty* station. She does service to your family name, exhibiting her superiority so superbly... with just the proper mix of arrogance and contempt. You would have been proud of her."

"Watch your tongue, *Sin*-clair."

"Are you now convinced? Would a man in love speak of his betrothed in such a fashion, especially to an intimate family member? When next you see her, you should commend her on the degradation she dispensed upon me months ago, so effortlessly... in public. I still remember it well. She may be admired by all for her physical beauty, but I see no beauty in her person."

Taken aback by Nathan's remonstration, Charlesworth's demeanor changed. With no apology intended, he said more to himself than Nathan, "It's not like her to trifle in such matters."

Roderick Charlesworth turned and left, without a bow or another word.

In the aftermath of the shocking visit, Nathan experienced a strange arousal of feelings. On the one hand, he still bore the scar from his unpleasant encounter with Jocelyn so many months before. It had been deeply buried, but it was still present. On the other hand, he remembered with precision her startling beauty: beauty that was impossible, unimaginable, and ineffable. He permitted himself a brief taste of flattery that such a bewitchingly beautiful woman of rank could have confessed her love for him—a penniless architect with no family or rank—despite the utter absurdity of such a notion. It was a tantalizing paradox.

Nathan wondered, *Could she truly have feelings for me? Why ever would she?* He shook his head with a silly grin, but then wondered, *Is she as beautiful as I remember?*

Nathan was surprised that his mind could dwell upon the attentions of another woman, when it was Regina who had stolen his heart. He immediately repented of his frivolous thoughts and put Jocelyn Charlesworth out of his mind altogether.

Chapter 25

It had been more than six months since the Debtors Act had passed, and Sedgwick had nearly given up hope of finding a way to exploit the perceived loophole. His lawyer had sent him a cryptic note two days earlier: "I heard about a recent case in Manchester that might interest you." He further indicated that he would be stopping by Sedgwick's office at two o'clock.

"Where is he?" Sedgwick stomped around his office impatiently. It was twenty minutes past two.

Sedgwick wrung his hands. "This had better be good."

Mr. Baumgarten arrived thirty-five minutes after the hour. "Sorry, detained in court."

Sedgwick had heard that excuse a hundred times before and wondered if it were really true, or if Mr. *Esquire* had been at the local tavern having a Friday afternoon drink.

The lawyer sat down across from Sedgwick.

"I have been researching court judgments during the past few months, hoping to find something that might give precedent in moving forward on your Mr. Sinclair." Sedgwick wondered how much *that* research was going to cost him.

"I had to sort through an endless list of judgments in the county courts of London and Manchester. I have been checking weekly. It's been a bit tedious."

Yes, I know you are laying the foundation for a massive invoice—one that I am going to contest and negotiate to a manageable fraction.

"Well, after many, many hours of poring through verdicts and judgments..."

Yes, yes. Get to the point. He could see the British Sterling symbol flashing in each of the barrister's eyes.

"...I came across a judgment near Manchester, where the judge ordered the imprisonment of a debtor for twelve pounds. It is apparently the first such judgment following the passage of the act last August."

Sedgwick was all ears.

"I am told he had no means to pay for it, but the creditor's lawyer found three witnesses who claimed that they had seen the debtor living an extravagant lifestyle, spending money on fine clothes..."

"Sinclair has done that, all right," Sedgwick interrupted.

"The debtor, being penniless, had a country lawyer. Out of his depth. Court found he had the means. First published case under Clause 5. We may be able to do the same with Sinclair. I shall introduce into court a certified copy of the Manchester decision."

A smile began to form on Sedgwick's face. "Sinclair has been living *extravagantly* and ignoring his debts. The sniffling scoundrel should be in prison. I tracked down his tailor—I am sure he will testify with the right *incentive*. We should also subpoena the restaurant manager at Verrey's."

Baumgarten chimed in. "We know Allenby owes Sinclair enough to pay the debt. Through Allenby, Sinclair has the means to pay. If we can show they are in bed together or that Sinclair is not taking appropriate legal action to collect the debt, or perhaps intentionally delaying the payment to avoid seizure from you..."

Finally, an original idea from Mr. Esquire.

"I shall need to interview the witnesses," Mr. Baumgarten continued. "The tailor, the restaurateur, and Mr. Allenby. I shall get sworn declarations to perpetuate their testimony. In the meantime, we should have him followed... see where he goes to dine. Does he attend concerts, theatre... We need to show him living lavishly, ignoring the debt altogether."

"Excellent work!" Sedgwick instantly regretted the praise, knowing that Baumgarten would add an extra pound or two on his next statement for good measure. "Press forward with haste. I want to get a hearing calendared as soon as possible and watch the blood drain out of Sinclair's face when I personally serve him with the summons."

Chapter 26

On the following Saturday, Nathan had plans to meet Regina at Kensington Gardens. Several days had passed since the peculiar visit from Roderick Charlesworth. During that time, Nathan occasionally found his mind wandering to the bizarre encounter, even imagining at times that Miss Charlesworth was in love with him. He envisioned being part of a world of wealth and society, where his financial problems were a thing of the past. To conceive that the most beautiful woman on earth might be interested in him was a delightful and intriguing fantasy. What if it were true? Why would she feel that way after disposing of him so cavalierly at Lady Sommersby's so many months before? Of course, such a woman held no interest for him, even if there had been a shred of truth to Roderick Charlesworth's insinuations. His heart belonged to a woman of virtue and purity, not a woman whose beauty veiled a decayed interior full of conceit and pretension. Nevertheless, the mark left by Miss Charlesworth seemed not so exquisite as before.

Preoccupied with these thoughts, Nathan traveled to Kensington Gardens on an early spring day, where the sun had finally broken through after a morning fog had blanketed the city. His pondering was interrupted when he observed Regina from afar, standing inside Queen Anne's Alcove, and he suddenly felt embarrassed for his whimsical fantasy with Miss Charlesworth.

Nathan greeted Regina. He was pleased to see her affable reaction at his coming. Nathan and Regina walked through the adjacent Italian Gardens and fountains. There were four fountains set in octagonal ponds around a smaller central fountain. The edges of the fountains were lined by stone urns with dolphins. At the south end of the Italian Gardens, the water cascaded down sculptured water nymphs into the Long Water.

He had not intended to mention it, but it was on his mind, and Nathan felt helpless to suppress the curious encounter with Roderick Charlesworth. "What could it possibly mean?"

Regina laughed. "You must have made quite an impression upon her at Lady Sommersby's. Do all women fall in love with you at first sight?"

"Quite the contrary, I would say."

"Or maybe, it was love at first *sound.*" Regina smiled. "I certainly fell in love with the music, before I..." Regina caught herself. Had she nearly declared her love? Nathan wondered.

She then finished the sentence, in a far more subdued tone: "...*noticed* the artist."

Even diluted, Nathan felt warm inside, having observed what he believed to be another unintended indication of her true affection.

They continued walking through the manicured grounds along the Long Water, with the view of the imposing Kensington Palace to their right.

"I wonder what Miss Charlesworth's brother would have done to you if it had been true. I presume there would have been quite a scuffle."

"Likely more than that. We would probably be dueling now."

"How dreadful. In such a duel, I suspect there could be no victory. Either you would die dueling or... die hanging from a scaffold, what with the Charlesworth power."

"Either alternative I could do without."

"It would have been such a shame to lose my frequent companion because of such a flirtatious misunderstanding. Are you hiding something from me, *Mr. Sinclair*?" Regina smiled, intentionally using his last name for the first time in months.

Before parting, Nathan asked Regina if she had recently attended the opera. She replied that it had been far too long since her last visit.

"I was very young when my mother stopped performing. Only six or seven, at the most. I have distant memories of watching her in cavernous halls. But, I do remember well her last performance. In Vienna. She was Rosina in *Il Barbiere.* Are you familiar with that opera?"

"Not really," Regina responded. "I have certainly heard of Rossini's opera, but know little of it."

"It is being performed this coming Tuesday night at the Drury Lane Theatre. I would love to have you accompany me." Nathan had been waiting all day to ask.

"Have you not heard it performed since you were a young child?"

"Never. I would love to have you at my side when I do."

"It would give me the greatest pleasure," Regina said gratefully.

As she spoke, Nathan heard the echo of his mother's sweet voice.

"Shall I arrange a ticket for your aunt?"

"I don't think that will be necessary."

As he made his way home in the cab, Nathan felt troubled that his mind had earlier turned to Miss Charlesworth.

Why do thoughts of her haunt me so? Regina is a goddess of inexpressible inner beauty; how could I ever be tempted by mere outward appearance?

He promised himself, once again, to extirpate ruminations of Jocelyn Charlesworth altogether. Whatever rubbish Roderick Charlesworth had accused him of mattered no more.

Chapter 27

Since being liberated from debtors' prison, Nathan had been experiencing creative surges in architecture and music unlike ever before. With just a few hours a day needed for his clients' work, Nathan expended much of the other workday hours toiling over drawings and plans of elegant mansions that he longed to build, but never expected to. At such times, his mind would run wild, taking flights of fantasy without limitation or restriction. He gained inspiration from the great chateaus of France, his forward-thinking professors in Switzerland, and nature itself. In his spare time, he had nearly completed the design of a mansion of breathtaking proportion, with stupendous height and grandeur, and many levels. But there had been something missing in the design. Something unique and revolutionary in thought. Something that would make such a dwelling immortal. Gradually, inspiration descended upon him.

Nathan purchased three long cords; one red, another blue, and the third yellow. It had been many weeks, but something about his Christmas Eve visit with Regina to the orphanage had inspired him to make the purchase. He remembered observing Regina braiding little Marta's hair. Using the same simple technique he had observed Regina employing, he began weaving the cords together.

Nathan had always been intrigued by the way a grand staircase could bring great beauty and drama to the interior of a structure, and he particularly appreciated long curving stairs that provided a bold architectural flair. He remembered how fascinated he had been by the dual staircases of the majestic Chateau de Chambord in the Loire Valley, where his mother had taken him as a youth. Later in life, he marveled that such an architectural fantasy of da Vinci's would have ever become a reality and focal point of a king's summer palace. In fact, Chambord was famous, in part, due to the dual staircases that were woven together but never met. Nathan now imagined a design that trumped even da Vinci's. Why not *three* interlocking circular staircases instead of two, that would never meet, like the braids of Marta's hair?

As he wove the colored cords together, he followed the descent of each through the braid. He was intrigued to find the cords making a figure eight, as the material curved, then changed direction heading toward the opposite circle. Nathan imagined the striking appearance such a display of three interlocking staircases would offer, if visible several stories high. He considered bridges that would offload from the stairs at appropriate intervals, never obscuring the majesty of the entwining steps. He imagined iron railings that would allow the spectator to pierce through to the rear-curving strand of the steps. Excited, he began to put pencil to paper and designed the appearance of the stairs from the ground floor, weaving up to a height of seven floors.

Oh, to actually have a commission where I could introduce such an extraordinary architectural marvel!

***

With spring struggling mightily for rebirth, Nathan hoped to see his career blossom as well. Some mornings, with the promise of spring and warmer weather in the air, he would awaken with his mind brimming with optimism. As the day dragged on, feelings of despair would often return with violence. However, there continued to be small indications of progress. He had acquired a new customer and had a proposal pending with another prospective client. He had even made a second payment to Sedgwick of ten more pounds, although he knew that the payment would only apply to the accrued interest and not the principle. He had also paid a portion of Stumbolt's back wages.

Despite this very modest improvement, his financial and professional struggles continued to blight hope of a future with Regina. His debt with Sedgwick nagged at him daily. Even with the two payments of ten pounds, Nathan knew the debt was still sixty pounds or more, with the interest. If he ever obtained any meaningful asset, Nathan had no doubt that Sedgwick would surely do his best to possess it through judicial levy. His dream with Regina would be to own a home some day, but there would be no real estate until his debts were clear.

Nathan was breathless to pledge his undying love and devotion to Regina, but knew that he must wait until he had some reasonable expectation of providing a secure home and future. He pondered whether Regina was becoming impatient with him, whether she was disappointed that he hadn't declared his love and made a proposal of marriage. Nathan knew he had put it off long enough.

It was time to disclose his precarious financial station to Regina, though she had never once inquired on that subject. Months ago, her aunt had ventured down this path at Verrey's, but those inquiries had been interrupted when Nathan was asked to perform. The topic had never been resumed.

Regina must be wondering why I have not yet proposed after all the time we have spent together. That would explain her muted behavior—she is disappointed in me. She may conclude that I am seeking friendship only, if I don't reveal the fragile circumstances that prevent me from offering a proposal of marriage.

To be sure, there had been subtle clues, accidental ones, that Regina's feelings went beyond friendship, but none had been manifest of late. During recent weeks, he had become slightly better acquainted with Regina's past, though rarely from her directly, and on those infrequent occasions the impromptu remark seemed regretted. He learned that she had become orphaned at the age of eight and had gone to live with her uncle and aunt. He discovered how her uncle had taken her into his home and treated her like one of his own children. Nathan never inquired about her past, honoring Sir Lancaster's admonition, despite a keen desire to know more.

But, it was now time for him to act. Nathan dared not delay further his declaration of ardent affection. It was time to disclose his own circumstances, to let her know of the obstacle that stood in the way of their union. He made a covenant to talk to Regina during their next evening together, at the opera.

Chapter 28

The following Tuesday, as planned, Nathan and Regina arrived at the Drury Lane Theatre in Westminster, part of London's West End. The original theatre had been built in 1663 but destroyed by fire ten years later. Rebuilt in 1674, it was London's leading theatre for the next hundred twenty years, until it was demolished and rebuilt in the late eighteenth century. It survived only fifteen years before burning to the ground once more in 1809. Rebuilt yet again in 1812 to accommodate three thousand patrons, it was one of the most popular venues in London.

As Nathan and Regina entered the sold-out theatre, their progress was soon arrested by the throng of people gathered in the large rotunda, which contained plaster statues of famous actors and poets under a majestic dome. Next to the rotunda was a grand staircase leading to the boxes, where foot traffic was headed from all directions. The couple fought their way through the crowd toward their seats in the gallery. On either side of the proscenium before them were two demi-columns of Corinthian architecture and a massive stage. It was a sight to behold, measuring nearly a hundred feet from the orchestra to the back wall, while rising majestically to a height of eighty feet—a stage that often relied more on scenery and crowd-pleasing effects than on acting or plot.

For the new season, curtains of amber satin had been installed, box-fronts had been covered with white and gold, and the parterre had been dressed with crimson. The interior was tastefully decorated with richly appointed gold embellishments throughout. The theatre had opened its season with Italian opera: first *Rigoletto*, then *Lucia*, and now *Il Barbiere*.

Mezzo-soprano Madame Monbelli was in the lead female role. She had performed in various locations throughout London to excellent reviews and had now earned the prestigious role of Rosina in Rossini's opera. The crowd was eager with anticipation over her operatic début.

As they finally took their seats minutes before the commencement, Regina leaned over to Nathan and whispered, "Can we expect to see the 'Man in Grey' tonight?" She was referring to the nobleman of the late eighteenth century, with powdered wig, a tricorne hat, grey coat, cape, and silver sword, whose remains had been found some twenty years earlier in a walled-up passage of the theatre, with evidence of foul play.

Nathan smiled. "Well, this has a reputation as the most haunted theatre in the world."

"If he does appear, that should be a sign of good luck for tonight's performance," Regina responded. "I so hope you have arranged for his visit. I have never seen a ghost before."

"If you watch carefully in the back shadows of the theatre during the first scene of act 2, I am certain you will see him standing there... but just for the blink of an eye."

"I shall keep careful vigil." Regina returned her gaze to the stage as the opera commenced.

Act 1 opened in a public square outside Dr. Bartolo's house, where a band of musicians and poor student Lindoro were serenading at the window of Rosina, Dr. Bartolo's ward. Lindoro, who was really the Count of Almaviva in disguise, hoped to make the beautiful Rosina love him for himself and not for his rank and wealth. However, no response to his serenade was forthcoming from Rosina. Figaro soon approached, singing. Since he used to be a servant of the Count, the Count asked him for his assistance in arranging to meet Rosina. Figaro suggested the Count disguise himself as a drunken soldier, ordered to be billeted by Dr. Bartolo, in order to gain entrance to the house.

The next scene began with Rosina's cavatina, which Nathan had been waiting for. He remembered his mother singing the cavatina the evening of her last stage performance. He was delighted that Madame Monbelli paid proper tribute to the cavatina with her pure voice and fluent execution, hitting even the high F with perfect intensity and beauty.

Knowing the Count only by the name Lindoro, Rosina wrote to him. Before being ejected from the house, the Count (disguised as the drunken soldier) had a quick word with Rosina, whispering that he was Lindoro, and gave her a letter.

In act 2, the Count returned to Dr. Bartolo's house a second time, now disguised as a singing tutor for Rosina. Dr. Bartolo confided in the Count (disguised as the tutor) of his plan to discredit Lindoro, believing Lindoro to be one of the Count's servants intent on pursuing women for his master. Dr. Bartolo soon learned of the Count's deception, drew up a marriage contract for himself to marry his ward, Rosina, and convinced her that Lindoro was merely a facilitator to find women for the Count.

The stage next erupted in a musical thunderstorm, as the Count and Figaro climbed a ladder to the balcony and entered Rosina's room. Rosina expressed her feelings of betrayal and heartbreak to the Count, who immediately revealed his dual identity, and the two reconciled. Figaro urged the two enraptured lovebirds to leave by the ladder, only to soon realize it had been removed. The notary, sent for by Dr. Bartolo to document his planned marriage to Rosina, was bribed instead to memorialize the marriage of the Count and Rosina seconds before Dr. Bartolo could prevent it.

The entire evening's performance was masterful, and the finale was greeted by rousing acclaim by the audience. The strongest applause was reserved for the consummate début performance of Madame Monbelli. Regina turned to an emotional Nathan and said gently, "It must be like seeing your mother again, witnessing this spectacle."

Despite the lighthearted mood of the opera, the performance had profoundly affected him. He had relived his vivid boyhood memory of his mother's last performance on stage. When Madame Monbelli had sung, it had been his mother he had seen and heard. Nearly twenty years later, the memory of her final performance was still seared in his mind.

"It has been a memorable night, particularly because I have been able to share it with you," Nathan spoke with great feeling.

Regina changed the mood. "Except the Man in Grey did not appear."

"Next time, we must hide in an abandoned dressing room after the performance and search the theatre for him, in the dark," suggested Nathan, continuing the charade.

"Is he harmless?"

"Like most ghosts, I am certain he must be, unless he mistakes us for his murderers."

"Then you shall have to search for him alone. I have no wish to deflect the advances of his sword." Regina shook her head with a smile. The mass of spectators pressed upon them and they did not speak again until reaching their carriage.

Assisting Regina into the carriage bound for the Lancaster estate, it was nearly time for Nathan to present the speech he had rehearsed for much of the day. After shutting the door for Regina, Nathan turned and saw a man with a thick mustache standing forty feet behind him next to a street lamp, staring directly at Nathan. As soon as their eyes met, the man jerked his head away, as if not wanting to be seen. Nathan had the distinct sensation that he had seen the man before, but couldn't place the face.

He discarded the thought. He no longer had to be worried about being followed; his freedom was no longer an issue. He entered the carriage on the opposite side, wondering why the presence of the man disturbed him. Once inside, he stole another look backward through the window as the carriage started down the road. When Nathan saw the mustached man's piercing stare again directed at him, he felt the back of his head tingle with a dread he couldn't quite explain or place. The look on the man's face bothered him—it had been a look of triumph.

Refocusing his mind to the task at hand, Nathan took a deep breath.

Now was the time.

There was awkward silence while Regina's face was turned away, looking out the opposite window.

Nathan needed a perfect delivery of his lines. He waited for a few moments, taking another deep breath to gather his thoughts. Before any words were spoken, Regina's face turned back toward his, and Nathan saw a look of veiled fear in her face. The look froze Nathan, momentarily paralyzing his declaration. The silence was awkward as neither spoke for some minutes, the only sound being the horses' hooves and whinnies and the trundling of carriage wheels underneath. Nathan stared out the window again, took a deep breath, and decided to proceed with his rehearsed statement, despite misgivings that there might be a better time.

"My dear Regina. I have been meaning to talk to you... for some time... about us." Regina turned away from the window and looked at Nathan, before casting her eyes downward. Nathan's mind suddenly went blank.

She is telling me not to continue, but I must.

"...I wish I could tell you that my business is thriving..."

That is not the way I wished to begin.

Regina kept her eyes lowered.

"...But that would not be the truth. Unfortunately, it has been a mighty struggle these two years..."

Regina raised her eyes to meet Nathan's, and Nathan saw her face suddenly relax.

I was supposed to speak to her of my affection first. Damn!

"Recently there has been some small progress, but I have a far path yet before I can gain a measure of financial security. For some time now, I have wanted to talk to you of my circumstances."

Everything is jumbled. Backward. This is not coming out well.

Regina seemed to sense his nervousness and put her fingers to Nathan's lips. "You have no obligation to reveal that to me."

Nathan felt a pang of disappointment from her response. "Well, I was *hoping* that I might owe you such an obligation."

Again, Regina turned away from Nathan and looked out the window into the dark of the night, preventing Nathan from seeing her reaction to his statement.

Nathan proceeded, as his delivery started to flow more naturally: "I have grown so very fond of you over the past months, and desperately hope you feel the same toward me." With those words spoken, Regina turned back to meet his hopeful eyes. Even in the evening light, Nathan could tell from the intensity of expression in her eyes that the feeling was mutual, though her lips were silent and her head was subtly shaking "No." Aware that Regina knew not how to deceive, Nathan sensed a struggle within her.

Why is she resisting her feelings? Nathan knew it was incumbent on him to proceed with caution and great tenderness.

"I have a dream... and a hope of a future together... some day." As Nathan paused, Regina lowered her eyes once more.

Is it shyness, or is it something else?

"I wish with all my heart that such a day will come soon, but I fear that it may be prolonged unduly because of my fragile finances. My work, thus far, has been very disappointing—I hope that will soon change." Nathan voiced the words with a pained look but was puzzled when Regina's face appeared to express relief.

In her soothing tender voice, Regina spoke. "Nathan. Sh-h-h. You mustn't talk so. I have such faith in you. You're a brilliant man. I am sure you will soon see a marvelous change in your fortunes. There is no reason to rush matters. All things will come to pass in their appointed time. In the meantime, let us continue to enjoy each other's company. Let us remain friends."

The word "friends" entered Nathan's heart like a dagger. He wanted to be much more than that and had sensed that Regina shared that feeling. To now hear the word "friends" from her had shattered him inwardly, even as he tried to hide his feelings of disappointment.

Regina looked at him tenderly and seemed to sense his disappointment. "We are the best of friends, are we not?"

The statement gave Nathan hope. He smiled back at her and nodded. At least there would be no pressure from her, while they continued to become better acquainted. He had let her know how much he cared for her, and she hadn't rejected him.

Maybe she is too shy to express her true feelings, Nathan pondered. Hadn't he felt the mutuality of their feelings just moments earlier, when their eyes had met? Hadn't the windows of her soul showed him that she loved him too?

***

Baumgarten had been busy. He had obtained statements from the tailor and the headwaiter at Verrey's. The maître d'hôtel hadn't been willing to assist, but the headwaiter at the restaurant consented to signing a declaration after being prompted by a gratuity. He had noted that Nathan had eaten at the restaurant more than ten times, although the statement omitted the fact that Nathan had also been performing at the piano those evenings and his meals had been merely an accommodation. Nor was there any mention of the fact that Nathan had never been charged for a single meal. With Baumgarten's embellishments and omissions, the sworn affidavit depicted Nathan dining regularly at London's most expensive restaurant.

A private detective had also documented dates and times when Nathan and a lady friend had attended concerts and theatre. Although only a few outings were specifically identified, the implication was that Nathan was a regular patron of the arts. But Baumgarten wasn't through. The following day he would be visiting Mr. Allenby—a man whom he understood to be in desperation.

With the statements in hand, Baumgarten needed to spend a few more hours preparing his client's motion, quoting excerpts from the declarations and making comparisons to the factual summary from the Manchester case. If Allenby had something to contribute the following day, he would work it into the papers. There would be a tidy bill for this work. His mind quickly tallied the hours and he added a few more for good measure. He included his dinner tab and gratuity from Verrey's, all in the pursuit of his client's best interest.

Chapter 29

Nathan's office had grown more comfortable since the weather began warming, as the pages of the calendar turned to May. Today, however, there had been nothing but rain. Steady, unrelenting, constant rain. The overcast weather mirrored his dreary concerns about his practice. The hoped-for dramatic change in his fortunes was still off in some distant future. His future life and happiness was dependent on a monumental upturn in his business, not the tediously gradual progress he had experienced during the past few months. Such a career-altering opportunity seemed more improbable and unattainable with each passing day. He was certain Regina would wait, but he couldn't expect her to wait forever.

Nathan had been focused intently on the drafting papers in front of him for the past few hours, after having consumed lunch from a nearby street vendor. Taking a break from his work, he rose from his seat and walked over to the window. He was surprised to see that a soft drizzle had replaced the heavy rain, and that the light of the sun was visible from the horizon. Seeking to refresh the stale air in his office, he lifted up the window and leaned out, breathing in air made clean from the heavy rain. As he looked out, he saw a beautiful rainbow in the afternoon sky. The sunlight had caused each tiny raindrop to act as a prism, forming a wondrous arc of red, yellow, and green. He stared at the fragile rainbow, not wanting it to disappear. It had been raining steadily on his practice, and he hoped the rainbow was an omen of better things to come.

While Nathan was enjoying the rainbow's prism of colors and a subconscious hope for a better future, a knock at the door interrupted his thoughts. The door opened and Stumbolt walked in. Ceremoniously delivering a letter to Nathan, Stumbolt suggested, "It appears you are being summoned once again to perform as a pianist. Too bad you are rarely summoned to perform as an architect."

Nathan didn't allow Stumbolt to affect his pleasant mood, and he even laughed inwardly at the slight. *He's right.*

Examining the letter, Nathan was intrigued by the beautifully embroidered border around the envelope, unlike any he had ever seen. The seal was also unique and beautiful—too pretty to be violated. There was no return address. Who was inviting him to perform? Another emolument would be welcome.

Doing his best to preserve the impress, he carefully loosened the wax, opened the envelope, and instantly smelled a sweet fragrance from within. Inside was a card, upon which was written in beautiful calligraphy the following short message:

> You are cordially invited to the 19th Birthday Party of
> our daughter,
> Miss Jocelyn Charlesworth
>
> The Charlesworth London estate,
> 8 o'clock Wednesday evening, May 25th

Nathan was dumbfounded. Why had he received an invitation to such an elite affair? Doubting his eyes, he looked again at the envelope to verify that it had truly been addressed to him. The elegant handwriting on the envelope undisputedly conveyed his name and address. Could there be some connection between the unwelcome intrusion of Roderick Charlesworth and this unexpected proffer? Nathan speculated that he might be the victim of someone's misguided sense of humor.

Jocelyn's affront had largely faded away by now; it had been blunted by the enigmatic declaration of love her brother had conveyed. But the invitation brought back the sting of Nathan's only encounter with her. The imprint on his mind of the beauty he had observed during their one brief meeting came back fiercely, once again, as he breached his vow to put Jocelyn out of his mind. He was overwhelmingly intrigued by the prospect of meeting her once more, under much different circumstances than before. After further reflection, his mercurial mind pondered whether the purpose of the invitation was another discomfiture, this time in front of a larger audience.

***

Seated at his desk the next day, Nathan picked up the invitation and examined it again. It had been two months since he had been accused of being Jocelyn's lover. Now he was invited, in a little more than three weeks' time, to attend what certainly must be one of the most exclusive events in all of London. In a moment of clarity, Nathan realized that acting on the invitation was utterly ridiculous, and he tossed it into the wastebasket.

Struggling to keep the invitation out of his mind, his thoughts spurned his will and kept wandering back to it. Later that afternoon, Nathan fished the invitation out of the wastebasket and turned it over in his hand. The words on the card hadn't changed since he had first read them. The envelope remained addressed to him.

Could there be any parcel of truth that Jocelyn has romantic feelings toward me? It doesn't matter, of course. It is wholly irrelevant. It is Regina who has stolen my heart.

Try as he might, he couldn't get the picture of Jocelyn's face out of his mind. Nathan recalled fondly the perfection of her face, her luminous golden hair, her exquisite figure. His artist's mind remembered her eyes, her lips, her nose, her ears. It was a face imprinted so well in his mind that he knew he could draw her portrait. He picked up a pencil and quickly sketched her face from memory. It was a good likeness, and even the picture itself was an extraordinary display of her beauty. He felt a yearning to view that beauty again. Catching himself, he repented: *What am I doing?* He took the parchment upon which the sketch had been drawn and tossed it into the fire.

I must be mad to fantasize about her.

Despite his firm mental denials, a part of Nathan desired Jocelyn to be in love with him, if only to salve the remnants of the poignant memory from so many months before. Maybe it was the fantasy that a woman of such extraordinary fairness would choose to lavish her affections upon *him*. Even if the absurd were true and she had undergone a transformation in her affections toward him, he would not go; defying the petition would give him some small measure of revenge for her previous insult. Yet, if he ignored the request, he might never discover the answer to the riddle. He fantasized about entering the Charlesworth estate just to see Jocelyn once more. No sooner had that fantasy graced his mind, than reality sank in and he knew with certainty that if he ventured forth, he would be questioned as a trespasser and summarily removed. Whom was he fooling? He had no part among the English gentry.

There it is... finished! I have exhausted utterly too much time on a foolish fancy. I have made up my mind. I won't go.

Should he even mention the invitation to Regina? There was no need. He had positively no intention of going. The three weeks would surely come and go, and when the event had passed, he wouldn't trouble his mind on the subject any further.

***

Sedgwick's lawyer had filed an application for imprisonment under Clause 5 with supporting declarations. The matter was scheduled for hearing. After the clerk stamped the summons, Baumgarten paid a special visit to Sedgwick in Whitechapel without an appointment.

"Counselor, you have a smile on your face," Sedgwick noted eagerly.

"I have it! The hearing is set for ten o'clock on the eighth of June." Baumgarten handed the summons over.

"Well done, Counselor. I shall count the days, but first, I can't wait to see the expression on his face when he is served."

"Just make sure to have another person serve him. You may be present, but service by a party is not lawfully effective."

"Understood," Sedgwick remarked. "Now that he is living openly, he obviously feels immune from incarceration. It should be a simple task to have him served."

Sedgwick could barely wait to hire a cab with one of his soldiers and cross the Thames into Bermondsey.

"Now, if Sinclair doesn't show..."

"Then the court will rule without any opposition. But you should expect him to be present and have counsel."

Sedgwick nodded.

"We are in excellent shape. The witnesses are all committed to their testimony with written declarations under oath." Baumgarten exuded confidence.

"Excellent." There was no reason to delay service to the following morning. He would see Sinclair today.

Chapter 30

Nathan was busy at work in his office, when Stumbolt knocked on his door.

"Mr. Sedgwick, sir, and Mr. Jones."

Nathan instantly felt anxiety. Why was Sedgwick visiting him? Did he have a court order attaching some of his property? In the back of his mind, he had wondered if and when Sedgwick would strike again. But after all, he had paid Sedgwick twenty pounds during the past several months; surely that would be appreciated. Nathan steeled himself for the encounter, preparing to assure Sedgwick that he would fully discharge the debt, although it might take another year or two to do so, with the burdensome rate of interest.

"Send them in."

Sedgwick walked in with a wide grin on his face. Nathan instantly recognized the other gentleman—the man with the thick mustache he had observed in the presence of Regina when they had attended the opera. Something was amiss.

"Mr. Sinclair. I trust you have been enjoying your freedom."

Nathan ignored the statement, but nevertheless offered both visitors a chair in front of his desk.

"You have received my payments, sir?"

Sedgwick gave Nathan a deathly stare. "A mere pittance. I lent you the money two years ago and you haven't yet dented the principal."

Can there be no compassion in this man?

"I'm glad you are here," Nathan lied. "I have been meaning to discuss with you a possible negotiation of the rate of interest. The present rate makes repayment extremely burdensome—would you be willing to reduce it to the pre-default level? I am still struggling to grow my practice."

"You neglect your legal obligation over an extended period and have the audacity to seek leniency?"

Nathan held his peace, but Sedgwick wasn't finished.

"All the while leading a life of luxury and opulence, frequenting the city's finest restaurants, attending concerts and the like?"

Nathan bit his upper lip.

"And Mr. Allenby?" Sedgwick demanded.

"He's on the verge of losing his home in foreclosure."

"Pity, pity. Well, Mr. Sinclair. You have a month to pay the debt in full."

"A month?"

Sedgwick turned to the mustached man. "Jones, hand him the summons."

Jones tossed a thick stack of bound papers onto Nathan's desk.

"Consider yerself served, Sin-clair," Jones smiled.

"What is this?" Nathan was visibly shocked.

"Clause 5 of the Debtors Act," Sedgwick exhaled triumphantly. "Order to show cause why you should not be imprisoned for fraud."

"Fraud! What are you talking about?"

"It's all there. Enjoy your last days of freedom. I've already made arrangements to have you housed in your old cell in Coldbath Fields. And your old job of washing the hallway floors awaits you. Warden said you seemed mighty comfortable there... that you particularly liked the fine cuisine."

Nathan was speechless.

"No need to show us out," Sedgwick said cordially. "We'll manage."

Moments later, Nathan sat alone in his office.

My God! I thought it was over.

Nathan read through the motion and declaration. He studied the language of Clause 5 from the act. The more he read, the more sickened he felt. The Manchester case provided a compelling precedent. It was all very convincing. He couldn't deny the facts contained within the affidavits, although they only told part of the story. When he had finished reading, he felt shortness of breath and his stomach was churning.

I need a lawyer. This time, I won't allow the court to make a decision without my voice being heard.

Every dream began to dissemble. His former anxiety, uncertainty, and angst returned with a vengeance. He didn't dare tell Regina. He would have to defeat the motion in order to have any peace. Could he obtain competent counsel for a few pounds?

***

Nathan's friend who worked in the courts recommended a

young lawyer, Michael Collier. Nathan arranged an appointment to see him two days after Sedgwick's visit.

Mr. Collier shared office space with several other young lawyers in an old building near the courthouse. At the appointed hour, Nathan was ushered into the lawyer's office. Mr. Collier looked to be in his early thirties. He was of slender build with prematurely greying hair worn short, and he stood several inches shorter than Nathan. He had a friendly demeanor and gave Nathan a vigorous shake, inviting him to install himself in a brown upholstered chair opposite his desk. Mr. Collier inquired of the purpose for his visit and Nathan proceeded to explain his history with Sedgwick, including the brief imprisonment.

"Ah," Mr. Collier smiled as he leaned back in his leather chair. "You were one of the fortunate few, who *barely* tasted of the horrors of prison."

If you would call being imprisoned fortunate!

"I must say, I am surprised that Mr. Sedgwick has become so focused on you. You say you have paid him twenty pounds toward the debt?"

"Yes, but it has only barely covered the interest."

"The default rate of interest places a heavy burden upon you. Perhaps we could negotiate a payment schedule with Mr. Sedgwick that would lower it to the pre-default level. I could arrange a meeting with his counsel to see if we can avoid this unpleasant hearing and work out a repayment plan that you can live with."

Nathan shook his head. "I have already suggested that, to no avail. For some reason, he has become obsessed with getting me back into Coldbath Fields. I rather believe he would prefer my imprisonment than repayment."

"Hard to imagine a creditor who would not want his money returned," Mr. Collier shrugged his shoulders.

"You should have seen him when the papers were served. He was jollier than Father Christmas."

"So you think it would be a waste of time for me to talk with his lawyer?"

"I rather think so," Nathan offered. "But, if you think something good may come of it..."

"I shall pay him a visit."

"My main concern, Mr. Collier, is to avoid imprisonment. It would destroy my life. I must never return there. I have met a very special young lady..."

"I understand. Let me take a moment to read through the documents."

Nathan handed him the papers. For the next fifteen minutes, the attorney flipped through pages, occasionally returning to a page earlier reviewed.

"First case I have seen under the act which seeks imprisonment." Collier read through the decision issued in the Manchester case. "We must find facts distinguishing your circumstances from that ruling."

Nathan and the attorney continued their discussion for another thirty minutes.

"I think we have some excellent defenses. In the wake of the act abolishing imprisonment, I would think most judges would go out of their way to avoid putting a man of your background and education in prison. Based upon your income, you have made significant payments toward the debt. You should make a good witness on your own behalf. I believe there is a good chance of defeating the motion. In any event, incarceration is limited to six weeks under Clause 5."

Nathan felt little comfort with that comment. To disappear for six weeks would ruin his life. What would he tell Regina? What about his business?

"Of course, there is nothing here that prevents Mr. Sedgwick from bringing another motion once you are released."

Nathan gave a pained look. "Is that possible?"

"Well, yes, it is possible. I would think highly unlikely in most cases. But if Mr. Sedgwick is hell-bent on keeping you behind bars, he may renew this motion on a regular basis. The danger is that the first incarceration may lead to others, as the judge routinely re-affirms each decision, based upon the prior findings. Even if another judge is later assigned the case... the pathway of least resistance."

Nathan's feelings of hope drifted away. The specter of intermittent stays at Coldbath's seemed even more depressing than his former station. It was imperative he prevail at the upcoming hearing, or all would be lost. After paying the five-pound retainer, Nathan tried to reassure himself, based on his attorney's optimism, that the motion would be defeated. He couldn't imagine living on the run again; the thought of being handcuffed and led into Coldbath Fields gave him a nervous sweat. Thoughts of escaping to France returned, but he knew that he could never go there. He would never forsake his love. He would stand and defend himself, relying on the mercy of the court.

Chapter 31

Nathan visited Regina soon after his meeting with Mr. Collier. The upcoming hearing continued to weigh heavily on his mind. After several minutes, Regina sensed something was wrong.

"Nathan, you seem distracted this evening. Is something the matter?"

Nathan dared not share his grave concerns regarding Sedgwick's motion. As he searched for a response, Jocelyn Charlesworth's birthday invitation crossed his mind as a more prudent source for his distraction, though he had given it little thought since Sedgwick's visit. Nathan did his best to lighten his demeanor.

"Nothing is the matter," Nathan responded with little hesitation. "But, there is something that did divert me. I received, by post, an invitation to attend the nineteenth birthday party of Jocelyn Charlesworth. I have been trying to figure out why."

Regina laughed, but showed disbelief. "Perhaps it was addressed to you in error?"

"You are probably right."

Regina looked at Nathan, striking an investigative pose. "Or perhaps not. First you receive a visit from the brother of Miss Charlesworth, confessing his sister's undying devotion to you. And now you have received an invitation to her birthday." She was clearly enjoying herself. "Are you telling me everything, *Mr. Sinclair*?" Regina knew that Nathan much preferred the use of his given name. She continued, with a raised eyebrow and artificially melodramatic tone. "Are you employing your powers of charm beyond the confines of the Lancaster estate?"

Regina's comment put a smile on Nathan's face and he returned the favor, elevating his chin. "*Miss Lancaster*. I appear to be in much demand among the fairer sex."

Regina turned away as if she were *totally* disinterested. Then she looked back with a devilish smile. "Oh, a woman can be *very* demanding when she wants to."

Nathan took the bait. "*Whatever* you demand, shall be my command."

Regina gave a short curtsy, then turned serious. "Have you ever visited the Charlesworth estate?"

"Never."

"I have heard it is a property of incomparable beauty."

"Undoubtedly."

"Are you not in the least bit curious to inspect its architecture?"

Nathan tried to appear as if the thought had never crossed him mind, which was untrue. "I suppose it would be interesting to view it firsthand."

"You should go," she said in a serious tone.

Nathan was taken aback. "I should?"

"I am dying to know the answer to this mystery. Maybe it's someone's idea of an elaborate prank—perhaps a lady friend of Miss Charlesworth's, hoping to liven up the party after your last encounter. Or..." Regina paused, "... maybe Miss Charlesworth is, indeed, *passionate* about you." With the emphasis on "passionate," she opened her eyes wide with a provocative regard. "Don't you want to know?"

"It is curious."

"Then, go. Perhaps you shall get some answers and even gain some inspiration for future designs. And, if you fall instantly in love with her, you must send me a card, so that I may know why you no longer call upon me."

"It would be rude not to. Let me make sure I have your correct address," Nathan appeared to be in deep thought as he intentionally blurted out the wrong street and number. "It is, ummm, 43 or 44 Chesterfield Lane?"

Regina lightly slapped him on the upper arm, shaking her head. "Fickle man."

Even with Regina's blessing, Nathan had serious reservations about attending the party, now just two weeks away. Nevertheless, the intrigue of Jocelyn Charlesworth provided a welcome distraction from his preoccupation with the upcoming court date.

Chapter 32

The sun shone brightly the morning of Jocelyn's party. On waking, Nathan felt foolish about even entertaining the notion of appearing. He certainly had more important things to attend to. But as the morning wore on, he found himself laying his newly pressed pants on the bed. He later went to the barber for a fresh shave and haircut.

I have no intention of going. His acts argued the contrary.

Later in the day, he said to himself aloud, "What am I doing getting dressed? This is madness!" Nevertheless, he proceeded to put on his white starched shirt with new winged collar, white bow tie, pants and waistcoat. He was pleased with his hair length and overall appearance.

At half past seven, he descended the stairs of the building that served as his residence and office, and hailed a cab. "I have just wasted six shillings," he thought as he directed the driver to the Charlesworth estate.

I have no intention of going inside. I'll just examine the exterior of the property and then return home.

The cab soon left the commercial area where Nathan's office was located, progressing into neighboring residential quarters. The attached dwellings of nearby homes were old, modest, and neglected. Soon, the cab reached the Waterloo Bridge, named in honor of the English victory at the beginning of the century. Built from Cornish granite except for the Aberdeen granite balustrades, it had an appearance of uncommon grandeur. After crossing the twelve-hundred-foot bridge, the cab continued northward until reaching New Oxford Street, then turned westward. Nathan noted an amelioration in the size and handsomeness of the residential dwellings. They turned north onto Regent Street and soon passed through upscale Portland Place, which displayed truly elegant mansions, now detached, with separating walls and manicured grounds, not dissimilar from the Lancaster property. Nathan was not prepared, however, for the transformation in the mansions that soon befell his eyes. He had never seen such a neighborhood! Many homes were set back from the road a good distance, with high iron fences and trees obscuring the structures. The size and scope of residences continued to expand until the cab approached the elaborate iron gate of the Charlesworth estate. The building was almost entirely secluded by a ten-foot-high brick wall and greenery, except for a dome extending skyward beyond the reach of the trees. Showing his invitation to the suspicious guard, Nathan gasped at the height of the structure, having never observed a property of such grandeur outside royal abodes.

As the cab entered the long winding road up the entrance, Nathan became aware of carriages exiting on the opposite path, having deposited their guests. Soon his cab came to a halt behind a procession of carriages awaiting their turn at the front of the estate. The conveyances were elegant beyond measure, with coachmen in rich attire. As the cab advanced and the queue shortened, the residence started coming into view. Nathan was incredulous at the height and stature of the mansion. It had been worth the trip! But his mind was made up. Shortly, he would instruct the driver to "Drive on." He had no place among the London gentry; that had already been made abundantly clear.

The sun was low in the heavens amidst scattered clouds, and it was still light as his cab advanced to the head of the line. Candles and gas lamps were visible in the windows, foretelling the approaching darkness. One of the richly attired Charlesworth attendants opened the door of his cab before Nathan was able to order his driver to proceed. Ignoring his prior resolve, Nathan paid the driver, and found his legs moving out of the chaise and toward the entrance. He was thunderstruck by the property! It rivaled some of the great chateaus he had visited in France; the architecture was intricate, mysterious, and incredibly beautiful. With no intention of going in, Nathan felt drawn up the steps to the entrance. If the exterior was so magnificent, mustn't he at least gain a glimpse of the interior before leaving?

I will leave in five minutes, Nathan promised himself as he entered. *No one will even take notice of me among the large crowd and expanse of this edifice.*

Entering the palatial manor, Nathan inhaled the delicious scent from an array of geraniums, wisteria, and lilacs, which bordered the walls of the circular entry area, heralding the passage from aromatic purgatory into paradise. Nathan's jaw dropped as his gaze lifted up sixty feet to a beautifully muraled dome. Shortly beyond the entry area were two grand sweeping staircases curving up not just to the next floor, but an additional level beyond. In the gap between the two ascending staircases, a majestic staircase descended downward nearly thirty feet. Newly arrived guests were migrating down the descending staircase to the ballroom below. The view from the entry was an extraordinary vista of beauty upward and downward with balconies, murals, statutes, tapestries, and other objets d'art. The vast majority of guests were gathered below in the sumptuous ballroom. Balconies extending out from the entry level circled the ballroom below. There were second, third and fourth floor balconies above, also reaching over the ballroom, each one higher than its predecessor. As Nathan edged toward the brink of the downward stairs, he marveled at a dome above the ballroom much larger than that of the entry, which rose more than a hundred feet above the ballroom floor. He had never imagined anything on this scale; his own grandiose designs paled by comparison. This was a residence worthy of kings and queens.

Transfixed by the splendor of the interior, all thoughts of making a hasty departure faded. Nathan was intent on exploring every corner of the dwelling open to guests. He ascended the grand winding staircase on the right of the entry, marveling at the detailed ironwork of its railing. Above the din of the crowd, Nathan became aware of music emanating from the ballroom below. He heard the first movement from Mendelssohn's Italian Symphony as he leaned over the balcony balustrade two levels above the entry and more than sixty feet above the ballroom. Nathan was astonished to discern below a full orchestra performing Mendelssohn, with pulsing woodwinds creating a harmonic background for the violins.

At what cost?

Nathan had rarely attended concerts since his mother's passing four years before, but he relished the opportunity of hearing world-class musicians perform. And here he was, in the Charlesworth estate, a fortunate observer of a magnificent symphonic performance.

More guests arrived as Nathan made his way around the third-level balcony that encircled the ballroom far below. Not only was the interior architecture astonishing, but the decor, appointment, and detail of the walls and ceilings were extraordinary. He examined with awe priceless pieces of art, along with sculptures of great beauty adorning niches and oriels. Nathan looked out from the height of a third-level window that gave breathtaking views of the London metropolis. The Charlesworths had ordered a glorious sunset for Jocelyn's birthday; rarely had he seen such a spectacular mixture of red, orange, and amber interspersed so beautifully upon a patchwork of clouds.

One day, I shall attempt to recreate that on canvas, he thought.

He watched the sun dipping below the horizon to the accompaniment of the elegant Andante con moto, as Nathan completed his tour of the upper balcony and returned to the entry area. He felt propelled to the ballroom below and aspired to a view of the upper balconies and dome from that vantage. He waited several minutes for late-arriving guests, as the second movement came to an end, hoping to descend the staircase under their cover. The ballroom below now seemed nearly full of elegantly dressed guests, and Nathan surmised that most had likely arrived. He couldn't wait longer. The next movement, the Con moto moderato, was one of his favorite orchestral pieces, and he yearned to hear it in closer proximity. It was a few minutes past nine o'clock when Nathan began his descent of the majestic staircase leading to the ballroom below, as the painfully beautiful and graceful minuet of the third movement began. Despite his strikingly handsome appearance in his new dinner suit, Nathan felt nakedly self-conscious in descending the stairs with the accompaniment of no one, other than Mendelssohn's genius.

As he made his way down, Nathan's eyes looked upward, then side to side, taking in the astounding majesty of the residence, as his senses absorbed the haunting orchestral theme. *What a marvel!* His eyes spanned the upper balconies and became riveted on the intricate Florentine dome mural rising heavenward. A band of brilliant emerald and sapphire stained-glass windows shone just below the ring of the dome, between heraldic shields set in a silver monochrome. However, had this palace been constructed? How long had it taken to build? What a feat of engineering!

Nathan's ears continued to devour the orchestra's sublime serenade, which increased in volume and beauty with his every descending step, as he drew nearer the impassioned musicians. At midpoint on the grand staircase, his attention was diverted downward by the parting of the large crowd from the center of the ballroom and moving slowly toward him. Nathan was fascinated at the coincidence of the crowd parting at his descent, as if they were making room for a guest of honor. He angled his head to the left, wondering what important magistrate must be following him down. Finding himself still alone on the staircase, he continued tranquilly downward and noticed with mild surprise the migrating gap in the crowd moving still closer his way. With scarcely ten steps left, Nathan's eyes abruptly fixated on a personage walking toward him from the crowd's opening. Coming his way was the most beautiful woman he had ever seen, a golden goddess of indescribable beauty, in face, in dress, and in shape. She was wearing a stunning light-yellow evening gown, newly arrived from Paris, with elaborately draped overskirts and a form-fitting, long-waisted bodice that reached below the hips. She had complementary tight-fitting sleeves and white gloves. Her golden hair was gathered in a high knot, with plaited braids descending downward; her glorious face was fully exposed. Adorning her ears were deep red ruby earrings, while encircling her neck was a three-layered necklace with matching large luminous rubies reflecting the light from the chandeliers.

Not only was she walking directly toward Nathan, but she was staring directly into his eyes. And it wasn't just a stare! It was a gaze of total rapture and adoration. It was the most radiant, heavenly, pleasing, and spellbinding regard that he had ever seen, and it was *fixed on him*.

Unaware of the gawking, gasping, and bewildered bystanders following the elegant carriage of this angelic beauty, Nathan continued his descent until the two met at the bottom of the stairs. Nathan felt transported to another world, another level of consciousness, by the way that this staggeringly beautiful seraphim made love to him with her eyes. The smile on her face showed such intense delight and pleasure.

At length, the goddess spoke: "Mr. Sinclair, I didn't think you would come. But I am so delighted that you did." Before he could respond from his daze, Jocelyn Charlesworth took his right arm in hers and gently led him back in the direction from whence she had come.

Finally finding his voice, Nathan did his best to eject a natural response. "My fondest wishes on your nineteenth birthday, Miss Charlesworth." Bystanders were stepping on tiptoes and craning their necks to get a glimpse of the man who had captured the attention of England's most celebrated jewel. Every eye was on the couple, as Jocelyn navigated them back to the center of the ballroom.

Stopping there briefly, Jocelyn acknowledged his birthday wish and once again showered Nathan with a look of such love and adoration that Nathan felt his whole spirit illuminating. Against all restraint, a broad smile burst upon his face and he felt, at that moment, the most honored and fortunate of men. "If possible, your beauty tonight surpasses my previous recollection."

Jocelyn looked away and then back at Nathan, gave a playful

frown, squeezing his arm and smiling again. "I am so embarrassed about that," she said just loud enough for him to hear.

Before she could say anything further, they were interrupted by a distinguished older man, dressed in military attire. "My dearest Jocelyn. Who is this handsome young escort?"

"General McBean. May I present Nathan Sinclair." The general scrutinized Nathan, before smiling. "You must be an extraordinary young man, to have her attention."

Nathan bowed. He recognized the name of his new acquaintance, a decorated military hero, and responded. "A rare and memorable honor to make your acquaintance." Before he could say more, Jocelyn volunteered, "Mr. Sinclair is an extraordinarily talented young man. A masterful pianist." Nathan was surprised at the comment, but surmised that she had heard him perform Chopin at Lady Sommersby's. "He is also a rising architect with impressive commissions for one so young." Nathan was puzzled and flattered by the latter comment, though he knew it to be untrue.

His look told all, as Jocelyn whispered: "The commissions will be in hand soon enough." *What can she possibly mean?* Nathan's imagination ran wild.

Moments later, there was another introduction.

"Monsieur Lefontaine. *Ravi de vous voir ce soir.*"[18] Nathan was startled by Jocelyn's natural and flawless command of French. "*Permettez-moi de vous présenter Monsieur Nathan Sinclair.*"

Nathan responded himself in French, his first language, the tongue his mother had spoken. Jocelyn then whispered to him: "*Je suis tellement heureuse que **tu** parles la langue des anges.*"[19] The use of the intimate *tu* term stunned and excited Nathan.

He responded back to her in kind: "*Je savais que tu avais étudié à Paris, mais je ne savais pas que tu parlais si couramment le français.*"[20]

Jocelyn then repeated her praise of Nathan to the flamboyantly dressed Monsieur Lefontaine, in impeccable French.

More introductions and birthday salutations followed during the next thirty minutes as Nathan felt as if in a dream. They walked toward the far corner of the ballroom, which opened to a magnificent music room, several steps upward. Nathan craned his head in the direction of the music room, his mouth gaping at what he saw. "Could that possibly be the new Steinway piano?"

---

18   So delighted to see you tonight.
19   I am so pleased that you speak the tongue of angels.
20   I knew you had studied in Paris, but I didn't know you were so fluent in French.

"The very same. Imported from New York just a few weeks ago. Winner of the Grand Gold Medal of Honor at the Paris Exhibition. I saw it there and begged my father for one."

"So you also play the piano?" Nathan asked with surprised look.

"Not at all. But I adore music. Perhaps you shall have an opportunity to play it sometime."

"I would love nothing more," Nathan responded enthusiastically.

Soon after, Nathan became aware that Jocelyn had maneuvered him to the door leading to the outdoor terrace behind the ballroom. It was a windless and clear night, the evening air having cooled considerably from the day's earlier warmth. The sky was full of stars and a partial moon, enabling Nathan to see the extravagant and extensive gardens that stretched before them. They were all alone on the spacious terrace.

***

At half past nine, the Duke of Wilmont entered the Charlesworth residence. He stood at the top of the majestic stairway, feeling more alive than he had in years. He had purposely arrived late in order to accentuate the drama of his entrance. He stood in pose for a few minutes, his right hand inserted in his waistcoat, surveying the happy crowd in the ballroom below. Although of short stature, the Duke was a devastatingly handsome man with a light complexion, aquiline nose, black hair, and matching handlebar mustache. With his trademark black cape and cane, black tailored suit, white gloves, and blood-red cravat, he gloried in the striking presence he created. The Duke relished the effect he had on women at a first encounter and their impulsive stares and yearning. Once they also learned he was a Duke of great property and power, the conquest was inevitable. On closer inspection, however, the Duke's affectation of superiority, inflated ego, and exaggerated intelligence diminished his advantage of wealth and appearance. Born to privilege and an ancient dukedom pedigree, he considered himself the center of the universe. He felt his only flaw was his height, and it greatly irritated him that he was shorter than many women.

He began his slow descent of the grand staircase, waiting to be recognized from below. He spied one woman looking up, poking a nearby companion. As he continued down the staircase, he noticed others gazing his way. He smiled and took a deep breath, basking in the attention, but pretending to ignore their stares.

Halfway down, he stopped and scanned the crowd, looking for the stare of one particular woman. Where was she? She was nowhere to be found. Frustrated, he continued downward until he reached the ballroom floor.

***

Gliding to a balustrade at the end of the terrace balcony, Jocelyn spoke to Nathan: "My brother told me about his visit to you several weeks ago. I was mortified, as you might imagine. *Qu'as-tu du pensé de moi.*[21] Of course, it was a misunderstanding, but one for which I am directly responsible."

"Well, I assured your brother that he was mistaken..."

"And you assured him of much more than that, I was told," she said as she looked away, embarrassed. "One evening some weeks ago, I was in the sitting room after dinner with him alone. My brother asked me whom I fancied from the procession of suitors that had come calling since my return from Paris. I replied that I found them all the same. Reasonably handsome, wealthy, well-connected, arrogant, lacking in ambition, and terribly boring. Men who would make atrocious husbands, whose fidelity would not last a fortnight. Men who sought a pretty wife as an adornment or keepsake.

"He then entreated me for the hundredth time to allow his good friend, the Duke of Wilmont, to make advances toward me. He regaled me with all of the Duke's virtues: his looks, his wealth, his power, and his prestige. I remarked that I would be far better served by marrying a man with character, ambition, fidelity, and passion... someone who would love me for who I am, not for my money, position, family, or... my face. Someone to whom rank and position was not the end-all... a man with dreams... someone talented... someone truly devoted to *me*.

"Whereupon my brother asked, 'Oh, is there someone who fits that bill?' I told him, 'There just might be.'

"My brother kept pestering me nearly all night, asking who that person could be. I was playing with him, being coy, hoping to deflect his friend's advances, and at the same time having enormous fun at his expense. He became more ruffled and agitated, insisting 'There is someone, isn't there? You must tell me whom.' By now, I had taken the game too far and felt pressured to come up with a name or I would never get a moment's rest. For some reason, in

---

21   What you must of thought of me.

my attempt to propitiate him, your name surfaced and I gave it to him."

"Me?" Nathan responded with a baffled look. "Why on earth me? Our sole encounter consisted of you summarily dismissing me without a second thought."

"Well, for me it lasted longer. What you don't know is that your performance of Chopin, later that evening, brought me to tears." Then pausing, she continued briefly in French. *"La musique est, et a toujours été, mon premier amour."*[22] Jocelyn paused after the comment, breathing a sigh as if in reflection on that performance. "When I saw your face behind the keyboard, I felt sickened by the way I had treated you earlier, and hoped for an opportunity to redeem myself. I behaved abominably toward you, and I offer my sincerest apology."

Nathan nodded with a friendly smile. "Apology accepted."

Jocelyn continued where she had left off. "But you must understand, for some reason all of London considers me to be the most desirable prize for all marriage-minded men of high society—which I cannot comprehend at all. I am aware that I have a pretty face and *spectacular* hair," Jocelyn said laughing, "but certainly there must be hundreds of women in London just as handsome. No, for some reason, *je suis devenue le prix célèbre, la prise premier.*[23] It was fun and flattering for a while. But now it has become tedious and tiresome. To my chagrin, I must deal with endless requests for visits and rendez-vous. I cannot begin to tell you how many dinners to which I have been invited and which I am expected to attend, for fear of making offense. Not a week goes by that I am not induced by prominent families to meet another handsome, wealthy, boring, young—or not-so-young—man. And each time, I must be polite and pleasant, *before* firmly rejecting the advances."

Jocelyn continued: "I devote a few hours every day to politely declining, in writing, countless requests for introductions from other English noblemen—again, for fear of making an offense. Unfortunately, a respectful declination on my part is seen by many as just another stage in their courtship.

"I deal with most of those the same way—the way I dealt with you. Only a very firm *No* seems to convince them (most of them, that is) that I have no interest. But they know that I am single, available, and unengaged, and many keep persisting despite my protestations.

---

22   Music is, and always has been, my first love.
23   I have become the celebrity prize, the prime catch.

"*Dans ton cas, tu n'as pas persisté.*²⁴ You didn't follow me as I turned my back from you. You respected my wishes. You were just another suitor, in a procession of many, whom I needed to discourage. *Je suis navrée si je t'ai fait du mal.*"²⁵

Nathan looked into Jocelyn's hypnotic eyes. "*J'ai eu mal. Je me sentais moins homme à cause de ça.*"²⁶

"*Je ne devrais pas avoir un tel pouvoir.*"²⁷ Jocelyn blushed.

"But with your reception of me today... the pain has gone away." Nathan smiled.

"That night, my brother pestered me with questions about you. I told him about your talents—I had made some discreet inquiries following your performance. I told him you were an up-and-coming architect, that you were a concert-level pianist (he knows of my passion for music), that you were very handsome, and that you would make the finest husband a woman could ever find."

Nathan beamed at the flattery: "*Tu me connais à peine.*"²⁸

"*Tout le monde te tient en grand respect,*²⁹ so it must be true," Jocelyn laughed. "Of course, I have no interest in marriage, not at this stage of my life. So after I mentioned your name, my brother kept pressing further for details. Now, understand that I did my best to be obtuse and coy. Not admitting anything in words, my mannerisms and looks let him know that we were madly in love. Yes, I don't mind admitting it, I was enjoying it immensely. You would have to know my brother..."

"Hopefully no more so than I already do."

"Quite so. Watching him squirm—listening to him tell me what a scandal it would be for me to marry a... you'll excuse the reference... a mere commoner. When I saw his volcanic reaction, I tried to assure him that there was truly nothing between us, that I hardly knew you. That only fueled his fire and caused him to be even more suspicious. But I never imagined that he would confront you..."

Nathan pretended a look of hurt: "*Tout ce temps, je croyais que la plus belle femme en tout l'angleterre était tombée follement amoureuse de moi.*³⁰ Now you have truly irretrievably damaged my pride and broken my heart." Nathan laughed.

---

24   In your case, you didn't persist.
25   I'm sorry if I caused you any pain.
26   It did hurt. I felt less a man, because of it.
27   I shouldn't have such power.
28   You hardly know me.
29   Everyone holds you in high regard.
30   All this time, I was believing that the most beautiful woman in all of England had fallen madly in love with me.

"Oh, my brother told me everything you said. I know exactly what you think of me. That you have no interest in someone so vain and shallow. Your judgment must be commended, that the true worth of a woman is her inner beauty."

"I hardly knew you," Nathan said protesting.

"There is no need for you to apologize. You are absolutely right. *Je suis superficielle.*[31] I have been pampered and spoiled all my life. I am used to expensive things. I am demanding, stubborn, and fiercely independent. I have no inner beauty at all—I have never needed any to get by."

"Well, humility is one of the signs of inner beauty."

"And, pray tell, what else must a woman possess to have the *inner beauty* you desire?"

"I have never been asked that before. I suppose if a woman has such inner beauty, she cannot hide it or shield it. It comes across in all she does." Nathan thought of Regina, but spoke of his mother instead. "My mother had it in abundance; a kind, charitable heart; depth of character, enduring life's trials and challenges with grace and without complaints; a cheerful spirit..."

Jocelyn looked into Nathan's eyes, "So, have you met any young women who qualify?"

Nathan hesitated.

Before he could answer, Jocelyn turned toward the candlelit gardens overlooking the terrace. "*Donc, il y a quelqu'un de spécial,*"[32] she confirmed softly, her back to him.

"*Oui.*"

Jocelyn continued looking at the gardens in the moonlight and then turned around. "What a fortunate young lady. *Es-tu fiancé ou promis?*"[33]

"Neither. It would take much to win her heart. I don't know of a man worthy of her."

"Do you envision such an alliance in the future—in the near future? Forgive me for prying. I am inquiring in the strictest confidence, but there is an important reason—to me—that I must ask."

"Under my present circumstances, I am not in a position to make such a proposal. I hope to be deserving of her love some day. I must become more established in my profession."

"Well. That may influence the reason I particularly wanted you to come tonight. If it does so adversely, my hopes shall be forever

---

31   I am shallow.
32   So, there is someone special.
33   Are you engaged, or promised?

dashed."

Nathan looked intently at her, searching for an explanation.

"I have a *proposition* for you. I have always loved the theatre; if I were free to do what I want, I would adore being a play-actress. Unfortunately, such a profession in my circles is viewed as barely better than a woman of... easy virtue... a lady of the night. The *proposition* would give me a splendid opportunity to display my acting talents."

Jocelyn paused, then continued. "A rumor is taking hold that I am seeing someone. Until tonight, no one knew for sure who that *lucky man* was... or if the rumor were true. But after your entrance tonight and my welcoming you and introducing you to guests, I am quite certain that the *someone* will be assumed to be you. For my own personal reasons, I would love to see the charade continue."

"Which explains your radiant greeting..."

"It was so good of you to come—it made me very, *very* happy, because I never expected you would—but, by continuing this *déception délicieux*, I would be spared the endless procession of suitors and the pressure from my family to meet them all. It would put a stop to my brother's persistent demands to accept the Duke's advances. It will give me the perfect excuse to decline the introductions and put a halt to my tedious letter writing."

"But, can you stand the scandal of being linked to a '*mere commoner*' like me?" Nathan inquired humbly with half a smile.

"You are no 'mere commoner.' I heard you referred to as a '*forever gentleman.*' There can be no greater compliment than that." It was a term rarely used, and was reserved for men whose excellence and depth of character knew no bounds.

Nathan blushed. "I am no gentleman."

"You may not be a man of leisure, but a true gentleman is much more than that. After all, you are well educated. You are an exceptional pianist. From what I have been told, you personify the gentleness, kind disposition, and integrity of what that term truly embodies."

Nathan had never before received such a glowing compliment, and gave an embarrassed smile. "But with no wealth, no rank... there shall surely be those who strongly object. Your brother, for example."

"Those close to me will understand. They may disapprove, but they will honor my wishes. Those blinded by rank, wealth, and privilege may not—like my *dear* brother Roderick—but I can control him."

"And your father?"

"Oh, he is rarely home. He will be leaving tomorrow for another trip abroad. It will take months for word to reach him. At first he will not believe it; he knows how much I treasure a life of privilege and pampering. Once he takes it seriously, the charade will have served its purpose for both you and me, and we can bring it to an end without him wielding his formidable power," she finished with a smile.

"So, if I go along with this deception, I can expect future visits from your brother?"

"Oh, he is really rather harmless. Of course, despite my protestations that we are just friends, he will do his best to sabotage our *budding romance*. The beauty is that it won't really matter what subterfuge he employs; since this shall all be a game, our feelings cannot truly be hurt."

Nathan's expression indicated hesitation.

"*Il y aura, aussi, des avantages pour toi.*"[34] Jocelyn said seductively. Nathan was all ears.

"First, you may come to my home any time you wish and play the new piano you were admiring from afar, under the guise of making advances toward me. Second, I will be an ambassador for your business. In my circles I have occasion to meet many of the most prominent and wealthy businessmen in London, some of whom are looking to build elegant new mansions, expand their gardens, or engage in some other project. I shall praise your architectural prowess to them all. Knowing that you and I are *romantically* linked will encourage them to please me and my father in turn, leading to commissions that wouldn't come your way for years."

Nathan was warming up to the idea as he began contemplating the benefits.

"Plus, we may become such good friends. I could use a good male friend… one with a brilliant mind and exquisite musical talent. I will be delighted to hear you perform whenever you do come. *J'aimerais avoir un ami avec qui je peux partager mes confidences, j'espère pouvoir être ta confidente.*"[35]

Nathan smiled, nodding his head.

"We shall attend concerts together. We'll go to dinner at the finest restaurants. With no expense to you. It shall be such fun!"

"How long will this *déception* go on?"

---

34 There will also be benefits for you.
35 I would love to have a special friend in whom I can disclose my confidences; hopefully I can be a similar companion to you.

"That is the beauty of it. For as long as we mutually desire. When either of us wishes to bring it to an end, we shall create an appropriate ending, with no hard feelings. Afterwards, even after our *liaison romantique* ends, we shall remain, I hope, good friends."

"Well, it is not my nature to deceive..." Nathan hesitated.

"No, I am certain it is not. The best part is that you never need express a falsehood. Be truthful; explain to anyone who may ask that you are only coming to my home... because of your love for our fabulous piano... and a grateful audience. Deny any romantic connection—that is a must! And it is also *the truth*. With the London rumor mills, such denials shall be perceived oppositely, but through no deceit on your part. You will see, the gossip columnists will do the rest."

"And what level of affection am I to show toward you when we go out in public?"

"Just treat me as you would any other lady. Be yourself."

Nathan reflected. "I see no harm in being truthful and being your friend."

Jocelyn smiled warmly as she directed Nathan to the terrace door leading back into the ballroom. "Oh, we shall become such good friends. And you must now refer to me as Jocelyn in public *and* private."

The intimacy of using her first name after such a short period of acquaintance was arousing. Nathan smiled, masking his embarrassment. "*Avec plaisir*, Jocelyn. And, of course, you shall call me Nathan."

"Yes, Nathan." Jocelyn looked adoringly into his eyes as they reentered the ballroom to the accompaniment of Beethoven.

***

On the ballroom floor, the Duke walked quickly through the crowd, annoyed whenever he was forced to stop to pay his respects, shake a hand, or endure an introduction. He was oblivious to the stares of the many women who recognized the handsome man of power and property. There was only one woman on his mind tonight. He fingered the velvet box inside his trousers pocket. He couldn't wait to present his birthday gift. It would astound her! It would make her eyes open wide! It would cause her to lips to spread in a glorious smile. It would send the precise message he wanted her to receive.

The Duke of Wilmont had always had a predilection for women with blonde hair, and Jocelyn Charlesworth was the ultimate blonde. He had known Jocelyn before her education in Paris, when she had already exhibited an extraordinary promise of beauty at the beginning of her teenage years. At that time, during his frequent visits to the Charlesworth estate, he had doted on her and developed what he considered to be a special bond; *even then* with the expectation some day of making her the Duchess of Wilmont. Upon her return from Paris, however, she had shown little interest in his advances, gifts, and flowers. In fact, she had largely ignored him during recent visits, speaking to him sparingly and frigidly. She had changed a great deal. Moreover, the Duke observed that she possessed a keenly educated mind, having mastered several languages and knowledge of history and the arts. She had also become the most desirable creature a man could ever dream of. Being the heiress of a large fortune made her all the more enticing to the Duke, due to his depleting monetary reserves. Unfortunately, the intervening years abroad had wrought upon her an independent and pertinacious maturity and an arresting freedom of thought and expression. He would need to rein her in and tame her. In time, with his guidance and control, she would make him a splendid wife. Yes, it was high time he had a duchess.

The Duke continued to navigate through the crowd, searching for the woman with blonde hair. Finally, his eyes recognized the glorious hair and the priceless ruby earrings from afar. As he approached from behind, he saw her stunning shape draped with a yellow evening gown and felt his heart begin to beat rapidly.

There was a tall man standing to her left. As the Duke approached, he noticed that Miss Charlesworth had inserted her arm between the man's waist and elbow.

Who is he? Why, on God's earth, is she attached to him?

Her brother Edward was of similar height and hair color. Had he come all the way from Manchester?

The Duke hesitated and decided to remain a spectator for a few more moments before approaching. Jocelyn turned toward the man standing at her side. The Duke's face turned pale. Her eyes were sparkling and she was staring at her escort with a look of delight. No, it was more than that. It was a regard he had never seen on her face or, for that matter, the face of any woman. It was a look of adoration, a look of intense, soulful, and utter rapture and love. It aroused an eruption of jealousy in the Duke, and his face grimaced in anguish.

He tried to catch his breath.

Who is this man?! he asked himself again. He had to see. He changed directions, walking quickly to his right, to get a better look at the man's face.

It wasn't Edward.

He didn't recognize the face.

A handsome man, much younger than he.

And much taller!

Miss Charlesworth's face glowed, her hair glowed, her jewels glowed in the reflection of the powerful gas lighting of the ballroom. She had never looked more beautiful. Mixed with the Duke's anger was an overpowering hunger and lust. The Duke caressed the small package in his pocket with his left hand—a black pearl necklace worth several thousand pounds, intended to take Jocelyn's breath away, to let her know of his ardent affection and admiration. With baubles of this price, the message would be clear—she was destined to be his duchess. No woman could refuse such a gift! But now, her eyes were making love to a rival. The Duke followed Jocelyn's path upon the ballroom floor as she made introductions of her companion to the London elite. He needed an opportunity to separate them. As he closed in, she turned her head slightly and briefly caught his eye. Jocelyn's eyes tightened and her lips clenched; the amorous look in her eyes was replaced by a frown. She then turned away and plowed through the crowd in the opposite direction, hanging on the arm of that miserable man.

The Duke felt as though he had been stabbed with a knife. He then turned around, certain Jocelyn had been looking at someone else. Seeing no one who appeared to be the recipient of Jocelyn's contemptuous stare, the Duke felt panic—then anger. She had sent him a message that she did not want him near. Where had the young girl gone who always came running to see him? Where was the beautiful flower whose eyes shined when he produced a special gift? Hadn't they walked hand in hand, along the back gardens of her home? Didn't she know that someday they would be walking, hand in hand, in *his* gardens as husband and wife? How could she have forgotten those days?

He had first noticed a change upon Jocelyn's return from Paris. He had waited four long years to see her and had imagined the encounter a thousand times. He could hardly wait to see how her face and form had matured since her absence. But no imagination and daydreaming could have prepared him for what his eyes soon beheld. When the Duke's eyes devoured the vision of her beauty, he was thunderstruck! Her loveliness had surpassed his every expectation. For her part, there had been no look of delight at his coming; just a small smile. She had politely extended her hand, but there was no embrace. Why was her reception so muted? What had caused such a change? It must have been that institution in Paris that had contaminated her mind and instilled within her an independence and freedom of thought. Damn them!

Hastily, the Duke went in search of his close friend, Roderick Charlesworth. He found him flirting with two pretty women in a large room adjacent to the ballroom. Pulling him away, the Duke stated forcefully, "Do you have any idea who that impertinent man is to whom your sister is attached?"

Roderick returned a disgusted look. "A liar and a scoundrel. That's who he is."

"You know him?" the Duke inquired.

"He is a penniless architect. Nathan Sinclair." He enunciated the name as if the name alone repelled him. "A member of London's trash. I confronted him a couple of months ago about seeing my sister, assuring him of dire consequences if he persisted. The scoundrel lied to my face and denied any relationship. He even had the effrontery to impugn my sister's character."

"You stood silently by?"

"He was quite convincing."

The Duke raised his voice in a frenzy. "Do you have any idea the scandal this could bring upon the Charlesworth name?!"

"You can be certain I shall be talking with my sister when this night is over."

"If she were my sister, I would not wait for the evening to pass." The Duke persisted.

"I shall talk to her!" Roderick fired back.

The Duke smiled to himself. *And I shall make sure you do.*

Although it was still early, the Duke climbed the steps to the estate's entrance, called for his carriage, and left. There was no reason to stay, if not to see Jocelyn. It was clear she didn't want his presence tonight. He took out the small package containing the pearl necklace. He would find a more opportune time to present his gift. His mind raced furiously on the way home. She would soon want to see *him*—every night of her life.

Chapter 33

Nathan left the Charlesworth estate exhilarated and transfixed. He could still smell the ambrosial scent of Jocelyn's sweet perfume. He had been the man upon whom the most beautiful of all women had showered her charms and attention in front of England's elite, many of whom he had met through her introduction. He had graced the rooms and hallways of an estate that compared magnificently with the finest palaces of Europe, worlds apart from the haunts he frequented. He had been in the highest echelon of London's society, mixing with its wealthiest and most prominent citizenry. To have come from humble circumstances, without wealth, rank, or position, and having suffered public insult from the beguiling Jocelyn months earlier, then to have been miraculously favored into her exclusive and radiant company for an entire evening had given Nathan feelings of rapture and redemption.

***

The Duke of Wilmont left the Charlesworth estate in a rage. His grand scheme of marrying the most desirable of all women was in jeopardy. He always got his way. No woman was free from his charms, and Jocelyn Charlesworth would be no exception. He had imagined being the envy of every man, not to mention having the fame and fortune that would follow. She would bear his children, and every man would know that he alone had caressed her beautiful form and made love to her perfection at his leisure. At every social gathering, she would be his adornment, extending to him the same adoring gaze that he had coveted and seen at her party; a gaze that had been despicably sullied on another man. That would never happen again, not after he met with her and told her of his passion for her and his desire that she become the new Duchess of Wilmont. Every man would yearn to be in his shoes.

***

Sleep came easily that night for Nathan, with visions of an astounding future. But when he awakened the next morning, Jocelyn's party seemed just a dream, and the dread over his upcoming court hearing with Sedgwick, now less than two weeks away, arrested the fantasy of a prosperous future. Reflecting on the evening's events, it was all seemed so preposterous. As the minutes and hours passed and he replayed the magical evening over in his mind, it became increasingly surreal and improbable to him.

Was I really there last night? Could it have truly been, that this extraordinarily beautiful and enchanting angel chose to bestow her affection and attention on me?

Even his beloved Regina had receded temporarily into the background of his mind, the experience had been so profoundly overwhelming. In the clarity of the morning light, thoughts of Regina came flooding back. What had he been thinking? In the magic of the evening, he had fallen under the spell of another woman; not just any woman, but a woman whose beauty was beyond compare. For a few hours, he had even felt equal in rank and station. What was he doing, even considering being a participant in a *deceptive* relationship with Miss Charlesworth? In previous weeks, when his thoughts had migrated to Jocelyn after the visit of her brother, he had afterwards mildly chastened himself. Now, he felt a much more exquisite guilt—that he had betrayed Regina by his presence and conduct at the party. He reminded himself that it was Regina who had encouraged him to attend the party; that made him feel only moderately better. Did he actually consent to Jocelyn's provocative *proposition*? He had agreed to nothing deceitful, only to tell the truth about their new *friendship*. He could certainly be her friend, could he not? Was there any reason why he couldn't visit her residence and experience the amazing new Steinway piano?—*if I am still a free man.*

***

The Duke slept fitfully that night. He felt rejected and bruised. It was a strange new feeling for him. He despised the effect it had on him. Was it truly possible that Jocelyn had frowned at him? He began to second-guess the affront, but the stare from the evening before came back forcefully nonetheless. She had glared at him, with the power of a lightning bolt on a dark night, showing contempt at his presence—a look no woman had ever dared direct his way. It seemed so implausible.

Perhaps she had been looking elsewhere. No, damn it; that will not do!

She had made eye contact with him. The message had been clear.

There must be an explanation for her behavior. It had to be a mistake. He must have caught her eye when the architect had made an irresponsible remark, or when someone had given her offense. He needed the answer to the riddle. As long as her rejection was pending, he would have no peace. He needed to confront her. He would visit her, deliver the gift, and everything would be as it should.

***

For Nathan, there had been more to the evening than just the *proposition*; Jocelyn had raved to others about his musical talents and seemed genuinely interested in helping him with his business prospects. Could she actually make a difference?

As hour after hour passed, the events of the evening began to fade and took on a character so foreign and unimaginable that he began to doubt what Jocelyn had requested of him. He knew not how to follow up on her *proposition*, even if he decided to do so. He had no place among London's gentry. He had been granted a memorable evening, one that he would never forget; but there could be no future beyond that. He decided there was nothing more he could do, other than remain in his own world. To do anything more would be a betrayal to his beloved Regina. Moreover, he needed to get his mind and focus on defeating Sedgwick's motion. There was much work to be done in preparing for the hearing, and what he didn't need were more distractions or daydreams.

Peace! What I wouldn't give for peace.

Chapter 34

The morning after the birthday party, the Duke remained frustrated, angry, and tense. He needed to act immediately. He couldn't allow these maddening feelings to interrupt his normally confident and powerful mien. With a pleasant breeze blowing in from the open window of his bedchamber, he looked out upon his majestically landscaped grounds on a glorious Sunday morning. He was the ruler of this land. He was the Duke of Wilmont! He must visit her. Today!

The Duke finished dressing and dabbed some French cologne on his face that would make him irresistible. He would deliver her gift today, a day late. It infuriated him that he had not been able to present it to her on her birthday. It wasn't his fault. He had pertinaciously sought out Jocelyn, and she had been preoccupied with that damn architect. He would let her know what a profound mistake it was for her to be in the company of a man of far lower rank than his.

On the two-hour drive to the Charlesworth estate, the Duke reflected back on the first day he had met Jocelyn. She had accompanied her father, Lord Charlesworth, to the Wilmont castle. It had been a dark day for the Duke's father. Due to financial problems, he had been forced to place the magnificent *Ravensdale* on the market. It was the same land where the much younger Duke had spent many weeks hunting and fishing, while staying at the lodge. The Duke's father had discreetly disseminated word to some of the wealthiest individuals in the southern part of the British Isles that the property was available. There had been much interest, and the Duke's father had been able to recover a handsome price for the property. However, the loss of the property had been heartbreaking to the family.

He had despised Lord Charlesworth's name before ever meeting him, due to the impending sale of the precious property. However, when he had met Jocelyn, who was no more than eight years old, his attitude changed. Jocelyn was an incredibly captivating young girl of astonishing beauty, and she had charmed him by pulling on his mustache and insisting that he carry her around on his back. Even then, he had wondered what she would be like as a woman.

Over the coming months and years, the Duke's family had become well acquainted with the Charlesworths. He soon developed a close friendship with Roderick. The Duke had seen a younger version of himself in Roderick and had become his mentor. He had many occasions to see Jocelyn during the subsequent years, until her departure to Paris in her mid-teens. She had grown more handsome every year. By the time she left England, the Duke knew one day he would propose marriage.

The Duke arrived in his carriage in the middle of the afternoon. The beauty of the day held such promise. He couldn't wait to get the previous night's ugly feeling behind him. Seeing a smile from Jocelyn would confirm that it had all been an error. At the door, he inquired if Miss Charlesworth were home. The butler invited him inside and begged him to wait while he inquired. The Duke waited anxiously as the seconds slowly passed by. Several minutes later the butler returned and informed the Duke that Jocelyn was not feeling well and could receive no visitors.

The Duke was crestfallen. He had desperately needed to see her to regain his equilibrium and calm. *Perhaps she became exhausted from the excitement of the party*, he rationalized to himself. *Surely, she would not have hesitated to descend for me.*

The Duke's frustration increased. *I shall have no peace until I see her.* He left the estate, insecure, his confidence further diminished.

Rather than take the long trek back to his castle, the Duke instructed his driver to take him to his London apartment a short distance away. He would spend the evening there and return the following day to again call upon Jocelyn.

That night, he was in the company of friends in a nearby private gambling parlor. He tried to affect his normal regal demeanor, but tonight it was forced. He listened not at all to the banter of others, rarely spoke, gambled heavily, and lost repeatedly. He hadn't experienced a losing streak so disastrous in years. It was an ugly feeling and exacerbated his unsettled state. It annoyed him that his losses for the evening exceeded the cost of the black pearl necklace that he had purchased for Jocelyn. If she had just seen him earlier that day, he would have avoided suffering such losses and issuing more notes. It was the architect's fault. He vowed to make *him* pay. The oath helped requite his dark mood.

***

On Friday morning, a much different day dawned. It was gloomy, the clouds were dark and threatening, and by midmorning it was raining heavily. The Duke surmised that the contrast in weather from the day before was a good omen foretelling a contrast in his fortune. He would see Jocelyn and all would be well again.

Once again, the Duke arrived at the estate in the middle of the afternoon—this time in the midst of a downpour. Once again, the butler invited him in. The Duke did his best to dry himself from the rain, although his shoes and lower trouser legs were soaked.

Once again, the Duke waited several agonizing minutes. Once again, he was informed that Jocelyn was not well and could not receive him. Once again, the Duke felt rejection and rage—although magnified from the day before. He left the estate under heavy rain, to the furious accompaniment of thunder and lightning, convinced that Jocelyn was avoiding him, and his blood was boiling.

***

In the gambling parlor later that night, the Duke was determined to recoup his losses from the evening before. He bet more heavily than he had ever done. Eyebrows were raised as he escalated his bets after each losing hand. By the time he retired for bed, he had lost more than ten thousand pounds, an enormous loss for one evening; most men would never see that sum in their lifetime. For the Duke, it was a loss he could absorb, but not without exquisite pain and anger; it would require him to reorganize the priority of other obligations and compel him to encumber some land. For the third straight night, the Duke slept poorly.

***

When the sun arose in a cloudless sky the next day, the Duke was agitated and shaking with fever. He was more desperate than ever to see his future duchess. It would put an end to his downward spiral. Changing his previous pattern, the Duke arrived in late morning. It was a beautiful day and surprisingly warm, with the sun shining brightly. The beauty of the day gave him new optimism that he would finally see her, though he continued to tremble from fever. When he knocked on the door, the butler notified him that Miss Charlesworth was strolling in the gardens in back of the mansion.

The Duke was elated. *Perfect. She is well. I will finally see her!*

The Duke navigated his way to the grounds behind the residence, where a large pond dominated the scenery. In his feverish state, he felt uncomfortably warm and was annoyed that his frame was quivering. Between trees behind the pond, he spied Jocelyn walking with her mother.

At last! I can get on with my life.

He reassured himself that the gift was in his pocket, touching the box lightly. Coming from the rear, the Duke treaded quietly until he was a short distance behind the two ladies. They heard footsteps and turned around. When Jocelyn saw the Duke, she was clearly startled; he was the last person she had expected to see during her turn of the gardens. She was certain he had given up after two failed attempts. She gathered herself and forced a smile.

"Miss Charlesworth." The Duke was still shaking, with beads of sweat on his forehead. "I am so glad to see you are well." *He clearly wasn't well.* "I hope you have fully recovered from your brief illness."

Jocelyn and her mother nodded respectfully.

"I wanted to extend my choicest regards for your birthday Wednesday night, but was unable to gain your attention." He clenched his jaw, trying to stop his teeth from chattering.

Jocelyn made a stiff smile. "Thank you for remembering, your grace." The Duke had not received an invitation to the party, but *knew* he had been expected to attend.

"May I speak with you privately for a moment?" the Duke inquired, his frame beginning to quiver uncontrollably.

Jocelyn's mother obliged despite a betraying glance from Jocelyn, and walked just out of earshot.

"My dearest Jocelyn, I brought you a gift—the gift I intended to present to you on your birthday." Shorter than Jocelyn, the Duke looked up into her eyes. He was awestruck by her appearance and felt consumed with possessing her. His quivering stopped momentarily as he drank in her intoxicating beauty.

"Thank you. But no gifts were expected."

With a trembling hand, the Duke presented the purple velvet box to Jocelyn. "Please open it."

"I cannot accept this, your grace."

"Please, do me the honor of opening it."

Jocelyn reluctantly consented, opening the container, which revealed a stunning black pearl necklace.

"It is lovely, but I cannot possibly accept such a generous gift."

The Duke pressed his shaking hands over Jocelyn's, and as he spoke, his voice betrayed tremors. "You must, my dearest. These pearls are an expression of the strongest affection I have for you. Ever since you were a young girl, I have—"

Jocelyn interrupted him. "Please, no more. I cannot return that level of affection."

"Cannot? Or will not?!" The Duke retorted with exasperation, the tremors in his voice more noticeable than before. He paused, then softened his delivery with a pained look on his face. "But, when you were a young girl, you adored me."

"I am no longer that young girl."

His facing turning red, the Duke inquired, "Is it that penniless architect?"

Jocelyn stared down at the quivering man, imperceptibly shaking her head. "It is not something I care to discuss. Thank you for your generosity and your very kind words, but you must give these jewels to your future duchess." Jocelyn smiled politely, returning the pearls to his hands.

"You cannot refuse me!" Anger replaced the pleading look that had been in the Duke's eyes moments before.

"Please," Jocelyn said firmly, her eyes boring into the Duke's. "We were friends before, your grace. Let us remain so."

Defeated, the Duke turned and walked away. He felt weak. He felt disgraced. Rejection was a foreign feeling to him—a feeling he despised. He returned to his carriage, his trembling and fever now in full force. During the long ride home, he gradually regained his wits, and his trembling subsided.

By the time he had entered Wilmont, his only thoughts were, *You shall yet be my wife. I will make certain of that. I will not let one man—and such an unworthy man—stop me from possessing you.*

Chapter 35

The Duke invited Roderick Charlesworth to his grand estate in the village of Wilmont. It was a medieval castle dating back to the eleventh century and had been home to the Dukes of Wilmont and their ancestors for nearly eight hundred years. Much of the original castle had been built of wood, but over succeeding generations, the wood had been gradually replaced with stone, until the castle became a prominent fortification during the reign of Henry III. It had undergone extensive restoration at various times since, but the castle's present structure was largely faithful to the original fortress.

The castle had imposing height and size and was visible from great distance. Exterior walls were more than ten feet thick at the base, and the edifice featured high corner towers and a massive central tower stretching upward over a hundred and twenty feet. Impressive as the exterior was, the interior was damp, dark, and gloomy, with small windows and dusky glass. The furniture was antique, heavy, and uncomfortable. Nevertheless, the Duke maintained a valuable collection of tapestries, paintings, and sculptures amassed during many centuries, and had even added a few prime treasures of his own during his "reign." Every time he observed his impressive castle from afar on his return homeward, there was no question in his mind that it was the perfect domicile for a duke and duchess.

The Duke was still feverish from his earlier trip to the Charlesworth estate, and with each passing hour, his anger had continued to mount like a distended volcano. He despised the upstart architect who had been Jocelyn's constant companion the night of her birthday. He was also thoroughly disgusted with his future bride for throwing herself at such a man.

Over dinner with Roderick, the Duke's anger was palpable. "The papers are already getting hold of it. They have not yet identified him by name, but there was mention of a *mystery man* who has stolen Miss Charlesworth's affections and who spent most of the evening at her side. That man should be me!" The Duke cried viciously as beads of perspiration formed on his forehead. "She steered free of me all evening."

"Jocelyn assured me he is only a friend. She loves music, and apparently, he is an exceptional pianist. I wouldn't be too concerned." Roderick tried calming down his friend.

"Are you mad?!" the Duke erupted. "Did you see the look in her eyes when she was escorting him around, making all sorts of introductions? It was revolting!"

"You have nothing to worry about." Roderick extended his hands outwardly with palms down, trying to calm his friend. "You are more handsome than he. You have wealth and power. He has nothing. My God, you are a Duke! He has no title, no family. She cannot possibly prefer him to one of the grand Dukes of England."

"That's what I keep telling myself. But one never knows with the *fairer sex*." The Duke said with a frowning smirk, as he twisted his mustache. He needed sleep desperately, but dreaded going to bed an insomniac. In a softer, plaintive tone, he philosophized: "They sometimes fall for these whimsical artists or musicians. Why, I have no idea. But I will not dare risk losing her to an elopement."

"The man is penniless," Roderick responded. "He has a shabby office in east London, just south of the Thames. I saw it myself—he obviously cannot afford much rent. My sister would never cast her lot with such a man. She enjoys the accoutrements of privilege far too much."

The Duke was not convinced, as he wiped the sweat off his brow. "Can you be so sure? Did you see her the eve of her birthday?"

"He is heavily in debt. One creditor is trying to imprison him." Roderick hoped to impress the Duke with his research.

"I thought Parliament did away with that?"

"Apparently the law has provided some exceptions."

"Bravo! That may be the end of him." The Duke's face relaxed.

"Let us hope so. But we must not take any chances. I shall find which judge has been assigned the case. Then we can exercise some friendly persuasion and guarantee the right decision is made."

"Well done, Lord Roderick!"

They continued eating. Sleep would come tonight, after all.

"You must protect your sister and your family's name," the Duke persisted. "It is clear that this Sinclair fellow hopes to wiggle his way into the family fortune. How does that sit with you?"

Roderick gave a disgusted look.

"You know, I have such plans for you, *Lord* Roderick. It's a curse to be the second son. Your father's land holdings will pass to your brother Edward, and you will be lucky to inherit a burrow in Cheapside. Once I am married to Jocelyn, I shall take care of you as I have always promised. I will give you Atherton Gardens and you shall be my neighbor. With your help, I will rule Wilmont just as my ancestors did hundreds of years ago. All shall fear and revere the great Duke of Wilmont... and worship his duchess. I shall need a good man at my side, a trusted and respected advisor. You must help bring all this to pass."

Chapter 36

By the middle of the week following Jocelyn's birthday party, the aura and glow had nearly faded completely away for Nathan. The upcoming hearing with Sedgwick continued to plague his mind and brought him down from the clouds to his real world. In his office in the middle of the morning, Stumbolt stealthily crept in. He exhibited a respectful attitude toward Nathan that he had never displayed before.

"You have a visitor. Monsieur Lefontaine wishes to discuss engaging your services."

"Show him in, at once," said Nathan with great anticipation, after having done precious little work in his office in the days subsequent to the Charlesworth affair.

Nathan remembered the brief introduction to Monsieur Lefontaine the night of Jocelyn's birthday. He had been wearing a burgundy suit containing gold embroidery, with a black silk shirt and white cravat. His attire today was more bright. The middle-aged man sported a heavily padded pale yellow frock coat with French redingotes, single breasted and knee length; with white vest, notched collars, and blue trousers. It was clear that Monsieur Lefontaine had a versatile wardrobe with an eye for setting fashion.

After introductions, Monsieur Lefontaine explained the purpose of his visit. He had recently acquired a summer estate in Buckinghamshire County. The mansion was quite acceptable, but the neglected gardens and landscape were not in keeping with his tastes and the splendor of the dwelling. There were fifty acres that he wished to completely redo. He inquired about Nathan's interest in creating and supervising a complete rework of the grounds.

"*Cela me ferait grand plaisir de vous aider dans ce project,*"[36] Nathan offered.

"*Pourriez-vous me donner une présentation préliminaire?*"[37]

"*Naturellement.*"

"*Quand êtes-vous disponible pour inspecter la propriété? Je suis à votre service.*"[38]

---

36   It would be my great pleasure to assist you in this project.
37   Could you provide me some preliminary drawings?
38   When would you be free to inspect the property? I am at your

Trying not to act too eager, Nathan reflected momentarily. It would be better for him to visit after the hearing. Otherwise, his mind would be too preoccupied. The hearing loomed drearily the following Tuesday. He would suggest a day after the hearing—by then he hoped to be free from Sedgwick's shackles.

"*Puis-je proposer mercredi ou jeudi prochain?*"[39] Nathan volunteered with a smile.

Monsieur Lefontaine replied, "*Devons-nous attendre si longtemps? N'êtes-vous pas disponible plus tôt dans la semaine?*"[40]

Nathan opened his journal, not wanting to appear too available or eager. *I will do it before the hearing. I will just need to clear my mind.*

"*Je pourrais reporter un rendez-vous le lundi et rendre cette date disponible.*"[41]

"*Parfait. Je vais envoyer un carosse à votre bureau à neuf heures? Nous prendrons le train de dix heures Wycombe. Ça devrait nous donner suffisamment de temps pour inspecter le terrain.*"[42]

It would be the day before the hearing. Nathan desperately prayed that it would not be his last day of freedom.

***

Roderick's only hope for a secure future depended on the Duke's approbation. He knew that if he facilitated his sister's liaison with the Duke, the Duke would reward him handsomely. And the Duke would be delighted at the recent development.

"The Sinclair case is scheduled to be heard before Judge Tanneyhill," Roderick informed the Duke at his next visit to Wilmont.

"Judge Tanneyhill. Who the bloody hell is that?"

"*Your* most dutiful servant."

"How did you arrange that?"

Roderick smiled. "Let us say a contribution has been made to his 'favorite charity.'" Roderick patted the wallet inside his jacket.

"What was his price?"

"A thousand pounds."

The Duke winced at the price.

---

service.
39   May I suggest next Wednesday or Thursday?
40   Must we wait that long? Are you not free earlier in the week?
41   I could re-schedule a rendezvous on Monday and make that date available.
42   Perfect. I will send a carriage to your office at nine o'clock. We'll take the ten o'clock train to Wycombe. That should give us plenty of time to inspect the grounds.

It had only cost Roderick's intermediary half that amount, consuming the lion's share of his monthly allowance, but he could make good use of the extra five hundred pounds the Duke would reimburse him. The Duke would never know.

The Duke grabbed a quill and check, and hurriedly scribbled on it, making it payable to Roderick Charlesworth. "Worth every penny to get rid of that scalawag!"

He then stood up, wandered over to the window, and looked out. "So, we are assured he will rule in our favor?"

Roderick nodded.

"And that the *architect* shall be immediately cast into prison?"

"Yes, your grace."

The Duke took a deep breath. A smile slowly began to form on his face.

"The day after, I shall pay a visit to console your sister."

The hearing was just three days away.

Chapter 37

The day before the hearing, Nathan was on the grounds of Lefontaine's newly acquired summer residence, inspecting the property. With the Clause 5 hearing preoccupying much of his waking moments, he was now glad to have the distraction of work, though he had originally desired to delay the visit. He tried to take comfort in his lawyer's optimism, and particularly in Mr. Collier's belief that he could prove Nathan lacked adequate means to pay the debt. Nathan, however, was far less confident and couldn't forget the trauma from his prior experience. His nervousness was compounded by the witnesses' affidavits portraying a lavish lifestyle. He couldn't bear dwelling on the consequences of an adverse result, knowing it would surely destroy his life.

Nathan forced his mind back to the landscape project. The grandeur and magnificence of the mansion was readily apparent, but the grounds were definitely lacking. Even if the present landscaping were brought up to proper standards, it would do little to complement the structure. English oak, mountain ash, and common alder trees were scattered haphazardly on the property. There was a small lake, more aptly described as a large pond, several hundred yards from the structure. However, the mansion was well positioned, sitting on a higher promontory than the rest of the property.

Nathan envisioned expanding the lake extensively, so that it would front the property and dramatize the elegance and height of the residence. He visualized the water reflecting the grandeur of the residence through the iron gate in front, with roads circumnavigating the expanded lake and leading to the grand entrance of the structure itself. He also imagined separate gardens, at various levels and with various themes, which would accentuate the architecture of the structure. The project he contemplated would dwarf anything he had ever been associated with, including past projects at Calemby & Co. And, it would cost a fortune!

Monsieur Lefontaine arranged for lunch inside the mansion. Over lunch, he explored Nathan's grandiose thoughts and concepts for the grounds. Throwing caution to the wind, Nathan maintained the integrity of some of his previously conceived lavish and costly concepts; designs which had only been realized on paper for no client in particular. Rather than shying from the magnitude of the ideas presented, Monsieur Lefontaine was energized by Nathan's creative and extravagant suggestions.

"*Extraordinaire!*" Lefontaine could hardly contain himself. "*Nous sommes du même avis. Votre vision est à la même dimension que la mienne. D'autre que j'ai consultés, on été limités par la conception existante. Cependant, vous proposez un nouveau départ avec le manoir comme unique référence. C'est précisément ce que je recherche. Votre formation en Suisse (Lausanne, n'est-ce pas) était bien placé.*"[43]

Nathan nodded and thanked Lefontaine for his compliment.

"*Je suis très impressioné. Votre créativité est rafraîchissante et audacieuse. Avec votre influence et votre direction… cette propriété va retenir l'attention et l'enthousiasme de tous ceux qui viennent la visiter.*"[44]

Nathan was flattered. He was also relieved that he had followed his first instinct to not hold back. But Nathan felt nervous about the inevitable question of fees, having no idea what he should propose and what Monsieur Lefontaine would accept. Would fifty pounds be too much for such a project? Did he dare ask for that sum?

As if reading his mind, Monsieur Lefontaine took a checkbook from his vest, scribbled quickly, and presented the check to Nathan.

Nathan looked at the check in disbelief.

"*Ça suffira pour commencer?*"[45] It was *ten times* what Nathan was prepared to ask for.

Five hundred pounds sterling! The amount represented exactly the unrealistic and ambitious goal that Nathan had set for his first year of practice; a target that he had missed miserably. Now he held that entire sum in his hand. And it was just "*pour commencer.*"

Doing his best to maintain his composure, Nathan muted his astonishment: "*C'est très généreux de votre part, Monsieur Lefontaine. C'est plus que suffisant, et je vais commencer immédiatement.*"[46]

This was life changing! It was a miracle! The check would easily

---

43   We are of the same mind. Your presentation is on the same scale as my own. Others I have consulted have been limited by the existing design. You are suggesting starting anew with the mansion as the sole reference. That is precisely what I have been looking for. Your education in Switzerland (Lausanne, wasn't it) was well placed.
44   I am very impressed. Your creativity is refreshing and bold. With your influence and guidance, this property will command the attention and excitement of all who come within its boundaries.
45   Will that be enough to get started?
46   That is very generous of you, Monsieur Lefontaine. It is more than enough and I shall get started immediately.

clear his debt with Sedgwick and still leave him with an enormous sum. A future with his beloved Regina seemed no longer a distant dream.

It had only been a week and a half, and Jocelyn's promise of "new commissions" had already come true, to a degree he had never imagined possible.

Chapter 38

During the night, he dreamed of the beautiful Jocelyn. Her face was irresistible. Her form was perfection itself. The golden lustre of her hair outshone the brightness of the sun. He imagined dancing with her in the Charlesworth ballroom to the accompaniment of a full orchestra and in the presence of the London gentry. He imagined her bejeweled glimmering golden hair, her exquisite white gown; he was holding her in his arms, dance after dance. He could smell her intoxicating fragrance as she showered him with looks of overwhelming devotion and love. Numerous guests, dressed in the finest fashions, were standing around them and staring. He was the center of attention, the envy of every man. There was no other woman on earth who could compare. She had bewitched him.

He woke from bed, still in a state of enchantment. Lying next to him was a slumbering young woman with golden hair. It all came back to him. He had been searching for a tonic to get his mind off Jocelyn the night before. Drowned with drink, he had even imagined *her* as his bride-to-be. She had been very pretty, very blonde, very willing, very interested in his wealth, and very interested in becoming his duchess. A suitable replacement for Jocelyn. He had taken her to bed, certain that Jocelyn's sorcery over him would finally come to an end.

In the morning light, she was no longer so very pretty, her hair hardly blonde at all. She was no Jocelyn, not even a poor imitation. The Duke rose from his bed shivering, put on a heavy robe, and walked toward the window.

My God, it is cold in here. It's the middle of summer and I'm freezing inside my castle.

At least he had slept well. But he felt the tremors coming back; tremors that had never plagued him until Jocelyn had rejected him. His life felt in disarray. Until he could win her back, he would have no peace. Until she looked at him with her adoring eyes—the way she had when she was twelve years old—he would be unable to attend to any other meaningful task.

So, it must be his music that has bewitched her so. I played the piano when I was a young boy. I am a man of immense talent, ability, and brilliance. It cannot be that difficult to bewitch her with my skill.

Now he had something to seize upon. Of course! Jocelyn loved music. He had always known that. He would show her how much he shared her passion. He would show her that he had talent equal to his rival.

How good a pianist can this Sinclair fellow be, anyway? With a little practice, I shall be able to outshine him.

Excited and energized, the Duke walked out of his bedchamber, into the hall, and down the grand winding staircase to the castle's parlor below. There was the pianoforte. He hadn't touched it in years. There was no time like the present.

The Duke sat down on the bench and looked at the keyboard. The instrument could be tamed. He had shown talent as a pianist. His mother had told him so repeatedly. He remembered playing "Für Elise" for her and her guests when he was but nine years old. He recalled the applause and praise. But soon, he had grown tired of the piano and never returned to it.

The Duke put his fingers on the white ivory keys. They were trembling lightly. Even after all these years, he still remembered the beginning. His right hand touched the E and D sharp in the treble clef a little more than an octave above middle C. He moved them in rapid sequence. Then the B, D natural, the C and A, as his left hand joined another A two octaves below. The notes moved upward first with the left hand and then the right. It was coming back, it was flowing... The first few measures were a bit rusty, but he managed to get the tune out. He couldn't remember the rest. He just needed the music.

The Duke called his butler. "Where is the music to 'Für Elise'!" he screamed. "I must have it at once!"

A few minutes later, the beaming butler arrived with the music score in hand.

"Ah, now I shall perform it as if Jocelyn were present," he said to himself. He looked at the music. It was a jumble of notes, sharps and flats. It made little sense now. "But I can read music!" he protested loudly.

Willing himself to remember, he charted the first note of the piece. "That is here." And continued laboriously to find the other notes. A half hour later, he had finished the first page, but now his hands were trembling mightily.

Why is this so difficult?

His fingers seemed inflexible and rigid.

Just a bit more practice!

He started page two of the music. After striking wrong notes several times, his shaking fingers managed to complete the first line.

This will never do. It will take me weeks just to relearn this piece.

A stark awakening of his total lack of musical ability suddenly fell upon him in full force. He brought both hands down on the keys with full strength. He sat at the piano for a long time staring vacantly at the music, until he finally sank his head down onto his hands, perched upon the ivory keys.

Chapter 39

Nathan and his lawyer arrived at the courthouse fifteen minutes early. A few minutes before the appointed hour, the courtroom doors opened. In the hallway, Nathan spied Sedgwick with a distinguished-looking man wearing a wig. There were others he recognized: his tailor, the headwaiter from Verrey's, and Mr. Allenby. None of them looked his way. Nathan shook his head.

The case of *Sedgwick v. Sinclair* was called, Judge Tanneyhill presiding.

"Court of Common Pleas, Case No. 24-01278. Sedgwick v. Sinclair. Order to Show Cause Why Nathaniel Sinclair should not be imprisoned under Clause 5 of the Debtors Act."

"Appearances, please."

"Aloysius Baumgarten for petitioner."

"Michael Collier for respondent."

"I have set aside the morning for the hearing. Mr. Baumgarten, do you have an opening statement?"

Baumgarten began striding to the lectern.

"Excuse me, your honor," Mr. Collier interrupted. "May I save the court and respondent the necessity for a hearing? Mr. Sinclair is prepared to pay the debt in full."

Judge Tanneyhill wiped his brow and gave a nervous twitch.

Sedgwick's spectacles nearly dropped off his nose.

Baumgarten was speechless.

Mr. Collier continued. "Mr. Sinclair has a check for fifty pounds payable to Mr. Sedgwick, the amount of the plaint."

Sedgwick whispered to Baumgarten.

Baumgarten addressed the court. "Your honor, we have every reason to believe that Mr. Sinclair's check is not good. Mr. Sedgwick will not accept a personal check from respondent. May we proceed?"

"He is stony broke," Sedgwick said loud enough for the judge to hear. Baumgarten gave Sedgwick an angry look, ordering him to keep quiet.

Judge Tanneyhill cleared his voice. "Mr. Baumgarten is correct.

His client is under no duty to accept a personal check. Unless your client has certified funds payable by an acceptable bank, we shall proceed. Mr. Baumgarten, please."

Nathan's attorney raised his hand, waving a check, interrupting again. He then walked over to Mr. Baumgarten. "Perhaps your client would accept a cashier's check issued by the Royal Bank of England." He handed the check over.

Baumgarten took off his spectacles and began examining the check.

The judge appeared skeptical. "Bailiff, please bring me the check, so that I may inspect it."

The bailiff complied with the request and presented the check to the judge. The judge put on his reading glasses and examined the check, holding it up to the light. "Well, it appears authentic. Payable to Mr. Sedgwick in certified funds for fifty pounds. Drawn on the Royal Bank of England."

"Isn't there something you can do?" Sedgwick whispered to Baumgarten. It was no longer about the money.

"Your honor, Mr. Sedgwick has accrued interest on this debt, bringing the sum due to sixty-four pounds. Mr. Sinclair is still fourteen pounds short. May we proceed?"

Before the judge could respond, Mr. Collier jumped up. "Your Honor. The petition states the sum of fifty pounds, not sixty-four. As Mr. Baumgarten well knows, Clause 5 applies only to debts of fifty pounds or less. His client has waived the interest by bringing this petition."

The judge opened the book containing the new legislation. The courtroom was completely silent for several minutes until the judge found the appropriate page.

In an apologetic tone, Judge Tanneyhill said: "Curious. But Mr. Collier is correct. It does limit imprisonment under Clause 5 for debts of fifty pounds or less. I cannot order Mr. Sinclair to pay more."

"May I see the check, your honor?" Mr. Sedgwick spoke in a loud voice, prompting another angry look from his lawyer.

The judge nodded and the bailiff retrieved the check and delivered it to Mr. Sedgwick. With a suspicious face, Sedgwick pulled on it, touched the ink, also held it up to the light, and examined every letter. "How can I be sure it is not a clever forgery?"

"If that is the case, then the charges against Mr. Sinclair will be far more egregious," the judge responded in overt satisfaction.

Sedgwick kept the evidence and left the courtroom fuming, his lawyer trailing.

Not only does he owe me fourteen more pounds interest, but I have had to pay my imbecile attorney another twenty. You have not seen the last of me, Sinclair.

Chapter 40

The visit and new commission from Lefontaine added a new element of reality to the memorable evening Nathan spent in the company of Miss Charlesworth.

I have Jocelyn to thank for this miraculous project. I should let her know that she has already changed my life. And when word spreads that I am in charge of such a magnificent project, more work will surely follow.

Yet, Nathan still shrank from visiting her, fearing a further visit might dilute the vivid remembrance of that magical evening. Moreover, his thoughts turned to Regina and her purity of heart and inner beauty. He could never compromise the love and devotion he felt for her. He welcomed the great reward of Monsieur Lefontaine's visit, a visit that could transform his practice and future; a visit that had liberated him forever from the shackles of debt and imprisonment. He owed a great deal to Jocelyn and would never forget her kindness. He would write to her and thank her from the bottom of his heart. But it was over. He would never see her again.

***

On Sunday evening, Nathan visited Regina at the Lancaster residence, accompanied by a feeling of jubilation. He could scarcely believe he was truly free from debt, something that had seemed impossible just a few days before. It was a feeling as wondrous as the *ecstacy* he had experienced upon his release from Coldbath Fields months before; he now had Sedgwick out of his life forever. Nathan contemplated moving his office to a more respectable part of London and considered taking more suitable living quarters. Most of all, he looked forward to sharing his extraordinary good fortune with Regina. It wasn't quite time yet, but soon he would propose.

Regina could sense something grand had happened to Nathan when the butler announced his entrance in the parlor. His face was aglow and he was smiling broadly, an even more generous display of pleasure at seeing her than normal. Regina smiled warmly and wasted no time in asking Nathan about Miss Charlesworth's party.

"So, did you go?" Regina looked anxiously at Nathan, dying to know.

"As you encouraged me to do," Nathan nodded.

"Yet, you are here, in person! I wasn't sure I would ever see you again. I waited each day for the postman to arrive, expecting the letter you had promised. When it didn't come, I assumed you had forgotten my address."

Nathan couldn't help laughing. "Well, after all the time we've spent together, it would have been rude not to come by in person..."

"And apparently you *did* remember the street and number where I live. Impressive."

"I must confess before last departing, I copied the address down."

"Brilliant. So, are there wedding bells in the future?"

"Most definitely!"

"Will I be invited?"

"You must come... but only if you are dressed in white."

If there had been a message intended, Regina refused to take the bait. "No, I shall wear scarlet, to camouflage my bleeding heart." She made an attempt to convey a look of rejection but couldn't hold the pose, and a smile broke through.

"Is she every man's dream?" Regina inquired.

"Did you not see her at Lady Sommersby's?" Nathan asked.

"Only from a great distance and only from behind. I think she was of far more interest to her legion of male followers than to the fairer sex. My uncle and I left early that night, shortly after your performance. So tell me, is she the most beautiful of all women?" Regina asked with her eyes open wide, anxious to hear the truth.

"All of London thinks so."

"And what do you think? Honestly!" Regina's expression demanded an answer.

"Her physical beauty is beyond compare."

"Have you also fallen under her spell?" Regina inquired in an artificially wistful tone.

"Quite so," Nathan expelled a quick laugh, but couldn't help reflecting on the memorable welcome he had received. "She is much different than I had imagined. I saw none of the elevated pride and condescension that she displayed at my first encounter."

"So, she did not indulge herself by humiliating you, once more, in front of her friends and family?"

"She did not."

"You *did* see her?" Regina gave an earnest look.

"I did."

"Well..." Regina showed impatience at Nathan's parsing of words.

"She surprised me. She was apologetic and embarrassed about our first encounter. She was quite pleasant."

"She no longer has a withered soul and decayed heart?"

"They weren't on display."

"What was on display?"

"Well, she actually exhibited poise and maturity in mingling with dignitaries and high-ranking members of society. She shared with me her love for music."

"So, *Mr. Sinclair*. Why were you invited? I must hear everything! Do not omit a single detail." Regina looked intently, waiting for the mystery to be revealed.

How much dare I reveal? Nathan thought to himself.

"Miss Charlesworth made me a *proposition*." Nathan paused for dramatic effect.

Regina's raised eyebrows signaled: *Get on with it!*

"Since returning from France, she has been besieged with solicitations from the male public, wishing for an introduction or even a proposal of marriage. She has no interest in marriage and tires from all the attention and time she must devote to arranged introductions and writing respectful letters of rejection. She has asked me to be her *fictitious* fiancé, so that she will no longer be perceived as *available*."

Regina gave him a skeptical look.

"I'm not speaking in jest, I swear. I told her that I would never engage in any deception and she merely laughed. She assured me that I *should* tell the truth and positively deny any romantic attachment, and that the newspapers would assume the denials were lies and perpetuate the myth."

"And in return?" Regina couldn't wait for the rest.

"Her father just purchased an exquisite Steinway pianoforte, the very same instrument that was awarded the Gold Medal at the Paris Exhibition a short time ago. She has invited me to come to her home weekly, to perform on the piano, thereby further corroborating the liaison."

"So, you are granted the opportunity to play this wondrous instrument, in exchange for denying any romantic attachment?" Regina now was skeptical.

"That's not all. I have saved the best part for last. She has also promised to regale my architectural brilliance to members of the English gentry."

Regina's surprise was evident by her curious look. "This young lady believes she can promote your business?"

"She already has. I have the most wonderful news. One of the gentlemen I met that night has already engaged my services for a fabulous new project."

Regina looked at Nathan with a sly smile, waiting for Nathan to end the charade.

"I swear it is true. A Monsieur Lefontaine. During our introduction, Miss Charlesworth lauded my architectural accomplishments, far beyond what I deserved. A week later, this same gentleman was in my office."

Regina's face did not register the delight Nathan had expected. After all, this was stupendous news!

"Regina, I must take you there. It is a massive landscape project for a statuesque country home he recently purchased. I have already received a handsome retainer."

Her skepticism vanished. "You have?"

Nathan couldn't resist telling her the sum in a low voice. Regina blinked her eyes in astonishment.

"You know what this means?" There was no more reason to delay. It was time to move things forward far more quickly than he had planned.

"It means you are deeply indebted to Miss Charlesworth." Once again, Regina refused the bait.

"Yes, I am."

"Then, you must honor her wishes," Regina spoke in a serious tone. "As long as you are not deceiving anyone and being truthful about the relationship, you should have a clear conscience. This is truly amazing! I think it would be fabulous to see you advance your profession so rapidly; it might otherwise take many long years to achieve similar projects. And you have already seen the fruits of the connection. Apparently, this young lady *does* have influence. You must take advantage of it."

Nathan felt a twinge of disappointment at Regina's insistence that he participate in the *proposition*.

"But I have already decided not to pursue it."

"How can that be, Nathan? Such an exquisite, unique opportunity is placed before you. And all you need do is play your role. Not a difficult one, at that. And, I'm certain you are dying to play her new pianoforte."

"Yes, that would be lovely. But, there is another reason that I *will not* pursue it," Nathan responded. "In furtherance of her designs, Miss Charlesworth expects us to attend public events, concerts, theatre, thereby perpetuating the fictitious engagement. I am not willing to pay that price. I want nothing that limits our time together, nothing that causes you any discomfort."

Regina gave Nathan a sweet smile. "You may still visit me, of course. We must merely be discreet while this *alliance* runs its course. If she can influence your business as well as she has already shown, it would be tragic not to pursue it. Of course, it is your decision. But I hope you are not rejecting it because of me."

Nathan was silent, once more sensing a fleeting feeling of regret. But before he could speak another word, Regina took his hands in hers.

"If it's because of me that you do not want to pursue this fabulous opportunity, then I give you my blessing." She then added with a mischievous grin, touching his cheek softly, "But you must promise me not to fall under her spell." Those were the words Nathan yearned to hear, and his feelings of doubt evaporated.

***

During the weekend, Nathan thrust himself into the new project. On Monday morning, he paid off his last debt, rewarding Stumbolt with a check that brought his salary current, with an added bonus of ten pounds. Stumbolt was gracious, insisting that the payment wasn't necessary, but still snatched the check as soon as it was tendered, fearing that his employer might change his mind. There was a subtle change in the way Stumbolt treated him from that day forth—a newfound respect that had never been present until the arrival of Monsieur Lefontaine.

***

The Duke received the day's mail in his library at midday. He was pleased to see a letter with Roderick's seal.

There must be some news already about Sinclair.

A few good nights of sleep had done wonders for his health, but his demeanor quickly changed as he read its contents:

> *I regret to inform you that we are too late. Inexplicably, Sinclair paid his debt in full at the hearing. There was nothing Judge Tanneyhill could do but release him and dismiss the case. Imprisonment is no longer an option. It is uncertain*

where the funds came from, but rumor has it he received a large advance on a new project.

"Just my bloody damned luck!" the Duke cursed aloud.

I must find another way to get rid of him and fast. These matters of the heart can move quickly. I shall check his background thoroughly, find his Achilles' heel. Everyone has one.

The Duke had the perfect man for the job. He quickly dispatched a letter to Nevius Tucker, a man who had come in handy before.

He looked at the velvet box on his desk. How had she been able to refuse such an exquisite gift? Women could not resist beautiful jewelry. Women could not resist him. Even Miss Charlesworth's rejection was only temporary and would soon change.

Chapter 41

On Tuesday's mail came a letter from Jocelyn. Instantly, the events from two weeks before came flooding forcibly back to Nathan. He held the letter for several minutes, delaying the intrigue of its contents. He returned to his sketches of Lefontaine's gardens, but his mind constantly wandered back to the letter. He finally succumbed, broke the seal, and smelled again the sweetly scented ink, before reading the words.

> *My dearest Nathan,*
>
> *I have been awaiting daily your visit. I am so very disappointed you haven't contacted me. It has been nearly two weeks and I yearn to hear you perform your magic on the Steinway. Remember our mutual pledge. I know Monsieur Lefontaine has paid you a visit and retained your services. You should know that I have great power to influence him. Now, if you will please honor me with the pleasure of your company. May I count on your visit Friday night for dinner? If you could arrive in the early evening, at seven o'clock, it would be my great joy to hear you perform before dinner is served.*
>
> *Yours, most affectionately,*
>
> *Jocelyn Charlesworth*

After reading the letter, Nathan felt ashamed and ungrateful, but also excited. He regretted neglecting to thank Jocelyn for the life-changing commission. But her letter also confirmed the reality of the magical evening, which had begun to seem like only a dream. The least he could do was accept the invitation; in his short message to her, he apologized, expressed his profound gratitude, and accepted her kind offer. He looked forward to paying his compliments to her in person and further relished the thought of performing on the new Steinway in the magnificent music room of the Charlesworth estate. And although refusing to admit it, part of him wanted to experience again the hypnotic spell of Jocelyn's company and beauty.

***

Nathan arrived at the Charlesworth estate precisely on time and was ushered in by the butler.

"I have been asked to escort you to the music room," the butler spoke in a stately voice.

Nathan followed the servant down the grand staircase to the ballroom and then continued on to music room, where the piano rested on an elevated circular platform in the center of the room. Standing in the music room, Nathan lifted his eyes to the circular balconies which extended upward three levels, with a mural-painted dome rising above the highest one—a repeat of the architectural majesty of the ballroom, but on a smaller scale.

Entering the music room, Nathan stared at the new Steinway & Sons piano, disbelieving his eyes. He had heard how Steinway had recently developed a rim-bending process that was said to give their pianos an extraordinary sound and character, but he had never encountered such an instrument until arriving at the Charlesworth estate. Now, the magnificent instrument was before him.

There was not another soul present in the room. Although he had observed and coveted the pianoforte from afar on the evening of Jocelyn's birthday party, he now felt intense excitement at the prospect of seducing it. He approached it tentatively, respecting it as if it were a highly treasured museum piece, off limits to human hands. He admired the beautifully stained rosewood finish, marveling at the intricate carvings starting with the piano legs and building up to the piano's undercarriage and sides, and the beautifully carved birds on the piano lyre where the pedals were placed. The music desk just above the keyboard was meticulously crafted, as were the ripple carvings on the sides, which extended the piano's full length. The size of the piano was astonishing, accommodating the deep strings expanded for the bass chords. He had never seen such an instrument! Standing next to it, he couldn't resist placing the palm of his hand on the right side of the piano where it curved away toward the deeper bass strings. He caressed the stunning rosewood finish, then examined the strings and hammers and imagined, before playing, the musical vibrations they would create. Delaying his pleasure at hearing its sound until the last possible moment, Nathan finally sat at the piano bench and observed the beautiful ivory keys, caressing the top of them silently.

He made love to the instrument for ten minutes before he finally raised his two hands above the keyboard. At length he chose Liszt's Concert Etude in D-flat Major, playing the arpeggios softly, and gradually building in power the beautiful romantic theme, aided by the impressive acoustics of the room. The timbre of the tones was unlike anything he'd ever heard before. The bass tones were remarkably rich and clear. The subtlety with which he was able to measure the dynamics of each note thrilled him. It felt effortless, playing on the extraordinary handiwork.

He remained alone in the music room as he continued with the third movement of Cramer's sonata *Le Retour à Londres*, followed by Beethoven's *Pathetique* Sonata. It had been nearly forty minutes when he finally paused. Instantly, a thunder of applause erupted from the balcony that extended over the music room, and Nathan observed a throng of faces peering over the balustrade, cheering and clapping enthusiastically. His upward glance manifested his complete surprise, and he rose quickly from the bench and gave a bow. He scanned the faces above him, searching for Jocelyn, but she was not there.

As the applause came to an end, he heard a lovely female voice from behind.

"*Quel grand plaisir de t'entendre jouer de nouveau.*"[47]

Nathan turned to see the angelic beauty of Jocelyn gracefully approaching him, wearing the same lavender dress she had worn the night he had first laid eyes upon her. He had a momentary flashback of that painful encounter, though it seemed so improbable and long ago, in the glow of her radiant welcome.

"Dinner is served." And with her arm extended, she motioned for him to join her.

"Do you remember this dress?" Jocelyn asked quietly as she inserted her arm in his.

"I do."

"I am wearing it tonight in honor of the night we first met."

"A night I shall never forget." Nathan squinted his eyes, as if he were still smarting from the pain.

"Nor shall I," Jocelyn said, as she squeezed his arm playfully. "After that evening, I wondered if I would ever hear you play again. And now I have," a long sigh accompanied her expression of pleasure, as though she were savoring each note he had played. "You performed so beautifully tonight."

---

47   What a great pleasure to hear you play again.

"It is hard not to play beautifully on such an instrument."

Nathan was soon ushered into a spacious and ornate dining room, where forty people were seated at the lengthy table. Another round of applause greeted his entry. Nathan nodded respectfully, unable to contain his smile. Never had he seen a dining room with such lavish decorations. Stuffed birds in cages, ceramic and china figurines, and potted plants graced the room, and priceless works of art hung upon the walls. On the table, adorned with a stunning centerpiece of summer flowers of all shades and colors in full bloom, a twenty-piece place setting with stemware, china, and polished silver had been laid for each guest. As was the case with many of the important chambers of the structure, there were three levels of balconies that encircled the dining room, crowned with another stunning domed mural.

Servants bordered the enormous dining room; their exquisite attire would have been the envy of military officers. Conspicuously absent was Roderick Charlesworth. In addition, Jocelyn's father was out of country, at the request of the realm, assisting in high-level trade discussions.

During dinner Nathan, seated directly across from Jocelyn, was introduced to many guests he had not yet met, including dignitaries and captains of industry. Nathan was also introduced for the first time to Lady Charlesworth, who warmly received Nathan, paying her compliments on his recital. It was apparent that Lady Charlesworth had been a great beauty in her prime, and now in middle age was exceedingly handsome. Although fluent in English, Nathan noticed the presence of a Swedish accent, reflective of the land where she had been born and raised, a cousin of King Charles XIV's offspring. It was evident where Jocelyn's golden hair had come from.

That evening, the guests enjoyed a twelve-course meal, beginning with a choice of julienne or vermicelli soup, and whitebait. Other offerings included broiled salmon, turbot in lobster sauce, canards à la rouennaise, braised beef, roast lamb, tongue, quail, roast saddle of mutton, compote of cherries, neopolitan cakes, charlotte russe, and madeira wine. Nathan had never dined on such a grand scale, with an army of impeccably dressed servants serving each course à la russe. During the dinner, Nathan conversed freely with the guests and felt eminently comfortable in their company. This was in large part due to Jocelyn's attentions toward him and her frequent participation in the discussions. After dinner, the male guests congregated in one of the nearby parlor rooms, separating from the female members. In that setting, Nathan had many opportunities, in the natural flow of conversation, to promote his architectural ideas and concepts, passing out several of his cards.

Before departing, Nathan inquired if he might bid Jocelyn farewell. The butler was dispatched to the women's parlor with the request, and Jocelyn joined Nathan in the conservatory shortly thereafter. It mildly surprised him that Jocelyn required no chaperone while alone in a room with another man.

He thanked her heartily for the recent commission from Monsieur Lefontaine.

"Our plan is off to an excellent start. You have already benefitted in your business, I'm so delighted to see. You can expect more business in the near future, I am certain. I have spread the word among many of my father's friends."

"I am deeply indebted to you. You have no way of knowing the impact this will have on my career and my life."

Jocelyn smiled. "And... there has already been an article about *us* in the *Daily News*. My birthday party made the society page, and it described a 'handsome young man who had the attention of the feted young lady during much of the evening.' Are you ready to become fodder for journalists?"

Nathan looked surprised. "Was anything more said?"

"The article left your identity a mystery, but you can expect your name to appear soon in print. Since my party, I have been declining all requests for introductions, and the requests have fallen sharply. I expect there will soon be rumors spreading that my affections are directed toward that 'handsome young man' and that an engagement may soon be in the offing. You and I have already benefitted from the 'proposition.'"

"I'm glad to have been of service to you," Nathan responded with pleasure.

"We must create an aura of mystery about you," Jocelyn said, her eyes widening. "I know very little of your past and circumstances. I have been told that your mother was a well-known singer of opera?"

"She was. She performed for many years in Europe, mainly in France, her home country. But when I was still young, she retired from the opera, regretting her frequent absences from her only child."

"And your father?"

"I never knew my father. He passed away before I was born."

"How sad you never knew him." Jocelyn thought of the loving

relationship she had with her own father. "What do you know of him?"

"My mother rarely spoke of him. His death affected her profoundly, and she deflected any inquiries I made of him. I know he was an artist... and an Englishman. Just before passing away, she wrote me a letter telling me she had something very important to tell me about him. Unfortunately, I never learned what that was."

"It must have been difficult to grow up without a father."

"My mother more than made up for it. She was an amazing woman. Now that she is gone, I do wish I knew more of my father. Whenever I inquired of him when I was a child, it was obvious she was pained greatly by memories of him, and I soon learned not to question her."

"Have you no idea what she wanted to tell you?"

"None at all."

Jocelyn walked directly in front of Nathan and boldly asked: "Forgive me for asking, but has it ever crossed your mind that the artist was not your father?"

Nathan reacted with mild indignation. "Whatever do you mean?" He instantly thought back to his mother's last words, wondering if that were possible.

"A woman's intuition. Is it possible that your mother fell in love with another man, perhaps someone prominent, wealthy, of rank, who could not marry her because of the difference in social standing?"

"Such an assertion would place a serious stain on her name," Nathan responded defensively.

Jocelyn softened her musings with an apologetic look. "I am not insinuating anything of the sort, mind you." After a pause, she followed up. "Have you ever had occasion to meet any members of your father's family later in life?"

"No... I never have."

"Do you not find it odd that you never had contact with his brothers, sisters, uncles, aunts, grandparents...?"

"I never truly thought of it that way. My mother and I traveled often, while she was performing... that is, until we moved to London. It would have been difficult to remain in contact with them."

"But, if your father was English, would you not have expected your mother to have made contact with his family when you settled in London?"

"I suppose so. But his early death pained her greatly."

"Did she ever tell you where in England he was from?"

"No. Only that they met in Paris."

"And, why then did your mother choose to move to London, if not to renew contact with her husband's family, when her own family lived in France?"

"You ask some interesting questions. She told me that we were making a new start. She felt there would be less pressure to resume her singing there. Before we moved, she had often promised retirement, only to be swayed otherwise."

Jocelyn's mind was actively reflecting what she had just learned.

"You can expect the newspapers to inquire into your background. *Cela te dérangera?*"[48]

"*Je n'ai rien à cacher.*"[49]

After their brief exchange, Nathan left with a promise to return soon.

---

48   Would that bother you?
49   I have nothing to hide.

Chapter 42

A few days later, Nathan descended the stairs of his apartment, shortly to begin his forty-minute ride to Rue Faubourg to see Regina. As he exited the ground floor, the heavy air and malodorous stench overwhelmed his senses. It had been far worse in recent days as construction on the south-side Thames Aqueduct neared completion. Laborers had dammed the sewage flow at various spots to enable subterranean work. With nowhere to go, random cesspools of filth formed, poisoning the nearby air.

It was a warm humid day and the street traffic was heavy. Thick steam rose from a team of livestock moving sluggishly through the manure on the streets, as the discordant racket from street merchants and vendors also rose. Standing on the sidewalk waiting for a cab, Nathan noticed a man with a grizzled face across the street who made brief eye contact with him and then turned away. The man wore a grey hat and cloak. A hansom cab stopped and Nathan boarded the conveyance. As it started down the road, he turned and saw the man running across the street, hailing a cab.

A coincidence. Why in heaven's name would I be followed? Who could possibly have interest in me now?

He excised the thought from his mind and took a deep breath when the cab crossed the London Bridge and the putrid odor of Bermondsey vanished. He relaxed and pondered with contentment his forthcoming visit with Regina.

***

Thirty minutes later, Nathan was delighted to be in the company of Regina once again. She had something on her mind. "You have been hiding your past from me," she shot him a playful look that said: *How dare you!*

Nathan looked bewildered.

"You never told me of your noble birthright." Regina showed him the *Daily News* article.

"That must be you they are speaking of."

Nathan read the morning newspaper. The *Daily News*, a publication that chronicled all movements of the city's elite, reported that the mystery man seen at Jocelyn's birthday party was a young architect and musician, whose mother had been a famous French opera singer and whose father was rumored to be of elevated birth: likely the son of a baron or baronet. Descriptions of Nathan included such adjectives as "dashing, brilliant, reserved, incredibly talented..." Reports indicated that an engagement was on the horizon.

"She has really gone too far," Nathan said under his breath, controlling his anger.

"She?"

"This rumor must be the creation of Miss Charlesworth. I was telling her about the letter I received from my mother shortly before her passing. She wrote that she had something important to tell me about my father."

"My, you *are* having intimate conversations with her," Regina said in a voice reeking with feigned jealousy.

Nathan winced. "When last we met, she told me that 'we needed to create an aura of mystery' about me. I guess this was her way of doing it."

"So, there is no truth to it?"

"None whatsoever. All I know of my father is that he was an artist."

"You have never wondered what your mother wished to tell you?"

"Many times."

"Were there no clues among her papers or possessions?"

"None that I could uncover."

"How sad her life was cut short, before she could tell you more. And, so tragic that you never knew your father. Even though they are gone, I have, at least, many fond memories of my parents. I remember their faces, their hearts, their dreams, their charity..." Regina's eyes started welling up as she talked of them.

Nathan took Regina's hands in his. "I wish I could have known them. I wish I could have known the extraordinary parents who gave birth to such a miracle as you."

Regina let out a short laugh. "I'm no miracle. You have yet to see my warts and scales."

"You do keep them well hidden."

"Nathan, you place me on too high a pedestal. I fear when you know me better, I shall come crashing down, and you will walk away."

"Never. I *do* know you well enough. Unfortunately, the more I know you, the higher I must elevate the pedestal. If it gets any higher, I will be forced to carry with me a stepladder, just so my eyes may grace your toes."

"The pedestal is no higher than a stepladder?"

"A very tall stepladder."

"How tall is it, exactly?"

Nathan's eyes looked up to the ceiling of the parlor room.

"That is not so very high," Regina's face expressed hurt.

"The stepladder does not stop at the ceiling."

"How high does it go?"

"Into the clouds."

"Oh, that *is* quite high. It shall indeed take you a very long time to see my warts and scales."

Chapter 43

During Nathan's recent visit to the Charlesworth estate, Jocelyn asked him if he would accompany her and her mother to an upcoming ball. It was all part of the *proposition,* for them to be seen together in high society, she explained. Soon afterwards, Nathan traveled to the Charlesworth estate to escort Jocelyn and her mother to a ball organized by Lord and Lady Polkinghorn. The Polkinghorns' stately early-nineteenth-century mansion was located just a half mile from the Charlesworths. They annually hosted a ball on the first Saturday in the month of July, *by invitation only.*

When Nathan arrived at the Charlesworth estate, Jocelyn greeted him with exceptional warmth. She was wearing a shimmering silver satin gown with off-the-shoulder sleeves and large crinolines; on her hands were matching lace gloves. Lying loose around her shoulders was a black paisley shawl folded on the diagonal. Her jewelry consisted of an elegant emerald necklace with matching earrings. Nathan was blinded by her ravishing beauty and shifted his regard to Lady Charlesworth to regain his bearings, who herself made a striking impression in an understated high-neck white satin gown. Lady Charlesworth expressed delight at renewing his acquaintance.

They traveled the short distance to the Polkinghorns' estate in the Charlesworths' luxurious gold-plated barouche drawn by four horses and guided by uniformed coachmen. As they exited the carriage, Jocelyn spoke quietly to Nathan: "Now, Nathan, I expect you to spend all evening at my side."

"There's no other place I would prefer to be."

"I have been so looking forward to our first dance together," Jocelyn whispered.

Minutes later, they advanced toward the spacious ballroom floor and began dancing a waltz. Nathan was impressed by Jocelyn's graceful and elegant movement. "Wherever did you learn such lightness of foot?"

"You would be surprised what they taught us at Chateau d'Écouen." Jocelyn smiled. "And, I must say, you distinguish yourself well enough on the dance floor." Nathan's manner on the dance floor was dignified and elegant, but more reserved than hers.

"My mother often danced with me when I was young."

Nathan sensed a newfound respect from the surrounding crowd, in recognition of his "recently reported noble heritage," as he glided with Jocelyn on the floor.

Too bad it's all fiction, he thought to himself.

After dancing a quadrille, Nathan gave Jocelyn a serious look. "There is something upsetting I need to discuss with you."

"*Ai-je été méchante?*"[50] Jocelyn asked coquettishly, batting her azure-blue eyes.

"You know you have. You should not be taking such liberties with my past."

"But you told me yourself that your mother had an important secret she wanted to share with you concerning your father. I simply imagined what the secret must have been and speculated about it with some friends. The next thing I know, it's in print. Truly, it hardly takes anything more than thinking out loud."

"Are you sure that is all you have done?"

Jocelyn again batted her eyes at him in response, leaving Nathan to wonder whether she was being truthful or not.

"You must promise me that you will be more careful," Nathan gently prodded—it was hard to stay angry with such a playful and stunning young lady. "You're trifling with my name. When it comes out that there is no nobility in my blood, my reputation may be sullied. I can't countenance any falsehood."

"Then don't. Has anyone asked you about it?"

"No. Not really." In fact, if it hadn't been for Regina mentioning it, he wouldn't be *au courant*. "I mean... in my circles, I don't really meet anyone who would. I will have to deny it if asked, you know."

"Are you certain it could not be true? My imagination has been running wild. And, who knows, maybe I *am* right. Your mother had something important to tell you about your father. You said yourself that your mother was an amazing woman. Wouldn't she have mingled with ardent admirers who were well connected among the aristocracy or the like?

"She *was* an amazing woman. She sacrificed her career for me and paid for my education," Nathan paused. "But I want no part of your deceit in this matter."

Jocelyn looked hurt for a few seconds, then her demeanor returned to playfulness.

---

50   Have I been bad?

"You must find me intensely mischievous... and childish." Jocelyn said with a puerile affect. "I have been told I have an *elastic* disposition, whatever is meant by that." Then she changed the subject, seeking to excuse her impropriety. "I have never really had to make any decisions in my life. They have all been made for me. I sometimes tire of all the grandeur, excess, and wealth."

"Do you? I cannot imagine that ever becoming tiresome."

"I suppose I take it all for granted. I am certain that when I get married someday, I shall take my husband for granted. Pity the poor man who is entranced enough by my beauty to marry me." Jocelyn mused.

"Sometimes you seem just twelve years old... other times thirty-two."

"Oh, twelve maybe. Hopefully never so old as thirty-two."

"Promise me no more surprises?"

"If I make such a promise, I may break it tomorrow," Jocelyn laughed whimsically. "You can never ask me for that."

"What then may I ask of you?"

"I am sure that I shall *conceive* of something."

As they continued to dance, Nathan continually looked away from Jocelyn. Her beauty was so beguiling that he feared falling under her spell. When he looked away, Jocelyn would shake her head or grasp his hand to get his attention back. She would open her eyes wide, staring at him hard, trying to get him to maintain her stare. Nathan knew what she was doing, but continued to look away, focusing on nearby dancers or scanning the crowd and architecture as they moved on the floor.

Nathan could tell Jocelyn was getting frustrated with him, and she approached him with an earnest expression.

"You really *must* gaze into my eyes when we are dancing. Don't you understand, *un homme amoureux ne peut pas quitter des yeux hors de l'objet de sa dévotion.*"[51] It was all part of the plan.

Nathan understood. He struggled to obey Jocelyn's request during the remaining dances they shared. It was a battle for him, because the more he gazed into her eyes, the more he felt himself being drawn into her sorcery. He had never experienced such powerful physical attraction. What's more, he could tell by her reaction that she knew the full depth of her power and her ability to charm any man.

When she exerted the full force of her adoring gaze, there was not a man alive who could withstand it for any appreciable time,

---

51 A man in love cannot keep his eyes off the object of his devotion.

Nathan knew. When he felt his control vanishing, as he did several times during the evening, he forced himself to glance away, to regain his balance. When he returned his eyes to the sorceress, he could read her thoughts: *You are at my mercy.*

Late in the evening, Jocelyn whispered to him. "I have it!"

"You have what?" The enchantment was broken, leaving Nathan's mind blank.

"What you may ask of me. You may ask me to a concert at St. James's Hall a week from next Monday. It will be the last performance by the Philharmonic Society this season. And then all concertgoers shall be without music for four months... All except me, of course." Jocelyn looked at Nathan impishly.

"I have never attended a concert there." Nathan reflected, but he vividly recalled walking through it when he visited the adjacent restaurant a short time ago. The thought of seeing a concert in the magnificent hall excited him.

"It is very large, but the acoustics are magnificent. We have excellent reserved seats. I have heard that a talented young female pianist, Madame Goddard, will be at the piano for Beethoven's Choral Fantasia."

Although familiar with the piano portion, Nathan had never heard the Choral Fantasia performed with a chorus and orchestra. The prospect of hearing it for the first time intrigued him.

"A shame Sir Charles Hallé will not be performing," Nathan commented. "I would love to have heard him play Beethoven."

"So, you are of a mind that only male pianists have talent?"

"I did not mean that at all," Nathan gave an innocent look.

"Would it shock you to find that there are some members of the fairer sex who are gifted musically?"

"Jocelyn, my comment was not intended as an aspersion on *your* sex..."

"You may find that Madame Goddard provides a more sensitive interpretation than *Sir Hallé*," Jocelyn persisted.

"I am certain she must be exceptional to be performing with the Philharmonic," Nathan said in an apologetic tone.

"And, Sir Hallé has just completed his Beethoven series. I think he is retired for the summer, so you have no choice but to hear a female play. If she plays poorly, perhaps you may interrupt her in the middle of her performance and finish it yourself," Jocelyn challenged Nathan with her eyes.

"In that case, I had better practice the composition."

"Yes. I would not want you to disappoint me or the other two thousand guests."

"We shall need front row seats, so that I can easily jump on stage and discreetly push her off the piano bench... if necessary."

"When you do that, it would be best if you wait for a break in the piano accompaniment, so that it doesn't interrupt the chorus and orchestra."

"An excellent idea. I will note several spots in the Fantasia where there shall be such opportune moments." Nathan made a motion with his hand as if he were jotting down notes in an invisible score.

"Oh, I hope *she does* let my sex down," Jocelyn said longingly. "It would be quite a scene to have a member from the gallery take over mid-performance."

"I may get my name in the papers. That should be good for business."

"Unless you make a serious mistake. Dare you run the risk?"

"Certainly."

"Good. It is time that we be seen *in public*... if only you will petition me to attend," Jocelyn requested with an air of exaggerated modesty.

"Petition you, I shall." Nathan obediently extended his right arm forward with his palm upward, in a flowery display. "Miss Charlesworth, I will be most honored if you will accompany me to the concert at St. James's Hall."

"Beaucoup mieux. J'accepte avec reconnaissance ton requête humble."[52]

"And you promise to behave?"

Jocelyn only smiled.

---

52   Much better. I gratefully accept your humble entreaty.

Chapter 44

On a cold summer's day, Nathan took a cab to Cheapside. The streets were teeming with merchants and customers. Traffic came pouring in from many arteries: Oxford Street, Holborn, the Strand, Fleet Street, Bishopsgate, Leadenhall, Moorgate, and King Williams Street. Produce and poultry were being sold side by side, as vendors called out their offerings. It was organized chaos, everyone pursuing their own purpose, oblivious to the cares and despair of others. Nathan vividly remembered the street and the building he had visited there more than a year before. It brought back a flood of memories of another time—a time full of desperation, fear, and insecurity.

He stepped out of the cab with his scarf tightly wrapped around his neck. He walked past a nondescript building, debating whether or not to enter. Part of him wanted to get on his way to the South Kensington Museum, where he had arranged to meet Regina in the early afternoon. He wasn't rushed for time, but wondered if he was playing the part of a fool by knocking on the entrance door.

Nathan stood at the front door and exhaled; he watched his warm breath mist in the frigid air. He shivered before engaging the knocker, then prayed no one would answer. He breathed a sigh of relief when there was no response and turned. But before he could take a step away, he heard the creak of the door opening.

A thin, scrawny young clerk with eyeglasses appeared. "May I help you, sir?"

"Is Mr. Sedgwick in?" Nathan asked, hoping he wasn't.

"May I ask who's calling?"

"A former client." Nathan handed the clerk his card.

A moment later, the clerk motioned Nathan to enter and led him into another room where Sedgwick was seated behind a desk covered with papers.

It seemed to Nathan that Sedgwick had grown wider since he had seen him last. Sedgwick looked up. "Came to gloat, did you?" he asked angrily, with no other acknowledgment of Nathan's presence.

"No sir."

"Well, if it's another loan you are looking for, get out before I call the police!" Sedgwick fumed with a look of blood in his eyes.

"I am not here to borrow money."

Sedgwick gave him an exasperated look. "Well? Get on with it. What is it?"

Nathan took a deep breath. "I have come to offer my sincere apologies. It was wrong of me to ignore my debt to you. I can offer no worthy explanation for my inexcusable behavior."

Sedgwick's growled response was undecipherable.

Nathan pulled out a blank check from his coat pocket. "I wish to the pay the accrued interest on the loan—the interest you were forced to waive in court."

Sedgwick sat up with a stunned look. "You what?"

"I know that I am no longer legally obligated to pay it. My lawyer explained it all to me."

Sedgwick studied Nathan with crossed eyes. "Is this your idea of amusement?"

"Please," Nathan spoke solemnly. "The amount due."

Sedgwick stared intensely at Nathan for several long moments, trying to gauge what was going through the visitor's mind. Shaking his head, he then turned to his right, opened a drawer in his desk, and fingered through some files before finally pulling one out.

"So, what madness has triggered this *mea culpa*?"

"It is the honorable thing to do. The amount of interest, please."

Sedgwick glanced through the papers. "As of the court hearing, you owed fourteen pounds, six shillings, and four pence in excess of the fifty pounds paid."

"And how much did you pay your attorney?"

Sedgwick looked perplexed. "My attorney? What does that have to do with anything?"

"I will also reimburse his fee."

Sedgwick raised his eyebrows in disbelief. It was all in the file. He leafed through the papers in the folder. "Mr. Baumgarten received twenty-two pounds on this matter, give or take a few shillings."

"And the men you paid to track me down? How much were they paid?"

Sedgwick's eyes opened wider. He had to think. That *wasn't* reflected in the file.

"Ten pounds, maybe more, maybe less."

Nathan scribbled on the check and handed it to Sedgwick.

Fifty pounds.

"It only adds up to forty-seven pounds, six shillings." Sedgwick had quickly done the math in his head.

"In case you neglected some other expense," Nathan meekly offered.

Suddenly suspicion invaded Sedgwick's mind and he felt anger boiling inside. "Are you playing me for a fool, Mr. Sinclair? Trying to humiliate me. Right? No man in his right mind would do *this*."

Nathan's face maintained a solemn look. "You came to my aid when I needed help. I was desperate. Rather than repay your kindness, I ignored the debt. I pretended it didn't exist. When I did receive some money, I spent it elsewhere. I never paid a single shilling to you, forcing you to take the extreme action you did. It was *I* who was angry with *you* for my being led away in handcuffs to Coldbath Fields, when you had every right to take such action. I was at fault. I am truly sorry for the inconvenience and aggravation I caused you. I am making amends, I swear."

Sedgwick still had a suspicious look, but Sinclair was very convincing.

"I'll accompany you to the Royal Bank of England, if you'd like." Nathan said with conviction.

Sedgwick shook his head, finally convinced. "That won't be necessary." Sedgwick stared at the check in wonderment.

Nathan bowed. "Good day, sir." He left without another word.

On his ride to the museum, Nathan felt he might someday find a way to make himself worthy of Regina. Paying Sedgwick had been an atonement for more than just the debt. It had been an expiation for other past misdeeds, none of which were of any major consequence, but conduct which nonetheless caused him to feel unworthy of Regina. The restitution cleansed his soul, and he felt a better man for it.

Nathan had been looking forward to visiting the museum with Regina, as a major expansion, several years earlier, had created new galleries. The museum's new wings included a series of mosaic figures that depicted great European artists from the medieval era to the Renaissance. Other new rooms contained riches from the Orient.

The main entrance to the museum, with its mosaic pediment, was on the north façade of the massive building. Patrons entered through large paneled bronze doors, which depicted giants in chemistry, astronomy, sculpture, architecture, mechanics, and painting. The entry area of the museum was patterned after the Italian Renaissance, with extensive use of terra-cotta, mosaic, and brick. Upon entering the museum, patrons were greeted with a sweeping ceramic staircase. The walls and ceilings were covered with decorative and molded ceramic tile. In all, it was a remarkable sight, and one that left the patrons eager to discover the many treasures within.

Wanting to arrive in advance of her, Nathan waited in front of the museum for twenty minutes before Regina disembarked from a pony chaise. She was wearing a lovely pink-and-beige day dress with pagoda sleeves, a high neckline and lace collar, and a matching beige hat with a pink floral decoration in front.

Nathan led Regina into the stunning entry area of the museum and then through various galleries, wishing to first show her the massive collection of architectural drawings and small-scale models of great buildings. There was a model of Bramante's Tempietto of San Pietro in Montorio; the top two stories of the façade of Sir Paul Pindar's fifteenth-century house, with elaborately carved woodwork and leaded windows; a fourteenth-century dormer window from the Chateau of Montal; pillars from past great buildings of different periods; and architectural drawings and models by great British and European architects.

Inspecting the drawings inspired Regina to inquire: "Other than your sketches, have you ever created any paintings?"

"Being a good artist is an integral part of an architect's craft. I have to be able to put on paper what a building or a landscape will look like, before it is ever built. The building or landscape is first sketched, then colored and textured with paint. You may recall my telling you that I often did portraits, when I was younger. But I have not painted any portraits in years." Nathan gazed at Regina, studying her face, imagining painting *her* portrait.

As if she were reading his mind, she asked impulsively: "So, if I were to request that you paint my portrait...?" Her subsequent facial reaction showed a twinge of regret at the bold impulsive request.

"I seem to recall you had strong objections to such an undertaking," Nathan responded with a sly smile, reflecting on the sketch he made on his first visit.

"I didn't know then that you were such an accomplished artist."

"You would sit for me now?"

"Only if you promised to make me more beautiful than I am, as you did before."

"I don't think any artist could improve upon your beauty."

"Now I know you are speaking in jest," Regina looked away shyly.

Nathan and Regina continued on through galleries covering the Renaissance, Elizabethan, Jacobean, Restoration and Baroque styles of Tudor and Stuart Britain. They examined the terra-cotta bust of Henry VII dating back to 1510; from the same time period, the heraldic Dacre Beasts, twenty-foot carvings of a bull, a gryphon, a ram and a salmon; Bernini's bust of Thomas Baker; a wood relief of *The Stoning of Stephen*; and carpets, tapestries, and paintings.

There were galleries from Georgian Britain, covering Palladianism, rococo, chinoiserie, neoclassicism, regency, and other styles and influences. In these galleries, they viewed sculptures of Canova, *The Three Graces* and *Sleeping Nymph*; a painting of the Salisbury Cathedral; a lifelike colored-marble sculpture of the Earl of Dudley's dog trampling a snake made of bronze. Nathan shared with Regina his knowledge of various artists, sculptors, and architects as they passed through the priceless art.

Regina interrupted Nathan's exposition. "I have heard such reports of Miss Charlesworth. How are you even able to gaze upon me after being in her resplendent glow?"

Nathan loved the sound of her voice, its cadence and its melody.

"Well, of course I must shield my eyes in her presence, to avoid falling under her spell." Regina playfully hit Nathan.

It isn't far from the truth, he thought.

"I have heard she is quite charming, as well."

"She can be quite charming."

"And she comes from incredible wealth."

"There's no denying that."

"What more could you want in a woman?" Regina asked rhetorically.

"Beauty, charm, and wealth. You are right. I must go at once." Nathan started to get up.

"You're horrid!"

They continued their tour of galleries, next entering those devoted to paintings and drawings. There were thousands of British and other European oil paintings, watercolors, pastels, and miniatures. There were full-scale designs for tapestries in the Sistine Chapel of the lives of Peter and Paul, a fresco by Pietro Perugino, a collection of Spanish tempera on wood. They stood in awe of paintings by British artists Constable, Turner, Blake, Barry, Landseer, Ellison, and their contemporaries. Then it was the French artists who invaded their minds and eyes with paintings by Clouet, Dughet, Boucher, de Troy, Pater, and many others. In front of Carlo Crivelli's Virgin and Child, they finally rested and sat on a wooden bench.

Nathan took Regina's hands in his, following up on their earlier colloquy. "Except, someone else has already stolen my heart."

"What if this thief were to return it to you?" Regina articulated her response carefully, as though she were searching for a tiny crevasse in Nathan's reaction.

"I would never allow *her* to do that."

"Why not?"

"Because the thief would then leave me with a broken heart."

"You had better hope the thief takes good care of it, then."

"I know she will."

Regina stood up and approached the virgin and child for a closer inspection and prayer. With her back turned, Nathan wondered what thoughts were going through her mind.

The next room they entered included reproductions of Italian Renaissance sculpture and architecture. In the shadow of a full-size replica of Michelangelo's David, they sat on a marble bench.

The discussion changed to Nathan's recent evening at the ball with Jocelyn.

"And how does she dance?" Regina inquired.

"She is very accomplished," was all Nathan was willing to offer.

"Is there anything she can't do? And, you? I have yet to have the pleasure of being your partner."

"We should correct that at once," Nathan rose and extended his hand to Regina.

"Here? But there's no music," Regina laughed.

"Who needs music to dance?" and instantly Nathan was serenading Regina, full of laughter, on the floor in a quick waltz step between sculptures. They were the only spectators in the room. A few inches shorter than Jocelyn, Regina moved gracefully in Nathan's arms as they glided effortlessly around the room.

As they were dancing, Nathan spoke: "I have never heard your laughter. It's the sweetest sound I could ever imagine." Her laughter was a paroxysm of unpretentious happiness, unrestrained and free—a celebration of life. After enjoying it once, Nathan wanted to hear it again, again, and again.

"I only laugh when I am deliriously happy."

"So how may I keep you in a state of utter bliss?"

"By surprising me always with tokens of such delight. Then I shall laugh always." Regina's eyes sparkled.

"I must invent ways to surprise you, then." Suddenly, Nathan lifted her up in the air, keeping her suspended for an entire three-step waltz. He was surprised by how light she was. Regina erupted again in spontaneous laughter. Nathan brought her down gently.

"Yes, Nathan. Like that," Regina responded with a rapturous smile.

They continued waltzing until other patrons entered the room.

"You have nothing to worry about," Nathan said in comparing her ballroom skills to Jocelyn's.

"And you are a superb dancing partner, Nathan."

"The sign of a true musician."

Nathan and Regina returned to a nearby marble bench, now in the shadow of Michelangelo's The Slave. As they talked, Nathan became aware of a man on the far side of the room who stole several furtive glances their way. The face reminded him vaguely of the grey-cloaked man he had seen before, except this man was clean-shaven and in much different attire. The man remained in the room longer than other museum patrons and seemed to be paying more interest to them than to the works of art. It must be a coincidence, Nathan thought to himself, when he noted the man's departure moments later.

"I have never met a man like you." Regina interrupted his thoughts. "You have so many talents. Yet, you conduct yourself with such modesty and kindness. Your dear departed mother must be commended for bringing up such a man as you."

Nathan smiled at the compliment, all the more because he knew that Regina was speaking from her heart. It was then his turn to praise her. "And you are unlike any woman I have ever met. The first time I saw your extraordinary eyes, I knew that I had to meet you. Getting to know you has only strengthened my appreciation of your wonderful heart, goodness, and equanimity."

Regina could not hold back from Nathan an adoring look. Nor could she hold back the brilliant glow of her inner beauty as she smiled back at him. At that precise moment, Nathan thought for the first time, *she's truly more beautiful than Jocelyn*. A feeling of utter euphoria swept over Nathan as he allowed himself to fully believe, also for the first time, that Regina might return the same degree of deep affection that had been swelling within him.

Chapter 45

The fifty-eighth season of the Philharmonic Society was ending with a tribute to Beethoven in celebration of the centenary of his birth. The concert programme was highlighted by Beethoven's First and Ninth Symphonies. Other works included the Choral Fantasia, the *Lenore* Overture, "Dervish Chorus" from *The Ruins of Athens*, the powerful terzetto "Tremate, empi tremate," and the dramatic aria, "Ah! Perfido."

Nathan arrived at the Charlesworth estate in the late afternoon. Jocelyn and Nathan, accompanied by Jocelyn's mother, traveled to St. James's Hall on Piccadilly Street in the Charlesworths' elegant gold-plated barouche. The ladies each carried a lilac, which they held at nose level when exiting the carriage, to mask the unpleasant outdoor odor. The Hall's façade stood before them with a Gothic design and enormous arched roof. The interior of the structure was influenced by Florentine architecture, with horseshoe arches reminiscent of the Moorish Palace of the Alhambra. From the ceiling were suspended numerous gas light fixtures, providing excellent lighting as darkness descended.

The Hall held more than two thousand people, with seating distributed between the ground floor, balcony, gallery, and platform. At the rear of the Hall, behind the orchestra, was an organ with immense pipes rising more than thirty feet in the air. Nathan, Jocelyn, and her mother were ushered to reserved seats fifteen rows back on the ground floor, with a superb vision of the performers.

"My dearest Jocelyn, I was hoping you had arranged front row seats, in case Madame Goddard's performance is lacking," Nathan said lightheartedly, reminding her of their exchange from their previous encounter.

"But Nathan, it will be even more dramatic if you rush from *here* to the stage. The audience will be in wonderment as to your actions and the suspense will be breathless. This is a much better location for you."

"I suppose you are right. Well, we shall just have to wait and see."

They settled in the long narrow green upholstered benches for the long concert evening, as the orchestra members were tuning and tightening their instruments. The London elite were on hand, filling every seat in the concert hall.

Soon, the orchestra was ready and the conductor entered the stage to enthusiastic applause. The concert opened with Beethoven's Symphony no. 1.

Midway through the evening, a piano was wheeled out onto the stage, in preparation for Beethoven's Choral Fantasia.

"Are you ready, Nathan?" Jocelyn whispered in Nathan's ear.

Nathan brought his fingers up and began flexing his digits. "Absolutely."

As Madame Arabella Goddard entered from the side, the crowd applauded warmly. Soon she was seated at the piano. Jocelyn playfully poked Nathan. Madame Goddard positioned herself carefully on the bench, gathering herself as she stared straight ahead for a full twenty seconds. The entire building was deathly silent. She then looked at Mr. Cusins, the conductor, and nodded. He nodded back. She gracefully raised her fingers to the keyboard.

Madame Goddard began playing the slow solo introduction with exquisite dynamics, modulating back and forth between C minor and C major. She began to show more flair as the ornamental choral theme was introduced.

Jocelyn glanced at Nathan, with a look that asked: *Is she adequate?*

Nathan smiled back. He was impressed.

Soon, the piano took a respite as variations on the theme were played by flutes, oboes, clarinets, and string instruments. Jocelyn nodded to Nathan with a smile that suggested: *If you're going to replace her, now would be a good time.*

Nathan lurched forward as if he was getting up. Jocelyn was wholly unprepared for his sudden move and instantly put her hand hard on his knee, giving him a stern look. Nathan could barely restrain his laughter.

The full orchestra exploded with the theme and the piano joined shortly. Nathan looked back at Jocelyn helplessly, wiggled his fingers and then putting them in his trouser pockets with a shrug. He'd missed his chance.

The chorus soon entered with sopranos and altos singing the main theme, followed by the tenors and basses, until the entire orchestra and piano rejoined. A *presto* coda with all performers brought the piece to a close. The crowd exploded in thunderous applause. Nathan instantly stood up, clapping heartily. A few others took his cue and stood also, as the crowd continued to applaud and shout. In moments, the entire gallery was standing and cheering.

As the applause died down, Jocelyn looked at Nathan. "She seems to have met your standards."

"I wouldn't go so far as that, but I felt you might be upset with me if I didn't applaud a member of *your sex*." Jocelyn flashed a reprimanding look. Then, in a much more serious tone, he confessed: "She was brilliant."

"I thought so, as well."

Following the Choral Fantasia, there was a thirty-minute intermission. Nathan and Jocelyn walked into the gallery, mingling with the crowd. They were the center of attention, and Nathan again thrilled at having all eyes on him and his escort, knowing that he was the envy of every man and the curiosity of every woman. He felt the thick deep hunger of men standing near, who would sacrifice everything to be where Nathan was. The reactions to first sightings of Jocelyn were memorable: jaws dropping, eyes widening, the observer rustling a friend to share the experience, and the occasional leer of unvarnished lust. Nathan had seen it all before, but it always intrigued and amused him.

I, alone, am with her. Of all the eligible men in England, I am her escort.

Jocelyn draped upon him, leaning toward him frequently and conversing freely.

"You must take my hand and show me more affection," Jocelyn whispered to him, subtly removing her lace glove, as they strolled through the gaping crowd.

Nathan responded as instructed and was surprised to feel the flesh of her left hand for the first time. The warmth of her hand surprised him. The softness of her skin excited him. Her fingers aroused him, as they caressed the top of his hand.

"*Embrasse-moi. Agis comme un homme amoureux.*"[53] Jocelyn spoke to Nathan in a soft seductive tone. Feeling as an actor in a stage play, wanting to perform for the audience, and being *for the moment* in love, he grabbed Jocelyn from behind her waist and twirled her toward him, hugging her tightly.

"Now, kiss me," she whispered.

Despite himself, Nathan felt powerless to resist. He looked into her pleading azure-blue eyes and felt himself being drawn in to her power. Her beauty was at its most intense at close proximity when

---

53   Embrace me. Act as a man in love.

staring directly into her hypnotic eyes. Her lips held the promise of exquisite sensuality. Only inches separated their faces as Nathan stared down at her and lowered his head preparing to touch her lips, all willpower having evaporated.

Before contact was made, they were interrupted by a loud voice: "Miss Charlesworth!" The Duke of Wilmont advanced and sought Jocelyn's hand. "How lovely to see you tonight, Miss Charlesworth."

Jocelyn curtsied. "How do you do, your grace?"

"Never better, now that I have you in view." The Duke then glanced at Nathan and bowed.

Nathan bowed back.

"Permit me to introduce Mister Nathan Sinclair," Jocelyn politely stated, and then acknowledging the Duke to Nathan. "The Duke of Wilmont."

"Will you kindly allow me to borrow your lovely consort for a few minutes?" The Duke inquired of Nathan. Instantly, Jocelyn squeezed Nathan's arm, communicating: *Absolutely not!*

Grasping immediately the message conveyed, Nathan responded with a forced smile: "I must respectfully decline, your grace. I have promised Miss Charlesworth my full attentions this entire evening. And *I never* break a promise."

Stunned by the refusal, the Duke blushed and showed anger. Turning back to Jocelyn, he grabbed her free arm and declared inexorably under his breath, just loud enough for Nathan to hear. "It is scandalous for you to be in public with this man!"

Nathan instantly seized the Duke's hand in a powerful grip, forcing him to relinquish his hold on Jocelyn's arm. The Duke briefly lost his balance twisting halfway around, his mortified face on full display to the gawking concertgoers. Catching himself, he turned back again, ready to engage, but Nathan and Jocelyn had already advanced into the crowd, heading back to their seats as the chime sounded the end of the intermission.

"*Comme c'est galant de ta pars de venir à mon secours.*"[54]

Nathan smiled back, but considered that he had made an enemy.

The concert resumed until Beethoven's Ninth Symphony brought the evening to a dramatic conclusion. The crowd had been treated to a magnificent spectacle, even if the *Athenæum* would later have less than complimentary words to say about the two choral

---

54   How gallant of you to come to my rescue.

works. The weekly publication did, however, reserve praise for Madame Goddard's performance.

When the applause for the finale died down, Nathan and Jocelyn made their way through the large crowd and repaired to their carriage. Once inside, away from the preening crowd, Jocelyn turned to Nathan: "You distinguished yourself well, Mr. Sinclair. We should have all of London believing in our imminent engagement. You were truly wonderful tonight. I felt so proud and protected in your company."

"The pleasure was all mine. And it is you I must thank for the magnificent concert. Hearing the Fantasia was especially memorable."

"So, can you outplay Madame Goddard, Nathan?"

"She was fabulous. I could not have done better."

"How modest of you to so speak. But I would much prefer to hear you play."

"That is quite a compliment," Nathan smiled.

"Could you not have performed the Fantasia?"

"Of course. But she performed it superbly."

"Have you never performed with a full orchestra?" Jocelyn wondered.

"Never... but it has always been a dream of mine to do so some day."

After pausing, Jocelyn continued. "So, which composition would you perform, if you were given a full orchestra to accompany you?"

Nathan played along. "It would definitely be a piano concerto."

"And you have a preference?"

"A difficult choice. I am partial to Chopin, as you know. His Second Concerto is extremely lyrical, although the orchestration is limited. There's always Beethoven and Mozart." Reflecting further, he offered, "But I think I would choose Schumann. It is sublime. It may be my favorite concerto."

"I have never heard it performed."

"I am surprised to hear that. It was performed just a few months ago, before your birthday—here at the Hall. It is a shame we didn't know each other then. I would have loved to have taken you."

"If I had known it was your favorite, I would have certainly gone. Have you ever played it—the piano part?"

Nathan nodded. "I know it well. I have the score."

"Then you must play it for me."

"Someday... I should like to perform it with an orchestra. Now, if you will simply arrange for the orchestra, I shall be delighted to play it for you."

Jocelyn laughed. "So, when may I hear it? How long would it take you to get it ready?"

"Merely a week... or two. It's not technically difficult. I would just need a little time to brush it up."

"I can hardly wait."

***

The anxiety, insecurity, frustration, and anger from several weeks earlier came flooding back. He had been living a hellish existence since Jocelyn's birthday party, when he had seen his rival attached to his bride-to-be. Jocelyn's rejection a few days later, when he had merely attempted to present his extravagant gift, had sent him further into a state of despondency and anxiety. Then tonight, after learning of her plans to attend the concert and seeking her in public, he had been publicly disgraced.

The Duke of Wilmont did not stay for the remainder of the concert, leaving abruptly for his London apartment after the ugly encounter.

"I will destroy him!" he screamed in his apartment, smashing every object within grasp. Now that he had met his rival face to face, he felt more inadequate than ever. He hated the feeling. His rival was handsome; not as handsome as he, but much taller. He cursed his misfortune for having been born of diminutive parents. His rival had placed a vice grip upon him which had caused him to lose his balance. His rival had prevented him from talking with his future bride. He would pay dearly for that!

The Duke was aware of the print rumors, which reported that Sinclair was a member of the English aristocracy. He doubted the veracity of those rumors, having seen past instances of irresponsible journalism before.

He must be investigated. I must find his weakness. Every man has one. Where is Nevius Tucker?

Chapter 46

There was much to do in London for entertainment: theatre, concerts, mesmerism, magicians, minstrel shows, menageries, lectures, dioramas, circuses, magic lantern presentations. It was also an age of musical and artistic enlightenment. Hardly a day went by that Nathan did not hear of another work by a brilliant composer, a work he could hardly wait to hear, learn, and perform. He marveled at the deluge of creativity from all corners of the earth. It seemed to him as if God had touched the minds of the masters, inspiring them to heights never before attained. Nathan at times wondered if subsequent generations would ever fully recognize the remarkable era of which he was part, and if they would appreciate the magical and unforgettable times of the musical renaissance. Nathan felt honored and blessed to be alive during these extraordinary times.

Following the Beethoven concert, Nathan pondered his amazing good fortune. Through Jocelyn, he was living a dreamlike existence. He enjoyed rubbing shoulders with the London gentry. Because of Jocelyn, he was shown respect and even acceptance within that rarefied fraternity, aided by the rumors of nobility she had planted. He had never before dined on such a grand scale. He had never before attended concerts in the best seats. He had never before had such optimism for his business, after experiencing firsthand the power of Jocelyn's influence with London's elite. He also enjoyed being in the spotlight with Jocelyn. She had proven to be an intelligent, spontaneous, and fun companion. He wanted his new existence to continue indefinitely, at the same time longing to begin a new life with his beloved Regina. When his real life resumed and the fantasy ceased, he would look back fondly on the times he spent with Jocelyn, and sorely miss them. When it was over, he would become, once again, an invisible member of London's masses.

In the years to come, with Regina by my side, I shall remind all present how important I once was. I shall regale my disbelieving relations with the names of English gentry I have met and locales I have frequented. Perhaps then, I shall rival Stumbolt in pomposity!

.At night, Nathan went to sleep with such memories and

thoughts. He dreamed of events and experiences that had never crossed his psyche before. So far, he had profited well from Jocelyn's *proposition*; the new commission from Lefontaine had removed his financial gloom and allowed him to display his creative genius. He had even received a couple of small assignments from new clients who had learned of him through the London press. *His star was on the rise*, thanks to her. He relished the afternoons and occasional evenings when he lost himself in the world of music on the Charlesworths' Steinway, performing on an instrument envied by the world's greatest pianists.

Every morning held the promise of such excitement, such intrigue. He never knew what prominent member of the London gentry he might encounter during his frequent trips to the Charlesworth estate. He had already talked with several who had expressed an interest in his work. Could today be the day that he received the commission of his dreams? Could today be the day that transformed his life forever? Never had he felt such vigor in his work. The Lefontaine project had been an assignment that he would never have imagined possible at this stage in his career. He thrilled to watch it slowly taking shape. Moreover, Monsieur Lefontaine had now become another ambassador for his career, unable to contain his pleasure and delight at Nathan's genius.

It was all so intoxicating. He even wondered, one idle night, if there was a need to rush his romance with Regina. But his heart told him otherwise. He could not deny that he would forsake his new bewitching glamorous world to have the angelic Regina by his side, as his life's companion. He would never lose sight of the true path for which his life was destined.

***

Intrigued that it was Nathan's favorite piano concerto, Jocelyn had asked Nathan to bring the Schumann score on his next visit. Wanting to perform some samples from the concerto for her, Nathan played through the entire concerto several times in advance; he had mastered it several years earlier, and it came back to him more easily than expected.

He returned to the Charlesworth estate for his customary Friday evening visit. When he descended to the music room, he was surprised to see Jocelyn already waiting for him. Normally, she listened nearby, frequently from a balcony above out of sight, waiting until his concert had ended. When she saw he had the Schumann concerto score with him, her smile expressed exquisite delight.

"I have been so looking forward to hearing it. If you consider it your favorite, then it must be indescribably beautiful."

"I hope you will find it that way, as well. But, you do understand that it will be difficult to convey the full beauty of this work without the accompaniment of a full orchestra. Perhaps it will be performed in a coming concert and we can attend."

"That would be wonderful. I should love to go with you. But, please, may I hear you play it now? I have been anxious to hear it since you mentioned your preference."

Nathan sat down at the piano. Jocelyn stood next to him. "Let me, at least, turn the pages for you."

Nathan appreciated the favor, since he had not committed the entire piece to memory.

Before he began, Jocelyn spoke. "I'm imagining that we are in a concert hall before a thousand spectators, and you are the concert pianist."

Nathan adjusted the bench and took a deep breath as he contemplated the music he was about to perform. "Now, I shall play both the piano part and orchestral part, where possible. Where they overlap, I will endeavor to play as much of the orchestra's part as I can, so you can better appreciate the full concerto."

"No, Nathan. I want only to hear the piano part. I can read music well enough to imagine what the orchestration will sound like from the score itself."

"You read music *that well*?"

"That should not surprise you. *You know* how important music is to me."

Nathan nodded, and exercised his fingers slightly. He, too, tried to imagine that he was in a concert hall and closed his eyes for a few seconds, rehearsing in his mind the opening stanza that he was about to play—he wanted to perform the composition flawlessly for Jocelyn. The concerto was not rigorous; it required no great stamina and strength; it had its challenges, but those were related more to rhythm than prowess. He needed no warm-up. He observed, with mild surprise, the excitement evident on Jocelyn's face.

Nathan pondered the music, the key, the tempo, and the dynamics for a few moments, then raised his hands above the keyboard to begin. In his mind, he imagined the initial strike by strings and timpani, and then contact was made by his fingers on the gleaming white ivory keys as he executed the turbulent, descending solo attack of the piano.

As he played the final chords of the introductory passage, he was suddenly startled by the accompaniment of music from the balcony above. The orchestra's part was being played by what sounded like a full orchestra. Nathan was in shock. Jocelyn was laughing.

"You must not stop," she said, with a look of intense delight as the oboe and wind instruments introduced the opening theme. *"They are expecting you* to continue."

And continue Nathan did. He took over the theme with the piano. As the movement transitioned to the middle section in a harmonically remote key, the piece showed off its fantasia genesis as Nathan produced a frenetic piano cascade. It was otherworldly, having an invisible orchestra from above. Yet the orchestra was so close that the sound of the music was nearly on top of him, and he had little difficulty finding his cues and keeping in perfect rhythm. Then came the recapitulation, with a muting and slowing of the music. Nathan followed with an ornamental solo cadenza until the orchestra joined to close the movement with a quick coda.

The relaxed mood of the intermezzo followed the first movement, providing a wonderful contrast to the grandeur of the opening episode. Nathan and the strings from above engaged in a colloquy, joined then by the wind instruments. Nathan relaxed somewhat in the less-demanding movement, savoring the lyrical cello solo that preceded the final movement.

It was such a powerful and unexpected experience that Nathan felt intensely emotional as he continued to perform. He struggled mightily to maintain his composure, not wishing to have his view of the score blurred by tears. He had fantasized about such an experience many times, but never imagined it would ever happen. And it was happening now. He was living his dream. In the finale, Nathan announced the joyful main theme in A major, closely related to the opening movement's motif, although livelier this time. The most difficult piano part was on the horizon, in the form of a deliciously syncopated rhythm. He discharged his task well and the orchestra followed. Finally, a long coda brought the inspiring movement to its conclusion.

Thirty minutes after he had begun, he sounded the final chords of the concerto and immediately heard cheers from on high. The musicians leaned over the balustrade to peer down at the pianist, applauding and tapping the tops of their instruments with their bows and batons. Nathan was overcome with gratitude, his eyes moist with tears, bowing time and time again, placing his hand on his heart and extending his hand upward. With tears covering her face, Jocelyn came over and embraced him, clinging to him tightly, not wanting to be released. There were no words capable of expressing the preternatural moment they had shared.

When, at last, there was release from the long embrace, Nathan conveyed his heartfelt gratitude, not with words, but with his eyes: *How can I ever thank you?*

When he finally spoke, his first words came from his heart: "I truly never imagined such an experience during my lifetime."

"You shall have it again... and next time in a concert hall. It was so beautiful!"

Overcome, Nathan drew Jocelyn close again, kissing her forehead, his lips lingering on the delicacy of her skin.

The orchestra members and conductor joined them for dinner afterwards in the opulent Charlesworth dining room. During dinner, all conversed freely. Nathan learned that members of the society had arrived a couple of hours before, setting up music stands and chairs in the large circular balcony above the music room and rehearsing until his arrival. Having recently performed the concerto, the members of the orchestra needed little rehearsal. The conductor had easily followed Nathan's lead at the piano and the performance went off without let or hindrance.

Nathan received glowing praises for his impromptu performance and was encouraged to affiliate with the Philharmonic. One member told Nathan that he preferred his lyrical interpretation and dexterity over the cleverness of Madame Auspitz-Kolar, who had been the society's soloist in May.

Later that night, after the society members had departed, Nathan could hardly suppress his gratitude to Jocelyn. "However were you able to bring this amazing surprise together? The cost alone must have been staggering."

"In truth, it cost nothing. I merely sent a letter to the Director of the Society asking what would be required to arrange for such an event, explaining the circumstances. Since they had recently performed the composition, he assured me by return post, it would not be a problem."

"And they consented... just like that?"

"Yes. Perhaps it was aided by my beautiful penmanship or the infallible selection of words in my request." Jocelyn expressed her comments with a modest smile.

"Or your beauty and celebrity."

"That too."

"It must be extraordinary to wield such power."

"Oh, it is. I merely go around London asking for what I may and my every desire is granted." Jocelyn laughed. "I feel like a daughter of the Queen."

"I suspect you live far better than *her* daughters do."

"*Je suppose que tu as raison.*"[55] After a pause, she continued. "But, I must confess... it probably has *something* to do with my father. He is, after all, one of the largest benefactors of the Philharmonic. As you know, the society has performed at our home before. In his reply, the director simply asked for the day and hour to arrive. Nothing more."

"Well, thanks to your wonderful kindness and consideration, I have had an experience I will relive for the rest of my life. I shall never forget it."

"If we ever married," Jocelyn winked shyly, "we would have to replace our servants with musicians."

"A capital idea!" Nathan smiled. "Can you imagine being serenaded every night?"

"I fear you would have to start writing your own concertos."

"I plan to... some day." He remembered the triumphant movement he had been inspired to compose after his liberation from Coldbath Fields. *Perhaps I shall begin with that.*

"And you must promise to perform them for me when you do, whatever our circumstances may be."

"I promise."

"You should never make a promise you cannot keep," Jocelyn gave a wistful look.

---

55   I suspect that you are right.

Chapter 47

On midsummer's eve, dinner was about to be served at the Lancasters'. All of the Lancaster children were fully grown and married, living their own independent and busy lives — all except Estelle, the youngest. Estelle was four years younger than Regina and had recently returned from an extended stay with relatives in the northern part of England. All her life, Estelle had been unusually sociable, never hesitating to strike up a conversation with a total stranger even when she was barely old enough to speak. She had a disarming openness and honesty that permeated all she did; sometimes, her candor raised eyebrows and offense, although none was ever intended. She had a childlike beauty to her, despite her eighteen years. Regina had been an older sister to her since her earliest reminiscences.

When orphaned at eight years of age, Regina had immediately become an accepted and cherished member of their family. During the first months when she had come to live with them, when Regina had been withdrawn, despondent, and angry, there had been nothing but love and caring from the Lancasters. In large part due to their love and attention, she had eventually been able to put the terrible tragedy behind her, and had proven to be a remarkable young woman of depth, character, purity, charity, and service. Regina had never taken her adopted family for granted, and when she had reached her teenage years, she vowed that she would devote her life to helping other lost children find new families, too. She had never forsaken her calling and had been the beneficiary of great joy for the service she performed.

Regina sat in her room before dinner, pondering the recent changes in her life. She had never imagined meeting a man like Nathan. She had never truly reflected on love and romance. That was something *other* people experienced. In her world of gratitude and service, her greatest happiness was savoring vicariously the undefinable happiness of a young child gaining a happy home, and the corresponding delight of the new parents. Now, she had come to realize that there could be more to life than joy in the service she performed. At the same time, it was a blessedness in which she knew she could never partake.

Regina descended from her bedchamber to the dining room. Already seated were Sir Lancaster, Aunt Hélène, and Estelle. With Estelle's recent return, there were now four seated for dinner, instead of three. Regina sat at her customary seat and smiled at the others as the first course was served. Her contemplative mood vanished when her aunt first spoke.

"Regina, dear. What are these reports of Mr. Sinclair being in the company of a Miss Jocelyn Charlesworth? Could there be any truth to such rumors?"

"They are all true." Regina responded without hesitation or emotion, but inwardly she felt awkward at the inquiry.

"But, I don't understand. He has been a regular guest here, and yet he is in the company of another woman?" Aunt Hélène expressed consternation.

"Perhaps I, too, overestimated our Mr. Sinclair," Sir Lancaster conceded.

"No, please do not think any less of him, dear uncle."

I knew this would surface eventually. I had intended to tell my aunt and uncle before they learned from another source.

Regina felt herself blushing and struggled to find words to explain the unconventional liaison, but Estelle interrupted Regina before she could continue. "Oh, mother, it is such an intrigue. They are just friends, but Mr. Sinclair is playing the role of Miss Charlesworth's lover, to keep her suitors at bay."

"And why ever would he do that?" Aunt Hélène raised her eyebrow.

Estelle continued. "Because, she must devote such time to declining introductions and proposals of marriage. She has introduced him to society to help him with his business. He has already received a fabulous new commission."

"And he has *carte blanche* to perform on the Charlesworths' new piano—I have been told it is a marvel! A Steinway just delivered from New York," Regina felt obliged to add further justification to the arrangement, although when expressed in words it seemed so hollow.

"It sounds like *our* Mr. Sinclair is playing with fire." The explanation didn't satisfy Sir Lancaster.

"He was quite reluctant to participate in the arrangement," Regina confided, doing her best to rehabilitate Nathan's character. "In fact, he wanted none of it. It was I who insisted he pursue it. Such an alliance will surely help his career. In fact, it already has. He just received a lucrative new project from a friend of the Charlesworths'."

"Why, dear niece, I am surprised you would countenance such deceit. It isn't like you," Aunt Hélène persisted.

"In truth, there is no deceit on his part. He is merely befriending Miss Charlesworth. The London press may suggest otherwise, but he makes no pretense of anything other than friendship."

"But to be seen in public with another woman..."

"It's a small price to pay, if Mr. Sinclair is so handsomely rewarded in business. And it is only for a short time," Regina explained.

"Don't you fear that he might succumb to the wiles of the handsome Miss Charlesworth over time? I have heard her beauty is beyond compare."

"He may be the *one man* who can resist her charms." Though Regina spoke the words with conviction, she wondered if it were true.

Aunt Hélène shook her head. "Regina, goodness knows you can decide whom you wish to see. We would never stand in your way. But, you must be very careful. Being seen with him could be scandalous for you, while he is reported to be courting another woman."

"Yes, my dear aunt. We have agreed to be quite discreet."

There was soon a change in topic at the dinner table, but Regina's feeling of discomfort lingered on.

Chapter 48

The Duke anxiously awaited the arrival of Nevius Tucker. It had been five years since Tucker had left Scotland Yard in disgrace, following allegations that he had accepted graft to destroy evidence in a high-profile case. The allegations had never been proven, but the Duke assumed they had been true, based upon his dealings with the man. Tucker was a man to be trusted, *if* the pay was right. A man who invariably produced results, *if* the pay was right. During the past couple years, the roguish Tucker had been useful in collecting rent from delinquent tenants and helpful in sniffing out embarrassing secrets of other members of the gentry who crossed him or to whom he owed gambling debts. It was surprising how easy the threatened disclosure of a mistress could eliminate even an exceedingly large note. Tucker had served him well, but he knew that if didn't keep him employed, he might find himself on the receiving end of similar skullduggery.

Tucker entered the Duke's library. He had traveled extensively throughout Europe and could acquit himself well in the prominent European languages. He was a mercenary of average height, average weight, average looks, and average age—a chameleon, who changed his appearance and loyalty as easily as the weather. The Duke examined him as he entered. *The last time I saw him, he had a beard and mustache; now he is clean-shaven.* He remembered a grey cloak the last visit; now it was black.

"Have you any news?"

"It seems that your Mr. Sinclair is seeing another woman, your grace," Tucker began.

The Duke was elated at the disclosure, but also surprised. One would think a man seeing Jocelyn Charlesworth would not require the company of another woman. He wanted to hear more.

"Your source?"

"My own eyes. He was seated with a woman at the South Kensington Museum, in one of the sculpture halls... showing great interest in her."

"Your definition of 'great interest' is exactly what?"

"The look on his face... and her face... they were more than just friends."

"Describe her to me."

"Dark hair, early twenties. Dressed well, comes from money."

"Pretty?"

"No, I wouldn't call her that. Adequate, I suppose."

Merely adequate looks? The Duke frowned. It didn't make sense to him that Sinclair would be seeing a woman of just *adequate* appearance. If he could attract Jocelyn Charlesworth, he should have little difficulty finding other handsome women. It may not be what he was hoping for.

"Did you observe them holding hands, embracing, touching...?"

"No, your grace."

"How long did you observe them?"

"Long enough."

"You were discreet, I hope," the irritated Duke muttered, concerned that a surveillance of that close proximity was reckless. Tucker refused to dignify the insulting implication.

"Did you follow the lady?"

"I endeavored to, but when she suddenly boarded a fly, I was unable to catch her in time."

"You imbecile! That was your chance. You may not get another."

Tucker shrugged his shoulders. "Perhaps you should shadow her yourself, your grace."

"I need her name... where she lives. Do you understand?"

"That will cost you fifty more pounds." His price was going up. A year ago a similar assignment would have cost half that.

The Duke pulled out a fifty-pound note from his wallet, tendering it to Tucker without releasing it. "I had better see some results... and fast."

Tucker smiled, yanking the bill out of the Duke's hands. The Duke paid well.

***

Roderick Charlesworth rarely cast his shadow at the Charlesworth estate. It was simply not as convenient as his London apartment. He preferred being close to his circle of reprobates and the private gambling parlor. Tonight had been no exception. He had indulged in his favorite passions of drinking and gambling, but his luck had deserted him early on. Furthermore, he had reason to see Jocelyn—the Duke had made a special request. Roderick knew his sister. This latest revelation would do the trick. If ever there could be a *woman scorned*, his sister would be the prime example of that, with her turbulent temper. The Duke would be pleased to know his rival would soon be history.

Jocelyn was in the south sitting room reading, when Roderick entered the Charlesworth compound.

"My dear... dearest sister," Roderick bent over and greeted Jocelyn, kissing her on the cheek.

"Lord Roderick—you are drunk!"

"A few drinks, my dear sister... merely my usual allotment," his words slurred together, as he took a seat next to her.

"You should be in bed."

"Soon enough, dear sister... soon enough. And... your... Prince Charming. How is he doing?"

Jocelyn simply shook her head and looked away.

"Is he behaving himself?" Roderick continued.

"Far better than you, I'm certain. Don't you have some skirt to chase, or wager to make?" Jocelyn shot back with a sadistic expression.

"Do you know where... what he's doing... tonight?"

"It's none of your concern."

"Oh, I think it just might be," Roderick volunteered. "Shall I... tell you where he is?"

"I have no interest in talking to you in your frightful condition," Jocelyn refused to proffer even a look at her brother.

"He's with another lady."

"Keep your comments to yourself, *dear* brother," Jocelyn closed her book and started to get up.

Roderick leaned over to Jocelyn and grabbed her wrist, speaking in a low controlled voice. "You will hear... what I have to say!"

"You are hurting me."

Roderick kept his grip. "He's cheating on you... and you care not."

"Hold your peace!" Jocelyn screamed, as she wriggled her hand free.

"A lady with dark hair. Not at all attractive. Apparently, he's not a discerning man. At the South Kensington Museum... kissing... holding hands... such a tender scene..."

"I don't believe you." Jocelyn's eyes began to tear.

"Not yet engaged and he's already seeing another lady... thought you should know... just trying to protect you, *sister*." Roderick staggered briefly as he walked away.

"Protect me? Protect yourself! Stay out of my affairs!" shouted a visibly upset Jocelyn after him.

Roderick laughed loudly as he left the room. He had planted a seed of doubt in his sister's mind; she had reacted. The Duke would be grateful.

***

The following day, Nathan traveled to the Charleston estate for a routine visit. He migrated to the music room, as was his custom. He began playing Bizet's melancholy F Major Nocturne, with long flowing arpeggios alternating between the major and minor key, soon followed by Beethoven's dramatic *Pathétique* Sonata.

Roderick Charlesworth was in his bedchamber, rousing from the previous night's extended slumber, the prolonged sleep further induced by the claret consumed in his room after his encounter with Jocelyn. Although his room was high above the music room, he could discern the powerful first movement of the Beethoven sonata being played below.

Good God, is that him *below? Not for long, I'm sure. Once Jocelyn confronts him with his infidelity, she will crush him with her titanic temper. I almost pity him. This should be interesting to observe.*

Roderick put on his tunic, brushed his hair quickly, exited his room on the third floor, and walked onto the indoor balcony overlooking the music room. Far below, he saw the pianist playing. Jocelyn would undoubtedly arrive momentarily.

I can't wait for the fireworks!

Nathan moved on to the second movement of the sonata.

Damn, can that man play! Roderick was struck by the music he heard. *No wonder she has fallen for him! Where the bloody hell is she?* Roderick thought to himself impatiently. *She would have heard him by now. What is she waiting for?*

After enduring the second and third movements of the sonata, he gave up.

Apparently, she won't even acknowledge his presence. That may be better. Roderick snickered as he reentered his chamber for further slumber.

Shortly after Roderick's return to his room, Lady Charlesworth entered the music room below, where she sat quietly on a deeply-cushioned chair nearby, not wishing to disturb Nathan midway through Dobrzynski's D-flat Major Nocturne. Nathan sensed that she wanted to talk, causing him to pause and look her way when he had finished.

"That was lovely, Mr. Sinclair. My daughter is not feeling well this afternoon and sends her regrets for not being able to descend to hear you play."

"I pray it is nothing serious, my lady." Nathan studied her face. There was a strong resemblance between mother and daughter, although Lady Charlesworth's angular features were not as soft as Jocelyn's, nor was her hair as luminous as her daughter's. Nevertheless, for a woman turning fifty, she was still quite beautiful.

"Nothing of concern, really. But, I have been looking forward to talking with you. I know how much she enjoys your company and loves to hear you perform. But, please be gentle with her. She has been sheltered and protected all her life and still has much to learn. She is really just a child in many respects, despite her age." Lady Charlesworth's Swedish accent gave her words an exotic flair.

"Lady Charlesworth," Nathan responded benignantly. "I assume you know that Miss Charlesworth and I are merely friends. I would never presume to trifle with her feelings in such a way."

"As she also reassures me. All women envy the beauty of my daughter. But beauty can be a curse as well. Similar to wealth and rank, it attracts the least desirable of men... I know from personal experience. In my daughter's case, she is cursed with all three gifts. As her mother, I must be on guard against unworthy, designing men, who seek to possess her for all the wrong reasons."

"You have nothing to fear from me," Nathan offered in a tender voice and regard.

"No, you are not clever and cunning like the others. You appear to be a man of probity. *Now* you are just friends. But prolonged togetherness can breed affection. Few men have the capacity to withstand the beauty and charm of my daughter, if exposed to her for any length of time."

Nathan paused, wondering if he should tell Lady Charlesworth more.

"Do not worry about breaking a confidence. Jocelyn keeps nothing from me. Unlike many mothers of privilege, I have always been very close to my daughter and know her better than she does herself. I know her purpose in seeing you—and I heartily approve. My husband would not, but that is another matter. I also know there is another woman in your life. But affections can change over time. She is comfortable in your presence and looks forward, very much, to your visits. Already she is opening up to you far more than she has to anyone outside our intimate circle. You must promise me never to harm her, never to betray her..."

"I am quite in love with another woman..."

"Then, be on your guard that you never signal anything more than friendship to Jocelyn. I fear that in your company, she may unknowingly open up the tender layers of her heart and may find herself developing an affection that was never intended. When you turn away from her, as you must someday soon, she may feel such exquisite agony that her heart will turn to stone and never be revived. For the man she cherishes one day, she will radiate like the noonday sun. But, if her heart is ever broken, her sun may never shine. Despite her beauty and poise, she is just a tender, fragile flower yearning to bloom, while fearing to wither and die."

Lady Charlesworth wasn't finished. Looking Nathan squarely in the eyes, she said in slow and steady voice, "One more thing, Mr. Sinclair. Beware of my husband. If Lord Charlesworth were ever to believe that you were romantically attached to our daughter, the consequences would be dire. He holds such lofty expectations for Jocelyn. Nothing less than a king's son will merit his approbation. Be on your guard. If ever you incur his wrath, the world will not be large enough for you to hide. He has ruined men far greater than you for a simple affront."

Nathan shivered.

When Lady Charlesworth left, Nathan admonished himself to be watchful as he resumed playing, moving on to Wölfl's Piano Sonata in C Minor. As he performed, he pondered the Jocelyn he had come to know. It did not comport with the portrait her mother had painted. Jocelyn was whimsical, highly intelligent, and at times exhibited a maturity far beyond her years, while at other times her behavior was quite puerile. But he had never observed or sensed the fragility of which her mother spoke.

Chapter 49

Roderick sent word to the Duke that he had informed Jocelyn of Nathan's betrayal. He invited the Duke to dinner without consulting Jocelyn or any of the household staff. With the architect out of the way, Jocelyn would be receptive to the Duke's advances. A woman jilted often sought revenge against her lover by seeing another man. He had been on the receiving end of such conduct himself. His ownership of Atherton Gardens depended on his sister reacting similarly.

The Duke was delighted at the invitation, but even more pleased that his surveillance had paid off. All afternoon, he perfected his appearance. His jacket and trousers had been pressed, along with his cape. A new shave and an abundance of cologne would make him irresistible. His trembling had finally stopped. He felt at ease. He felt the same calm and suavité that came to him so easily with women. Jocelyn had been the lone exception, but tonight that would change. Staring at himself in the mirror for the tenth time, he smiled at his striking looks. Yes, things would be different from this day forward. He would soon take possession of England's most precious jewel.

On the ride over, the Duke reminisced about the cherished moments he had spent with Jocelyn when she had been a young girl. He recalled her delight at the trinkets he dispensed to her on each visit and her sitting on his lap, once placing her arms around his neck. He remembered going for walks with her in the back gardens of the Charlesworth estate where Jocelyn had told him how handsome he was. He had returned the favor by telling her she was going to grow into the most beautiful woman in all the world. He had been right. As she grew older, however, she had stopped sitting on his lap and had shown less interest in conversing with him. During the last couple of years before her studies in Paris, she had become moody and far less animated at his arrival.

He remembered Jocelyn at fourteen years of age, just before her departure. Already a young woman, he had been irremediably smitten by her beauty. While she had been gone, he had thought of her often, imagining what an extraordinary young lady she would be when he saw her again. He had been electrified when he had first laid eyes upon her after the four-year hiatus. In fact, she had been so incredibly captivating that he had discovered a seizure of tongue—an inability to speak to her without stammering, and then, regretting every infantile comment. As handsome and polished as he was, she had dismantled his easy confidence with women and made him feel inadequate in her presence.

***

Roderick had not seen Jocelyn since the evening of his disclosure. He had been told that she had not been feeling well. That was surely a good sign. The disclosure had affected her far more than she had let on. She had even snubbed Sinclair when he had come to the estate a couple of days before. Maybe that was more effective than one of her tantrums. Just ignoring him and refusing to descend for him. Perfect! She should be well enough to join them for dinner tonight. The Duke's visit would be a surprise to all; he would arrive just after dinner started. Decorum would require he be invited in to dine. It would be like old times, *before* Jocelyn left for Paris. He looked forward to her reaction at the Duke's arrival, now that Sinclair's infidelity had been exposed.

***

Jocelyn did descend for dinner. Roderick expected to see remnants of tears and crying, but none were present.

Well, she has recovered quickly. Maybe her attachment to the architect wasn't that strong, after all.

Roderick looked her way, but she refused to look back.

She is angry with me for having been the bearer of bad tidings. So be it. She shall forgive me soon enough.

The first course of the dinner arrived. The servants brought white soup, boiled salmon in shrimp sauce with dressed cucumbers, along with baked bullets in paper cases. While Jocelyn was partaking of the salmon, the butler entered the dining room.

"The Duke of Wilmont has arrived and sends his compliments."

Those dining expressed surprise, particularly Roderick. Jocelyn's reaction was not what he was expecting. "How insolent of him to visit without an invitation!"

"My dear sister," Roderick responded. "The Duke is my dearest friend. He needs no invitation."

"He has offended me!" Jocelyn's voice crescendoed defiantly. She rose from her seat and stared menacingly at her brother. She could tell from his guilty look that he had arranged for the visit. She screamed at him: "How dare you!"

Failing miserably at his attempt to maintain an appearance of innocence, Roderick responded, "We dare not offend the Duke."

"To *hell* with you and your Duke!" She picked up her wine glass, and in a fit of rage, flung it at her brother. The glass barely missed, but the wine did not. She ran from the dining room before Roderick could utter another word. He picked up a cloth napkin and dried the wine from his neck, face, and tunic.

Now what do I do?

Roderick was more worried about the Duke's insult than the drops that had stained his tunic. He raced after Jocelyn. She was already ascending the steps to her room in a rush. He gulped up steps three at a time in his haste to catch her. When he reached the floor of her chamber, he heard her door slam shut and the lock bolted.

Roderick pounded on the door. "Sister! Open the door! You will offend the Duke! He wishes to see you!" No sooner had he spoken than he heard a large object forcefully hitting the door and crashing to the floor, followed by another and yet another in rapid succession.

"He is a Duke of England, damn it! You cannot turn your back on a Duke!"

Jocelyn screamed from inside the door, "Toast your blooming eyebrows!" with such intensity and volume that Roderick winced and knew it was useless to continue trying.

Defeated, Roderick walked down the winding staircase wondering what excuse he would tell his friend. The truth would only enrage him. And Roderick would bear the brunt of that anger, after having invited him all the way from his castle to woo a supposedly pliant Jocelyn.

A pliant Jocelyn, my eye! She must still be in love with that excrement. I can't tell the Duke that.

Gathering his thoughts, Roderick put on a brave face and made his way into the entry area where the Duke was impatiently pacing back and forth, with a bouquet of flowers in hand.

"Why are you making me wait here *like a servant*?!" The Duke demanded indignantly in an angry voice, his face full of rage.

"A thousand apologies, your grace," Roderick humbly responded. "My sister has taken ill. I was at her room, entreating her to come down, but she is too weak. She sends her respects."

"Truly?" the Duke's eyes lit up.

Roderick nodded. "Oh yes, your grace. I am sure she would like very much to see you."

The Duke breathed a sigh of relief. "So, she is truly over the architect?"

"If you had seen her reaction the other night, you would not be asking such a question." *A white lie won't hurt.*

"Excellent. You must inform me the moment her health is restored. It is imperative that I see her face," the Duke demanded.

Roderick nodded dutifully. "You will join us for dinner, of course."

"Not without your sister," the Duke responded coolly.

The Duke took leave. On his ride home he thought: *She sends her respects.* He smiled. That was enough. *She will send me more than that, the next time I see her.* He tossed the bouquet of flowers out the carriage window and wondered why Lord Roderick had wine stains on his tunic.

Chapter 50

The following week, Nathan and Jocelyn had arranged another appearance in public, this time at the Vaudeville Theatre, where they had premier seats for the performance of *The Two Roses*. Nathan arrived at the Charlesworth home at the appointed hour in the early evening of a warm summer's day. He waited patiently in the entry area for Jocelyn. It wasn't like her to keep him waiting. It had been nearly two weeks since he had last seen her, inasmuch as she had been ill on his last visit.

Perhaps she's still not feeling well, Nathan thought. He felt a pang of disappointment that their evening out might be canceled, and regret at missing Jocelyn's beauty and charm.

Ten minutes later, he heard footsteps descending from the upper left staircase and looked up to see Jocelyn. Her eyes were staring down, away from Nathan. There was no smile on her face; this surprised Nathan, because in the past she had always shown delight at his presence. Her countenance held a tight, controlled regard, with no emotion. However, her beauty was not the least diminished, enhanced by the ravishing beige satin evening gown with a garland of pink roses and lace.

"Good evening, Jocelyn," Nathan greeted her with a bow and smile.

She curtsied and flashed a brief factitious smile, making eye contact with Nathan for just a moment.

Nathan felt a chill. "My dear Jocelyn, is something the matter?"

Jocelyn gave a quick shrug, keeping her eyes away from Nathan.

"We can go to the theatre another time, if you prefer,"

Jocelyn responded in a cold tone, as her gaze returned to Nathan briefly. "No, I am well enough. Let us depart." Rather than taking his arm, as she had in the past, she continued toward the front door on her own. Nathan followed behind, perplexed at her behavior.

They boarded one of the fashionable Charlesworth curricles. On the trip to the theatre, Jocelyn remained taciturn and her gaze was fixated on the scenery outside the carriage. Nathan made several attempts at conversation, but received only monosyllabic replies. They sat quietly in awkward silence for more than fifteen minutes, hearing only the whinnies and snorts of the horses and the grinding of the carriage wheels underfoot on cobblestone streets. Jocelyn rarely made eye contact, and when she did, she just glanced at Nathan for an instant and then turned away.

Have I already fallen out of favor with her? Nathan wondered. He had a painful flashback to his first encounter with Jocelyn.

"Please Jocelyn, tell me. Is there something troubling you?" Nathan finally inquired.

"I'm concerned that my *proposition* is not proceeding as planned." Jocelyn responded sternly. Nathan gave a curious look.

"Were you at South Kensington Museum recently?" she continued.

Nathan felt his privacy invaded and hesitated. "I was. But how would you know that?"

"And in the company of another woman?"

"Yes." The line of inquiry felt awkward to him.

"My brother is apparently having you followed. Last week, he confronted me with news of your visit to the museum... *and* your companion."

Nathan instantly thought of the grey-cloaked man. "I remember a man inside, who seemed to take an unusual interest in us." Nathan related the earlier incident in the street and the gallery.

"He said the woman had dark hair."

"That is correct."

"Was it *her*?"

"It was."

"I was told you were making quite a scene. Holding hands, kissing and fawning all over her." Jocelyn's face distorted into an unpleasant scowl.

Nathan started laughing nervously. "Surely you jest! In public, with museum patrons looking on?"

Jocelyn was not amused. "Is it wise for you to be seen in public with her, while you are 'courting' me?"

Embarrassed, Nathan nodded. "You are right. I must take care..."

"You must be discreet. If you are seen *making love* to another woman, our *liaison* may come into question. It could prove embarrassing for all, including your lady friend."

"That would not do well." Nathan thought of Regina being scandalized.

"Nathan, I know you're in love with another woman, but it undermines our spectacle if you do not play your part in public."

Nathan nodded slowly. She was right.

"Have I not done my part?" Jocelyn asked plaintively.

"You have... and *how well* you have." Nathan thought of the Lefontaine commission and felt as though he had let Jocelyn down. "Please forgive me. You have my word that I shall exercise excessive discretion in the future."

The carriage reached its destination. The Vaudeville was set behind two houses on the Strand. Jocelyn and Nathan exited a street adjacent to the houses, passing a large crowd forging toward the main entrance. To attract London's elite, the theatre had separate entrances for the expensive boxes, so that the upper class could avoid mingling with the lower. Entrance was made through narrow corridors, leading to the boxes where they would be viewing the play. The theatre seated over a thousand guests, but in a confined space. The interior was decorated in a Romanesque style, with a fan-shaped paneled ceiling and innovative concealed gas footlights. Four levels of patrons filed into the horseshoe-shaped auditorium.

Nathan instantly became aware that all eyes were upon Jocelyn and him, as they exited the carriage. Jocelyn's expression instantly changed. He had never seen her more serious or somber than in the ride over, but now suddenly she was magnifying a loving regard toward Nathan and smiling at all the onlookers.

She can change moods in the blink of an eye, Nathan thought to himself.

Nathan found all the attention intoxicating. It was an exhilarating feeling, being respected and revered as *part* of the English gentry.

Their box was just above the gallery, offering both excellent views of the stage, and privacy. The chairs were superbly appointed with soft stuffed cushions. Narrow tables were set against the box walls; one supported a silver receptacle full of ice and a bottle of wine, with two crystal wine glasses; the other had a white china vase filled with red roses. *How fitting,* Nathan thought, since the play was entitled *The Two Roses.*

So, this is how London's elite live.

The comedy began. Henry Irving, an up-and-coming play-actor, assumed the role of Digby Grant, a man of good family, but mean-spirited and shifty. Grant had two daughters who were referred to as the "Two Roses" by their two male suitors. Of the suitors, one was blind. The suitors did their best to minister to the needs of the father, who wished the marriages to occur without delay so that he might profit thereby. During the play, a visitor arrived, informing Grant that he would soon be heir to a huge fortune, provided the appearance of another person did not manifest. The suitors, formerly welcome, were summarily dismissed by Grant, who no longer had need for their money, and expected his daughters to now marry in a much higher stratum. During much of the play, Grant contrived to make everyone miserable, including his daughters and the suitors, who remained still very much in love. Finally, as the play neared its climax, the blind suitor was discovered to be the missing heir to the fortune, and the father's consent to the matches was soon forthcoming, to the delight of the audience.

"Which rose am I?" Jocelyn asked afterward.

"Pardon me?"

"There are two roses in your life, are there not?"

Nathan made the connection and responded. "You are the rose of unparalleled beauty, who has just bloomed in the prime of life. Everyone wants to possess you."

"But it is the other rose with the intoxicating fragrance," lamented Jocelyn, hinting at Regina's great inner beauty.

Nathan selected a single rose from the vase nearby and pulled it carefully from the bouquet. The rose was in full bloom and Nathan put it to his nose, taking a prolonged smell of its delicious fragrance. He handed the rose to Jocelyn. "Oh, your fragrance is quite provocative."

She accepted the rose and smiled politely.

And you are the blind man.

On the return home, Jocelyn spirits were much improved from before. "It must be so titillating to be an actor on stage."

"I should think it would be rather intimidating, especially before a large audience," Nathan responded.

"I would love to perform. I would love a leading role... I would love to lose myself in the character I played."

After a few moments of silence, she ventured to ask: "May I solicit your complicity in a daring endeavor?" Jocelyn gave Nathan a devilish smile.

Nathan's ears perked up. "Whatever do you have in mind?"

"You must be my partner in crime."

"And what crime shall we commit?" Nathan played along.

"You shall help me break out of my prison."

Not understanding, Nathan asked, "Your prison?"

"My home... my life."

"Is your home truly such a prison?" For an instant, Nathan remembered his brief tenure at Coldbath Fields. *Would that I could have had the misfortune of being jailed in the Charlesworth estate.*

"If you had my life, you wouldn't pose such a question." Jocelyn responded with a melancholy tone. "I must play the role that has been assigned to me by birth—not the role I would play if I were free."

"What role would you play, if you were given your freedom?" Nathan inquired.

"I should love to be a play-actress." Jocelyn responded as if she were eating her favorite dessert.

Reflecting on how Jocelyn had helped him fulfill a lifelong dream of playing before a full orchestra, Nathan wanted to reciprocate. "How may I help you fulfill your dream?"

Jocelyn looked at him intensely. "I wish to audition for a part in *The Lancashire Lass*. I would love to play the role of the *lass*, Ruth Kirby. Auditions are taking place a week from Saturday."

"You could never appear in public as a play-actress. Imagine the scandal that would cause." Nathan could see the headlines in the London newspapers.

"I would appear *in secret*." Jocelyn whispered the last two words.

"I don't think you could ever appear *in secret*."

"I shall be in disguise."

Nathan registered surprise. "Even with a disguise, you would be instantly recognized."

"You would be amazed what a wig and a little makeup will do. I shouldn't confess this, but my golden hair is the secret to my beauty. Without it, I am just another pretty face." Jocelyn distorted her face playfully.

No, she is definitely not just another pretty face, Nathan thought.

"Sneaking out alone with me? You shall be at my mercy? *Que feras-tu si je décide de te ravir?*"[56] Nathan made his best attempt at play-acting.

"*Ça serait délicieux. Fais-le, s'il te plaît.*"[57] Jocelyn smiled coquettishly.

Nathan felt, for an instant, the power of her sensual attraction.

---

56   What if I decide to ravish you?
57   "That would be delicious. Please do."

He had surprised *himself* by his bold provocative remark made in jest, but he was even more intrigued at Jocelyn's response. Not daring to venture further, he asked: "And how shall you escape from your prison?"

"That should be easily done. My home is so large, I could easily be 'lost' for hours at a time. Just have a pony chaise ready at the east gate at two o'clock sharp."

Chapter 51

As the cab crossed the Westminster Bridge, Sir Rochester raised his handkerchief to his nose to mask the malodorous stench that assaulted his senses. It was always unpleasant venturing on the south side of the Thames. Recent news articles indicated that the massive construction work on the southside aqueducts was nearing completion, but if the stench in the air was any indicator, those reports were unduly optimistic. The cab plodded along on Westminster Bridge Road, navigating its way in a northeasterly direction through the thick traffic and livestock. The nauseating odor worsened as the coach approached Bermondsey in the glaring afternoon sun. Sir Rochester dabbed the moisture forming on his forehead, shaking his head in regret at his decision to make the trip.

Twenty minutes later, the cab turned onto Dockhead Road. It was a dismal street, with buildings on either side of the street covered in black soot. The haunting faces of frowning pedestrians in dirty, threadbare clothing conveyed a daily struggle with poverty. Taking a deep breath, Sir Rochester decided, against his better judgment, to exit the cab. Opening the door before setting foot on the filthy ground, he motioned to a young street sweeper a short distance away. The dirty-faced boy scampered through the grime-covered street with a wide smile. With precision and finesse, the boy carefully cleared a path from the street to the sidewalk. When completed, he bowed and motioned respectfully for his new patron to proceed. Sir Rochester exited the cab, handed a couple of shillings to the delighted sweeper, and walked onto the sidewalk.

Sir Rochester checked the street number twice, comparing it to the handwritten note in his pocket. Could this be the building of the architect who was serenading the beautiful and wealthy Jocelyn Charlesworth? He shook his head and lingered on the sidewalk for a few minutes. Tentatively, he entered the building and started up the steps to the second floor. The corridor was musty, and the steps creaked under his weight as he ascended. He located the third door down the dark hallway with the sign "Sinclair, Architect." Most of the stain on the door had faded. He stood still for a few moments, debating whether to enter. Reluctantly, he placed his gloved hand on the doorknob and turned it slowly, opening the door. Walking into the reception area, the faded wallpaper, cracked moldings, and sparse furnishings on their last legs nearly caused Sir Rochester to retrace his steps. His strong instinct was to leave abruptly, until the clerk noticed him. Now it was too late.

The clerk had looked up from his desk and eyed the visitor from top to bottom. Immediately, Stumbolt knew he was in the presence of wealth and high station; it was evident from the immaculately tailored suit, cloak, and top hat that the visitor wore. It was further confirmed from the gentleman's grandiloquent pose and demeanor.

Like a private who had just recognized an unexpected general, Stumbolt stood up so quickly that his upper thigh noisily pushed the desk up a couple of inches as he rose. He then produced a lengthy bow and spoke in his most respectful tone. "Percy Stumbolt at your service. How may I be of assistance?"

"Sir Augustus Rochester," he announced, producing a card. "Is this the office of Mr. Nathan Sinclair?"

"Yes, your..." Stumbolt almost said: *Your grace.* Not knowing how to address the visitor, he tried "...your lordship."

"Is Mr. Sinclair available?"

"One moment, sir."

Seconds later, Stumbolt invited him into Nathan's private office with great deference. As Sir Rochester entered, he looked about the room. The room was clean, but the stains on the ceiling, the threadbare carpet, and the chipped window behind Nathan's desk did not inspire confidence. *At least the man's overhead must be a paltry sum*, he thought to himself.

Nathan came forward and introduced himself. Nathan vaguely recalled having briefly met him the night of Jocelyn's birthday party. Sir Rochester was a distinguished-looking gentleman, with a mustache and neatly trimmed beard. He appeared to be in his midfifties. On the strength of the glowing recommendation from Miss Charlesworth alone, he told Nathan of his plan to erect a lavish summer home in the London outskirts and wished to view some of Nathan's designs. He felt compelled to also justify his presence in the shabby quarters by expressing his strong attachment with the Charlesworth family.

"I must see for myself if Miss Charlesworth has exaggerated your talents."

"I expect she has," Nathan responded humbly.

Sir Rochester gave a brief guttural response, wanting to get on with it. He had little interest in staying more than a few minutes. "Show me your work."

Nathan showed him several designs he had created for no client in particular, merely in the process of honing his design skills. There were exterior designs of magnificent edifices and adorning landscapes painted in watercolors. Sir Rochester raised his eyebrows at the sight and wondered how an architect in such shabby quarters could mastermind such beauty.

After forty minutes of poring over artist renderings and floor plans of extravagant dwellings that only existed in Nathan's mind, Sir Rochester had completely forgotten about the questionable location of the office, the dilapidated interior, and the passage of far more time with the architect than he had intended.

Could this young man be the one who may allow my dreams to take flight? Sir Rochester allowed himself to think.

"I want you to see the land yourself. After you have spent time there, walked its terrain, draw me a design that will astonish me and cause me to *covet* your services. I want a property that will be an architectural masterpiece; something historic... something unique... something memorable."

Nathan could barely suppress his enthusiasm, and he made arrangements to visit Sir Rochester's land the following day.

***

Arriving at the property in midmorning of a cloudy day, Nathan began surveying Sir Rochester's land. It was a magnificent property, with heavily wooded areas surrounding a large meadow. Nathan envisioned the manner of residence that belonged there. It could be glorious! He imagined the stone exterior, the symmetry of windows, the majestic height of the domicile. He became excited as he contemplated the edifice taking form in its various phases of construction. While standing at the foot of the road below, he considered the view that passers-by would have. From that perspective, he took out a pencil and paper and began sketching a design that would take full advantage of the upward slope and surrounding terrain. This would be the type of project that would transform a career! While Monsieur Lefontaine's project was devoted to landscape renovation, this project would be a building of stone and mortar. When completed in a few years' time, it would stand as a monument to his creative genius. It would be a landmark in the county and beyond—a beacon for business. Nathan contemplated, with great excitement and anticipation, the supreme effort he would undertake to create a breathtaking and imaginative residence, which would be without peer in all of the United Kingdom. They agreed to meet in ten days' time for initial designs and concept drawings.

***

During the next week and a half, Nathan devoted the vast majority of his waking time to the exterior renderings and floor plan of Sir Rochester's proposed new structure. He felt a creative surge unlike anything he had ever experienced. At night, when he sat at the piano, his fingers felt on fire as he played with a passion and energy that surpassed even his normal high levels. At times, he interrupted a piece in mid-play, something he almost never did, to leap from the bench and race over to the adjoining office, where he would set down on paper the latest bolt of creative inspiration that had reached his psyche. Eating dinner at the local pub, he never failed to carry a pencil and paper with him, never knowing where and when a brilliant concept or idea would germinate. His pockets were full of the frequent notes he made outside his office. Even in separate visits to Regina and Jocelyn during those ten days, his mind was distracted with design concepts. He did his best to keep his mind on his hostess, rather than anticipating the evening's conclusion when he could return to his creative high. He vowed not to breathe a word of the potential project to either woman until his position was secured.

It was a time of creative combustion unlike any other in his life. Nathan knew that Sir Rochester's project might be the pivotal moment of his professional career: the greatest opportunity he might ever have. If he failed at this incredible undertaking, he would regret it for as long as he lived. The best and most bold ideas he had ever contemplated, since developing a passion for architecture years ago, found expression in the renderings that he was now putting to paper. At times, he couldn't believe the harmony and symmetry that were growing, hand in hand, in his designs. It was almost as if the touch of providence had already designed the property, and he was merely the instrument setting it to paper.

As he put the finishing touches on the punctilious drawings and reviewed the designs one final time, Nathan could not wait for Sir Rochester's reaction. He knew that he had designed a transforming property that no discerning man could ignore.

***

The appointed day and time arrived, and Sir Rochester paid his second visit to Nathan's humble office. On this visit, none of the shabbiness of Nathan's office registered on Sir Rochester's mind. He entered with great expectation.

"Prepare to be astonished," Nathan unabashedly said to his prospective client.

He first showed Sir Rochester an exterior color drawing of the proposed residence from the vantage of a planned gated entrance from the highway below, which displayed unalloyed imagination and dramatic flair. Inspired by classical architectural concepts, it layered elevations and exterior walls in unprecedented fashion. The design showed complexity and purity, side by side. The drawings depicted a residence extending to great heights, with each upward floor smaller than the level preceding. Large windows were placed symmetrically on each level, intended to bring nature's beauty into the interior. Sir Rochester could not hide his enthusiasm.

"Now show me the floor plans."

"You have been to Chambord, southwest of Paris, I'm sure."

"I have."

"The proper use of a staircase can transform an interior. You are obviously familiar with the dual grand curving stairs of the Charlesworth estate, da Vinci's design—the helix staircase?"

"It is a marvel," Sir Rochester responded. "Two staircases interlocked together, but never meeting."

"I propose going one better," Nathan offered. "The use of not two staircases, but three."

Sir Rochester was taken aback. "Three?"

"Imagine the braids of a young girl's hair, interlocked together, but extending upward. The braid contains three separate strands of hair, all joined together but never connecting, similar to da Vinci's design. Imagine the centerpiece of your residence with three interlocking staircases, going up not just one level or two, but a full five floors up to the highest balcony, all visible from the entrance. An intricate and bold marriage of the three circular staircases into one, each independent yet related. With your land sloping upward, we dig into the hillside, and create an interior of amazing height. At each level, we have narrow bridges extending outward from the staircase to other rooms or corridors, keeping the stairway in full view to its apex." Nathan then explained how the dome above the stairs would be made of stained glass with steel framing, and that the interior would include a grand atrium with enormously tall plants, trees, and fountains, bringing nature's beauty inside.

His potential client was now wide-eyed with interest.

"Now, let me show you other exterior drawings. From here you can see the manifold towers and turrets that will create the impression of a celestial city extending skyward."

Sir Rochester examined the drawings with disbelief. "Can this be built? Can you truly create a building identical to your drawings?"

"Without question. If you dedicate a budget to match the design."

"How long will it take to build?"

"Part of that is based upon your allocation of funding. If there is unlimited access to resources at all times, you could see it erected within four to five years' time."

"Extraordinary."

At the conclusion of the presentation, Sir Rochester could not suppress his enthusiasm, "You have surpassed even my lofty expectations, not a simple task." Smiling broadly, he continued. "You have earned the commission. But, you must promise me that this project will be given your utmost devotion and care."

Nathan responded unwaveringly.

"As to fees. I was quoted six thousand pounds by the esteemed firm of Quincy & Quincy for the design and all drawings of a comparably sized property. Judging from your *modest* quarters, I assume your overhead is a tiny fraction of theirs. If you will do it for five, then the job is yours. I expect a 50-percent retainer will be acceptable to get you started?"

Nathan tried to maintain his composure as he contemplated a fee that would dramatically transform his life. He humbly accepted the generous offer with grace and gratitude.

"Then, proceed at once."

***

After Sir Rochester left, Nathan stared at the £2,500 check from Sir Rochester. Was he dreaming? He studied each digit on the draft to ensure that his eyes were not deceiving him. He had never imagined such a sum! Even in his moments of runaway fantasy, such a payment and project were not within his expectation. His shock and disbelief soon gave way to intense gratitude and wonder at his dramatic change in fortune. That his financial burden had been lifted via Monsieur Lefontaine had been miraculous. But now, five times that sum! How could he have been blessed with such prosperity?

The magnitude and scope of this new project also infused him with awe and thankfulness. Were there any architects in Western Europe who had free creative rein with such a project? Moreover, as the project took form, his name and standing as an architect would spread rapidly, dwarfing even the impact of Lefontaine's project.

He would make other sweeping changes in his life. First, he would begin searching for a more respectable location for his office—a larger space, commensurate with the fame and new standing he would soon enjoy. He would hire a draftsman at once, maybe two.

His thoughts next turned to finding suitable living quarters for a future life with Regina, if she would have him. He couldn't wait to share the wonderful news with her. All obstacles to marrying the woman of his dreams had now been removed. All obstacles, except Jocelyn. He must meet with her first, and thank her, sincerely, for her generosity—generosity he would never forget. For Regina's sake, it was time to bring the deception to an end. Together, Jocelyn and he would devise an appropriate ending to their liaison. There could be no more visits to the Charlesworth household, there could be no more public outings with Jocelyn. He must break off all connection with her for the time being; after a passage of time, hopefully they could resume their relationship as friends. Jocelyn would understand. The public must know that they were no longer "seeing" each other, to ensure that both women's characters remain unblemished, and remove any hint of scandal.

After reflecting fully, Nathan decided to delay sharing the wonderful news of the Rochester commission with Regina until he was able to ask for her hand in marriage.

Chapter 52

On the day of the audition, Nathan arrived several minutes before the appointed hour at the east gate of the Charlesworth estate. He was still on an emotional high, filled with gratitude for the Rochester commission. He had purchased a bouquet of orchids and daisies as an expression of his deep appreciation, and looked forward to thanking Jocelyn personally for the wondrous good fortune. He remained inside the cab for several minutes, wanting to keep his presence inconspicuous, while savoring the flowers' sweet fragrance.

By the time it was a quarter past two, he became concerned. He left the cab and walked onto the sidewalk next to the tall brick wall, peering through the locked iron gate. It was a windy, overcast summer day with leaves whisking around. Nathan had difficulty seeing through the heavy foliage. After a second look, he observed movement. Moments later, he saw a young shapely woman hurrying through the trees and plants. The woman inserted a key into the lock, opened the gate, and emerged.

Nathan scarcely recognized her, the transformation was so complete. The brunette wig gave her a startlingly different look. It completely smothered her natural hair, and obscured the sides of her face and ears with looped braids. Her blue eyes and dark hair gave her an unusual and exotic blend. She was wearing an ordinary dress by her standards, completely different from her normal attire. Still, she had her extraordinary beauty, but it was a much different look. She was no longer Jocelyn Charlesworth.

"We're late," she said as she rushed past Nathan into the waiting cab. Nathan scarcely had time to open the door before she flung herself inside. By the time Nathan entered, a beaming Jocelyn had appropriated the bouquet and was smelling the fragrance.

"How did you know these were my favorite flowers?"

"What makes you believe they are for you?" Nathan joked.

Jocelyn took one flower from the bunch and tossed it playfully at Nathan.

"Of course, you are not supposed to give flowers until *after* the performance."

"These flowers have nothing to do with your performance." Nathan turned serious. "I have you to thank for the most amazing commission from Sir Rochester. I am still in shock over it. Beyond my wildest dreams. It's an undertaking most architects will never see in their lifetimes. I don't know how to thank you. You are amazing!" Nathan gave Jocelyn details about the project.

"I am glad to see that you are reaping such benefits from my *proposition*," Jocelyn beamed radiantly.

"I think I am benefitting far more than you."

"*J'ai tout ce que je veux.*"[58] Jocelyn responded with a smile.

Jocelyn then explained her tardiness. "My mother's timing couldn't have been worse. She insisted on having lunch with me today—something we haven't done together in weeks. She was asking about you!" Jocelyn said as she pointed her finger into Nathan's mid-section.

"And what did she ask?"

"She wanted to know how our *liaison* is going, making sure that I don't fall in love with you."

"And have you?" Nathan asked with a smile.

"Hopelessly and helplessly, of course." Jocelyn responded with a wink of the eye. "You made quite an impression on her yourself, when the two of you had your little *tête à tête*. Except for your *lowly* station..." She said "lowly" very slowly and in an artificially low voice. "...She says you would be an ideal partner: the perfect gentleman, an amazing musician, and a brilliant architect. If she only knew you as I do," Jocelyn gave a sly smile.

"I hope you did not disillusion her," Nathan responded.

"Well, I had to tell her the truth. I heard you play a wrong note last month in a Beethoven sonata."

Nathan had a mortified look on his face. "Oh no! I thought the G flat had escaped detection."

Jocelyn shook her head. "Nothing escapes my detection."

"I dare never play again. Should I make another mistake, you will certainly shun me forever."

"On that point, you are correct. But, you must continue playing, to atone for your error."

"And how long shall my atonement last?"

"A very, very long time," Jocelyn responded dreamily. Nathan had a fleeting wish that Jocelyn's statement were true.

"Well, I can understand your mother commenting on my being a *perfect gentleman* and an *amazing musician*," Nathan grinned with a

---

58   I have everything I want.

mock display of vastly elevated pride, "but brilliant architect? How would she know about that?"

"Oh, *we've heard about you.* Monsieur Lefontaine has been raving about your designs to everyone."

"Including to Sir Rochester, apparently. I will also need to thank Monsieur Lefontaine for that. What else did you two discuss?"

"She told me to be careful. She said: 'Jocelyn dear, you have such a fragile heart, you must find someone you can love, honor, and trust. If your heart is ever broken, you would never survive.'" Jocelyn imitated her mother's voice and accent. *"Elle pense que je suis si fragile."*[59]

"Are you?"

"You know better."

"So, how did you escape?"

"My usual excuse. 'I am not feeling well; I need to go to my room and rest.'"

"Well, you have done an excellent job with your disguise. I hardly recognized you."

"Perfect. I am so excited… and nervous."

"And your lines are memorized?"

"A hundred times over."

The cab arrived at the Queen's Theatre, where auditions were being conducted for H. J. Byron's *The Lancashire Lass*. The theatre was newly constructed after a fire had destroyed it a couple of years before. Only the walls of the theatre had remained standing after the fire, and the new building had been erected within the shell of the old theatre at the cost of fifty thousand pounds. Constructed with iron and concrete to reduce future risk of fire, the new theatre was enormous, containing four balcony tiers and seating for over two thousand five hundred patrons.

The Lancashire Lass was a hugely ambitious production. The action ranged from Liverpool to the Australian outback, highlighted by a dramatic drowning at a pier. Included in the plot were criminals, blackmailers, a hero wrongfully accused of a heinous crime, and a lovely, innocent heroine. The stage was so massive in width and in height that theatre promoters were contemplating using a real ferry steamer, which would actually sail before and after dispensing its passengers in one of the critical scenes.

Nathan and Jocelyn exited the cab and entered the huge theatre hall. Hopeful actors filled the front rows, with nearly a hundred

---

59   She thinks I'm so fragile.

people seated near the stage. Two actors were onstage, in animated rehearsal, going through a scene.

Jocelyn quickly walked up the aisleway toward the stage area. Her arrival was duly noted by another member of the ensemble, and she was directed to sit near the front. Nathan remained in the back of the theatre, anxious to observe her performance.

Nathan sat patiently, observing actors working hard to impress the play's director. Finally, after an hour and a half wait, he saw Jocelyn walk forward to the stage; a male actor joined her. They climbed onto the stage. In seconds, they began rehearsing.

> A chair was placed in the center of the stage. Jocelyn staggered in from the side of the stage, sinking onto the chair.
>
> "Wait a minute, don't speak to me yet." Jocelyn put her hand to her heart. "I am better now. I was frightened. I fancied someone followed me, but it was only fancy, perhaps. Are we alone?"

Awestruck, Nathan could scarcely believe the transformation in Jocelyn's demeanor and manner.

> "Quite—except." The male actor said pointing away. Jocelyn rose suddenly from the chair. "Is he here?"
>
> The male actor was standing close to her. "Yes. I did all I could to soften down the severity of his position. Ruth, I did more than I'd any right to do, in order to make him comfortable."
>
> Jocelyn seized the man's hand. "Bless you, Mr. Jellick, you are a good man—a kind, generous man—a kind, generous man always. Heavens! Will the truth ever be known?"

Nathan stared spellbound, finding himself drawn into the drama as though it were unfolding in reality before his very eyes.

> "It must and will be known someday, Ruth."
>
> "But when?—When? When he no longer lives to hear his innocence declared? When the law has wreaked its vengeance on the guiltless? What comfort is that to those who care for him?" Jocelyn became very agitated. "And that door alone stands between him and liberty.

One turn of the key—" Jocelyn moved toward an imaginary door.

The male actor moved to intercept Jocelyn. "Ruth, what would you do?"

Jocelyn looked dazed, paused, and said with a blank look. "Nothing, nothing."

"Heaven knows I would do anything to help him, but I am powerless—completely powerless."

"Not so—you are all powerful. You can, if you please, save his life and mine."

"Tell me how, Ruth."

Jocelyn (as Ruth) grasped the male actor's arm. "Prisoners have escaped before now."

"What?" The male actor showed alarm.

"Within that room lies one accused of a crime, that, were he guilty, would rightly doom him to an ignominious death, but he is innocent. By cheating the law of its hapless, *guiltless* victim, you will be doing a simple act of common justice." Jocelyn began speaking hurriedly. "It will *never* be known; people have *broken* out of this place before *now; who* is to know that *you* aided his escape? By tomorrow, when you discover your prisoner's flight, he will be far away—out of the country." Jocelyn kneeled and grasped the male actor's hand, pleading with all her might; the male actor was greatly agitated. "For my sake, do this generous deed; dear, *dear* old friend. It will break my heart—it will *kill* me should he suffer for another's crime. Let him escape and my life shall be *devoted to you.*"

The great sacrifice Ruth was willing to make registered within Nathan and he felt the gravity conveyed by Jocelyn. His eyes misted over, as he looked on in astonishment.

"Ruth, Ruth, what are you saying? Do you mean to say that if I let him escape, you will—"

With her hands before her eyes, Jocelyn responded in anguish. "Yes, yes, give me but his life, and—" Jocelyn gave a mighty struggle, nearly choking. "—and take mine." On her knees, she stretched forth her arms to the male actor.

"You do not know the danger involved in such a

course."

"One turn of the key and he is free! Can you deny me this?" Jocelyn was pleading. "*Can* you refuse to do a deed of which your own conscience will acquit you, though all the judges in the land shall call it a crime?"

The male actor gazed intently at Jocelyn. "And, if I do this, Ruth; if I run this fearful risk, you will keep your word, Ruth?" He walked over to the imaginary door of the imaginary room. "Listen; and be sure the sergeant does not hear."

"One moment; he must not know that *I* am here; he must not know of our bargain. He would never purchase his liberty at such a price." Jocelyn pretended to hide.

There was silence for a few seconds. Suddenly the other actors and spectators exploded in a rousing ovation, adding lustful cheers for the performance. Previously, there had been polite applause for other actors rehearsing scenes—nothing like this.

Nathan was in awe! Jocelyn's acting skill was far superior to all the others who had gone before her, including veteran theatre actors. Her idiosyncratic performance had been breathtakingly convincing. In the five-minute audition on the setless stage, Nathan had found himself pleading for the male actor, who had played the jailer, to release Jocelyn's (Ruth's) lover. She had a natural delivery and inflection and changed her facial expressions and voice so well that it had all been painfully real and believable. Adding to her rousing talent was her amazing beauty. Even in disguise, her features and form were stunning. After the applause died down, there was still a buzz among the ensemble. The director jumped onto the stage and approached Jocelyn. His facial expressions and excitable movements conveyed that he had been mightily impressed.

Minutes later, Jocelyn ran down the aisleway, her face beaming. She came to Nathan and hugged him tightly.

Breaking the embrace, she was breathless. "They have offered me the part of Ruth. It's *the* leading role. I am so thrilled!"

Nathan would have been shocked if they had not. He could hardly restrain his praise. "You were amazing! You were utterly believable. I've never seen such a convincing performance."

"I cannot believe they have offered me the part." Jocelyn was jumping up and down with excitement. Fellow actors and spectators were still looking her way, not wanting to lose sight of the actor who would be the key to a successful theatrical run. Taking Nathan by the arm, they walked from the building. Jocelyn looked as if she had been reborn.

On the trip back, Jocelyn was ebullient and Nathan could barely contain his praise. "I am astonished at your acting ability!" he gushed.

"You shouldn't be," Jocelyn smiled. "I had many opportunities to perform at Écouen. We had our own underground performances—the handicap being that we ladies often had to play the male roles."

"I would love to have seen you as a man." Nathan grinned widely.

"Oh, you would be surprised. I can make a very handsome man, especially with a beard and mustache." Jocelyn placed one finger horizontally over her mouth and the other vertically pulling on her chin. "Would you kiss me if I had a mustache and beard?"

Nathan's face expressed horror at the thought.

"*Je pense que je pourrais te séduire, même avec une barbe et moustache.*"[60] Jocelyn said in a provocatively sensual tone.

Nathan laughed. "And your hair?"

"Simple. I merely place my *priceless* tresses under a hat."

"It must take a very tall hat."

"Although once the hat fell off in a duel."

"So, can you also fence?" Nathan inquired playfully.

"Did I not ever tell you? I took a fencing course at Écouen... disguised as a man," Jocelyn looked at Nathan, opening her eyes large, daring him to doubt her. Nathan could not contain his laughter.

"You think I'm speaking in jest? Cross me, sometime, and I will challenge you to a duel. Then you shall see." Jocelyn put her arm forth in a slashing motion.

"I must never make you angry."

"No. You absolutely must never do that. But, no one could make me angry today... Can you imagine? I will be performing before thousands, several nights a week. The play premieres in just four weeks."

Nathan wondered to himself how she would *ever* be able to accomplish *that*.

Jocelyn looked at him. "The play reminds me of us."

Nathan looked at her quizzically.

"Ruth is of high birth and is in love with a man of low station.

---

60   I think I could seduce you, even with a beard and mustache.

Another man, a charming but deceitful man, wants to purchase her love."

"That would be the Duke."

"Precisely. Ruth is willing to forsake her love to save the life of her lover, and pledge her affections for another man, the man who will set her lover free from prison and death. She is willing to be with another man, to save the one she truly cares for."

"I see our difference in station, but otherwise I'm not sure what role I have in the script," Nathan laughed.

"Don't you see, you have broken me out of prison. You have saved me from an *ignominious* fate—consignment to a man I despise. And, you have consented to be with me, another woman, though your heart lies elsewhere. You are the hero in my play."

"I assure you that I have been the major beneficiary," Nathan said, thinking of the amazing commissions he had received through her efforts.

Looking out the carriage window, Jocelyn changed the subject. "There will be rehearsals to attend."

"How often?"

"A mere four per week."

Nathan winced.

"I shall need assistance for those."

Taking up the bait, Nathan replied without hesitation, despite the inconvenience it would create for his suddenly thriving practice. Surely, it was the least he could do after her magnanimous generosity.

"It shall be my pleasure to be of assistance. I shall make sure you don't miss a single one." He wondered to himself how she would ever be able to disappear from her home four times a week.

"You would really do that for me? How lovely you are." Jocelyn gave him a kiss on the cheek. Caught by surprise, Nathan looked away, his face flushed.

Jocelyn became more subdued and the two were silent for several minutes, as the carriage jostled over cobblestone, the horses snorting aggravation in the summer heat.

"Of course, I cannot return," Jocelyn said, her face looking downcast.

Nathan remained silent.

Minutes later, she spoke again. Tears were welling in her eyes. "It's so sad. They shall expect me the day after tomorrow, and I shall never return. They shall wonder what happened to the *Lancashire Lass*. They shall go in search of her, publish advertisements in the newspaper, but she shall never return."

Nathan knew what a great dream it was to her, and felt her sadness, imagining what it would be like if he lost his wonderful new commissions. Taking her hand in his, he spoke softly. "You are quite sure of that? There must be some way to make this wondrous dream of yours come true."

Jocelyn immediately changed her affect, brushing away a fallen tear. Her face lit up as the cab came to a stop at the side gate of the Charlesworth estate.

"It's time for me to return to 'my prison.' It was enough to be offered the part. I shall be quite content with that." Moments later, she disappeared inside the gate.

Chapter 53

Nevius Tucker was feverish and his stomach upside down. He hated being on the water, and particularly detested crossing the channel—it was always choppy, especially now. He would manage, though, with the extravagant payment he had extracted from the Duke, along with a promise of much more if he succeeded. It was clear that the Sinclair matter was of utmost importance to the Duke. Those were always the best projects, when so much was at stake. The Duke had shelved the task of looking into the other woman, seeing that it had not produced the desired effect, and now wanted to launch a thorough investigation into Sinclair's past.

The investigation led him to Paris, where Allysandra Mercier, Sinclair's mother, had been well known. Surely, among the opera performers, he would gain the scent he was looking for. After a week of dead-end inquiries, he found the pivotal lead. The man was singing in a three-penny theatre, with barely enough patrons to justify the production. Nevius opened the man's lips with food and drink.

The balding, swarthy man's tongue loosened after the third glass of cheap wine.

"I remember Madame Mercier well. I sang with her in Don Giovanni." It had been more than twenty years ago.

Tucker shoved another drink his way.

"Tell me everything you remember about her."

***

Nathan was on the sidewalk watching workmen install a sign above his new ground-floor office: "Sinclair, Architect." He felt pride in seeing his name so prominently displayed on King's Road. Before, it had just been a second-story window with letters barely large enough to read from the street below. An office in Chelsea was a major step up for him in respectability. He had a reception and clerk area, and three separate offices. He had moved in his desk and files the previous day. He now had room to grow his business.

Despite misgivings, he had decided to bring Stumbolt to his new quarters. Stumbolt's imperiousness and ego might actually be an advantage with the London gentry who were now gaining prominence on his client list. Stumbolt could convey a certain kindred aloofness and arrogance.

Nathan also retained a young draftsman by the name of James Allen, with whom he had become casually acquainted during the past year. A studious sort, Allen had no lofty ambitions. He wore spectacles and seemed at home spending hours poring over drawings with his rulers, compass, and protractors. Allen had already begun work on the time-consuming and detailed construction drawings necessary for the Rochester residence. Each perspective — north, south, east, and west — of every room had to be sketched, including floor and ceiling. The load of each balcony, ceiling, and deck had to be carefully engineered and assessed, and Allen would work closely with a structural engineer with whom Nathan had contracted to ensure that the Rochester edifice would stand a thousand years. Nathan already had plans to hire a second draftsman; the Rochester project would be very demanding, and he wanted nothing to delay its fulfillment.

At the same time, Nathan had been fortunate in locating the ideal apartment for his new life. It was a convenient walking distance from his office. He had entered into a year's lease for the two-story abode, with options to extend the occupancy further. It would do fine for the first few years of his marriage to Regina. In addition to a pleasant entry area, it had a spacious parlor room, kitchen, and library on the ground floor. The second level added three bedrooms.

***

Nevius Tucker's investigation led him to the small medieval village of Moret-sur-Loing, located on the edge of the forest of Fontainebleau, an hour from Paris by train. The community was located by the banks of the Loing, which emptied into the Seine a short distance downstream. Tucker had learned that Allysandra Mercier, Nathan's mother, had spent several years in the charming village. She had been a celebrity in the community and there were a number of people who remembered her well.

There was also an aura of mystery about her that he couldn't quite piece together. Conflicting accounts from residents remembering her sojourn there more than twenty years ago made it difficult to complete the puzzle. What had been certain was that she had disappeared for a time, only to return with a newborn son and no husband. Several residents recalled hearing that her husband had died tragically soon after she gave birth to a son. Others weren't certain if the death was fact or fiction. Tucker realized that if he could uncover the secret, and if the secret was what the Duke wanted, it would be explosive. But first, there were leads to follow up and questions to answer. He needed to locate the former nanny and an elderly priest, if they were still living. What role did the infamous Guy LaJeunesse play in Madame Mercier's life? His instinct told him he was on the verge of an important discovery. If the findings were what he expected, the Duke would reward him handsomely.

Chapter 54

It had been nearly impossible to keep things from her. Regina had remarked that Nathan was hiding something from her. On previous visits, Regina had asked Nathan how the Lefontaine project was coming along, and he had promised to take her there. This would be the perfect opportunity! Today would be the day.

It was on a bright Saturday morning that Nathan picked up Regina and her cousin, Estelle, to visit Lefontaine's landscaping renovation. It had been more than two months since Monsieur Lefontaine had retained Nathan. During the first couple of weeks, Nathan had finalized detailed sketches of the transforming landscaping for the estate. Monsieur Lefontaine had been giddy with delight at what he saw on paper and wanted to begin the work immediately. A team of cheap laborers had been hired to begin the laborious task of expanding the existing lake, while a company specializing in demolition was tearing down walls and other structures in order to allow the sketched plans to come alive. The process was in its infancy, but with the army of laborers, it was clear to bystanders that a massive rework was underway. Nathan showed Regina and Estelle drawings of the finished project. Both ladies were mightily impressed.

"How long will it take to complete?" Regina queried.

"With Monsieur Lefontaine's vast resources and ability to provide a huge crew of workers, we may be close to completion within a year or two's time. Of course, it will take much longer for the plants, trees, and shrubs to grow to maturity."

"Will it truly look like this?" Estelle asked with admiration, pointing to the drawings.

"If I do my job correctly, it should look infinitely better."

Estelle was an independent soul, and trudged along the grounds inspecting the work and enjoying the stares from the laborers, leaving Regina and Nathan at some distance.

Regina had something on her mind.

"Now that you are known to be courting Miss Charlesworth,

our meetings will need to be exceedingly discreet. It would bring dishonor upon you *and* me, if word leaks of our friendship."

"I suppose you are right. I certainly wish to protect you from any scandal."

"And such a scandal would likely end your strategic alliance with Miss Charlesworth."

"Regina, that may be over sooner than you think."

"Whatever do you mean?"

"Regina, I can hardly wait until we can be seen in public... until the world knows how I feel about you."

Putting her fingers to his lips, Regina responded. "Sh-h-h-h. We must wait for your 'courtship' with Jocelyn to run its course, before we consider such matters."

Regina's mind was active with trepidation. *The longer the courtship, the more days I shall be with my sweet prince. I must remember every day, every hour, every minute, we have together. Upon these memories will I build my future happiness, when finally we must part.*

Nathan was nearly bursting inside, impatient to tell Regina of the fabulous new commission. But that would have to wait until the afternoon.

***

After leaving Lefontaine's property, Nathan took his guests to lunch at an upscale restaurant within a short walk of his new living quarters. After lunch, he suggested a promenade in the neighborhood. Several blocks later, they came upon the intended street. The homes were newly built identical brownstone, yet quite attractive. To the surprise of the two women, Nathan started walking up the steps of one of the residences. Regina and Estelle stared at each other with a surprised look. He pulled out a key and opened the door.

"My new living quarters."

Regina showed surprise. "Can you afford such a place?"

"Well, my dear, I have some exciting news I have been saving to tell you."

"What is it, Nathan?" Regina asked her eyes all a wonder.

Nathan proceeded to tell her about the Rochester commission. Regina was amazed at the scope of the project and the size of the retainer. "How wonderful for you, Nathan! You have been blessed abundantly by your alliance with Miss Charlesworth. This project shall place you in an echelon reserved for the elite London firms."

Nathan nodded. It would pave the way for their future together.

"You have been keeping this from me all this time?" Regina scolded. "Shame on you."

Nathan feigned an apology, but his smile gave away his true intentions. They entered the furnished apartment.

"How do you like the parlor?"

"It's beautiful."

Nathan motioned toward the window. "And here I shall place my mother's dear pianoforte."

"It's been far too long since I heard you play," Regina noted.

They continued touring the apartment. Most of it was bare, but there were several pieces of furniture which he had purchased from the former tenant. He was also in negotiations to retain the former household staff: a chef who also served as housekeeper, and a butler.

Nathan showed Regina the library. There were a large desk and chair on one side of the room, and ample bookshelves. Opposite the desk was a wall with curtains, but no window. Nathan pulled up the horizontal curtains, which revealed a blank wall, with a large nail suggesting a painting had hung there before. It was evident that the landlord had placed a treasured work of art on the wall, one considered to be too valuable to leave in the custody of the new tenant.

"I have plans for this wall," said Nathan, looking at Regina.

"And what plans are those?"

"You shall see."

As they continued their tour of the rooms in the apartment, Regina could tell that Nathan was looking for her approbation. She did her best to show enthusiasm and pleasure, but inside she was mourning the imminent loss of her love.

Nathan sensed a sadness in Regina. Interpreting her reaction, he said: "My love, if this dwelling is not adequate, *we* can find another."

"Oh, no! No! Nathan. It is perfect."

"Then you must know that I am prepared to stop seeing Jocelyn, if that is what troubles you. This commission removes any further obstacle between us."

"Nathan. You must not talk so, until it is truly over. We must not talk further of our feelings until it has come to an end." Regina had not the fortitude to end it today.

"Of course, my love."

I should have ended it before now and spared him such pain! How weak I am! Dear God, how I have tried to tell him.

Chapter 55

The Duke looked over the "Confidential Report" he had received from Tucker via post. He learned that Tucker's travels had taken him to Moret-sur-Loing, a small village near Paris. Tucker had interviewed a number of inhabitants there, receiving sworn affidavits. The statements were all in French, but Tucker had provided a translation for each. It was clear that Tucker was still trading off his Scotland Yard credentials, although they were no longer current; the French had respect for the Yard inspectors. The Duke read the first six translations and smiled. He paused at the seventh, from an elderly priest. He wouldn't need that one, so he tossed both the priest's affidavit and its translation into the fire. He needed more information on one man: *Guy LaJeunesse.*

The Duke grabbed his quill and dispatched further instructions to Mr. Tucker.

***

After showing Regina *their* future residence, Nathan knew it was time to bring his relationship with Jocelyn to a close. Tomorrow would be the day. He had been the recipient of great benefits from Jocelyn's proposal. The commissions alone, from Monsieur Lefontaine and Sir Rochester, assured him of a brilliant future as an architect, along with financial security. He would always be grateful to her, but it was also time for him to move on with his life, to resume openly courting his beloved Regina.

***

On his trek to the Charlesworth estate on a late Monday afternoon, he pondered how to break the news to Jocelyn that their liaison had run its course. He wondered how she would react. Would she plead with him to continue the charade, or would she release him with a smile? He would offer friendship after marriage, if she still desired it. Perhaps that would ease their parting.

Nathan was a regular visitor at the Charlesworth estate on late

Friday afternoons and evenings. He was such a frequent guest that he was now virtually invisible to the butler and other servants within and without the grounds. Rarely, however, had he ventured there on other days of the week, but this could wait no longer. He began his customary descent of the staircase leading to the ballroom below and the adjoining music room. But after just a few steps downward, he sensed the faintest strain of a pure and sweet vibration of sound emanating from the balcony to the right. He arrested his descent and returned upward, straining his ear, seeking the direction of its source. Pure and sublime. His perfect pitch told him it was B flat. He could scarcely discern the nature and origin of the divine sound. It sounded like the voice of an angel. Or was it the vibration of an instrument? It was so very faint that it was hard to tell. The sound was coming from the corridor to the right, which led to the library. His keen ear heard next a discordant middle C, six and a half notes lower, then repeated, yet also of the purest vibration. Another B flat, followed by a note a half step higher than middle C, D flat, repeated more quickly this time. As the barely perceptible tones continued, he heard a melody so transcendent, yet completely unrecognizable, that he thought his ear had pierced the veil of heaven. He had never heard music of such extraordinary beauty mingled with such melancholy heartbreak.

He yearned for the source of this mysterious bittersweet serenade. Continuing silently down the corridor, the music grew in volume and he knew he was getting closer to the source. The theme was now repeating, but an octave higher. As he advanced, the awareness grew within him that he was listening to a master playing a stringed instrument. The perfection of each note of the performance overcame him with such emotion that he felt a spiritual current electrifying his frame.

Nathan soon arrived at the entrance to the library. His eyes beheld the back of a lady in white with golden hair down to her waist, the bow of the violin moving back and forth as she continued the mournful music.

Astonished, Nathan thought, *It can't possibly be Jocelyn, can it?*

He waited silently, hidden in the shadow of the hallway, leaning discreetly beyond the doorframe in utmost admiration of the virtuoso performance. With the melody finished, the lady in white lowered the bow and turned slowly to the setting sun reflected in the window. Nathan's suspicions were immediately confirmed, as he recognized Jocelyn. He had never seen her in such glory! It was a portrait of incredible beauty; Jocelyn dressed in white, her magnificent hair hanging unrestrained to her waist, holding a violin and bow in her hands. It was the first time Nathan had seen all her hair down, and it glorified the perfection of her loveliness.

I can't break off with her tonight, he thought to himself. *Not after hearing this.*

Nathan stole one more glance at the angel in white with golden hair, continuing her private concert with music not meant for human ears. It was the last image in his mind as he turned and quietly followed the corridor back to the entryway and exited the opulent residence.

***

Not wanting anything or anyone to disrupt his recollection of the genius he had just heard, he continued to replay in his mind the theme Jocelyn had performed. All thoughts of ending the relationship that day had faded. Rather than hail a cab, he made the long trek home on foot, though it took him several hours. In the dark and stillness of his journey home, his mind was preoccupied with the musical feast he had observed.

How could this be? I have spent many nights with her and never once did she hint at any musical talent, let alone one so extraordinary. How is it possible that she could have such an exceptional gift?

***

It wasn't until the end of the next day that Nathan could even approach his dull, hollow-sounding box piano. His first attempts at playing caused insult to his ears and distracted the delicate perfection of the performance he had witnessed. His feeble attempt at Schubert's Sonata in A Minor, Opus 42, seemed tedious and hollow. After progressing several stanzas, he stopped cold, abruptly rose from the keyboard, and again replayed in his mind Jocelyn's virtuoso performance. He sat down again and played the tune he had heard on the violin, with single detached notes, and committed the theme to memory.

More days passed as Nathan continued to be haunted by Jocelyn's extraordinary talent, so pure and beautiful was the music that had graced his ears. At odd moments of the day, he allowed his thoughts to reflect on Jocelyn, her beauty, and her music.

I have never truly known her.

His unpremeditated reflections advanced to an image of the

two of them playing together, by the light of the fire in their own home—Jocelyn on the violin, dressed in white, her golden hair hanging down to her waist, to his pianoforte accompaniment.

What am I thinking? He caught himself. *How dare I be unfaithful to my dear Regina with such thoughts?!*

Chapter 56

A week earlier, Regina had invited Nathan to meet her at a troubled orphanage. Due to her need to maintain a good rapport with the operators, she did not take an active role in orphanage reform. Her objective was to find a suitable match for child and parents, and realized that if she became too vocal in reform, she might lose her ability to operate freely among the various homes. She hoped that Nathan might be inspired to take up the cause and help champion the reforms that she could not, after their romance had run its course. She felt relief that it wouldn't end today. But her mind was now made up to end matters on their subsequent encounter — it was time.

The day scheduled for the visit arrived several days after Nathan heard Jocelyn play. He and Regina arrived at the orphanage separately. On the way over, Nathan's mind remained preoccupied with Jocelyn and the accidental discovery of her glorious talent, despite his best efforts to cast it from his mind. He longed to hear her play again, but knew it would never happen.

His thoughts were interrupted by the gig coming to a stop in front of the orphanage. Nathan saw Regina standing near the entrance and walked over to her. While pleased to see her spontaneous reaction of happiness at his arrival, he wondered why it was inexplicably followed by a fleeting regard of sorrow. The pained expression had lasted but the blink of an eye and he wondered if he had been mistaken, especially as the bright smile instantly returned to Regina's face.

"The parents should arrive momentarily. Today is the day."

The grounds were a dark contrast from the Home on the Hill, which he recalled from his visit months before. Everywhere, there were signs of neglect. The small lawn in front was dying and full of weeds much taller than the sparse grass. Dirt, twigs, and leaves littered the sidewalk, and it looked as though the steps and porch hadn't been swept in months. The front door was covered in grime and dirty handprints, and the building itself showed signs of heavy deterioration.

Soon after, a couple arrived in a pony chaise. The man was in his late thirties and the woman several years younger. Regina introduced Nathan to Mr. and Mrs. Herschel. His first impression of the couple was favorable. They showed each other natural affection in their words and manners, and each displayed a pleasant countenance. They had little time to become acquainted before the director of the orphanage, Mr. Chadwick, came forward. Nathan's first impression of Mr. Chadwick was *not* favorable. He was tall and skeletal, with a haughty and unforgiving demeanor.

The four followed the director inside the building. Unfortunately, the interior was even more depressing than the exterior. Children were dirty, hungry, and in poor spirits. The director seemed oblivious to the conditions. He scolded several children for inconsequential misdemeanors in the brief trek from the entrance to his office. Once inside the office, he motioned for the parents and Regina to be seated; Nathan remained standing as there were only three chairs for the guests.

"We are prepared to relinquish custody of Avery. But there is the little matter of the donation."

Mr. Herschel removed several bank notes from his wallet, handing them over to the director. The director looked visibly upset. "I said fifty pounds! There is only thirty here."

Regina responded in her soothing, tender voice. "With your heavy responsibilities, Mr. Chadwick, I am sure you've forgotten. You requested fifty. I informed you that the couple could afford only twenty. After further discussion, you displayed great charity and generosity by magnanimously agreeing to accept an amount well below the customary donation. I was greatly touched by the compassion and wisdom you showed that day. I am sure it is now coming back to you." Nathan was amazed by Regina's calm and soothing delivery.

The director was lulled into submission by Regina's sweet regard and voice, and he confessed that he had forgotten. In fact, he had not, but his practice was always to demand more than agreed when the adoption was assured, often to his pecuniary benefit.

"Now, you must commit to bringing up this child as a devout member of the Church of England." Nathan found it ironic that the self-proclaimed God-fearing director could allow the children to live in such squalor.

Mr. and Mrs. Herschel promised they would, just as they had promised during the initial visit.

"Do you attend church regularly—every week?"

The couple nodded, as they had before.

"Discipline is the next matter of priority to me," the director said emphatically. "You must be willing to use the rod with this young man. I cannot have his corruption on my conscience."

Regina responded on the couple's behalf. "I assure you that the parents will use all appropriate discipline with the child."

The director then inquired about education and the couple's income. Their income was modest, but manageable. It was all ground that had been dealt with before. It must have been for Nathan's edification, Regina surmised.

The director then produced a folder with various documents. There were adoption papers that the couple had to sign; other documents confirmed that Avery was in excellent health, releasing the facility from any legal liability.

When the process was completed, the director asked: "I suppose you would like to see the child?"

The couple nodded enthusiastically.

They followed the director to a large room in the back, where a dozen children were playing.

"Boys are easier to place than girls," Regina noted quietly to Nathan as they followed the director and couple.

"Why is that?"

"Childless parents often desire a male heir. Other couples may be looking for help on a farm or business."

"And these parents?"

"Probably more the former."

The director showed them to Avery.

"How long has Avery been here?" Nathan inquired.

"Nearly three years."

Avery looked emaciated. He was seated on the ground, playing lethargically with a couple of marbles. His hands were dirty, his face smudged. Young as he was, his eyes lit up when he saw the approaching couple; he recognized them well from their prior visit. It is every orphan's fantasy to be adopted, and Avery was no exception. Yet, such a miracle is rare. So many disappointments. So many visits from prospective parents and so few adoptions.

Young Avery looked up at the director, asking with his eyes if *he might truly go* with the couple. Nathan felt his heartstrings pulled. The couple walked up to Avery and both knelt down in front of him.

Avery looked wide-eyed, as he asked them a question: "You're not really going to be my mummy and daddy, are you?"

"Oh yes! We truly are." The new mother took Avery by his

hands and gave him a wondrous smile.

"When will you come back?" The couple had met with Avery a week before, and the mother sensed that the meeting had seemed like a lifetime ago to little Avery, and that their adopted son had given up hope of ever seeing them again. She felt her heart breaking.

"You are going with us now," the lady said softly.

Avery looked up at the director. "I'm not really going now, am I?"

Before the director could respond, the lady responded: "We have a beautiful room for you with lots of toys. Here. We brought you one." She produced a small toy soldier from her purse.

The director's eyes flared at the undeserved reward.

Avery's eyes lit up. Nathan watched the look of hope and joy painted across the young boy's face. Avery examined the wooden toy, placed it on the ground, maneuvered it into battlefield position, and then attacked. "Can I play with it for a while? I will give it back when you go, I promise."

The new father's eyes could no longer remain dry. "Don't you understand, Avery? You are going to be *our* little boy. We love you and you are coming home with us. Now." With that, the man picked up Avery. Avery's face first showed disbelief and surprise, then his face broke into a wide smile. The couple started down the corridor. Avery looked back at the director, hoping against hope that the director had not changed his mind.

As they proceeded further down the corridor, a flicker of understanding began sinking in. "I must say good-bye to my friends," Avery said, wiping his tearing eyes with his arm. During the next fifteen minutes, Avery said his good-byes. Some children displayed happiness at his good fortune, some showed sadness, and others, envy.

The new family, followed by Nathan and Regina, left the building. One of the children, a young girl of no more than five, tugged on Regina's arm. She had seen Regina leaving before with new parents and was pleading to her with her eyes.

Nathan heard Regina tell the child in a soft, loving voice, "I promise I will come back for you. Very soon." A look of utter delight descended upon her face and she let go of Regina's arm.

Outside, Avery asked his new parents, "How long shall I stay with you?"

"Always!" the mother said loudly. "You shall always be our little boy and we shall always be your mummy and daddy." Avery's look of incomprehensible delight was painted all over his face. Now he understood.

Nathan looked at Regina and thought how many times she must have witnessed such a touching spectacle. Her face was streaming with tears as she observed the indescribable happiness of the three new family members.

"You won't recognize him in a month or two," she whispered to Nathan. "Every child I place from *this* orphanage is a life saved."

***

On her separate path home, Regina dwelt upon the experience and committed every feeling, every expression on the faces of the child and parents, every utterance made by either, to memory. It would serve as another sublime reward for her efforts. *My life is so fulfilling, even without Nathan. I must never forget that. I have such treasured memories from every child I place.*

Every night before falling to sleep, Regina would choose one child to ponder. She would start by reflecting on the first time she saw the child. She would remember the child's eyes lighting up when he or she started to believe in the impossible. She would remember the new parents picking up the child for the first time, loving and hugging the child. She would relive the new family leaving together, their lives forever enriched. Then, she would visualize meeting the family months or even years after, the child fully integrated into his or her new home and environment. Every night when she retired, among all the orphans she had placed, one child would be commemorated. One child remembered. One child would linger on her mind as she fell into peaceful slumber.

Nathan, you disturb my peace... you invade my happiness. I love you so tenderly, but I know that I can never be yours. I wish you could save my life, as I help save the life of an orphan child. You have allowed me to taste romantic love—it is exquisite and miraculous and... wonderful. But, the next time we are together shall be our last. Will I ever be able to go to sleep again in peace, knowing I broke your heart and mine? Will I be able to ponder an orphan child without you distracting my sweet serenity? Will I ever know such happiness again... once you are gone?

Chapter 57

Nathan was working intensely on the interior drawings of the Rochester residence. It was awe-inspiring to be the architect of such a structure. He envisioned moving about the rooms as if it were his own palace. It truly was a palace that he was creating! If his vision was too bold or too costly, it would be up to Sir Rochester to tone it down. For now, there was no limitation on his creativity.

One of the three braided staircases was shrouded in mystery. It appeared to come from nowhere. In reality, it disappeared into the ground floor and was accessible only by secret hallways or doors on the second and fourth floors. Certain areas of the dwelling could be gained only from this staircase. Some of the areas would be nearly invisible—the upper clerestory balconies on either side of significant hallways, and upper floor balconies near the tops of domes. Other rooms accessible only from the secret hallways would be concealed within the architecture. It had been a concept that Sir Rochester had championed.

James Allen had proven to be an exceedingly competent young draftsman. He was quiet, soft-spoken, and showed little overt personality, but he was a hard worker, and his drawings nearly always captured the integrity and substance of Nathan's grandiose designs. The industry and energy of the new projects elevated even Stumbolt's performance, as his erratic record of attendance seemed a thing of the past. Nathan was interviewing for a second draftsman, due to the sudden expansion of work that had descended upon the office.

In his third full week at the new location, Nathan had already developed a routine. Unlike his first year and a half of practice, Nathan could barely wait to get to work each day and move the new projects along. He became an early riser, reaching the office often before seven o'clock. He would customarily continue work without break until the noon hour, or shortly after. His housekeeper-chef prepared breakfast and dinner at home, but after the first few days of walking home during the noon hour for lunch, he decided to save time by getting victuals for lunch from street vendors. The food was fast and tasty and enabled him to save thirty minutes.

He found the stall of one street vendor particularly to his liking. Run by a man of large stature who went by the nickname "Dutch," the stall was the largest one on the corner, and offered fresh bread and butter, sandwiches and cake. Dutch had painted his stall a bright green, and had erected a large canopy that extended six feet outward, to shield customers from the hot sun during summer days or rain during inclemency. An immigrant from Holland when he was a youth, he had no trace of an accent, but had always been called by his country of origin. He had labored in the shipyards for twenty years before finally saving enough money to purchase the wagon and equipment. Now in his tenth year as a vendor, he had an established spot inherited from his deceased partner and had built a clientele based on good food, reasonable prices, and friendly service. Nathan preferred the Dutch's smoked ham sandwiches and currant cake to the offerings from other nearby vendors. Being a regular customer had its perquisites—Dutch always provided Nathan the best cut of ham and made sure he received the freshest watercress and the hottest cakes.

Returning to the office after lunch, Nathan noticed the arrival of a letter from Jocelyn, reminding him of the passage of time since their last meeting and requesting *politely* that he come again to the Charlesworth estate. Nathan realized that it had been two weeks since his last visit, excepting his memorable witness of her musical gift a week before, of which she, of course, knew nothing. He could delay no longer; it was time to tell her that their "relationship" needed to end. Nathan decided he would write her a letter, to properly express his utmost gratitude for her kindness in changing his life forever. He would deliver the letter in person.

What words could he use to express himself? Words seemed so inadequate. He needed inspiration. Music would provide that, as it had so many times before. He walked from his library to the parlor, where his newly installed box piano stood lonely in a room with few furnishings. It had been his constant companion all his life. He had played it nearly every day of his life, except when he had been running from Sedgwick. Now, seven days had come and gone without a sound or a touch, since hearing Jocelyn's secret virtuoso performance. He had wished not to destroy the exquisite melody and memory of the week before, but it was time to move on. He placed his fingers on the top of the yellowing ivory keys—piano keys that had been brightly white years ago, when his mother had unlocked the mystery of music to him.

Nathan remembered vividly the melody he had heard on the violin, for it had been playing over and over in his mind since witnessing Jocelyn. With a single finger, he outlined each note just as he had done the night of her private performance. He played the theme a second time, adding a note in the bass clef for texture. A third time the melody was played, as Nathan accompanied the theme with left hand arpeggios. Then, a fourth time, he enhanced the melody in the treble clef, now an octave above. He played the piece again and again, each time improving and expanding it, imagining a duet with Jocelyn at the violin. He was finally liberated to play other pieces, but he needed to start slowly, and he did so playing Beethoven's first movement of the *Moonlight* Sonata from heart. He followed with the piano score from Schubert's Piano Trio no. 2, then brightened his mood with several Hummel Preludes and a Chopin Scherzo.

For two hours, he renewed his intimacy with the piano. Inspiration would rarely forsake him while playing, and when he retreated to the library he knew what to write. He sat down at his desk and the words flowed with facility. This was the farewell Jocelyn deserved.

***

In the meantime, another farewell was being rehearsed. Regina could delay it no longer. It wasn't fair to Nathan to keep prolonging her good-bye. Already it had gone on far too long. She felt such regret that she hadn't ended it many months earlier, before her mind became obsessed with thoughts of him. She felt guilty that he had acquired a new home with her in mind. If she had only had the courage to end it during the infancy of their friendship, when she knew that their mutual feelings would deepen, it would have saved him the exquisite pain he would surely feel in his lonely new home once she was no longer part of his life.

Nathan would be coming tomorrow. The dreary fall day mirrored her feelings. She bundled up and walked out into the gardens behind the Lancaster residence. The fragrance of delphiniums and chrysanthemums mocked the cloudy sky that hid the sun.

There is such beauty in the world. Life is a miracle. Why should I be so sad?

She often fantasized about married life with Nathan, even though she knew it would never happen. She imagined sitting by the fire, listening to him play Mozart or Chopin. She imagined him holding her tenderly and kissing her. She imagined a house full of laughing children, with parents devoted to each other and to their children. She imagined following, with excitement, the rise of his career, visiting his architectural projects, watching them take shape and form. She imagined continuing her work with orphans, perhaps even adopting one with Nathan someday. Life would be so happy and complete. Then her mind would wander to more intimate moments, and she knew that such wondrous times would never occur. Her future life with him was only in her dreams.

It depressed her greatly to know that tomorrow would be the last day that she would ever see him. How would she tell him? What words would she choose? How would she make him understand? She thought of telling him that her work with London orphans could never take second place to a husband and a family. That was a lie, of course. Could she be so cruel as to lie to him? He would see right through her. Nathan was so gentle and caring. He might not fully understand the reasons for her decision, but he would abide by her request, with grace and dignity.

Why ever did I have to meet him? she thought. *I had been content and fulfilled before I heard him on the piano. Yet, I'll never regret the time I've shared with him. In my private moments, I will relive those memories. If a blind man were given sight for a year, would he curse the year of sight he had been blessed with, when the miracle of sight had caused him to understand the beauty of nature, the visual identity of loved ones, the miracle of color, which had all been a mystery to him before? No, he would treasure that time, and use it as a reference for the rest of his life. The same holds true for me. Knowing Nathan has opened a dimension I never knew existed. I had never known romantic love until I met him. Painful, wondrous, and glorious love. Thank the Lord, I have experienced it. Dear God, help me to end it without causing him too much pain.*

She thought of the orphans. *That* usually gave her such happiness—reflecting on the happiness of a forsaken child embraced by a loving family. It helped her gloom, but her mind continually turned back to tomorrow. She felt like a condemned prisoner, knowing that life would end tomorrow on the gallows.

"Don't be so melodramatic, Regina," she reprimanded herself aloud.

Life will go on. I have so much to live for. So much to do. So many lives to serve.

Chapter 58

Despite her wishes otherwise, the next day dawned. Nathan would be arriving in early evening. She still had not resolved precisely how to end matters, but her resolve did not waver. Today would be the day. Time passed that day as if in a dream. She attended church with the remnants of the Lancaster family, a prayer in her heart all during the service; a petition that she would be given what to say at the very hour. She had lunch on the terrace, the sun shining brightly. She had tea in the afternoon in the parlor. No one present perceived of her anxious mind and the heartbreak soon to follow. The evening came. Regina put on her pale blue chiffon dress. She opened her jewelry box, looking for the right accompaniment to her dress. In one corner, there was the silver locket necklace Nathan had given her many months before. She had never worn it, never even placed it around her neck. By doing so, she knew that she would be deceiving him and herself, committing to a future that could never happen. She picked it up and placed it in her silk reticule. She would return it to Nathan when she bid him farewell. She found jeweled clips for her hair and powdered her face. She had never felt more dread.

As the sun neared the horizon, the butler announced the arrival of her beloved Nathan. She put on her best smile and welcomed him, but she could display no deceit. This would be their final visit together. They made small talk for several minutes, before Nathan asked: "Something is troubling you, my dear. What is it?"

Regina turned away and fought back the tears.

"Please tell me how I can help," he touched her lightly above her wrist.

Regina turned back to him, her eyes moist, but her eyes looked downward as she spoke. "Oh Nathan. We have spent such lovely times together. We have created so many wonderful memories."

"And we shall create many, many more, my love."

No, today shall be the last memory I shall have of you. It is a memory that shall never leave my heart and mind. It is a memory that I shall take with me to the grave.

Their eyes met, as she continued. "How does one endure the

loss of a dear one, one who is treasured with all one's heart?"

Nathan sensed that Regina had lost someone dear to her. Could it be that Avery, the emaciated young boy who had just been joined to new parents, had not been restored to health? Or could it be another orphan child who had contracted a deadly disease?

"It is never easy. We cannot help but mourn the loss, but we should take comfort in the times and memories that we have shared."

Regina searched for guidance.

God, give me the words to say, to tell him tenderly. Spare him pain, please.

Suddenly, inspiration distilled upon her like the morning's dew, and she knew how to proceed: "You told me once of a childhood friend, your first love. Whatever happened to her?"

"She came to the park often during that summer and then she was gone. I never saw her again."

"She moved away?"

Nathan's countenance darkened. "No." It was Nathan who was unsure what to say next. He wanted to spare Regina the tragic story.

"Whatever do you mean?"

Nathan hesitated, as the painful memory vividly returned to his mind. "She died."

"How ghastly! You were so very young, the loss must have caused you great pain."

Nathan looked mournfully away. He remembered with great clarity the emotions he had felt when he had learned of his dear young friend's death. "It had only been one summer of my life, but to this day I remember the exquisite sadness at her passing. For years afterward, I would go to the park, wishing against reason that I might see her again or hear her sweet voice."

"How did she die?" Regina asked gently.

"It was a terrible tragedy." Nathan paused, reliving the day he learned of her death. "Her home burned to the ground. She and her family all perished."

Regina's face turned ashen. Abruptly, she stood up and walked toward the window. Nathan followed, putting his arms lightly around her waist and kissing her neck gently from behind.

"It was many years ago, my love."

"You never told me her name."

"Ginny."

Regina's strength left her and Nathan caught her before she collapsed. He gently led her to the sofa nearby. Tears flooded Regina's eyes, and she began sobbing. "It can't be true," she spoke more to herself than Nathan between sobs. "That was my childhood name. I remember a shy boy I met in a park... many years ago... before my home burned. He had a slight accent." Distant dim memories that had long been put away in the deep recesses of her heart were reanimated with great clarity.

Nathan was in shock. He felt his hair standing on end. "But I saw the home myself. It was burned to the ground and I was told all had perished."

"All but me. I lost my parents and my six brothers and sisters that night." Regina could barely form the words, it ached so badly to speak of it. "My father saved my life sacrificing his."

Overcome with emotion, Nathan could say nothing for several minutes. He draped his arms around Regina, a myriad of feelings coursing through his veins.

Nathan pulled back from his embrace to study Regina's eyes and face once more.

"Can it really be you, Ginny? Can I have really have found you after all these years?"

She nodded between sobs.

"God has brought us together. Both of us, alone in the world. Both orphans of sorts. Together again after all these years." Nathan embraced Regina again, more tightly than before, and buried his head in her hair.

More minutes passed as neither spoke another word.

Can it be true? My dear Lord, have You truly brought us together? Is it even imaginable that Nathan and I met years ago in the great sprawling city of London and now have been reunited again? Did you spare me, that I might find this exquisite happiness? Is it possible that Nathan could be my life's companion? Is he the one man on earth who can love me?

Regina finally found her voice: "I remember how shy you were. And how thin—as thin as a *needle*."

Nathan smiled. He hadn't been called that nickname since his boyhood days.

Regina continued softly. "Unimaginable tragedy I have known. But, wondrous love, too— there was such love and affection in our home, such closeness. We didn't have much, but we had each other.

"For years, I wished the fire had consumed me, too." She paused. "But, I have also known unspeakable kindness. My mother's oldest brother—who had cast her aside, when she married my father—came rushing to my rescue, and he has since been the dearest man and a second father to me."

Still holding her hands, Nathan spoke gently. "I knew there was something familiar about you when our eyes first met."

She looked into Nathan's eyes. Struggling to maintain her composure, Regina was powerless to conceal her happiness. Her eyes brightened with joy and a smile burst forth in full bloom on her face and lips, overwhelming all restraint. Never before had she displayed such a smile and glow. Was it possible that destiny had brought them together for a purpose? Could Nathan truly be the one man on earth who could accept her and love her as his wife? A feeling of hope in a glorious future together grew within her breast, as she placed her head lightly against Nathan's chest. Today would *not* be the last day they shared, after all.

Chapter 59

Roderick took another sip of the Duke's newly imported Portuguese wine. He had never seen the Duke in such fine spirits. Sinclair's life among the English gentry would soon be over.

"It won't be long now," Roderick predicted.

The Duke smiled. His mind had been preoccupied with a fond memory of Jocelyn from years before. It had been in the early dawn of her beauty. She had just turned twelve and had asked the Duke about the faraway cities and exotic countries to which he had traveled. The Duke had regaled her with stories of visits to European capitals and the Orient. He had captivated her with tales of pirates, conspiracies, treasure, and betrayal; none of it was true, of course, but she had been exceedingly gullible and enchanted. If only she were as gullible now. If only she were so easily enchanted now.

He had seen the sun rise on Jocelyn's loveliness and witnessed its ascent to the full glory of her indescribable beauty. Did that not entitle him to possess her? He would see to it that she became as a child again, when she was crowned his duchess.

"I wish I could see his face when he finds out," Roderick laughed.

"That would be priceless." The Duke could sense victory. Once the architect was out of the way, his path back to Jocelyn would be assured.

"My dear Duke," Roderick smiled. "You should work on your *French*."

***

Tonight he would bid Jocelyn farewell. Nathan had not seen her since the mystical evening when he had witnessed her musical mastery. He had the farewell letter on his person, in his coat pocket. He would deliver it to her tonight. He perceived Jocelyn in a much different light than before; her musical gift gave her a new level of depth and maturity that she had previously been lacking in his eyes. He had underestimated her and undervalued her. *I never tru-*

ly knew her, he thought regretfully, realizing that his acquaintance with her would end tonight. She seemed as a stranger to him, and he felt a perplexing nervousness about seeing her again.

Tonight he would express his supreme gratitude to her and praise her for her amazing musical gift. But, he would also tell her it was time for him to move on with his life. Such thoughts of her preoccupied his mind on the trip over. He wondered how the evening would unfold.

***

From her high bedroom window, Jocelyn had an unobstructed view of the main gate. The trees obscured, especially in summer when the branches were heavy-laden with leaves, much of the long double road that led from the gate to the entry of the Charlesworth structure. On late Friday afternoons, and other random moments, she would often sit at the window seat of her chamber, hoping to glimpse Nathan's arrival. Whenever she saw him enter the gate and stroll up the long road through the intermittently blocking trees, she felt such delight at his arrival and the coming concert. On rare occasions, she would miss his entrance and discover the haunting melody echoing quietly through her bedroom door or perhaps into another room in the mansion; that was also delicious, because on those occasions, it was an unexpected surprise.

Today, she was particularly yearning for his visit. It had been two weeks since she had heard his musical genius. That had been far too long a separation for her from Nathan and his music. Would he be coming soon? It was Friday. It was late afternoon. That was usually when he appeared. From her window seat, Jocelyn glanced out upon the immaculate landscaping of the Charlesworth estate on a cloudy day. He was nowhere in sight. Jocelyn sighed.

She glanced back appreciatively at her luxurious room from her seat at the window. The walls were covered in a light-lavender fabric, and bordering the windows were pleated purple brocade drapes embroidered in gold, with tasseled tiebacks. Her Corbett bed, crafted in rich oak, stood high enough off the floor to avoid morning drafts from the fireplace, and laid upon it were silk sheets, a deep purple satin duvet, and matching satin pillows, flounce, and ribbons. The oak chairs and matching footstools were upholstered in the same light-lavender fabric as the walls. Cabinets and marble-topped tables held small sculptures of bronze, ebony, and ivory. Much of the floor was covered with a sumptuous burgundy Persian rug. A beautiful gold chandelier hung from the ceiling, and matching candlesticks stood on the night tables. There was a brightly painted bath, with a pure enamel lining; the toilet table was adorned with crystal decanters of perfume imported from Paris and Milan. The room held a sweet fragrance from the many fresh orchids, lilies, and roses on display. In the far corner of her chamber was an exquisitely carved oak jewelry chest. Each of its five drawers was brimming with trinkets of great value and beauty: settings in diamonds, rubies, sapphires, emeralds, pearls, and other gemstones, a collection to which Jocelyn's father was continually adding. Jocelyn wondered if there was any other woman on earth who possessed a bedchamber equal to hers.

She looked back out the window and noticed the front gate moving. Her heart leapt as she recognized Nathan's profile. She would be the recipient of another concert tonight. She followed Nathan's long march up the road, rose from her seat, and glanced in the ornately crafted mirror above her jewelry chest. Everything was in place. How blessed she must be among God's creations to have received such beauty, she thought to herself. Jocelyn opened the door, walked into the hallway, descended one flight of stairs, and inveterately took her spot perched on the ottoman on the balcony above the music room, beyond the view of Nathan.

***

As usual, Nathan descended to the music room without seeing a soul, except for the butler who admitted him in. He sat at the piano for several minutes before starting, pondering his life and his music, and the transformation that had occurred so miraculously because of his acquaintance with the most beautiful woman on the face of the earth. Nathan was unaware that Jocelyn was a short distance above, waiting with great expectation to hear him begin his concert.

Jocelyn had discreetly observed Nathan's stride into the ballroom below and his entry up the short stairs into the adjoining music room. She closed her eyes, waiting to savor the first sound from the piano. Softly and elegantly, Nathan began playing. Jocelyn sighed, entranced to hear his mastery once more.

Nathan had a unique performance planned tonight, but that would wait; he wanted to make sure that Jocelyn heard his special arrangement. First, he started with Mendelssohn, playing selected works from his *Songs Without Words*. Now, if she were listening near, she would soon know. He had developed a melodic accompaniment to shroud the theme at its inception, but ultimately Nathan exposed on the piano the same melancholy melody he had heard Jocelyn perform on the violin.

As the theme was gradually revealed, Jocelyn gasped in wonderment. How could Nathan be familiar with a piece that had just been written by Pyotr Tchaikovsky? Jocelyn had received the publication just days before from an obscure publisher in Moscow; Nathan couldn't possibly have a copy. Jocelyn was so bewildered at hearing the theme played that she needed to descend now to see Nathan. She made her way down to the music room, savoring every nuance of the beautiful melody on the way.

As Nathan completed the piece, he heard approaching footsteps; he had been expecting Jocelyn and her surprised reaction. The footsteps, though, were heavier and slower than Jocelyn's. Nathan spun around on the piano bench and saw the butler approaching.

"I have been instructed to escort you to the library, Mr. Sinclair."

Nathan was puzzled by the summons, but dutifully obeyed without a word.

By the time Jocelyn arrived at the music room, Nathan had vanished. Where had he gone? Could he possibly have left already? Certainly not. Not after playing *that* piece. She began searching for him in nearby rooms and corridors.

In the meantime, the butler had led Nathan up the main staircase and down the corridor to the right of the entryway, and into the library. On the long summer day, the sun was still hanging above the horizon, throwing bright light into the library's windows. For the first time, Nathan studied the room's interior. It consisted of three levels, with angular bookcases extending from the main level all the way to the ceiling of the top level, housing easily a thousand books or more. The deep-stained wood paneling gave way to windows on the right side, which opened up to a garden atrium. Nathan was amazed at the architectural beauty. Straight ahead, sitting in front of a library window, was the silhouette of a man seated behind a desk. The light from the window behind made it difficult for Nathan to fully discern his features at first. Nevertheless, Nathan immediately surmised the identity of the man behind the large, intricately engraved mahogany desk, and he felt his blood turn cold.

"My lord," the butler said to the man seated, and then looking Nathan's way, introduced "Mr. Sinclair."

The butler left, shutting the heavy door behind him. Lord Charlesworth briefly proffered an inscrutable glance upward at Nathan, before returning his eyes to a document he was studying. Despite frequent visits to the Charlesworth residence, Nathan had never met Jocelyn's father, although he knew his face well from the portrait hanging in the sitting room and his appearance at Lady Sommersby's months before. He sensed at once that he was in the presence of a man of immense power and purpose.

Nathan remained standing for several minutes, until Lord Charlesworth finally motioned for him to take a chair directly in front of his elegant desk. As his eyes adjusted to the light, Nathan could discern Lord Charlesworth's full set of dark hair, turned silver at the temples. He wore a black dinner jacket, white shirt, and dark tie. Around his neck was an ivory satin scarf that lay untied on either side of his chest.

Setting the document aside, Lord Charlesworth's eyes seared into Nathan's. "So, at last we meet. The *infamous* Nathan Sinclair. The man who presumes to court my daughter."

Nathan nodded meekly.

"You invade the privacy of my home as though you were a member of the family. You trespass the chambers of *my abode* with abandon. You caress the precious instrument I purchased for my daughter. You finesse *my daughter's* weakness and exploit it for profit. I always feared a musician might cast a spell upon her," Lord Charlesworth paused, sizing up the man seated across from him. "But you are much more than that, aren't you?"

The blood drained from Nathan's face.

"You want more than the spoils you have gained thus far. You wish to be a partaker in all things that pertain to the Charlesworth name and glory. You seek to ascend to the pinnacle of power, prestige, and wealth. You yearn to be ordained with nobility, when you are nothing more than a miserable fraud."

Nathan broke eye contact with Lord Charlesworth, feeling as though the wind had been knocked out of him.

"I know who you truly are," Lord Charlesworth said slowly with a despicable frown. "An imposter, and a poor imitation at that. A bastard son with a blemished birthright worth less than a bowl of porridge. Look at me, coward! Hold my stare!"

Nathan felt the power and force of the command and raised his eyes to hold Lord Charlesworth's glare of contempt, trying to make sense of the defamatory remarks that had just violated his ears.

"The man who dares to scandalize *my* name, who seeks to share in *my* wealth..." Nathan held his stare, his heart beating rapidly.

Lord Charlesworth moved forward in his chair, boring into Nathan's soul in fury. "How dare you!"

Nathan felt the walls of the library closing in around him. He had been warned that Lord Charlesworth would rage against him if he ever found out, but Nathan had never truly imagined it would happen, *and not like this!*

Lord Charlesworth reclined back into his chair, and returned to his natural voice. "Tell me, *Mister* Sinclair, what is your price... for the time you have devoted to this hopeless enterprise? What amount do you require to disappear forever? To never see my daughter again?" Lord Charlesworth opened a drawer and retrieved a check.

Nathan was taken aback by the sudden change in the interview.

"Go ahead. Let us be done with you!"

Nathan's throat was dry. He opened his mouth and no words came out.

"Speak up, boy!"

Clearing his throat, Nathan tentatively spoke his first words. "Your grace, you are mistaken. I seek no financial gain..."

"Yes, only the affection of my beautiful daughter. I know how this masquerade works. The sincerity, the protestation of love, all for the purpose of increasing the price. Name your price!"

Nathan shook his head. "I swear, your grace, I seek no recompense. If it is your wish that I disappear and never see Miss Charlesworth again, I shall comply at once."

"Very well! You won't set a price; I will set one for you." Lord Charlesworth grabbed a quill, dipping it in ink, and began writing. He stood up and walked over to Nathan.

"That should be adequate." Lord Charlesworth tendered the check.

Nathan held up his right palm, indicating he wouldn't accept it.

"It is an extraordinary amount for any man. Look at the sum. Take it, and be gone!" Lord Charlesworth demanded in an angry voice.

Nathan looked down, refusing the temptation of even glancing at the sum inscribed on the check. Keeping his eyes lowered, Nathan spoke quietly. "Please, your grace. I will not accept any sum, though you should offer me a fortune."

It was clear Sinclair was no fool, Lord Charlesworth thought. It was evident he had played this ruse before and knew that *proof of extortion, by way of a canceled check,* would send him to prison for the rest of his natural life. Lord Charlesworth walked back to his desk and sat down.

"You're a pathetically transparent fraud. You have already reaped a fortune from *my personal friends,* as we both know, and now you hope to disappear without consequence."

Nathan tried to speak again, but nothing decipherable emerged from his throat.

"Silence! And you renounce my daughter's love so readily? Proof you have abused her heart. Proof your motive is nothing more than financial gain."

"Your grace, Miss Charlesworth and I... we share a love of music, nothing more."

"So, you've scripted the response for this day—your day of reckoning. Shrewd. Planned for the day when this artifice must end, *a far richer man now than before.* Am I not correct?" Lord Charlesworth's voice boomed.

"Yes, your grace. I am. But, I never intended any reward..."

"Hold your peace! I have heard enough. Did you actually believe that you would succeed in this fraudulent scheme? Did you actually imagine that my daughter would marry a common guttersnipe? Trying to fabricate noble birth is an old trick, one that never endures. The aspirant of nobility is inevitably revealed and his state is far worse than before. Which is precisely what will happen to you, when you shall be exposed in all your glorious deceit tomorrow."

Nathan's heart was beating madly, nearly shaking his whole frame, and he felt his impending destruction.

"You may wish to leave the British Isles tonight, *Mister* Sinclair, before it is made public," Lord Charlesworth said in a lower tone. Nathan looked at him with trepidation. What was coming next?

"When the morning dawns, the *Times* will tell your story and reveal your sordid past. Imprisonment at Coldbath Fields. That should be a great boon to your business."

It had been a hidden fear of Nathan's that his incarceration might someday see the light of day—but never like this.

"But that is only the beginning..."

Nathan braced himself for what was next to come.

"The world will learn the truth about you. Your father's imprisonment for fraud."

Nathan couldn't believe what he was hearing.

"Like father, like son. It will be public tomorrow. The *Times* shall tell the tale of your contraband father, who forged master artwork for a living, deceiving art collectors throughout France... and... your mother giving birth to you out of wedlock..."

With the last comment, Nathan felt a dagger piercing his heart.

"The editor paid me a visit earlier today, just the welcome home gift I was hoping for," Lord Charlesworth added sarcastically. "He asked my permission to run the story, fearing my wrath because he believed that *with my blessing* you are courting my daughter. But that will no longer be the case, once you leave this room."

Nathan felt a wave of nausea come over him. *How does Lord Charlesworth know about my parents, when I know nothing at all?*

Lord Charlesworth suddenly raised his voice with great power and authority, as if he were the Queen's prosecutor seeking the penalty of death. "How dare you think that you can succeed in stealing the affections of my beautiful daughter with your fraud and deceit?!" The force of those words caused Nathan to cower in fear.

"So you have nothing more to say on your own behalf. At least in that regard, you are commended. I have little time for the likes of you, but hear me now!" The power and volume of his voice crescendoed beyond his previous thunder, as he gave Nathan a deathly stare. "From this moment forward, I *forbid* any further contact with Miss Charlesworth—in person, by letter, by intermediary. If you venture so much as a look her way, you will incur the full brunt of my wrath. If you disobey me, I promise your personal destruction! I will have you arrested for fraud, and when and if you are able to extricate yourself someday from prison, when your hair has turned far greyer than mine, your only harbor will be on some unknown island thousands of miles away, begging for scraps of rotting food and filthy drink.

"You think you can purloin the crown jewel of my life without consequence? Have no doubt of my power and influence, Mr. Sinclair." He slowly enunciated both syllables of Nathan's name as if he were the most reviled man on earth, bringing the stinging indictment to a close. The silence was deafening.

Nathan waited several seconds to see if there was more. Meekly, Nathan looked at the defiant lord.

"May I speak, your grace?" Nathan inquired delicately. Lord Charlesworth looked indignantly at him. But, when no objection was uttered aloud, Nathan pressed forth timidly. "I fear you and know that you can and will do as you say. I solemnly swear to fully abide by your edict from this moment forth. But know that this evening I came to end matters with Miss Charlesworth, having no expectation of encountering you."

From his expression, it was clear that Lord Charlesworth doubted the veracity of his assertion. Nathan produced the envelope from inside his pocket. It was addressed to Jocelyn. "It is all here in this letter, your grace. My farewell to your daughter. You may do with this letter as you wish, but know that tonight I came to deliver this letter to her, never to see her again. I covenant upon my life, to never look upon the face of your daughter for so long as I shall live. You shall never be troubled by me again." Nathan placed the sealed letter on the desk.

"May heaven help you keep your oath." Lord Charlesworth said defiantly, and then whispered under his breath. "At your peril."

Nathan stood, bowed, and escaped the library, feeling as if he had been physically bruised and beaten. His very existence felt as fragile as that of a porcelain doll perched on the bureau's edge. As he hastily passed through the library door, his head lowered in shame, Nathan heard Jocelyn's voice calling his name and her quick footsteps from behind. He turned not in her direction, but rather departed the house and ran toward the front gate. Jocelyn hastened to the front door, hysterically shouting his name. Nathan ignored her calls, refusing to take a final glimpse of Lord Charlesworth's daughter, fleeing like an escaped convict from captors in hot pursuit. It was not until he was well beyond the Charlesworth compound that Nathan finally stopped to catch his breath and felt with full force the crushing suffocation of the interview.

***

Lord Charlesworth took the sealed envelope and tossed it into the fire. He had no time or interest in reading the self-serving contents from the pathetic cretin. Nathan Sinclair's life would be over, for all intents and purposes, soon enough.

Sinclair will live to regret the day he ever deigned to see my daughter's face.

But before the letter ignited, Lord Charlesworth thought better of himself, and picked up a fireplace poker nearby to maneuver the singed envelope away from the flames.

Maybe the lies in this letter will seal his destruction.

He took the warm envelope in his hand and broke the seal.

Chapter 60

On his homeward trek, Nathan felt as if he were being pulled into a cesspool of sewage and filth, though the cobbled roads upon which he walked were free of grime. With every step, he felt himself sinking lower into the excrement and refuse. The longer he walked, the deeper he sank, until his extremities seemed fully immersed, the putrefaction invading even the pores of his skin. He imagined thick black muck rising to his chin, mouth, and nose—cloaking all senses. Though the outer air was unusually clean, Nathan struggled mightily to breathe, so intense was his feeling of suffocation in the miasmic filth.

When he reached home, Nathan collapsed on his newly purchased couch in the parlor, next to where his mother's box piano stood, wondering how he could endure the coming shame. Should he leave in the morning light, never to set foot upon the British Isles again, as Lord Charlesworth had suggested? He felt the most hopeless of souls and knew that the coming humiliation might well ruin every dream he had and any prospect of a life worth living. His hope to conceal forever the incarceration had now been dissembled, and the coming revelation would be particularly painful, because Regina would know that he had not been honest with her about his past. As damning as that disclosure would be, the wild assertions about his parents, if true, would doom his self-respect and his inner being forever. Could it be true? Lord Charlesworth was certainly convinced.

He further speculated about what Lord Charlesworth might do, *even if* Nathan honored his solemn oath; it left him with an uneasy feeling. Although his objective of ending the affair with Jocelyn had been achieved, the means of fulfillment had been unspeakably bitter, having been shamed to his inner core. Despite his professional success, for the first time Nathan regretted mightily having acted on Jocelyn's birthday invitation. *Lord Charlesworth is right. I have been deceitful. I should never have accepted her proposition. If I had not, my stay at Coldbath would never have seen the light of day.*

Nathan's tortured mind anguished over how Regina could possibly love a man as despicable as he. Her fine opinion of him would be forever shattered.

Nathan feared losing his new clients—the ones who were "well connected" to the Charlesworth clan. That would *also* devastate his hopes and dreams.

I remember so clearly the degradation that I suffered from Jocelyn a year ago. Although she has redeemed herself in every way since, now her father has dispensed upon me a wound from which I fear I may never recover. How can any man absorb such a blow? Will this pain and angst fade with time? It did with Jocelyn, but that was only a graze to my ego and confidence. Lord Charlesworth has lacerated my soul. This curse shall follow me all the days of my life.

Nathan walked lethargically over to his piano and sat on the bench. He remained motionless for several minutes, his hands at his side. No one, not even Lord Charlesworth, could ever take away his musical gift. It was a God-given talent, one that his mother had nurtured in him from a young age. If all else failed, maybe he could earn a living as a musician. That thought depressed him; not because he didn't love music and performing, but because it would be admitting he had failed as an architect. He wasn't ready, yet, to abandon his vocation.

Music always lifts my spirit, Nathan thought to himself. He struggled to think of a composition that would raise the heavy weight, but music seemed so insignificant, suddenly, in light of Lord Charlesworth's revelations. Nathan stood up from the bench and walked away.

A half hour later, he returned to the bench.

Dear God, find me the music that will pull me out of this ditch.

Chopin's Scherzo in B-flat Minor would get him started. He began with a flourish, but felt his interest in the piece wane soon after he began. The suffocation of his soul was too overpowering.

Don't let go.

He forced himself to concentrate on playing the piece perfectly, and ultimately made it all the way through. It did nothing to brighten his mood. Instead, his coming claustrophobic collapse seemed imminent. He must try again.

Nathan mentally searched through his repertoire of pieces. He played each movement of Beethoven's *Tempest* Sonata. He hoped the music's "tempest" would overpower his inner storm. It did not. Surely Mozart could rescue him. He started with Regina's favorite: Sonata in C Major. The lightness and delicate simplicity of the music helped briefly, until it brought memories of his beloved Regina. As he reflected on her, he had a vivid premonition that she would turn away from him once the ugly disclosure foretold by Lord Charlesworth became public. He abandoned the composition before completing the first movement.

Dear God, how will I ever get over this oppressive gloom?

As he sat at the piano, Nathan only felt darkness and doom. Almost without thinking, Nathan began playing single notes with his right hand, in the middle register of the keyboard. The simple tune evoked such sadness that Nathan felt tears welling in his eyes.

Why, dear God? Why has this curse come upon me?

He repeated the theme in thirds and then triads with his right hand. Next, the left hand followed in accompaniment, painting a portrait of utter hopelessness. The slow and quiet theme continued as Nathan improvised subconsciously in a distant key. With his fingers, he then chronicled his gradual descent into darkness, reflected by the theme, which became even darker, deep in the bass register of the keyboard. The theme carried no hope, only dread. There would be no moment of triumph in this composition. The left hand was now alone, first triads then thirds, then single notes, until the last sound faded away unresolved — no tonic, no supertonic. That's how his life would someday end.

Nathan left the bench, but the hopeless theme continued in his mind, so melancholy, so heartbreakingly sad — a kindred accompaniment to his own feelings.

His mother's piano had failed him when he needed it most. Cherished as it was, it was just a pathetic imitation of what he had become accustomed to at the Charlesworth estate.

I shall never play such an instrument again, he lamented.

He would miss the frequent recitals on an instrument that made him feel like the greatest pianist in the world. *What would such a piano cost?* He had no idea, but knew that it must be a king's ransom. During his lifetime, he would never possess such a piano.

The hole he found himself in was too deep. Music had given him no respite from his waking nightmare. For only the second time he could remember, it had failed to work its magic. He flopped again onto his couch. He felt mentally and physically drained. He dreaded the imminent disclosure in the *Times* and wished he could disappear. The heavy cares and worries of the day finally dulled his exhausted mind and he fell asleep.

Chapter 61

Nathan would never forget the day he learned about his father. When he arrived in his office the following day under a black cloud, Stumbolt was absent from the reception area. Entering his private office, he saw that the morning newspaper had been placed on his desk. The paper was opened to an article on the society page that was circled in black. He didn't even have the luxury of trying to locate the report on his own. There it was, published and highlighted. Every word of the article would become part of his legacy and would soon sound in all corners of London. He saw the headline. It sickened him.

IMPOSTER UNMASKED.

Then in smaller print, "Miss Charlesworth's Escort a Fraud."

Nathan sat at his new desk, the one he purchased shortly after moving into his new upscale office in Chelsea. He looked out the window. Maybe it would be better not to read the article. It would surely wound him and destroy the illusion of his father being a great man, a man worthy of his dear mother. How dare anyone or anything cast such a terrible stain upon the memory of his angel mother?

Dear God, give me strength now, when I need it most. Help me navigate through this dark hour.

Nathan looked down again at the circled article.

I must read it, for if I don't, I will never understand the mystery my mother meant to tell me. If only she had lived to warn me, I would have lived a quiet and peaceful life, taking care to avoid the public eye. Surely, this horror could have been suppressed from those I know and love.

His mind began to conjure up all sorts of evils that lurked in the small print. Before Nathan had the courage to begin examining the damning article, Stumbolt entered his office, without knocking. Showing mild aggravation for being interrupted without a knock, Nathan looked up. "What is it, Stumbolt?"

"I tender my resignation, sir."

Nathan didn't even bother to ask why.

"I can no longer be associated with... you..." Stumbolt explained. In the blink of an eye, he was gone. Stumbolt had never moved so quickly before, clearly wanting to distance himself from Nathan's employ as quickly as possible.

At least I am now rid of him, Nathan thought.

Then a far more frightening thought occurred. *Is this only the beginning of the defections?*

***

With growing dread, Nathan read the damning words.

> Credible sources have confirmed that Nathan Sinclair, the man linked romantically with Jocelyn Charlesworth, has a sordid heritage. On these pages several months ago, we first reported that Mr. Sinclair was a frequent companion of the beautiful Miss Charlesworth. Initial reports revealed little about him, but there were indications, never confirmed, that his father was a member of the English gentry. It appears now that Mr. Sinclair himself was the author of such rumors, hoping to facilitate his entry to London society and his attachment to Miss Charlesworth. Recently, our sources learned of their "secret engagement"; Mr. Sinclair appeared on the verge of pulling off one of the most presumptuous and extraordinary frauds in English history, hoping to exploit the vast wealth of the Charlesworth family in the process.

> Compelling evidence has come forth that Mr. Sinclair's paternal heritage is quite the opposite of his claims. A review of the marriage registry from Moret-sur-Loing, France, indicates a purported union between an apparent Englishman, Stephen Sinclair, and his mother, Allysandra Mercier. However, it has been confirmed that there is no record of anyone by his father's name existing anywhere in the region. Furthermore, residents of the small medieval village who were interviewed by interested parties confirm no knowledge of any Englishman residing in that village or neighboring areas before or after the time of Mr. Sinclair's birth. In fact, interviews of residents have disclosed that Madame Mercier leased a home alone near the tiny village of Châtenay-sur-Seine, a short distance from Moret-sur-Loing, and

then disappeared for some time, returning with a baby boy that was first claimed to be her sister's son, and later treated as her own.

Further research has revealed the likely identity of Mr. Sinclair's father. An intruder in the region at the time of the apparent marriage, a Guy LaJeunesse, was engaged in creating copies of paintings of great masters, representing the paintings as originals, pocketing vast sums for what turned out later to be forgeries. He was apprehended near Moret-sur-Loing and sent to prison for twenty years, where he died before his sentence was completed. Reports confirmed that it was shortly after his apprehension that Madame Mercier disappeared from Monet-sur-Loing, only to return some time later with the child. Witnesses recall her having been in the company of LaJeunesse before his fraud was discovered. The inescapable conclusion is that the parents of Mr. Nathan Sinclair were never married and that his father was a charlatan, imprisoned for fraud.

It appears that the son has adopted the sins of the father. Not only has he perpetuated the myth of noble birth for personal gain, but he has concealed his own sordid past as a fraudulent debtor who served time at Coldbath Fields Prison, released only after the act abolished debtors' confinement.

Nathan was shattered by the article. As horrific as was the revelation about his parents, he felt an even more violent degradation from the publicity of his incarceration. Now everyone knew, including Regina, Aunt Hélène, and Sir Lancaster. There would be no more visits to the Lancaster residence.

I am no better than my father, Nathan told himself. Years ago, he had constructed a fantasy of his father as a great and noble man. He had always been confident that learning about his father would give him great pride. He was also certain that his mother would have only fallen in love with a remarkable man, one who would have complemented her many virtues. Now, he understood why his mother had shrouded his identity in secrecy. She had obviously been fooled by a man with conniving and deceitful charms. At least she had been truthful about the fact that his father was an artist, apparently an exceptionally good one; but she had hidden the fact that he was one who had perniciously exploited his talents for personal gain. His mother had been trying to warn him on her deathbed, but had been unable to whisper more than a few isolated words. *So, that's what my mother meant when she said "ton père... français,"* Nathan thought. *She was telling me that my father was a Frenchman, not an Englishman. It made sense now.* It also explained why there had never been any attempt to contact his father's family in England—there *was* no family in England. Whatever family remained from his father obviously resided in France, undoubtedly hoping to efface any association with the convicted forger.

He thought back to his mother's wedding ring. Had she purchased the ring herself, and engraved the initials of a fictitious Englishman, to perpetuate the fiction of a marriage? That was the only logical explanation. *How could she have lived a lie for so many years?* Undoubtedly, that was why he never remembered her wearing the wedding ring—it was all a fabrication. But why, then, had she given him the ring? It made no sense. Nathan knew he would never know the answer to that riddle.

Nathan also knew that his mother would never have knowingly fallen for such a charlatan. But, if that weren't slanderous enough, the article implied that his mother had conceived out of wedlock; was it possible his mother could have been seduced by such a man?

Until I know for certain, I shall never accept the fact that I was born a bastard. I will never doubt the virtue of my mother, unless she so confesses with her own lips in the world to come.

What did all this ugliness mean? The thought of losing Regina caused Nathan to cry out in anguish.

Not only will she never forgive me for deceiving her about my past; she will see that I have inherited that deception from my father. I cannot bear to see her face when she learns the news.

Nathan also pondered his future as an architect. There was little question that his practice would suffer mightily from the adverse publicity. His grand commissions were at risk. Who would want to deal with an imposter, a fraud? He felt a claustrophobic insecurity and a darkening pall over his life and future.

Had he lost his dear Regina forever? Surely, she had seen the article. What was she thinking now? Could a woman of her purity and virtue be attached to a man with such scandal?

Just when my life was coming together so miraculously!

If I lose Regina, I lose everything.

Nathan cloistered himself in his office, without a clerk. At least Mr. Allen, the draftsman he had hired, seemed oblivious to his problems; as long as he was paid, Nathan expected no defection there. Nathan thrust himself into his projects, working until late at night, striving to take his mind off the sordid disclosure.

He had been expected at the Lancaster residence on Sunday afternoon. Nathan would save them the embarrassment and not intrude.

Will I ever have the courage to call upon Regina again? Surely, she must be hoping that I never do. With her honor and purity, she must realize that any association with me will come at a heavy cost. She must know that any children brought into the world through our future union would be similarly tarnished by this curse. It may take generations for the ugliness to pass. Perhaps I could talk with her about leaving England and forging a fresh start in the Americas? Dare I ask her to leave her family, her work? No. That would be too much of a sacrifice to ask, even if she were willing to do so for my sake.

During the weekend, he immersed himself in his office, working on projects that he feared would soon be canceled. There would be nothing more to live for, when the work dried up and the love of his life turned her back on him.

Chapter 62

All day Monday, Nathan worked with his draftsman on Sir Rochester's residence. The draftsman relocated to the front office, to receive visitors if any arrived. With each passing hour, Nathan expected an unpleasant and uncomfortable visit from Sir Rochester, Monsieur Lefontaine, or both. When he heard the door to his office open in midmorning, he was certain that it was one of his two prime clients defecting. He breathed a sigh of relief when he learned it was merely the delivery of the *Times*.

Nathan took the occasion to open the newspapers, wondering if there were any other articles about him in the aftermath of the *Times* report. He breathed a sigh of relief after scanning the headlines and finding no follow-up article. Soon he would be forgotten; it was just a matter of time. As he leafed through the pages, he noticed the *Sinclair* name in print. It had been almost a subconsciously discovery, and he studied the page trying to locate the name again in the sea of small print.

There it was, in a letter to the editor.

It's not over yet, Nathan closed his eyes for a moment wondering when it would ever end. With his heart beating, Nathan read the letter, fearing the oncoming wrath of the aristocracy.

> Dear Editor,
>
> To the chorus of English gentry conversing about Mr. Nathan Sinclair, I add my voice. But it is a much different voice from most, as you shall see. It was I who labored unceasingly to have Mr. Sinclair imprisoned when he failed to pay a substantial debt. It was I who rejoiced when he was arrested, handcuffed, and led to prison. When the Act of Parliament released him, it was I who was angered and continued my crusade to have him returned to jail. My lawyer took steps to have him arrested as a fraudulent debtor, which required me to waive a fair amount of interest. Inexplicably, in court Mr. Sinclair escaped imprisonment by paying the sum

due, except for the interest which I had been forced to legally discharge.

A few weeks later, this same Mr. Sinclair paid me an unexpected visit. To my astonishment, he asked for the amount of the waived interest, the amount of the attorney's fees I had expended, and even the cost of the men I had hired to track him down. He then proceeded to hand me a check for a sum in excess of my costs, wanting to make sure that I hadn't overlooked any other expense. He then humbly asked my pardon and left. The check was duly honored by the bank.

Some might find it odd that an "imposter" would pay a debt he didn't legally owe.

I most certainly do.

Respectfully yours,

Winston Sedgwick

Nathan's eyes misted over. One kind act had returned another. From Mr. Sedgwick, of all people. *The last man on earth from whom I might ever expect a favor.*

Nathan prayed that Regina might read Sedgwick's letter. Perhaps, in the maelstrom of defamatory print, the letter would reach her and soften her heart. Perhaps she would not see him as a man without redemption.

There had been no defections in his business yet. Nathan allowed himself a glimmer of hope that he might yet salvage his career and that he might yet see Regina again. But it had only been a few days. It was possible news hadn't yet reached his clients.

***

On Tuesday, Nathan continued to dread that the inevitable visit from his treasured clients could occur at any time. No matter. He would continue laboring until he was told to stop. He would continue to lose himself in his creative energy for so long as he could. It was midmorning when the mail was delivered.

Included in the mail was a letter from Regina.

Nathan's hands trembled as he held the envelope. He hadn't expected to hear from her so soon. He knew the contents. She would be informing him that she had great affection for him, but that she could not continue their liaison in view of the loathsome allegations concerning his father. She would wish him well with every success, but she would ask him politely and firmly to call no more. Nathan knew not how he could endure a rejection from the woman he loved. It would be the most devastating setback of his life—a tragedy from which he would never recover, for as long as he lived.

He put the letter down on his desk and prayed that he had never been born. It would have been better not to have come into the world under such a stain. As he continued to torment his soul, his mind turned to the terrible grief and heartache his mother must have endured. He imagined the shame that had caused her to leave the country of her birth and start life anew where no one would know of the scandal. His heart went out to her. All these years she had harbored the terrible secret. She had wanted to tell him, to protect him, knowing that some day the secret would be revealed to the world. She had wished to forewarn him, to enable him to make preparations for its divulgence and to disclose it in his own way to those close to him. She had anticipated that public exposure of a secret like this could scar his life and future forever. A feeling of profound sorrow for his mother overwhelmed him, and he was ashamed at his selfishness about his own meager distress. He vowed to go on living, to prove that the sins of the father didn't necessarily carry over to the next generation. He would overcome.

With renewed strength and fortitude, he gained the courage to read Regina's letter. He would ache mightily from the priceless loss of one so dear to him, but would move on with his life and persevere, to honor his mother. He broke the seal, his hand still trembling, and he slowly read the contents.

> *My dearest Nathan;*
>
> *You must be hurting so. I feel such pain for you. How humiliating for you to have these matters made public. The news of your father must have been devastating to you, and I feel profound sorrow to learn of your earlier financial distress. How could I possibly judge you or your circumstances, when I have been blessed with such abundance?*
>
> *I understand why you did not visit on Sunday. You believe*

that I no longer care for you, that I no longer wish to be associated with you. You are certain that no respectable woman would dare be in your company. In these assumptions, you are mistaken.

Your father's misdeeds are not your own. Your father's deceit and fraud have no succor in your soul. I know you are a man of great talent and ability, unlike any man I have ever met. I know you are a man of integrity, despite what the journalists may write. I feel no shame at your side. I feel only honor and pride.

Let me nurse your wounded heart and mind. I know you. I had great respect and admiration for you before news of your father surfaced. My respect and admiration have not diminished in any way since.

You will be welcomed as always at the Lancaster house. Please honor me with your presence soon.

Affectionately yours,

Regina Lancaster

Nathan was astonished by the contents of the letter. A surge of relief and euphoria washed over him. He read it a second time, then a third, to make sure the words didn't change with each reading.

What nobility of heart she has! What an extraordinary young lady, who is willing to abide the stain upon me. Nathan felt as if he had awakened from a nightmare.

Whatever the other terrible consequences to these horrible revelations, I can endure them with Regina at my side.

Chapter 63

Regina pondered recent events. She had been on the verge of cutting off her relationship with Nathan during their last time together, until they had discovered to their mutual astonishment how their paths had crossed years earlier, before the fire had devastated her life. That discovery had caused her to believe that destiny had brought them together for a purpose and had given her a hope that she had never before allowed herself to feel. Soon after, she had learned of the stain of Nathan's paternal heritage and his brief confinement, which had caused her exquisite pain because she knew the horrific impact such a disclosure would have on Nathan. But ironically, it had also given her a feeling of hope that Nathan would accept her. That both of them, though damaged, could build a life together. With renewed hope, she found the power within herself to write him a letter, asking him to call. Still, she shrank from having to bare her soul to Nathan. From what reservoir of her life's experiences would she gain the courage to do that?

***

After writing her letter, she had hoped for a visit from Nathan, and her hopes were fulfilled the day after the letter was sent. Nathan called upon her in the early evening. She welcomed him warmly into the parlor of the Lancaster residence.

"Though I knew nothing of my father, I had no right to conceal my embarrassing past imprisonment. I'm ashamed to say I hoped you would never know."

Regina looked at Nathan with compassion. "How could I ever imagine what such an experience must have been like for you? I have never had to worry about my next meal, or about where I would sleep. It must have been frightful."

"But I had no right to conceal it." Nathan took pains to explain how he had fallen in debt, and readily admitted his neglect in repaying it. Although he referenced the twenty-pound advance to Allenby as a contributing cause for his misfortune, he made it clear to Regina that he was directly responsible for the unfortunate matter.

"Did you intentionally steal from Mr. Sedgwick?" Regina asked.

"No, of course not."

"Did you borrow from him, intending never to repay?" she followed up.

"No; at the time, I had every intention to repay."

"If Mr. Allenby had paid his debt to you, would you have repaid Mr. Sedgwick?"

"In full, including interest."

"Then I am satisfied. You rightfully expected Mr. Allenby to discharge his obligation to you, especially when you had come to his rescue, and if he had, there would have been no more issue with Mr. Sedgwick. When Mr. Allenby failed to honor his obligation, your debt with Mr. Sedgwick went into default and grew at such an alarming rate that it must have seemed hopeless on your part to ever repay it."

Nathan nodded. Regina had grasped the matter perfectly.

"Mr. Allenby bears the guilt in this matter." Regina's summation salved Nathan's shame of incarceration. He marveled at her wisdom and grace.

"I never imagined that you would see me again after you learned of the allegations against my father... and my mother." Nathan stared into Regina's dark eyes, wanting to hear her response.

"Then you don't know me as well as you think," Regina smiled. "Why should I hold you accountable for conduct in which you had no part? Regardless of whether you are born of a criminal or a king, what matters is who *you* are."

"The son of a criminal carries the stigma of the father's crime."

"Many might think so. But are we to be judged by our own actions, or the actions of our parents? Would a just God condemn you for crimes you never committed?"

"Surely not," Nathan had to admit.

"Then why should I condemn you?"

"Others have." Nathan related his encounter with Lord Charlesworth.

"Are you not the same man who is an extraordinary musician, artist, and architect? Have all your talents abandoned you?" Regina asked in earnest.

"They have not."

"You still have your dreams and ambition, do you not?"

"I hope to."

"Are you not the same modest, thoughtful, honest, good-natured man I have come to know and care for these many months?"

"I am the same man."

"And is it not you who was once a shy stammering boy, so many years ago—my sweet *Needle Nate*?" Regina broke the serious mood with her childhood reminiscence.

It did what Regina had hoped; it changed his mood. "All this time, I thought my embarrassing nickname safe. My dear Ginny, you may call me that anytime you wish—but never in public," Nathan bantered back playfully.

"All right, *Needle Nate*. But it doesn't really suit you now. You are no longer so thin as a needle. I shall have to find a new, more suitable nickname for you."

"But may I still refer to you as Ginny?"

"Anytime you wish—*especially* in public." Regina smiled and then paused. "I would never have imagined that my Needle Nate would have become the man he is today. Needle Nate was so shy and unsure of himself. You must have already been an accomplished pianist at the age I met you, but you never mentioned anything about it."

"None of the other boys played. Frankly, it embarrassed me then."

"And what an amazing young man you have become. So accomplished, so erudite, so charming and handsome. I have never met a man like you. I have never met a man as fine as you. There must have been an endless number of women attracted to you." Regina's charm was a balm for Nathan's hurt, and he temporarily forgot about the painful disclosures.

"Well, actually, there is only one woman whom I *care* to attract."

"And who might that woman be?"

"That's another well-protected secret."

"Just like your nickname?"

"Just like my nickname."

Later that evening, Regina opened up to Nathan as she never had before. "I have often wondered why I was spared from the fire. For a long time, I was angry to have survived; I longed to join my family in the hereafter. I felt so lonely. It took a long time for me to overcome the tragedy."

"Thank God you were spared," Nathan said earnestly as he pulled Regina to his breast. "And now, there's no longer the need to maintain the illusion of the Charlesworth alliance. *That*, at least, is over. I can openly court you. We can be seen in public together."

Regina felt such powerful conflicting emotions. She thrilled at the words Nathan spoke, but trembled at the disclosure of her own secret that might yet change everything. That could wait.

She continued where she had left off. "My dear father and mother were examples of great nobility and charity, even though our means were modest. I can't recall my parents refusing aid to a stranger or beggar. Often, we would have less to eat, because of their kindness. There were seven children in my family who were taught to think of others first and to make a difference. But they are all gone... all but me. I have dedicated my life to taking up their yoke. I have dedicated my life to doing the good works of all seven. And in so doing, I have been blessed seventy times over." Regina's mood and melodic voice touched Nathan to his core.

Can there be any woman alive who compares to your nobility and charity? Nathan thought to himself. *Can any man be worthy of you?*

For the first time, Regina shared the names of her deceased brothers and sisters, relating fond memories of each. Through tears of love and sadness, she celebrated the lives of each of her dearly departed family members with Nathan. His heart broke as he heard reminiscences of the twin boys, who would always have a special place in her heart—they were only four years old when they left this world. Each brother and sister came alive to Nathan, as she described his or her appearance, personality, dreams, and passions. Regina reserved her most revered respect for her parents, sharing stories of small but heroic acts of kindness and compassion that never would be published or known to the world, except in the hearts of the grateful beneficiaries. What greatness and nobility her parents had possessed! Though they were of modest and humble circumstances, their legacy surpassed that of kings and rulers. Regina was their shining bequest to the world, and there could be no greater gift than she.

Chapter 64

Lord Charlesworth sat behind his desk. He needed to tie up some loose ends and so began writing letters to Monsieur Lefontaine and Sir Rochester. He had learned how Sinclair had exploited the influence of the Charlesworth family in order to line his pockets with wealth from *his* friends. It angered him that Sinclair had gained such a career boost at their expense, especially on the premise that *his* friends were pleasing *him*. They had certainly heard about Sinclair's father by now; in his letters he condemned Sinclair's fraud in the strongest possible terms and urged them to distance themselves from him. That should do the job. Sinclair had probably spent any retainers and would be hard-pressed to return the funds. Lord Charlesworth knew some skillful lawyers who could recover the advances. If Sinclair couldn't pay, he would be returned to prison for fraud, where he would languish for years.

Thirty minutes later, the letters were handed to the butler for posting. That afternoon, the letters were picked up by the postman for delivery.

***

"I thought I'd find you here," Roderick said to the Duke, who was playing chemin de fer in the smoke-filled gambling parlor. He admired the stack of currency in front of the Duke. "Your luck has changed, I can tell."

The Duke's mood was bright. "Ever since the newspaper report, I've had ridiculously good luck. And your efforts with Lord Charlesworth?"

"I have been singing your praises to him. My father shares my opinion that a quick marriage to a bachelor of high rank will help suppress any scandal."

"And who might that high-ranking bachelor be?"

Roderick smiled.

"And Jocelyn?"

"She would never defy her father."

"So it has been arranged?"

"Lord Charlesworth is expecting you tomorrow evening."

Excellent, thought the Duke. *It is only* his *permission I need.*

That night, the Duke slept more soundly than he had in months. He dreamt of his beautiful new duchess, her wealth, and *his* legion of admirers.

Chapter 65

The Duke of Wilmont had never felt better. He had been on a horrendous losing streak, one that had run to nearly fifty thousand pounds; an amount that had caused a serious strain on his liquidity and might force a sale of dukedom property to pay the debt. But after news of Sinclair's father had become known, his fortunes had changed. He had already made up half of his losses and expected to recover the balance in a week or two, at the rate he was winning.

His best carriage was painted and primed for his trip to London, where he would ask Lord Charlesworth for the hand of his daughter in marriage. He had been a friend of Roderick's and the Charlesworths' for over ten years. During that period, he had met the head of the family a number of times, despite Lord Charlesworth's frequent travels.

Both families went back many generations. The first Duke of Wilmont had been installed near the end of the eleventh century. Even the Charlesworth family was not as ancient. The Duke had always been extremely respectful of Lord Charlesworth, who was his senior by twenty years. Lord Charlesworth had known the Duke's father well. The relationship had begun when Lord Charlesworth had come to his father's rescue, years ago, by purchasing Ravensdale—the most desirable parcel of land in the south of England. The easternmost portion of the vast property bordered the sea, and the grounds included several large freshwater lakes, enormous dense forests, and vast meadows. A promontory offered breathtaking views of valleys, cliffs, and the sea, and a magnificent and unparalleled building site for the fortunate owner lay where the remnants of an eleventh century castle still remained.

The proceeds from the sale of Ravensdale had given the Duke's father financial freedom during the latter years of his life. Unfortunately, the Duke had mismanaged much of the estate after his father's passing several years later, encumbering, although never selling, land holdings. The loss of Ravensdale had always pained him, but with the impending marriage to Jocelyn, perhaps Lord Charlesworth would present a dowry of the property, returning the property back to the rightful owner.

He had asked Roderick to plant the seed with his father. Roderick had much to gain from the marriage, the Duke surmised. He would convey Atherton Gardens to Roderick if the marriage to Jocelyn took place. Well, he wouldn't actually convey title to the Gardens; rather, he would grant Roderick a living in the property. With Roderick's ruinous way of living, the Duke expected to outlive him by ten or twenty years, despite Roderick's younger age. Ravensdale, even with its dearth of desirable structures (there was a hunter's lodge in the forest) was a property infinitely more precious than Atherton Gardens. The castle remnants had a particular history with his forefathers, the castle having been burned and plundered by one of the Duke's ancestors in the thirteenth century (the property's name contained the only link to the plundered family's raven crest). The Wilmont family had maintained steady ownership of the property for the following six hundred years. A bequest to Jocelyn of that property would be a means of keeping it in *both* families. With Lord Charlesworth's vast land holdings, a transfer of Ravensdale would hardly be noticed, and a bequest to Jocelyn would keep Lord Charlesworth's descendants owning the property for generations to come.

It was still light when his carriage reached its destination. The Duke was soon ushered into Lord Charlesworth's library. It had been more than a year since the two had met face to face. The Duke of Wilmont gave a prolonged bow of ultimate respect. Lord Charlesworth nodded and smiled.

"A pleasure to see you."

"The pleasure is all mine, your grace," the Duke replied.

Lord Charlesworth inquired of the health of the Duke's siblings and their families. "It has been some time since our paths have crossed. Roderick has told me of your desire to ask for Jocelyn's hand in marriage."

"Your grace, I have known her since she was a young girl. Even then, I fancied that a union between our families would be a wonderful thing: uniting two of the oldest families of the Empire."

"Your father was a good man; I held him in high esteem. His kindness and fairness to his tenants was well known. He had a reputation for honor and integrity."

The Duke nodded. The relationship with his father had become stormy as the Duke matured into manhood. His father had been disappointed in his errant ways, his gambling, his womanizing.

More than once, his father had come to his rescue to avoid embarrassment to the family, and had threatened on several occasions to disinherit him if he didn't change his ways. His father's weakness was believing in his son. The Duke always repented; his father always forgave and genuinely believed each time that his son had reformed, until the next fall from grace. Fortunately, his father had died believing that his son had finally reformed his life—that had been a most uncomfortable year for the Duke, being on probation while his father was ill. He had been forced to limit his wild ways, at least openly. Surely, Lord Charlesworth's good opinion of his father had been carried over to him. He could imagine no reason that Lord Charlesworth would refuse his request: he was incredibly handsome, wealthy, from an ancient family, and a grand Duke of England. And, he would bring the title of "Duchess" to his wife.

"I had great admiration for my father," the Duke lied. His father had been weak. More than twenty percent of the Wilmont land had been sold during his father's reign. His father had frequently forgiven debts of his tenants, and granted payment extensions during times of poor harvest and hardship. That generosity had come to an abrupt halt with his father's death. If the Duke had lived as frugally as his father, his bank reserves would have been heavily laden. Unfortunately, the Duke's lavish lifestyle had exacted a large toll on those reserves, forcing him heavily into debt.

"My daughter is more precious to me than all my wealth," Lord Charlesworth continued.

"I hold her in the same regard, your grace."

"Her future husband must be a man of exceptional probity, honor, and strength. Your father would have qualified. Do you?"

"Perhaps you have heard that I sowed my oats during my younger years, but I made a vow to my father before his death that I would honor his life and follow in his footsteps."

"Have you honored that pledge?"

The Duke looked directly into Lord Charlesworth's eyes and said with deep conviction, "I swear upon my father's life that I have." The lie came easily, as it does for those whose lives are built upon deceit. Lord Charlesworth held the Duke's stare.

The Duke was not finished. "Your grace, something must be done with this Sinclair fellow. He charmed his way into your daughter's life hoping to exploit your family's wealth."

Lord Charlesworth nodded.

"I fear there are many in our circles who have never made his acquaintance or seen his face. It would be truly tragic if he is allowed to continue to foster his pernicious ways and ingratiate himself with other unsuspecting souls. He must be publicly exposed to society as the fraud he is. That way, he'll be excluded at any society gatherings, and we may save other trusting souls from a similar fate." The Duke's desire to humiliate Sinclair was registered all over his face; he particularly wanted to ensure that the architect never had occasion to charm Jocelyn again with his music. "Hopefully he'll have sense enough to leave London."

Lord Charlesworth nodded. "I have in mind the perfect time and place for that. He shall never dare show his face in the British Isles once I am finished with him."

The Duke gave a satisfied smile.

Lord Charlesworth continued. "I know you have been a frequent associate of my son's. Roderick has been a major disappointment to me. Unlike his elder brother, Edward, he seems to have little interest in matters of finance, investment, and stewardship."

"Perhaps it is the lot of fathers to underestimate their sons," making a veiled reference to his own father's opinion of him. The Duke knew the converse had been true in his case; his father had *overestimated* him. "I think Roderick will surprise you yet. Like some second sons, he is jealous of his older brother's inheritance. He has always lived in your shadow, your grace, and the shadow of an elder brother who has more than adequately acquitted himself."

"True. Roderick was a difficult child. Like many fathers, I was too indulgent with my children. He stopped listening to me long ago. I would be deeply indebted to you if you could help instill within him a commitment to honor, integrity, and industry."

"I believe that I am ideally situated for that task. I know that he looks up to me as the older brother that Edward never was to him. If I am granted the honor of being his future brother-in-law, you will elevate my status in his eyes. He will strive more readily to follow my example." That part was true, although the example was not the one Lord Charlesworth had in mind. "I accept your request with the greatest humility and solemnity."

Lord Charlesworth looked pleased.

***

Upon leaving the Charlesworth estate, the Duke breathed a sigh of relief. Narcissist though he was, the Duke was aware that his reputation for honor and integrity was far different from his father's, and he was grateful that Lord Charlesworth traveled in different circles than he. He had expected to receive Lord Charlesworth's consent and his blessing. He had not expected Lord Charlesworth to arrange for an engagement party two weeks hence, celebrating the upcoming marriage—that had been a pleasant surprise. Nor had he expected Lord Charlesworth to propose a date for the wedding, and a location—Westminster Abbey! The place where kings and queens had been crowned and wedded. The Duke had offered his undying gratitude, with a showing of profound humility and respect. Undoubtedly, Lord Charlesworth wanted to suppress any embarrassment that had been caused by Jocelyn's relationship with the architect. Everything was going perfectly. His marriage to Jocelyn was now a virtual certainty.

The Duke imagined a thousand members of the London aristocracy descending on Westminster Abbey for the wedding... *his* wedding. He imagined Jocelyn dressed in white, kneeling at his side, consenting to be his wife. The most beautiful woman on earth would soon be his duchess. The Duke and Duchess of Wilmont would mingle with kings and queens, presidents and potentates. His celebrity and glory would grow until it extended to the far corners of the Empire.

Chapter 66

Over the ensuing days, Nathan and Regina spent much time together, as Nathan noticed a freedom in her affection toward him. It was time to meet with Sir Lancaster. He dropped by the Lancaster residence when he knew that Regina was away visiting a family seeking to adopt.

The butler ushered Nathan to Sir Lancaster's library, a room Nathan had never entered before. The library was noticeably more modest than Lord Charlesworth's, but still handsome with paneled walls and high ceilings, a large fireplace, and ample shelves filled with books.

"I have been expecting you," Sir Lancaster greeted Nathan with a smile and bade him to sit.

Nathan boldly pressed forth on the topic of his father. "Sir Lancaster, I am certain, by now, you have heard the reports of my father. I never knew him; he died before I was born. His life was always a mystery to me, because of my mother's extreme reluctance to speak of him. I have great difficulty accepting the rumors circulating about him and my mother, but unfortunately, I have no evidence to contradict them. If what the *Times* said is true about my parents, some may feel that it will stigmatize me... and everyone who associates with me."

Sir Lancaster looked Nathan up and down. He reflected for a short time, taking a deep puff on his pipe. Then he removed his pipe. He philosophized for several minutes, taking his time to reach the conclusion: "One should not be condemned for the sins of one's parents."

Nathan's face expressed relief.

"But, I am deeply troubled that you fell heavily into debt and had to suffer the consequences."

Nathan's relief was replaced by anxiety. "Sir Lancaster, I can offer no excuses for that lapse of judgment. In mitigation, I will say that I advanced funds to aid a client who was in desperate need and who has never repaid. If that client had repaid his debt to me, I would have been able to discharge my obligation in full. Nevertheless, I did not deal with the debt responsibly, and it soon became too large a debt to discharge. The debt has now been paid in full."

"Yes. I read your creditor's letter in the *Times* and shared it with my niece. But for that letter, I would have cautioned her never to see you again."

Nathan said another silent *thank you* to Mr. Sedgwick, nodding his head solemnly. "Fortunately, I have made great strides in my practice recently and feel to be in a position financially to properly provide for Miss Lancaster."

"So I have surmised."

"You must know that I have gained the greatest admiration for your niece," Nathan began.

Sir Lancaster smiled. "She's an extraordinary young woman. Has she opened up to you about her past?"

Nathan nodded. "She has. We recently discovered to our mutual astonishment that our paths crossed as children. Years ago, before the fire, she befriended a shy young boy who was terrified of girls. I remember fondly her kindness and goodness. I had been told that the entire family had perished in the fire and it left me with a deep scar."

Sir Lancaster removed the pipe from his mouth. "It was a terrible tragedy. It breaks my heart to think of it even now, so many years later. Her father, a man I had foolishly repudiated, died heroically. He awoke with the home in flames. He rushed into the blaze to the room where Regina's younger twin brothers slept. He carried them in his arms and navigated through the flames, placing them in the hands of concerned neighbors, never realizing that they had already succumbed. Though covered with severe burns, he went back into the house to rescue his other children. Upon entering the girls' bedroom, he picked up Regina, the next youngest of his children; the other girls were likely already dead. When he carried her out, he was in flames. A neighbor took Regina from him and he staggered into the flaming home one last time, desperate to rescue his other children. He never returned.

"When Regina's mother, my youngest sister, chose to marry, she married far below the family's station. I argued strenuously against the union, because the man she loved came from poor working-class parents. My father threatened to disown her if she proceeded with the marriage. We never met her fiancé. She defied my parent's wishes, eloped, and married in secret. Not until she had borne a child did she and her husband return to London. They chose to live in obscurity. I was the eldest and only son. My older sister and I were forbidden to contact her. Even after my father died several years later, we continued to honor our pledge and never knew her family. It wasn't until the tragedy occurred that my prideful heart melted and I forsake the pledge."

Nathan was overcome with sadness. "However did Regina deal with such a tragedy at such a young age?"

"For several years she kept to herself and rarely spoke or smiled. She carried with her such heavy sadness. One Christmas, during her twelfth year, we took her to an orphanage, where she passed out gifts to young children. From that day on, she was a changed person and *began living*. A few years later, she devoted her life to their cause."

Nathan nodded. It was time for him to express the purpose of his visit. "As you undoubtedly know, I am now free from my attachment to Miss Charlesworth..."

"So I have heard. I understand that her engagement to the Duke of Wilmont will be formally announced the evening after tomorrow."

Nathan had not heard that yet, but it did not surprise him. He felt sadness for Jocelyn, knowing that she must feel like a condemned convict sentenced to a life in prison. He regretted that he could do nothing more to save her from her dreary fate.

Sir Lancaster knew what was coming next. He had seen it before, with his three married daughters—the nervous suitor, searching for words, trying to demonstrate his worthiness for the heart of his daughter. It was never comfortable for him. No man had ever been worthy in his eyes, although each of his daughters now seemed happily married. Nathan was exceptional, by comparison. He would have heartily endorsed Nathan's advances toward any one of his daughters. Too bad Estelle was so young and immature. Sir Lancaster wondered if she would ever find half the man as Nathan.

After a lengthy pause, his mind turning once again to Regina, Nathan continued: "I have seen firsthand the fruits of Regina's great and noble service. She has touched the lives of so many. She has touched my life in the most profound manner. I have fallen in love with her, heart and soul. I have come tonight to seek permission for her hand in marriage... to ask for your blessing. I know how she adores and reveres you."

Sir Lancaster leaned back in his chair, exhaling smoke from his pipe. "Regina is of age. I would never stand in the way of her happiness. From all that I have observed, you are a fine young man, supremely talented and ambitious... with a serious and mature mind.

If she returns your love, as I suspect she does, then you have my wholehearted blessing and consent."

Nathan thanked him for his kind words and blessing, and walked out into the glorious afternoon sun, with plans to return later that day.

Regina, her uncle, and her aunt all greeted Nathan warmly upon his arrival in the early evening. After several minutes of small talk, Sir Lancaster discreetly motioned for his wife to join him in the library, leaving Nathan alone with Regina in the parlor.

Regina noticed the abrupt departure of her aunt and uncle and her heart started beating rapidly as she sensed what was to come next. *God, give me the strength to tell him now. Give him the strength to understand.*

Nathan stared tenderly into Regina's eyes and took her gloved hands in his.

Nathan dropped to one knee. Regina felt her heart skip a beat.

"I fell in love with you a lifetime ago. Through God's grace, we met again. When my eyes met yours at Lady Sommersby's, I knew there was something familiar about you and I became obsessed to see you again. Then soon after, heaven smiled on me once more and I saw your face from across the street. I ran after your cab and discovered where you lived, and then your name."

The tears started flowing down Regina's cheeks.

"I petitioned Countess von Brandt to include you in her dinner party. I did all this, because I knew I could never live without you. There is not a woman on earth with your charity and virtue. I have the most ardent admiration and affection for you, and love you with my whole being. When I go to bed at night, I want your eyes to send me to a peaceful repose. When I awaken in the morning, I want your smile to be my first welcome to the coming day. I ask you to trust me with all of life's happiness and sorrows, as I shall also trust my life to you. I love you." Then, declaring his fervent love in his native tongue, which conveyed more intensity for him than the English version, he spoke softly: "*Je t'aime.*"

Regina held Nathan's stare through a steady stream of tears. Nathan then paused, searching for the perfect combination of words: "Will you do me the great honor of becoming my wedded wife?"

Regina's heart was beating madly, her face now covered in tears. She tried, but could form no words.

"Are your tears an expression of happiness?" Nathan gently

tugged at the white gloves Regina was wearing, removed them, and began caressing her hands, still kneeling before her.

After freeing her hands from his and turning her face away, Regina continued to sob. Nathan felt a sudden doubt about the level of affection Regina returned. His world was about to crumble and he felt his confidence failing. But it was Regina's confidence that had deserted her. She no longer had the courage to share her secret. She would have to refuse his love, even though she was helpless in her devotion to him.

She turned back toward Nathan, her eyes looking downward. "Oh Nathan. You could never marry me." She forced herself to speak, groaning in an unnatural voice: "I am much too ugly."

Believing she was comparing herself to Jocelyn, Nathan spoke tenderly. "That's preposterous. There is no more beautiful woman to me under the heavens than you. You are more beautiful to me every time I see you. You have the finest eyes of any woman I have ever known."

"I'm ugly in ways that I could never express in words." Her soft sweet natural voice returned, but it was quaking. Slowly, with her hand trembling, drawing upon every ounce of courage she had, Regina untied the cuff of her left sleeve and pulled it up ever so slowly, as she turned her face completely away from Nathan; she couldn't bear to see his reaction. She was revealing skin ravaged and disfigured the length of her left arm, from the top of her wrist up to her shoulder, a permanent reminder of the burns she had sustained so many years before.

But Nathan did not withdraw. Rather, he tenderly took hold of her left arm. She struggled mightily for release, but he wouldn't let go. He began gently caressing the scars, then touched the disfigured flesh with his lips, going from her wrist to the top of her arm. "Oh, precious. This is of no consequence. It is your soul I love. Though you were burned all over, I would love you still."

"There is more," Regina said still trembling, her face yet turned away.

Slowly, and with every resource of strength she had remaining, she extended her right hand over to her left side, and patted softly the lower abdomen on her left side, continuing up her side, touching the side of her left breast to just under her shoulder. "That too," was all she could manage to eject between sobs.

Nathan instantly took Regina in his arms. "Don't you understand?! I love *you* with all my heart and soul. I could never bear to be without you. I want you to be my life's companion."

Regina continued sobbing and trembling in their embrace. Finally, she spoke softly in his ear, her voice breaking. "Can you love a woman as damaged as I? Can you truly?"

"We are both damaged. My heritage is a stain on my life, yet it bothers you not at all. How could I possibly be bothered by the flesh that God chose to spare you with?"

"You might find yourself repulsed on our wedding night." This she whispered in his ear as their embrace continued.

"Never. I shall love your scars more than your smooth skin. It shall always remind me of God's miracle in sparing your precious life."

Regina pushed back from the embrace, staring with her large brown eyes into Nathan's for the first time since she had turned away. "Then you still wish to marry me?" At that instant, Nathan felt the unfathomable depth of her innocence, sorrow, and hope.

His eyes told her all she needed to know, and the words then formed the confirmation: "With all my heart, my dearest truest love."

Nathan and Regina kissed for the first time. It was a kiss of such power and emotion, such mutual longing, and such pure love, that neither wanted to break the embrace.

I can't believe this is real. Never could I have imagined that I would experience such happiness. Thank you, Lord. Thank you for sparing my life so that I might be so blessed.

It was the first time since the terrible fire fifteen years ago, that Regina had thanked God for sparing her life.

Chapter 67

The morning after, seated in his office, Nathan could not contain his great happiness. He was enthralled with his challenging new architectural projects. His income had increased dramatically. It had been a few weeks since the humiliating article about his father, and not a single client had deserted him. He was in love with the most amazing woman on earth. She had consented to be his wife. Had any man ever been as blessed as he?

The day continued with brilliant hope and promise. His creativity was burgeoning—he couldn't put down on paper fast enough the rush of illumination pouring forth on Sir Rochester's project. He found himself smiling and laughing, at odd moments of the day, as he contemplated his glorious future. He had survived his father's stain and come out the other side stronger and more appreciative of people who accepted him for who he was, and who didn't judge him for the misdeeds of a man who died before his birth.

In the afternoon, Nathan reviewed the structural engineer's calculations and recommendations for the footings, foundation, and walls of the Rochester residence, and made notations on the working drawings where he needed to make modifications to conform to the engineer's recommendations. While deep in thought, the draftsman entered his office with an envelope that had just been delivered by special courier.

Without a second thought, Nathan tore the letter open.

Dear Mr. Sinclair,

I regret to inform you that I must terminate your professional services at once. Please cease all work on the project.

I respectfully request a prompt refund of the retainer. Inasmuch as you have performed some limited work, I authorize your retention of ten percent of the retainer.

Please forward your check for the balance to the office of my solicitor below:

Percy Chambers & Milton
48 Canton Lane
Sussex

Yours ever truly,

Sir Augustus Rochester

The letter shattered Nathan's exquisite happiness. It was the event that he had been dreading but had begun to believe would never occur. Nathan felt a sinking feeling in the pit of his stomach. He had already spent or committed a good portion of the retainer in renting his new office and apartment, far more than the ten percent his client permitted him to retain. How would he come up with the balance? How could he break the terrible news to Regina? What would this mean to his new office and apartment? He vowed to meet with Sir Rochester and try to convince him otherwise, but he feared the die had been cast.

Nathan was powerless to concentrate on his work. His past financial fears and security returned with a vengeance.

Why have I been cursed with such a stain upon my heritage? How could any father leave such a legacy of disgrace to a son? Did my father even know that I existed? While he languished in prison, did he feel remorse for the lives he had damaged? Now, my professional hopes and dreams lie in ruins. Can I ask Regina to cast her lot with a man without means?

Nathan left his office, still reeling from Sir Rochester's rescission.

This was not just any project—this was the project of a lifetime! A project that will never come my way again. The ache of disappointment was almost more than he could bear.

Is Lefontaine next? What future can there be here? Perhaps Regina and I should leave England and find a new life where the stigma is unknown. France is no longer a viable option; it would be too easy for the nightmare to resurface there.

Nathan walked into the humidity of the late summer's afternoon. He felt half a man. Regina's love and acceptance had filled him with such joy the night before—Rochester's cancelation now left him feeling hopeless.

Nathan's aimless wandering soon took him down familiar roads he had frequented as a youth. He wondered if the park had changed in the intervening fifteen years since his last visit there. He walked a few more blocks and turned right.

There it was.

Unchanged.

Preserved exactly as he remembered it.

Large oak trees extended heavenward with their bounteous leaf-laden branches, bordering the park. Nathan sauntered deeper into the park until he reached the small lake. Willow trees, in summer's abundant glory, stretched over the lake. A gentle breeze eased the stifling humidity and caressed the water's surface.

There was *the* bench.

Nathan walked over to it and sat down. He closed his eyes, imagining the sound of footsteps from behind. He imagined turning his head, as had done so many years before, and seeing a young girl with braided hair. Even then, her eyes had been extraordinary. The thought of young Regina staring back at him provoked a melancholy smile. He shook his head at the improbability of having met her again years later, and marveled that they were now destined to become man and wife.

Nathan rose from the bench and began a stroll around the lake. A flock of birds flew overhead while his mind remained troubled by the Rochester rescission. He dreaded telling Regina. He wondered how long their marriage would be delayed.

With his trek around the lake nearly complete, Nathan noticed a young man and woman seated on the bench. Holding hands and staring into each others' eyes, they appeared very much in love. Nathan imagined their simple life. They were likely starting a future together without a trace of the disgrace and misfortune that weighed oppressively on Nathan's mind.

If I were seated there, even with my father's sordid legacy, who would know? Who would care?

Unfortunately, he had become a celebrity in his own right—the London newspapers had deemed him worthy of print, eligible for a public hanging.

I would give anything to have remained forever in anonymity. I would give anything if I could change places with that man.

No sooner had these thoughts entered Nathan's mind, than the man stood up and walked away, leaving the woman visibly shattered. She began crying. Nathan watched from a distance, trying to imagine what had transpired. The woman was inconsolable, when only moments before her face had been radiant. Overcome with humanity and compassion, Nathan walked over to the bench and sat down opposite the sobbing woman.

Several minutes passed. Seeing the woman in extreme distress, Nathan felt compelled to ask, "Excuse me, ma'am. Is there anything I can do to help?"

The woman looked up from her tears at Nathan and shook her head.

Nathan remained seated and looked away from the woman, feeling embarrassed.

I had no right to intrude. Nathan glanced back at the reflection of the trees on the water, feeling a kindred sorrow for the woman. *Whatever troubles her so deeply, dear God, bless her.* He rose from the bench, preparing to walk away.

Suddenly the woman spoke, sensing a compassionate stranger. "My fiancé is losing his sight. The doctor told him there is nothing more they can do for him. In a matter of months, he will be totally blind." Nathan felt the weight of her distress and searched for something comforting to say. Before he could speak, she blurted out in a pained voice. "He has released me from our engagement." Between sobs, she painfully stated: "I *pleaded* with him not to..."

Nathan spoke soothingly. "I can tell you love him tenderly."

The woman nodded. "I told him that I will be his eyes." She tried to dry her tears, but could not stop sobbing.

"If you love him so, you must *never* give him up." Nathan thought of his love for Regina.

The woman exhaled her words slowly, between her soulful heaving. "He won't be able to work anymore, without his eyes. We will be destitute, but I don't care. I would sooner die than live without him."

Nathan's problems suddenly seemed so minor by comparison. He could not imagine being blind. His work as an architect was so squarely based on sight—without it, he would be utterly impotent. He could no longer draw or paint. Only his musical ability would remain from his talents, and even that would be challenged. Nathan often played in the dark, but learning a single new piece would be an enormous task, and only if there was someone to act as his eyes.

"Then you must convince him that you will never abandon him. You must overpower him with such a shower of love and affection that he will understand that you are making no sacrifice at all. It's because of his great love for *you* that he is releasing you." It all seemed so clear to Nathan.

The woman seemed to understand, for the first time, the enormity of her fiancé's selfless act in releasing her just minutes before.

"Of course. You are right."

The lady stood up, wiping away her tears. "I have been so obsessed with losing him, that I have failed to accept what is so obvious to you, a total stranger. He loves me so much that he can't bear to burden me with his handicap. I suppose I always knew that deep inside, but thank you for putting it into words." Nathan followed her with his eyes as she hurried from the park in the direction her fiancé had gone, turned a corner and disappeared. He wondered what the future would hold for the couple.

Would I trade places with him? Nathan repented of his earlier thought, as he remained alone on the bench.

No, I am yet blessed with my sight and the powerful love of an extraordinary woman.

With the day's light fading, Nathan started walking back home.

With Jocelyn no longer in my life, I will soon be forgotten by the public and the newspapers. I shall become anonymous once more, and my father's transgressions will no longer plague me. Surely, I will not lose every client. I will cherish those who remain and rebuild my practice. I should be no worse off financially than I was before I met Jocelyn.

It was dark when he entered his dwelling. He would not run away. He would prove to all that the sins of his father would never invade his soul. He would overcome the loss of the Rochester commission and any other defections that might come. He would put his full energies into his work and his life. He would create a heritage of honor, industry, and integrity for his descendants. His father's stigma would not pass to the next generation.

Chapter 68

Upon awakening the following morning, the desolation of losing a project that would have been the culmination of any architect's career descended upon him with renewed force. He would need to inform Regina of the devastating loss, but that could wait. He did not want to cause her distress just two days after his proposal of marriage and her touching acceptance. Marriage would have to be postponed until he could regain some measure of financial stability; but he knew that he could count on her love and support, regardless of what obstacles might come their way.

Nathan went to his library and sat at his desk. Maybe he could persuade Sir Rochester to change his mind. Nathan knew his design was bold and brilliant. Was there any other architect who could ever hope to fulfill Sir Rochester's grandiose vision? He would compose a letter to him. What could he write that would convince his client to reconsider? Nathan felt a crisis of confidence, and began wondering if there were any words that could change his mind. Sir Rochester had spoken of his close affiliation with the Charlesworths at their first encounter. Had it been the influence of Lord Charlesworth that had pressured Sir Rochester to rescind the commission? Most likely. If so, Nathan knew he stood little chance of changing his mind; a letter to Sir Rochester would be futile.

Most troubling was that much of the retainer had been spent. Nathan knew he would need to be forthright with Sir Rochester. He seemed like a reasonable man. Hopefully he could convince him to defer the payment for a period of time or permit him to make periodic installments.

How long will it take to discharge such a debt? If he marshaled all of his capital, he could return more than half of the retainer. Still, a debt of nearly one thousand pounds would be an enormous burden. Furthermore, when the prepaid rent on his new apartment and office had been exhausted, his monthly obligations would be far higher, imposing a crushing financial burden far beyond anything he had ever experienced before. He would have to find a more humble abode, as before. It would be degrading, but he could manage that. Over time, the scandal of his father would eventually fade. No longer part of London society, there should be no renewal of interest in him. By maintaining a low profile, he could keep his name out of print, live in obscurity, and rebuild his career.

Nathan stood up from his desk and walked over to the parlor. He sat down at his mother's box piano and began playing Chopin's Nocturne in D-flat Major. Having tasted heaven's nectar in the form of the Charlesworths' incomparable Steinway, the box piano quenched little of Nathan's thirst for peace. He would never perform on such an instrument again, except in his mind. At least there would be the occasional privilege of performing on other well-strung claviers at the homes of his musical benefactors. Perhaps he could become more active in those recitals among the London gentry and also gain an increase in the generous honorariums routinely bestowed upon him. That would help ease the burden of debt, which now lay upon him. But, as he played Schubert's Serenade, the realization struck him forcefully. London aristocrats had shunned him. None would ever invite him back to their homes. How could they invite a man branded a fraud and an imposter by the London press? He was a leper. His mother's box piano would have to satisfy his refuge for music. Its sound was so weak and hollow, he felt as though his ears were clogged. As he played the second half of the composition, he used his ample imagination to illuminate the dull sound. He was back performing for Jocelyn; he knew she was seated in the balcony listening above and would soon come down to greet him with effusive praise and her glorious smile. That was another memory he needed to erase. Regina would have to be content with the music from his mother's piano—and she would be.

But will it be enough for me? Nathan wondered.

Not until late afternoon of the unusually cold and windy late summer's day did Nathan make his way to the street where his office was located. It was normally a ten-minute walk from his new apartment to his recently relocated office. Today, it took him twice as long to navigate the distance, his pace slowed by vexation of mind. Standing in front of the building, he examined the sign prominently displaying his name and profession: "Sinclair, Architect." When first the sign had been erected, he had felt such pride and enthusiasm—it had proclaimed to all that he was successful and in demand. Now, the sign mocked him. It was emblematic of his failure. Nathan wished he had never moved; it would have been easier to return to his previous location and hide in obscurity.

Entering the building, he knew that the day's mail had been languishing on his desk for much of the day. He dreaded another client defection. Passing through the reception area into his office, he saw that his draftsman had placed two letters on his desk.

I'd better take my medicine and see what ills lie within. He quickly tore them open, and was grateful to have been spared any more rescissions from clients.

How much will Sir Rochester accept by way of monthly payments against the balance of the retainer? He shall surely want at least fifty pounds a month. Under my present circumstances, I cannot begin to pay such a sum. Can I promise him any sum at all?

Nathan's desktop and adjoining table were still covered in Rochester drawings. *Perhaps I should throw them all in the fire*, Nathan thought. *What possible use can they serve me now?* In anger, he gathered the papers and walked toward the fire, where embers were still burning.

Can I destroy these brilliant designs? I must forget the day that Sir Rochester walked into my office. It is better that they burn. Otherwise, they shall be forever a painful reminder of what might have been. Nathan lowered himself with the papers and stared into the fire. He felt a bankruptcy of optimism and hope. There was no reason to save these designs. Sir Rochester's new architect would create a new design; these drawings would be of no value to anyone. Nathan extended the drawings over the ashes. In a moment, all remnants of Sir Rochester's magnificent palace would be just a memory.

Suddenly he heard a knock, and Mr. Allen burst into his office. The draftsman saw Nathan kneeling by the fire with the precious designs (many of which he himself had toiled over for endless hours) and divined instantly what Nathan intended. Nathan saw Allen's wide-eyed look of astonishment and instantly rose up, and, hoping to convey the opposite impression, placed the papers back on the table neatly. Mr. Allen's demeanor changed just as quickly — he must have been mistaken. He recovered and informed Nathan that there was someone to see him.

At least this client has the courage to cancel the commission in person. Putting on a brave face, Nathan motioned to his employee to invite the visitor in. Seconds later, Nathan saw a face he recognized.

"Mr. Sinclair, I presume?"

Nathan nodded. The man's features were familiar, but not his name.

"I am a footman in the employ of Lord Charlesworth. There is a carriage waiting outside. I have been sent to escort you to his estate. I have been instructed to wait here until you are ready to depart."

It took Nathan a few moments to register the bizarre request.

"There must be some mistake," Nathan protested. "Lord Charlesworth has made it quite clear that I am never to set foot on his property again."

"I was advised that you would respond so. No, I assure you, Lord Charlesworth spoke to me *personally* and made it clear that you must return with me, *at once*, to his residence."

"Did he offer an explanation why?"

The footman's face registered surprise at the question. "My task is only to gather you."

Nathan was not prepared to defy one of the most powerful men in all of England—a man who had already threatened to destroy his life.

"Give me a few minutes and I will join you," Nathan said to the footman, who instantly left his office. Nathan stood alone in his office in wonderment. He walked over to the window and peered out. There in the street was one of the Charlesworths' elegant curricles, painted burgundy with the gilded-peregrine crest, and two large grey snorting horses in front.

Nathan grabbed his coat and hat.

It was early evening when the carriage approached the Charlesworth gate. Nathan felt a strange intrigue about the summons. It took his mind off, temporarily, the shattering loss of the Rochester dream project and its corresponding financial complication. Was it possible that Jocelyn had intervened to plead his innocence? Would it have made a difference? He doubted it. He recalled with exquisite pain Lord Charlesworth's fury.

His carriage fell in line behind others depositing their guests at the main entrance.

Many others are coming tonight. What is the occasion?

His mind had been so distracted by the events of recent days that he had nearly forgotten Sir Lancaster's remarks. Of course, the engagement party. Tonight Jocelyn was to be formally engaged to the Duke of Wilmont. But why was he being asked to attend? Whatever the purpose, it could only be bad, and he wanted no part of it. Yet, Nathan dared not defy Lord Charlesworth.

Nathan recalled vividly the first time he had visited the estate and how he had nearly instructed the coachman to drive on, an option not available to him now. He regretted having ever responded to Jocelyn's birthday invitation. There had been a few scintillating months of excitement, success, and notoriety, but the aftermath had left him worse off than before. His carriage finally came to the head of the line. The footman opened the door. Nathan exited the carriage. In the weeks since his last visit, the leaves had changed color and many had fallen. The vines growing up the side of the mansion were yellowing, which cast a frigid hue on the residence. He trudged up the steps to the Charlesworth estate, wanting to turn back. It was an eerie feeling, climbing the steps again. It instantly struck him that Lord Charlesworth had some new degrading revelation to present or, more likely, a public denouncement in front of all of London's gentry, to ensure that he would never be welcome in society again. Sir Rochester's defection had been the first sign of that, and Lord Charlesworth would see to it that no other member of the elite would ever contract for his services.

As he entered the residence, Nathan was again reminded of his first visit to the Charlesworth estate. In many ways, it felt similar. He had felt like a trespasser then. He felt a trespasser now. He had no comprehension as to why he had been invited to Jocelyn's birthday in the first instance. Now, he lacked a similar comprehension for his summons tonight. As on his first visit, many of London's elite were present. Music was playing down below; it had also been present on his initial visit to the estate. Nathan immediately recognized the second movement of Beethoven's Seventh Symphony; a somber movement that mirrored his feeling of dread.

Seeing a large assembly of well-dressed guests below in the ballroom, he slipped down the stairs, hoping to blend in with the crowd. When he reached the ground floor, he heard fragments of conversation from persons anticipating the imminent engagement of Miss Charlesworth to the Duke of Wilmont. Some, who recognized him, appeared appalled to see the "imposter" and former companion of Miss Charlesworth at the engagement party. It was clear that the paternal disclosure had caused him to be shunned by London's elite.

Although Beethoven's third movement was a marked contrast to the preceding movement, with its spirited and optimistic flair, it did little to brighten Nathan's disquieted spirits. He tried his best to disappear behind the ballroom's grand pillars.

This must be Lord Charlesworth's way of gaining revenge upon me. He wants the public to see my reaction when Jocelyn's engagement to the Duke is announced. Poor Jocelyn. She must be in abject torment, being forced to marry him. I can endure this unpleasant evening, if this is what

Lord Charlesworth needs to balance the scales, but my agony must be nothing compared to Jocelyn's.

Over the course of the next half hour, more guests arrived. The mood of the crowd was lifted by music, which gently progressed to themes more optimistic and bright. Beethoven's Seventh Symphony was followed by Haydn's *Surprise* Symphony. Oblivious to the more uplifting melody, Nathan did his best to remain invisible, rarely making eye contact with any of the guests; he felt fortunate, at least, that there were many who did not recognize his face. Nathan's timorous mind was elsewhere, still pondering the loss of Rochester's glowing project; it pained him exquisitely and gave him grave concern for his future and for that of his intended bride. Their future, which had seemed so bright the morning before, was now threatened by darkening clouds.

Scanning the crowd briefly, he spied Roderick Charlesworth talking with a triumphant Duke of Wilmont. For an instant, his eyes met Roderick's and Roderick gave him a mischievous grin.

He must have prevailed on his father to invite me, Nathan thought.

Reacting to Roderick's expression, the Duke cast his eyes on Nathan, flashing an arrogant smirk conveying that he had succeeded in the Jocelyn lottery. It was clear that both the Duke and Roderick were pleased to see Nathan in attendance, for reasons yet unclear to Nathan, which magnified his anxious foreboding. There was something sinister afoot, and Nathan wanted no part of it.

At length, the crowd reacted and Nathan became aware that Lord Charlesworth and his daughter had entered the room from the opposite side of the grand staircase, where they were standing on a temporarily erected platform near the windows, several steps above the ballroom floor. Seeing Lord Charlesworth's face brought back vividly the exquisite pain and humiliation from the shameful revelation of his father's legacy. It had been his darkest hour. The feelings of poignant reproach and abject inferiority once again enveloped him with a suffocating intensity. It was now clear to him. Lord Charlesworth despised his very existence and planned a public hanging, where Nathan could be viewed and identified by all the London aristocracy, ensuring that his future would be one of misery and shame.

Nathan looked at Jocelyn from afar. She was dressed in a crimson evening dress, with large blood-red overskirts. Her arm-length gloves were a similar color, and Nathan imagined that Jocelyn had purposely chosen the color and dress to portray her bleeding heart. All of her hair was bound upward. There was no jeweled hairpiece nor any adornment on her ears or neck. Lord Charlesworth was expressionless, but Jocelyn was not. Nathan had never expected to see her again, and certainly not like this. Her eyes had a vacant stare, as if her mind were a thousand miles away. Her face was gaunt and sad; he had never seen her looking so morose, although she had a melancholy beauty nonetheless. He could tell by her puffy eyes that she had been crying. Nathan felt acute sorrow for her.

She fought so hard to avoid marriage, particularly to the Duke. And now this. What a tragedy. Such a beautiful woman wasted upon such a despicable man! Nathan instantly wished that he could leave; he didn't want to witness the spectacle of the great sadness of such a dear friend.

Lord Charlesworth raised his arms, motioning the crowd to be silent. The mass of people stopped buzzing and all eyes focused on the commanding and imperial Lord Charlesworth and his celebrity daughter.

"Honored guests, dear friends and family. Thank you for coming this evening. Tonight we celebrate the engagement of my beautiful daughter, Jocelyn." The crowd erupted in applause and cheers.

At the head of the crowd stood the Duke of Wilmont and Roderick Charlesworth.

I should depart now to thwart any act of revenge or humiliation that Lord Charlesworth has planned for this night.

"The Duke of Wilmont has asked for my daughter's hand in marriage." The Duke turned and faced the crowd smiling widely, and the crowd cheered. Nathan had heard enough, he slowly shuffled his way into the shadows and plotted his retreat.

I have endured enough. Surely, I may leave now...

Nathan wanted no part of the crowd's pity and scorn. The hostile mob slowed his departure as he made his way toward the grand stairway that ascended toward the entrance.

Lord Charlesworth continued, "He hails from among the noblest bloodlines of the United Kingdom, and of course, is sufficiently handsome and wealthy." The crowd laughed. "I have long considered him an excellent choice for my daughter..."

If he only knew the true character of this man, thought Nathan.

Nathan took one long last look at Jocelyn. He would never see her face again. It was unfortunate that his last memory of her would be with such tormented sadness etched upon her face. He turned toward the grand staircase, hesitating no longer, as Lord Charlesworth's voice droned on. Wishing he were invisible, Nathan began creeping up the long staircase that led to the entrance and his imminent departure, hugging the iron railing to the far left. He felt nakedly conspicuous alone on the grand staircase and sensed the eyes of the murmuring crowd upon his back, condemning the exit of a guest at the evening's climactic moment: the glorious announcement of engagement.

Departing before Lord Charlesworth could enact the execution of Nathan's abasement in front of London's elite, this would be his farewell to them. Leaving in shame. Cowering up the stairs, tiptoeing like a thief in the night—the enticing world of society, celebrity, status, and wealth forever behind him. With each ponderous movement up a seemingly endless staircase, a troubling and uncertain future loomed ahead.

Chapter 69

Lord Charlesworth spied Nathan beginning his ascent up the grand staircase on the far side of the ballroom, and frowned. He needed to act now.

In a booming voice, Lord Charlesworth interrupted his monologue and cried: "Mister Nathan Sinclair!"

Just ten scant steps from escape, Nathan's departure had been observed. He closed his eyes and froze on the steps, his back to Lord Charlesworth and the crowd. He had been so close to leaving it all behind, seconds from avoiding his public hanging. For an instant, he was tempted to ignore the summons, continue up the remaining steps, and flee. Who would try to stop him? But Nathan knew that defying Lord Charlesworth would have dire consequences.

Nathan slowly turned around and noticed all the eyes of the crowd upon him.

"Descend!" Lord Charlesworth commanded.

Nathan took one step down, then another, amid the loud murmuring of the crowd. It seemed as though time had slowed to a crawl, as a listless Nathan continued downward, suffering the scornful stares from the crowd. Nathan's eyes glanced at the Duke of Wilmont and Roderick, and he saw their malevolent smiles. His worst fears had been confirmed—this would be the moment of his public denunciation. He dreaded what was to come, reliving the stifling rebuke he had endured when last in the presence of Jocelyn's father.

When he reached the ballroom floor, he looked again at Lord Charlesworth. The imperious man had an intense look on his face and motioned to Nathan to come toward him. The crowd parted as Nathan approached the landing where Lord Charlesworth and his daughter stood. Jocelyn clearly wanted no part in the scene unfolding, and her eyes were cast downward.

"Up here," Lord Charlesworth demanded.

Nathan walked up the three steps of the landing, his heart beating madly, waiting for the flogging. He stood on the side opposite of Jocelyn.

"Turn around, that all may see."

Nathan was now facing the guests, composed of the upper echelon of London's elite, including many of the wealthiest and most powerful members of the Empire. With every ounce of inner strength he had, Nathan continued to hold his head high and looked directly into the staring crowd.

"Dear guests and friends, before I announce the engagement of my daughter, I introduce to you Mister Nathan Sinclair. Some of you know him already. But now, I ask you all to look well upon his countenance. Several weeks ago, the *Times* reported how this young man had been found to be an imposter, serenading my daughter with claims of nobility, exploiting the Charlesworth family fortune. The article revealed his father was a forger of artworks, who spent the last twenty years of his life in prison..."

Nathan's face turned red in humiliation as Lord Charlesworth's voice droned on. Although his head was still held high, he elevated his focus just above the murmuring crowd, no longer able to hold the multitude's contemptuous stare. Resigned to remain silent and say nothing in his defense, Nathan endeavored to retain what little dignity he had left.

"I want you all to study his face," Lord Charlesworth's voice boomed.

Nathan braced himself for the scathing pronouncement of his imprisonment and his scandalous birth, which was sure to follow.

"From this day forth, I want each of you to remember this man."

It will soon be over, Nathan thought.

"Look upon him. Look upon the face of the man who presumed to court my daughter. Look upon the man who bewitched her with his music. Look upon the man who stole my daughter's heart. Look upon..." Lord Charlesworth paused, turned his head to the left and stared directly at Nathan for several seconds before finishing the sentence.

"...My future son-in-law."

The guests were stunned to silence.

The Duke of Wilmont dropped his glass of champagne in utter shock—each shattering crystal echoing in the sudden silence.

Roderick Charlesworth cursed.

Jocelyn gasped, as if her life had been suddenly spared from the gallows.

The crowd began to murmur again. Lord Charlesworth's voice quieted them as he looked back upon the crowd. "My daughter deserves the finest of men. She deserves an extraordinary partner who shall be devoted to her, who shall cherish her and love her all the days of her life. I am delighted that such a man is standing at my side." Lord Charlesworth placed his left hand squarely on Nathan's shoulder.

As he felt the pressure on his shoulder and the words spoken, Nathan turned his head toward Lord Charlesworth in amazement. Instead of contempt, there was a look of softness on Lord Charlesworth's face, an expression of friendship, even a regard of *respect*.

Jocelyn's visage expressed equal astonishment and she stared at her father with a look of wonder.

What is happening? Nathan tried to regain his bearings.

"It gives me great pleasure to announce the engagement of my daughter to Mister Nathan Sinclair."

Nathan was certain that his ears had deceived him. What words were coming from the man who had, so recently, threatened his personal destruction?

Amid the stunned silence, a single clap of the hands was heard, followed by another and yet another from different corners of the room. Suddenly, the whole crowd ignited in deafening applause and cheering. Nathan's mind was reeling, as the reality began seeking in.

Jocelyn embraced her father and began sobbing, her head buried in his chest.

How can this be? I have just proposed to Regina.

The guests continued to cheer and applaud with gusto. In a display of tender affection, Lord Charlesworth stroked his daughter's hair as she clung to him.

"There is more I must say, much more," Lord Charlesworth's strong voice quieted the crowd and Jocelyn released her father from her embrace. "This part is unpleasant and unfortunate. A stain has been placed upon the name of my daughter's fiancé. He has been defamed in the newspapers and among some in this crowd... including myself. The stain to his reputation is *completely unfounded*. Moreover, there has been an evil conspiracy afoot to destroy his name and character. I am pained to confess that the conspirators are in this crowd tonight, and they are close to me."

Lord Charlesworth turned his gaze to the Duke of Wilmont, who stood frozen in bewilderment. "They have already paid a heavy price, suffering irrevocably the loss of my daughter's affections and respect, and mine as well. But I shall not dwell on those unfortunate revelations tonight." The Duke and Roderick Charlesworth abruptly turned their back on Lord Charlesworth and disappeared into the crowd, exiting the ballroom hastily through the music room's opening and a secondary staircase.

"I am sad to say that I also treated Mr. Sinclair shabbily, believing the scurrilous rumors about his past. An eloquent letter he wrote breaking off his attachment to my daughter caused me to pause at the authenticity of the rumors, as did a letter to the *Times* from a Mr. Sedgwick. I felt compelled to undertake an investigation; an investigation that would have given me the right to destroy him and forever brand him a charlatan if it had confirmed his hand in perpetrating a fraud. My investigators revealed a much different portrait of him."

Lord Charlesworth again turned his aspect directly to Nathan, his eyes burning into Nathan's very core. "He is of noble birth." The words rang with the power and authority of a judge acquitting a defendant of a capital crime. The crowd buzzed at the startling statement. Nathan's jaw dropped in astonishment as his eyes blinked hard.

Lord Charlesworth paused to allow his declaration to sink in, as the crowd began to murmur. "His father, Étienne de Saint Claire, was the firstborn from the house of the Marquis de Saint Claire, whose family had a peerage in Orléans before the French Revolution." Nathan felt his whole frame electrified from the base of his spine to the top of his scalp by the revelation, which instantly wiped away the stain of his paternal heritage and replaced it with nobility. His mind flashed back to the day his mother died and recalled her wedding ring; his initial impression had been that the first letter on the engraving was an "E," not an "S": *Étienne de Saint Claire*. It all made sense. His mother's reference to his father as being "French." Her last words had been an attempt to enunciate *"Il... marquis,"*[61] not *"il me manque."* So this was the answer to her riddle. A whirlwind of thoughts raced through his mind. Nathan was riveted on Lord Charlesworth's delivery, staring intently at him, desperate to learn what his mother had hoped to reveal before passing.

"Mr. Sinclair's father fell in love with and secretly married a French opera singer in a small village near Paris. Because of the family scandal that such an alliance would create, Mr. Sinclair's mother insisted, over her future husband's protests, that their union be kept secret. Just days after the secret ceremony, Lord Saint Claire died tragically in a most unfortunate accident. But not before he had conceived a son. To protect the family's name, Mr. Sinclair's mother never revealed the secret, keeping it even from her only child. All along, he believed his father was an Englishman named

---

61 He... Marquis.

Stephen Sinclair. Of course, his father's given name 'Étienne' translates to 'Stephen,' and his surname, 'Saint Claire,' has been anglicized to 'Sinclair.'" The crowd gasped in wonder.

"The parish registry from Moret-sur-Loing reveals the full name of the father, however with the *English* translation. Mr. Sinclair was born to the opera singer, Allysandra Mercier de Saint Claire, nine months and a day after the wedding. The priest who performed the ceremony is still living, and confirmed Lord Saint Claire's identity at the private wedding."

I am of noble blood? My mother married to the son of a marquis? Nathan could scarcely believe his ears.

The crowd was breathless as Lord Charlesworth continued to weave his narrative. "I wish I could add that Mr. Sinclair is the heir to great fortune. Unfortunately, the estate of Lord Saint Claire ended upon his death, when the Marquis's family fortune was left to his surviving children many years later. However, it would appear that destiny has balanced the scales by bringing Mr. Sinclair into the Charlesworth household. The tragic end to the love affair between Lord and Lady Saint Claire will be redeemed through the union of their son with my daughter." The crowd cheered and applauded.

Nathan was trying to assimilate all the information that he had just heard, hanging on every word, when Lord Charlesworth spoke again. "Mr. Sinclair, or may I say, *Lord* Saint Claire, take your rightful place at my daughter's side."

Lord Charlesworth stepped backward. Nathan's and Jocelyn's eyes met for the first time in weeks. Jocelyn was beaming and she rewarded Nathan with a look of rapture. They stepped forward together and Jocelyn suddenly threw her arms around Nathan's neck in a tight embrace, not wanting to let go. The crowd cheered again.

When they separated, Lord Charlesworth extracted an envelope from his coat pocket. "To quote from your letter." He removed the letter from the envelope and gave Nathan a loving look, then read: "*You* shall be the 'lifetime partner' of my dear daughter 'who shall be loved and revered by her family.' And may you both 'have such happiness that it will shine brightly from your faces, such that neither of you will be able to contain your exquisite joy.'" He then turned to Jocelyn: "This *extraordinary* letter I shall present to you on your wedding day."

Lord Charlesworth turned back to the crowd. "I shall expect to see all of you in attendance at the wedding." There was a chorus of cheers.

Lord Charlesworth raised both hands to silence the throng. "I have taken the liberty of reserving Westminster Abbey for the wedding the third Thursday of the coming month." The crowd cheered and he did not look for a response from the betrothed. That was less than forty-five days away!

Nathan and Jocelyn were soon besieged by guests congratulating them and wishing them well. His mind still spinning from the evening's events, Nathan played his role, accepting the plaudits and felicitations.

Sir Rochester came forward, facing both Jocelyn and Nathan. "Full steam ahead," he said with a huge grin, as he vigorously shook Nathan's hand. Nathan broke into a spontaneous wide smile. All had been forgiven.

The remainder of the evening was a blur, as guest after guest came up to the couple. Jocelyn was at Nathan's side all evening until there were finally no more guests present. She then bid him adieu, with another embrace and joyous smile, and asked breathlessly, her eyes wide, "Lord Nathan, whatever did you write in your letter?"

Then, just before his exit, she whispered. *"Veins me voir demain."*[62]

Leaving in the same carriage that had deposited him at the Charlesworth estate, Nathan realized that he had not mentioned to Jocelyn his engagement to Regina made two nights before.

As he traveled homeward, the revelation about Nathan's parents gave him a feeling of wonder and identity.

What happiness to know that my mother was the woman I always knew her to be. What joy to have a father to be proud of, after I believed myself to be the offspring of a criminal. I can finally say, with certitude, that my father was, indeed, an extraordinary man.

A sleepless night followed, as Nathan attempted to process all that had occurred in the previous twenty-four hours. Nathan's feelings went from euphoria to anxiety, from happiness to sorrow, from liberation to subjugation. The deluge of emotions was almost too much to bear. Regina had just accepted his marriage proposal, leaving Nathan euphoric. Now he was engaged to another woman! — a woman who just happened to be the most beautiful and celebrated woman in England.

How could this have ever happened? However will I break this news to Regina? I must tell her before she sees it in the Times.

---

62   Come to me tomorrow.

Nathan pondered his dilemma. *I'm engaged to two extraordinary women. Perhaps, I shall walk down the aisle at Westminster Abbey with Jocelyn on my left and Regina on my right. I shall then make my choice of bride in the midst of the procession to the altar. H-m-m-m. Whom shall I choose? The one with the prettiest dress? Or the one with the brightest smile? No! The one who promises to serve my every whim,* Nathan chuckled himself shaking his head. *I'm not so far removed from knowing that no worthy woman would ever take a second look at me.*

His predicament was eased by having the stain of his father purged in the blink of an eye, and discovering his noble birth. *Am I any different now than I was yesterday? Does the noble birthright make me a better man? Perhaps in the eyes of some, it does. But I remain the same man as before.* He marveled that he was a member of a noble family from France whom he had never met. He longed to meet his father's siblings. He longed to meet his new cousins, uncles, and aunts. But now was not the time for that. He must conclude his engagement with Miss Charlesworth before making their acquaintance. Otherwise, they might develop an attachment with the Charlesworth family, only to be disappointed when the marriage did not proceed—probably not the best way to get things started with his *new* family. Once his relationship with Jocelyn came to an end, there would be time enough for that.

If this delicate matter is not handled properly, I may lose them both. I may incur the wrath of both the Lancaster and Charlesworth households. And then, I may truly have to book passage to the Americas.

The dilemma had to be expertly resolved and quickly. His future depended on it.

Chapter 70

The next day Nathan came to Jocelyn, as he had promised. He arrived earlier than planned, unable to postpone the message of his engagement to Regina, whom he would see afterward. He found his familiar and comfortable spot, the Charlesworth music room, where he began performing Schubert's Impromptu in C Minor, Chopin's Nocturne in C-sharp Minor, then Liszt's "La Campanella" Etude followed by Chopin's Fantasy in F Minor. He waited impatiently for her arrival. Finally, after the Chopin Fantasy, he felt a light touch on the top of his shoulder. He turned his head and saw Jocelyn standing next to him. She greeted him.

"Lord Nathan, *pourquoi une telle humeur sombre?*"[63] Jocelyn's mood and face still expressed jubilation from her liberation. "You should be playing something liberating, something triumphant!"

By his brooding regard, Jocelyn could tell that Nathan did not share her emotions. She instantly felt selfish at her happiness, and her demeanor changed. "I'm so sorry. I was thinking only of myself last night. I thought my life was over, and then I found myself liberated, forever free from the Duke's grip. No one was more surprised than I when my father announced our engagement."

"My dearest Jocelyn, I rejoice that you have been released from the Duke's evil clutches and that he has been exposed for the despicable man he is. When I saw you last night looking as if your life was going to end, I felt such sorrow for you."

"My life *was* over," Jocelyn said her face expressing briefly the hopelessness she had felt the night before.

Nathan stood up from the piano bench. "But I have something I must tell you."

Jocelyn caught her breath and stared at Nathan.

"The night before last, I proposed to Miss Lancaster," Nathan spoke deliberately.

Jocelyn's face turned pale. "Oh, my Lord!" She turned away and asked softly: "She accepted?"

"Yes." Nathan spoke with an agonized look. "Can't you see? This whole charade of yours has placed me in an intolerable pre-

---

63   Why such a dark mood?

dicament."

"Oh, Nathan. It's all my fault. I concocted this mad scheme for my own selfish purposes. I never realized it would come to this. When my father told me of the *Times* article, it sickened me to the bone, and I wanted so desperately to write you, but he strictly forbade it, promising me that you would pay dearly if I did. And then, when he announced my punishment would be to marry the Duke, I felt my life was over. I pled with my father day and night to release me from the engagement. Trying desperately to change his mind, I begged him to allow me to keep seeing you. I stained his coat with my tears." Jocelyn's eyes were welling up in tears, causing Nathan's anger to soften.

There was more silence between them.

"You must be so happy. I envy you." Jocelyn spoke softly as she dried the tears from her eyes with a handkerchief. "I must release you from our engagement at once."

"But how?" Nathan inquired. "After your father's virtuoso performance?"

"In a way that spares you embarrassment *or* any repercussions from my father."

Jocelyn paused thoughtfully, then looked back to Nathan. Her tone changed as if she was sharing a great secret. "It must be very imaginative. We must carefully plan each step."

"We have little time. Your father has reserved Westminster Abbey in six weeks' time."

"I may yet have a grand performance to give—on *life's* stage," Jocelyn mused. "If I became suddenly ill and begged my father to send me to a warmer climate to recuperate..."

"But your father will have doctors waiting on you daily. They will find nothing wrong with you."

"I could tell him that I prefer to postpone the marriage..."

"But I have not even told my fiancée of *our* 'engagement.' Postponing things would also delay my real marriage."

"You are right. I could tell him I no longer love you," Jocelyn stated ruefully. "But that would humiliate my father, calling off the engagement after last night's spectacle. There must be another solution."

"You could tell him the truth."

"Oh, I could never do that. My father would never believe me. I had to be very convincing in my love for you. Your letter, also, had a profound impact on him. He would never be able to accept that you are not madly in love with me. And, if he learned of our deception, I fear his anger would be rekindled—*primarily* against you. I can't bear that to happen."

Nathan nodded. "But surely he would understand that you have no desire to marry at this time of your life? You are not yet twenty. Can't you convince him that you want to lead your own life and not be just another man's ornament?"

"I don't know if all men would treat me so," Jocelyn said dreamily as she looked into Nathan's eyes. "But after telling my father how desperate I was *to marry you*, even if he were to believe me, he would never allow me to break off the engagement. He would force me to lie in the bed I have made."

"So, we must think of something else."

Jocelyn became animated. "We shall devise a delicious script that will bring matters to a perfect ending. I am certain there is a way to do that. We have already enjoyed a very rousing act 1, have we not? I have been able to postpone marriage for nearly a year, and put an end to the unwanted attention from numerous men, and most importantly, I have been spared a devilish fate with the Duke. I owe you much, Nathan. You have always played your part well. I will not let you down, *my lord*," she said accentuating the last two words with a show of genuine respect.

"And I have been so richly rewarded as well, *my lady*. Not just in business, but in a very special friendship," Nathan said looking intently at Jocelyn. "When I marry, I shall miss our frequent rendezvous."

"But we must remain friends. Will she allow that?" Jocelyn inquired earnestly.

"Of course. I have told her so much about you. I cannot wait to introduce her to you. She will instantly fall in love with you."

"And I, her, I am sure. If she has won the love of a man such as you, she must be a great lady." Jocelyn pondered. "When we next meet, I shall have the outline for the final act."

Chapter 71

Nathan felt a measure of relief as he left the Charlesworth estate. Jocelyn had seemed determined to devise an appropriate resolution to ending their engagement. Surely, among the two of them, they could develop a solution. Jocelyn had also informed him of a spate of dinner and social engagements that her father expected both to attend in the weeks preceding the wedding.

I must see Regina now, before word of last night's engagement becomes public.

On the way over, his mind was burdened by the heartache and distress he would be bringing to Regina with the news of the engagement.

How do I tell her what happened last night? How do I make her understand?

Pure in heart and forgiving as she was, would not any woman respond with anger and suspicion to finding her fiancé engaged to another woman?

How would I bear it, if I were to discover that Regina was engaged to another man? Nathan dreaded the disclosure that he knew he must shortly make.

Nathan reached the Lancaster residence shortly before dinner. As he entered the parlor, Regina greeted him with a loving embrace and Nathan felt such intense happiness holding her that he refused to release her for a few moments. When at length he did, Regina gave him a glorious wondering smile. They made love to each other with their eyes and lips.

As they parted from their embrace, Nathan noticed that Regina was wearing the necklace he had given her on Christmas Eve. It was the first time she had worn it in his presence. He put his hand on the locket and lifted it up slightly above Regina's chest. "This was my mother's."

Regina looked at him lovingly. "You never told me."

"I thought I might scare you away."

"You could never have scared me away," Regina smiled. "But I feared you would run from me in fright, when you learned of my secret."

"I may yet," Nathan winked.

Regina playfully pushed Nathan away. "It's not too late to run."

"I'll wait for our wedding night."

"It will be too late then. I won't let you go." Regina's eyes opened wide and Nathan allowed himself to fall fully under her spell.

"You swear?" He asked whispering, before kissing her.

"I swear." She answered, after the kiss.

Regina continued caressing his lips with hers.

How do I tell her?

"Dearest Nathan, you have brought me such happiness. Such happiness that I cannot contain my feelings," Regina whispered to him between kisses.

"My dearest love, I cannot wait until we are sealed together as husband and wife." Nathan responded.

My God, give her strength to understand.

"We haven't talked of our honeymoon. Wherever do you wish to go, my love?"

"There are so many places I wish to show you," Nathan responded as they released their embrace. Inside, his heart was breaking. "I must take you to Switzerland, Austria, and Italy."

"I've always dreamed of traveling," Regina had a look of wonderment and innocence in her eyes. "And when shall we be married?"

Nathan knew he could wait no longer.

Regina continued: "And where? I am perfectly content with a small private wedding, but my uncle and aunt insist on sending invitations far and wide. And whom do you wish to invite, my love?"

"My relations in France, on my mother's side... and on my father's."

Regina gave Nathan a puzzled look. "Your father's side? You've always told me you've never met them... you don't even know who they are."

"My darling, I have the most incredible news. I have finally learned the truth about my father... about my parents. My father was *not* Guy LaJeunesse, the art forger. The *Times* article was in error—it was part of a conspiracy between the Duke of Wilmont and Miss Charlesworth's brother to discredit me, and in turn, discredit the fictitious liaison."

"But, how can this be?" Regina gasped at the news.

"I can scarcely believe it myself," Nathan responded with a

wide grin.

"You have learned your father's true identity?" Regina's expression of astonishment remained on her face.

"Yes, my love. My father was French, not English. His name was Étienne de Saint Claire, the son of a marquis. His family had a peerage in Orléans before the French Revolution."

"My dear Lord! If what you're telling me is true, you come from *noble blood*," Regina was stunned.

"My mother insisted they keep the relationship secret, because the family would have objected to him marrying an opera singer. Unfortunately, my father died soon after their marriage, which broke my mother's heart. This is what she was trying to tell me with her last breath."

"Nathan. It is so wonderful! I loved you, regardless of your heritage, but now *you* shall no longer be burdened with your father's supposed disgrace. I am so happy for you."

Regina embraced Nathan tightly.

She then looked up at him. "You must have many relations who know nothing of you. And you know nothing of them. How wonderful it will be for you to discover your family. Thank the Lord. You must find them all—we shall invite them all to the wedding."

Nathan nodded. "I can't wait to discover them. I am so anxious to meet every one of them. It shall give me such joy to learn from them about my father."

Regina was breathless to ask: "How ever did you discover this marvelous news?"

The question brought Nathan's mind back to the enormous and unpleasant disclosure that lay ahead of him. His expression suddenly changed from one of ecstacy to pain, causing Regina to ask, "What's wrong, my dearest?"

"My dear love, I have something else I must tell you." Nathan spoke in a solemn tone.

"That sounds ominous. You've already changed your mind?" Regina ejected a scared laugh, yet in the back of her mind, she had a fleeting doubt that his nobility might yet change everything.

"Never. But you will not laugh when I tell you how I learned the truth about my father." Nathan knew not where to start. He began with the bizarre summons he received to the Charlesworth estate, the evening where the Duke of Wilmont was to become engaged to Jocelyn Charlesworth. He told Regina that he believed the purpose had been to expose him to English society as an imposter, to ensure that he could never succeed in business.

He explained how he had been on the verge of leaving the estate, determined to defy Lord Charlesworth's attempt to humiliate him—how his name had been called and he had been ordered down the grand staircase. But, instead of exposing Nathan as an imposter, Lord Charlesworth announced that he had undertaken his own investigation, and had discovered the truth about Nathan's parents.

"*Lord Charlesworth* brought you this news?" Jocelyn's mouth opened wide in astonishment.

Nathan nodded. "And he also informed the crowd of the conspiracy that had been perpetrated to defame me. Although he didn't say so in words, it was clear who the conspirators were: the Duke and Miss Charlesworth's brother."

"How despicable of them to do that," Regina's face expressed contempt. "What evil men. Surely they shall be punished."

"They have certainly incurred the wrath of Lord Charlesworth. That shall be severe, indeed."

"So, what happened next?" Regina could hardly wait to hear.

"Something totally unexpected. My dearest sweetheart, you know how I deeply I love you. You know that I am counting the days until you become my wife."

Regina looked at him with a glimmer of foreboding, wondering what was coming next.

"Fear not, my love. But what I am about to tell you will cause you pain."

"Oh, Nathan! What is it?"

"To the surprise of everyone present, Lord Charlesworth announced the engagement of Miss Charlesworth, not to the Duke, but to..."

Regina's look showed that she feared the worst. "Don't tell me, Nathan... No! No!"

Nathan nodded slowly.

"*Why you?*" Regina groaned in a voice filled with pain.

"Because Miss Charlesworth had to be convincing in her 'love' for me, in order to persuade her father not to force her to marry the Duke. Then, when the Duke was revealed as a devious man, her father believed he was honoring her fervent wishes to marry me."

"*Nathan!*" Regina shrieked. "Lord Charlesworth will force you to marry his daughter!"

Nathan tried to calm her. "Here, here, my love. Miss Charlesworth has no interest in marriage. Together, we shall devise an ending to the engagement. Fear not, my darling. It shall be over soon." Nathan began caressing Regina's hair.

"I don't understand how it ever went this far," Regina said, her voice aching through her sobs.

"It was never supposed to," Nathan shook his head regretfully. "But I promise you I will bring it to an abrupt end."

"But how?" Her voice was breaking.

Nathan paused. "I don't know yet, but I will find a way."

"There is no way! Don't you see? You could never offend Lord Charlesworth without incurring his vengeance. Oh, Nathan. How could you have allowed this to happen?!" Regina had a look of anger and betrayal that seared Nathan's soul, and she turned away from him.

Nathan reached out to Regina, pulling her back, embracing her tightly, as she moaned woefully.

"I have told everyone," Regina protested between sobs. "Everyone has been so happy for me. There has been such joy in this house since you proposed."

"Sh-h-h-h," Nathan said soothingly. "It is you I love. It is you I shall marry."

"I can't bear to tell my uncle and aunt. It will be so humiliating. Whatever will they think when they find out?"

"I will talk to them and explain. Let me be the one to spare you any shame. I shall go to them at once."

Regina nodded. Nathan knew Regina would never have the courage.

"My dearest love, I promise you that I shall construct an ending that will do no disrespect to Lord Charlesworth... or his daughter."

They remained in a fragile embrace for several minutes, until Regina was finally able to control her sobbing.

She regained her composure, as her voiced softened. "I am so sorry. I had never imagined that I would find such precious love. And now having found it, I fear I shall lose you."

Nathan took Regina's hands in his. "I promise you that even should I be at the altar of marriage, kneeling before the priest in the face of the Charlesworth power, *I will walk away!* I will surely do it. Nothing shall prevent me from marrying you, my dearest love."

"Yes. It must end properly. We don't want any upset to your career or to the Charlesworth family." Regina dried her tears and looked Nathan directly in the eyes earnestly. "I believe in you. I trust you with all my heart. Let no more be said on this topic tonight."

Their lips met and they kissed passionately.

"Do you remember the night I first came to your home?" Nathan whispered after their lips parted.

"I shall never forget," Regina whispered back with a smile.

"I sketched your portrait?"

"Yes. You were intolerable! Against my express wishes."

"I have a space reserved in my... in *our* library... a blank wall across from my desk. I showed you that wall not long ago and you asked me what would be hanging there. Do you remember?"

"Of course."

"Would you permit me to draw a portrait of my beautiful wife-to-be that I may gaze on, at all times, to my heart's content?"

"But, my love, you will tire of me if you gaze at me so often."

"Whenever I tire of you, I shall merely pull the curtain down," Nathan said lightheartedly.

"You shall never do such a thing!"

"Only if you are angry with me, then."

"I can't imagine ever being angry with you."

"Or disappointed?"

"That either."

"Then I shall never draw the curtain down."

"You had better not, *if* I grant you permission to paint my portrait."

***

Fifteen minutes later, Nathan and Regina were in the presence of Sir and Lady Lancaster. As he had done before, Nathan first told of his noble birthright and they also rejoiced in the wonderful news. Nathan explained how he had been summoned to the engagement party of Miss Charlesworth and the Duke of Wilmont, expecting to be publicly denounced as an imposter by Lord Charlesworth. He related his desperate attempt to depart, only to be called back down the grand stairway. Regina's aunt and uncle had already been fully informed of the fictitious liaison with Miss Charlesworth and anticipated the conundrum Nathan had been placed in before it was announced. Their reactions were solemn and severe, but not accusatory. It was mutually decided that there would be no further word or announcement of Regina's betrothal to Nathan until the Charlesworth engagement had run its course. Sir Lancaster cautioned against the two being seen in public in the meantime.

"That went better than expected," Nathan spoke to Regina afterwards.

She smiled. She had expected nothing less from her dear aunt and uncle.

The rest of the evening passed tenderly and sublimely. Nathan and Regina talked again of their wedding. They talked of life several years into their marriage, being together in middle age and ending their lives together hand in hand. They discussed the children they would bring into the world. Regina wanted at least six and Nathan had no limit to the extent their family would grow. As they parted, a tearful and doubting Regina told Nathan, "I long for the day when I shall call you husband and you shall call me wife," as she silently prayed.

Chapter 72

The Duke reflected. "'Diseases desperate grown, by desperate alliances relieved.' I must find a way to dispose of Sinclair. The *son* of a *marquis*! Bah! With no money and no real title. He is leagues beneath me in stature. And you, my dear Roderick, are you going to allow this reprobate to marry your sister?"

Roderick was petrified. After last night's disaster, his father must have discovered his complicity with the Duke in perpetrating the fraud against Sinclair. Knowing his father, he knew that he could expect to be disinherited without a shilling. His gambling, his drinking, and his womanizing were at the mercy of the very generous allowance his father bestowed upon him—an allowance that would now abruptly come to an end. Roderick would rather die than give up his gluttonous and decadent lifestyle.

The Duke and Roderick had left the engagement party in a panic, fearing the inevitable consequences of having offended one of the most powerful men in the United Kingdom. But the Duke's fear soon turned to wrath, and it was directed against Lord Charlesworth's second son.

"You have failed miserably on delivering your sister. You have promised time and again to get Sinclair out of the way."

"Your grace, I have been your most obedient ally and friend. I have served you faithfully and despise the scoundrel infinitely more than do you! He has stolen my birthright; he has ripped my inheritance from my very hands. I will be cast off forever from my family because of him."

The Duke ignored Roderick's pathetic loss as his anger continued to rage; how could Roderick's deprivation possibly compare to his? "You have told me lies to appease my wrath. You have given me hope where there was none."

"Your grace, my sister has misled us both. He was no more than a friend. She assured me that it was his music that she adored."

"How can music bewitch a woman so, Lord Roderick?" The Duke asked with a defeated look. "Have you heard him play?"

"I have."

"And...?"

Roderick hesitated. Would another lie be better?

"Speak up!" The Duke shouted in exasperation.

"Your grace, he has exceptional talent..."

"Silence! Curse his talent! Damn his music!"

Maybe there was a way, Roderick thought. The Duke had unwittingly planted a seed, and an idea began to form in Roderick's mind that could put an end to Sinclair and his music.

I should have thought of this before.

"There is still time to dispose of our *Lord Sainte Claire,*" Roderick enunciated the name in a mocking voice. The idea was brilliant. He would keep it to himself until the deed was done. That way, he would receive all glory and gratitude from the Duke. Atherton Gardens would be his, and more, much more. He would allow no margin for error. This time, he would take care of it personally.

"Yes, my dear friend. Your whole future depends upon it."

***

In his new office, Nathan pored over the Rochester exterior drawings. So many thoughts invaded his mind that it was difficult to focus on the task at hand. So much had occurred in such a short span of time. Just a few days before, he had been informed that his services were no longer required. The very next day, the evening of the engagement, all had been forgiven. He remembered with exquisite clarity the pain and enormous disappointment that Sir Rochester's rescission letter had caused.

I almost burned those precious drawings. Thank God, Allen entered the room in time. Nathan shuddered at the thought.

How fortunate I am, that I may pursue this project to completion! The drawings were truly magnificent, he had to admit. There would be nothing like it in all of England.

But his thoughts then raced to the immediacy of the wedding, and on to forging a solution to break it off before it was too late.

Five weeks from now! There is little time to end it. However, will we manage to break off the engagement? If I do anything at all to offend Lord Charlesworth, this project and others will end and my career will be destroyed. Jocelyn certainly can have no interest in marriage, since she is scheming to devise an ending, too. She is the consummate actress. Could she pretend to fall in love with another man? Could she convince her father that she wishes to delay the marriage? We need more time!

His crowded mind then moved on to reflect upon his new heritage and a family he had never met. He yearned to know his cousins, uncles, and aunts on his father's side.

I will search my relations in France and let them know I have arrived at long last! Finally, the long lost relative, whom they don't even know exists, shall knock on their door. Oh what rapture! What welcome shall they express! Ha! Of course, they will turn me out! Surely, they will think me an imposter. Despite Lord Charlesworth's revelation, I still feel like one. I suppose I must write them first, Nathan mused, as he pondered the delight of making the acquaintance of his new family.

What stories shall they tell of my father? I shall want to know every detail about him.

His anxious thoughts then returned to Regina. *If only this last obstacle were removed. If only she and I were planning* our *wedding.* He imagined Regina in a white wedding dress. He could feel the warmth of her loving and adoring regard. He envisioned kneeling before the altar with her, taking her hands in his, and pronouncing his undying love. That blessed day could not arrive soon enough.

He forced himself back to the drawings. He took out the watercolors and began bringing the sketches to life with the colors and shading he added. It was imposing and impressive. The structure would gain a height rarely if ever seen in a personal residence. The arches, angles, and numerous windows made a powerful and dramatic statement. The residence would become known far and wide. Nathan's fame as an architect would spread. He couldn't wait to share the new exterior drawings with his client, showing north, south, east, and west perspectives, and in his mind's eye he could clearly see the finished project, which would take several years to build. It truly was a masterpiece. Many of the ideas and concepts that he had developed in years of study and in other creative moments now took form in Sir Rochester's design—*many* of his grand ideas and concepts, but certainly not all. The best and the boldest were still reserved for his own home one day. A home that never had any chance of being built until recent weeks. It now seemed possible that some day he might actually be able to design his personal palace. How that dwelling would shine! To share it with his wife and their children, what an extraordinary heaven that would be. Someday, he would find the perfect site for it.

He needed to get his mind back on more urgent matters.

I must find a way to bring it to an end. I can't rely on Jocelyn to do so. Based upon her reaction earlier, Nathan began to wonder if she would have gone through with *their* wedding, had he not revealed his marriage proposal to Regina. *Surely not! She concocted this whole relationship to buy her freedom. She must want to end it as desperately as*

I. Perhaps she may approach her father and tell him she would like to travel with her family before the wedding, and during that interval gradually "develop" a change of heart.

I will go to her tomorrow.

***

Roderick had sworn off drinking—for a time. He needed his wits to pull off his *brilliant* scheme, and time was running out. Unaware that Nathan had moved, Roderick first stopped by Nathan's old office. He looked into the second floor window where Nathan's business sign had appeared before. It was bare. Roderick wasn't surprised. He had half expected Nathan may have moved after appropriating new commissions from Charlesworth friends.

After making several inquiries, Roderick obtained an address for Nathan's new office. He hailed a cab and was soon on his way to Chelsea. He easily located the building on King's Road where Nathan had set up his new office, and spied the placard "Sinclair, Architect."

So this is where works the man who has destroyed my life! Roderick felt intense anger. He had never known such desperation and now was prepared to take whatever action was necessary to salvage the fortune he had been promised from the Duke.

Roderick surveyed the building in the late-afternoon light. Nathan's office was on the ground floor of a three-story building with marble walls. It was an impressive building and Roderick cursed the day Jocelyn had heard him on the piano. Life would have been infinitely different if their paths had never crossed. It infuriated him that Sinclair was prospering while his own life was falling apart. That would change soon.

Roderick located a tavern on the opposite side of the street. He found a table near a window where he could observe the front of Sinclair's building, and settled in for a lengthy vigil.

A waitress came over and asked what Roderick wanted to drink. It took every ounce of discipline he had to order tea instead of a bottle of claret. He needed to stay alert. Minutes passed into hours. Several times the main door of Sinclair's building opened, but each time it was someone unfamiliar. Hunger overtook Roderick and he ordered fish and chips from the limited menu. Between bites, he looked up and kept watch. The light of the day was soon fading and Roderick wondered if Nathan was even inside. A short time later, as he was cleaning his plate, Roderick finally observed

Nathan emerge from the building. Nathan turned to his left and started walking down the sidewalk. Roderick left some coins on the table and quickly exited the tavern. He hurried down the sidewalk, staying on the opposite side of the street, keeping a good distance behind. Nathan turned the corner, and some time later, Roderick saw Nathan enter a brown brick residence.

Roderick walked up to the residence as dusk descended and made note of the address.

I know where he lives, he thought as his lips curled up in a devious smile.

His day was done and Roderick took a cab to the Duke's London apartment. He would return on the morrow. Watching. Waiting.

Chapter 73

A week had passed since the public announcement of engagement. They needed to quickly develop a solution to end the engagement without embarrassment or offense to either side. Nathan felt compelled to impress on Jocelyn, once again, the urgency of developing such a resolution. Rather than advancing to his customary place in the music room, he asked the butler to announce his arrival to Jocelyn. Moments later, she entered the parlor, where Nathan had been waiting.

"What a pleasant surprise to see you so soon. I hadn't expected you until the day after tomorrow." Jocelyn smiled brightly, referring to Nathan's customary Friday visits.

It took his breath away. Every time he saw her, even after a day or two of separation, he could scarcely believe a woman could be so stunning.

Collecting himself, he told her, "We need to talk." Nathan confided to Jocelyn his concern that there was little time to devise a closure to their engagement.

"Perhaps you could tell your father you would like to travel... with your parents before marriage? That would give you time to gradually let him know your affections had waned."

Jocelyn paused as she considered Nathan's comment. "I don't know how he would react to that. After you departed the evening of our engagement, I hugged and kissed my father a thousand times. He has taken an active role in all the planning, something I would never have expected from him. Invitations have been sent out for pre-wedding dinners and gatherings. And reserving Westminster Abbey is no simple undertaking."

"We have just five weeks until then... Surely he could put it off a few months."

"I could ask, but I must give him a good reason and be convincing. Once my father has made up his mind, it takes an Act of Parliament to change it."

"Could you talk to him, at least?"

"Of course, I shall." Jocelyn pondered. After a pause, she said: "But, we may not need additional time. I have been plotting the perfect ending."

"And what is that?"

"When next we meet, I shall tell you."

"And not before?'

"There are a few details yet to be worked out in my mind, but once I figure those out, and I shall, it will be perfect." Jocelyn had a brilliant smile on her face.

She then stood up. "Now, since you are here, and since I have not heard your music during the past few weeks, may I hear from you tonight?" They walked together from the parlor, down the corridor, and to the long staircase into the ballroom.

As they were descending the stairs, Jocelyn's arm in Nathan's, she inquired, "Nathan, when you were here last, the night my father confronted you... that last piece you played. How did you become acquainted with that melody?"

Nathan realized she was referring to the melody he had imitated after observing her private performance on the violin. "One day I was in your home and I heard an angel playing it." He looked up toward the heavens as he spoke.

Jocelyn turned to him in the middle of their descent of the staircase. "You did not!"

"It's in my letter to you. You were dressed like an angel, your glorious hair down to your waist, and you were performing a melody of indescribable beauty."

"You were never to know." Jocelyn spoke softly.

"And why not?"

Jocelyn looked away, without responding. They continued their descent down the remaining stairs to the ballroom below.

When they entered the music room, she answered his question. "Because I promised myself no one outside my family would ever hear me play, except my future husband. Now I have broken my promise."

"But such an extraordinary talent. Why would you want to hide it?"

Jocelyn hesitated before responding and walked over to the high arched window of the music room, searching for the right words. "When I play, I bare my soul. I open my inner being... I expose my innermost thoughts."

"How did you come by that glorious piece?"

"It's Tchaikovsky. *"Nur wer die Sehnsucht kennt."*[64] I had just received it from the publisher earlier that week." Jocelyn paused. "Its

---

64   Only he knows what yearning is.

title... its theme... defines my heart."

"Is your heart truly so sad and lonely?"

Jocelyn only smiled.

"It would be my honor to hear you play again." Nathan gently proposed.

"If we were husband and wife, you would. Every day, if you wished. You would play the piano every evening. And I... the violin by the morning light." Jocelyn reflected dreamily.

Then she continued. "However would we pass the time in between? It is lovely to imagine what it would be like, at times. But, of course, I shall never marry. No man could endure me for any length of time, once he discovers my..." Jocelyn stopped mid-sentence, with a regard of mock concern that she had said too much.

Nathan was in suspense. "Discovers what?"

Jocelyn debated whether to tell Nathan. Then she came over to Nathan and whispered in his ear. "My temper."

"I didn't know you had a temper," Nathan responded aloud with a look of feigned surprise. Jocelyn put her finger to her mouth, playfully signaling that no one else within earshot should hear—of course, no one else was present. Then in full voice, she spoke: "It is a sight to behold. I lose control. I become a *wild animal*."

"Do I dare ask what animal?"

"A tigress, with teeth bared and claws ready to strike." Jocelyn's opened her mouth, baring her flawless teeth, and held out her hands and nails ready to claw. "If you were my husband for any length of time, you would have scars to prove it." She thrust her right hand down in a slashing motion.

"Is there no way to tame the tigress?"

"No one has succeeded yet."

"I suppose I would need to construct a cage, then... with strong steel bars."

"You would need to carry it with you at all times. You never know when I might erupt into a tantrum."

"Is there nothing that calms the beast?"

Jocelyn hesitated, not wanting to reveal too much. "Just one thing I know of."

"Which is?"

"I dare not share such a confidence with any man. I would never want him to have such power over me."

A sudden bolt of inspiration came upon Nathan. "Oh, you needn't tell me. I think I already know."

"Is my mystery so simple?"

"Yes. It is."

"Tell me, then. What calms the tigress?"

"First show me your temper, then I shall attempt the antidote."

"You must tempt me, to see the tempest."

Would I ever dare?

"I shall think of something," Nathan said with a smile, and then continued. "Is your temper the only thing that will cause your husband to turn his back on you?"

"Oh, no!" cried Jocelyn. "I have many other defects of person that will cause my future husband to tire of me—once my beauty wears off. My whimsical indulgences, my conceit... so many others, I can't begin to list them all."

Nathan was charmed by her modesty and humor. "All joking aside," he began. "You have so much to offer, besides your beauty. You are intelligent, spontaneous, playful, and so talented." Then in a lighter tone: "*Et tu parle un français parfait. C'est un énorme atout.*"[65]

"*Pour toi, peut-être.*[66] I suppose most eligible young men have no interest in languages. You, on the other hand... *Peut-être vais-je changer d'avis et t'épouser.*"[67]

Nathan laughed. "*Est-ce la seule exigence? Que ton futur mari parle français?*"[68]

"And appreciate my musical talent."

"Oh, I think most marriage-minded men would find that an extraordinary asset."

"*If* I ever choose to perform for them."

"It would be a shame not to."

"I suppose you're right. But, my music is so very personal to me... I don't know if I could expose myself so, even to my future husband."

"For the man you trust and love, you will want to expose yourself fully, in every way."

"Oh, is there such a man?" Jocelyn looked out the window wistfully. "I shall never find such a one as he. But it doesn't matter... I shall never marry."

Jocelyn walked back from the window and motioned politely to Nathan to be seated at the piano. "Now, it would be an honor for me to hear *you* play once more."

---

65   And you speak perfect French. That's a huge asset.
66   For you, maybe.
67   Maybe I'll change my mind, and marry you after all.
68   Is that the only requirement? That your future husband speaks French?

Chapter 74

During the past several days, Roderick had staked out Nathan's office from the tavern restaurant. Each day Roderick arrived mid-morning and noticed that Sinclair typically left the building and strolled to one of the corner street vendors for lunch. He kept track of the length of time Sinclair stood in the street; it averaged about twenty-five minutes. He noticed that Sinclair had a preference for one particular vendor. The location would work well. It was time to put his plan in motion, but he would need an accomplice.

***

Nathan needed to see Regina. He longed to see her eyes and hear her voice. He longed for her embrace. He longed to touch her soft lips with his. But before he saw her again, he needed to be able to explain how his engagement to Jocelyn would end. Nathan looked at the calendar in his office. Time was marching on. Had Jocelyn approached her father yet about delaying the wedding? What was the solution she had hinted at earlier? As he was pondering these thoughts, Nathan received a letter in the mail from Jocelyn, asking for his immediate visit. The letter was short and to the point, and in French:

J'ai imaginé un plan parfait. Viens tout de suite.[69]

Nathan locked his office and hired the first available cab, leaving immediately for the Charlesworth estate. It was midafternoon when the cab dropped him off at the entrance.

Moments later, Nathan and Jocelyn were in the parlor alone.

Jocelyn had a delightful smile on her face. "Lord Nathan, I have it! The perfect ending."

Nathan's expression showed impatient anticipation.

"But I have not yet decided if I should tell you now, or surprise you on our wedding day." Jocelyn said mischievously.

---

69   I have devised the perfect plan. Come at once.

"On *our* wedding day?" Nathan feigned horror.

"That's when the final act will unfold."

"Well, I suppose that I shall just have to trust you and allow the act to play out." He said, acting his part in the exchange.

"*As-tu une telle confiance en moi?*"[70]

"*Ne devrais-je pas?*"[71]

"*Et si je change d'avis et nous nous marier à la place?*"[72]

"Now that would be some final act. *Est-ce ta solution?*"[73]

"*À peine.*[74] I *suppose* I must tell you now."

"And spoil the surprise?"

"I may require your assistance."

"Oh. Shall I be offered a part?"

"If you promise not to outshine *my* performance, I may allow you a very small role."

"How generous of you. And is the script yet written?"

"Well, I must admit, I have been inspired by Shakespeare. I just need to visit a man of science and medicine—an apothecary—to verify it can be done. I have sent correspondence, under an assumed name and postal address of course, to one who has been discreetly recommended."

"You surely don't intend to fake your death in the tragic manner of Juliet?"

"No, but you are not far off."

"Would you mind terribly, confiding in your supporting actor?"

"All right, if you insist," Jocelyn said with mock reluctance. "I've been told that a combination of herbs may bring on the sudden onset of unconsciousness lasting nearly four and twenty hours."

Nathan changed his demeanor. "*Tu ne peux pas être sérieuse?*"[75]

"*Je suis tout à fait serieuse.*"[76]

"Surely you don't intend to trifle with your life…"

"I'm not that brave. But, I have been told it is very safe. An ingestion of laudanum and other herbs in just the right combination will create the effect in less than ten minutes' time."

"But, even if it works and you truly lose consciousness, that will only delay the inevitable for a short time."

---

70 Do you trust me so?
71 Should I not?
72 What if I change my mind and we marry instead?
73 Is that your solution?
74 Hardly.
75 You can't be serious.
76 I am absolutely serious.

"Not in this case. Upon waking, I will be suffering from total memory loss—I've heard it referred to as 'amnesia.' I shall have forgotten everything—even my name. You will try valiantly to help me remember, but I shall not. In a few short weeks, I shall prevail upon you to stop seeing me and shall ask that the engagement be broken. I will tell all those I know that I do not love you, and cannot marry you. You shall fulfill your duty by your unsuccessful, but valiant, efforts to restore my memory. There shall be no shame or disrespect to me or my family."

"I know you are an incredible actress, but can you be so utterly convincing that no one will suspect?"

"Oh, it shall be such fun. I shall enjoy every minute. I will know everything about everyone, but will pretend that I don't. I will, undoubtedly, see sides of people that I have never seen before. I will discover my true friends, and learn of those with other motives. Months later, when you are officially engaged to your beloved, my memory will slowly return. You shall be married before my full memory is restored. By then, I shall desire you as a friend, nothing more. Is it not the perfect ending?"

Nathan was impressed. The idea was brilliant; he would never have imagined such an ending. "All except the concoction. I am deeply concerned about that. I must accompany you to the apothecary and make sure that you suffer no harm. Perhaps a smaller sample can be administered first, well in advance of the wedding, to ensure no ill effect. And if the dose doesn't produce the desired effect, we will be forced to find another solution. Feigning unconsciousness would be no small task."

"I agree. Even the best actress could not pull that off over an extended period. I must actually lose consciousness for this to work. There will be attempts to revive me, but they shall not be successful. And I must have you by my side at all times, to make certain that nothing intrusive is done. I shall be breathing, of course, and have a pulse, so you must order them to find me a bed in the abbey where I may lie until I wake."

"There will be doctors to deal with."

"You must remain at my side when they are checking me and assure them that I will recover without any action on their part. And you must act well your part."

Nathan nodded, realizing that he would play an important role.

"Lord Nathan, you must be very convincing in your angst and distress. You must do your best to remind me of our mutual love. You will attempt to restore my memory by reciting all the events we've attended and the places we've gone. When I remember you not at all, you must show overwhelming heartbreak and grief. Are you prepared for such a role?"

"Perhaps we should rehearse," Nathan offered. "When next we meet, should we not test our drama skills?"

"An excellent idea! But remember, I am the *star* of this play. *I do not* want you stealing my scenes and getting all the great reviews!" Jocelyn laughed.

Nathan pretended a serious reflective pose. "I think that my role is far superior to yours. It is I who must run the gamut of emotions, from despair to love to despair again. It is I who must strive greatly, doing my best to convince you of my undying devoted love. All you shall be required to do is to pretend you don't know me. All you need do is ask, or insist, that I leave. You have so little emotion to display. You shall be merely a blank slate. Little talent shall be required for your role."

Jocelyn nodded her head with a delightful smile, then displayed a look of sudden illumination. "You are absolutely right. We must reverse the roles. You shall take the concoction and forget everything, including me, although I am not sure that would be possible, even for one who had truly suffered memory loss. *How could anyone forget such extraordinary beauty?*" The last sentence she said with an ugly accent, making her face as horrid looking as possible.

"But who shall take care of my business when my memory is gone?" Nathan feigned great concern.

"A minor detail. It shall survive for a couple of months. I shall make sure your treasured clients are placated... or they shall have *me* to deal with!" Jocelyn let out an involuntary giggle.

"So, then you must try to make me fall in love with you," Nathan smiled. "That should be very entertaining. How will you try to persuade me?"

Jocelyn considered her options with a sly smile.

"*Alors, je te parlerai en français d'une voix séduisante.*"[77]

"If you do that, I might forget my role. Too dangerous. *Tu ne devrais pas me parler en français.*"[78]

Jocelyn reflected further. "I shall play the violin."

"Oh no, not that! Too much of a risk... if you do that, I shall surely fall in love with your music and have instant recall."

"Then I shall look at you with a loving regard, holding your hands, staring into your eyes..."

---

77   Well, I shall speak French to you in a seductive voice.
78   You must not speak to me in French.

"But I shall have to look away. Otherwise your sorcery might bewitch me."

Jocelyn sighed. "My tears shall fall plentifully as I mourn the loss of my paramour."

"Then you shall weaken my resolve. You may not do that!"

"What then may I do? You deny me any opportunity to act at all!"

Nathan enjoyed fencing with Jocelyn. "You must take care not to look too beautiful, not to dress too well, not to smell too fragrant. You must show the same elevated bearing and pride you displayed on our first encounter." Jocelyn frowned and playfully hit Nathan. "You must give me no excuse to remember. If you act accordingly, then I shall be safe and my memory loss shall persist long enough for matters to come to the proper ending. You will then tire of my blank stare. You shall give up and leave me alone... and be *glad* to be rid of me."

"No," Jocelyn's eyes rolled in an upward arc briefly, mimicking careful reflection. "*Tu ne prendras pas la concoction.*[79] Not if you deny me any chance to perform. I suppose you must run your business. My *extraordinarily busy affairs* will just have to be put in abeyance while my mind remains blank," she added sarcastically.

"So, when do you expect to take the concoction?"

"As you and I are waiting in the back of Westminster Abbey; I will take the serum just minutes before our procession toward the altar. If timed correctly, I shall faint upon the slow and long walk forward. You must remain at my side at all times after I have taken it, even as I walk toward the altar."

"We shall walk together to the altar?"

"Yes. Just the way my parents did, when they married in Sweden. In that way, you shall be able to catch me when I lose consciousness. You *shall* catch me?"

"I shall do my best. But pinch my arm just before you lose consciousness... otherwise I may be distracted by the vainglorious guests and the majesty of the abbey."

"You are dreadful! You are trifling with my exquisite form and stunning features." Jocelyn *did* pinch Nathan, and powerfully.

"Ouch! All right." Nathan exaggerated his pain. "I shall promise to be vigilant and expect you to fall at any moment. If I fail, however, it shall only further dramatize the scene, shall it not?"

"At my expense! If I wake up the following day with a broken neck or bruised face, I just may change my mind and remember

---

79   You shall not take the concoction.

everything... for revenge. How would you like that?"

"H-m-m-m. Very tempting, I must say." Playing along, Nathan's thoughtful expression showed he was carefully pondering that option. "All right. You shall be holding my arm as we walk up the aisle, will you not?"

"Of course."

"Then, I shall clamp my hand over yours. I will be able to react quickly enough to keep you from falling, if I do that. We should rehearse that, also."

"Particularly that!"

"But, what if the concoction doesn't work?"

"We shall test it beforehand to ensure that it is *infaillible*."

Chapter 75

At his next visit to the Lancasters', Nathan brought a large canvas and oils. During the painting session, Regina was seated on one of the Lancasters' fine antique chairs, with a magnificent maidenhair fern to her left and a bouquet of jasmine, fuchsias, and flowering maple to her right, in front of an elegantly paneled wall. She felt extremely self-conscious having her portrait painted. It had never been attempted before, nor had she ever expected it to occur.

Aunt Hélène had purchased for Regina a brand new burgundy gown for the sitting. Regina's hair had been meticulously arranged; she felt that she looked her best when her hair bordered her face, accomplished by her closely curled fringe and an elegant loose chignon. She had long grown accustomed to her longer-than-average nose and had always felt that her eyes were too large for her face. Even so, Regina was surprised at how beautiful she looked. Her face glowed. She couldn't contain herself; she had discovered such happiness with Nathan. He knew her secret and loved her still.

Regina sat motionless for what seemed an eternity. After a couple of hours, Nathan told her that he was finished *for the day.*

"May I see it?" Regina inquired.

"It's bad luck to show the subject, until the painting is done," Nathan said, with an exaggeratedly serious tone.

"So, you are superstitious?"

"Absolutely."

"How shall I know that you are not making my nose too long or my eyes too large?"

"Oh, your eyes are very large indeed. In fact, I am still working on them and them alone."

"You have painted nothing else?"

"Your eyes have me mesmerized. I know that if I can capture your eyes perfectly, then everything else will follow."

"And how long shall it take for you to perfect my *extraordinary* eyes." Regina inquired, batting her eyelashes at the artist.

"Several months, at least."

"You liar! I have sat motionless for two hours. You better have done more than my eyes." Regina walked over toward the canvas. Nathan pretended to be guarding it with his life. "You will let me see, or no more sittings for you."

Nathan dressed his face in fright. "Oh, if you must. But we shall both have dreadful luck."

Regina glimpsed at the unfinished portrait and gasped. "You are amazing." Nathan had sketched her face lightly in pencil, and the likeness was a magnificent imitation of her in every way. He had not yet put paint to the depiction of her face, but her burgundy gown was resplendent. "I shall sit for you, anytime you wish, and for as long as you wish."

"Are you content so far?'

"I am in awe."

"So, shall I always keep the curtain open?"

"Always. I shall *always* want your eyes to gaze upon mine when you are seated at your desk. You shall have permission only to occasionally and infrequently look down when you *must* write a very short letter or read a *single* sentence from a book."

Nathan smiled. "I shall then remove all books from my shelves and assign the writing of all letters to a steward. That way I shall never look away."

As the evening wore on, Nathan and Regina found themselves alone in the sitting room, seated next to each other.

"My love. I have reserved the best news for now. I believe that an appropriate conclusion has been arranged to end my *other* attachment."

Regina playfully pushed Nathan. "I cannot believe that I am marrying a man engaged to another woman. I must be mad."

Nathan smiled. "Let me explain." Nathan described the concoction that Jocelyn would ingest, the resulting unconsciousness, and her feigned loss of memory.

When he had revealed the stratagem in detail, Regina reflected. "It sounds very dangerous. What if something dreadful happens to her?"

"We shall be quite certain before she takes it. It is merely a combination of common herbs and laudanum. Taken in a small dose, it should do no harm."

"And it shall happen at the wedding?" Regina pondered. "What if the concoction doesn't take effect?" Regina's face expressed grave concern.

"It shall be tested first, to make sure."

"And after Jocelyn regains her consciousness. Are you certain that she will be convincing?"

"I told you of her audition. She is the consummate actress."

"But for so long?"

"If you knew Miss Charlesworth, you would know that she will enjoy play-acting, even for several weeks. She expects to discover all sorts of interesting things about herself from others. I truly think she is looking forward to the performance."

"But you must also be very convincing. You will need to visit her often, bring her flowers and gifts, and do your best to persuade her that she is madly in love with you." Regina looked intently into his eyes, then a smile started forming. "And what kind of a play-actor are you?"

"My part shall be simple. I shall play the role of the heartbroken fiancé. Which I shall truly be, because when I shall be absent from you, my heart shall be aching."

Regina softly struck Nathan again. "It had better be. And you had better think of me every second of every visit when you are speaking of your undying love for her. If not, you shall never have me."

"You shall always be on my mind."

"And you must promise me not to try too hard to convince the 'forgetful' Miss Charlesworth. It would truly be tragic if, due to your valiant efforts, she ended up suddenly 'remembering' and truly falling in love with you." Regina said with a smile.

"If you only knew Miss Charlesworth..." Nathan just shook his head.

"Promise me that no harm will befall her, if that is the plan you undertake. I would never want you to be responsible for any injury to her. It would be better for you to marry her than for her to suffer harm."

"Do not fear, my beautiful bride-to-be. We shall be certain of that."

Chapter 76

The weather cooled considerably as the sun's heavenly trek fell more southerly in the heavens. Leaves were as plentiful on the ground as in the trees. October had passed and the wedding day was on the horizon. Much of Nathan's free time was preoccupied with exciting new commissions and creative outbursts, as he began the fulfillment of his professional dreams at such a remarkably young age. He had time enough, though, to daydream about his future life with Regina, and time enough to worry about the efficacy of Jocelyn's solution.

One day, Nathan had spent a busy morning reviewing the Rochester construction drawings drafted by Allen. Everything had to be perfect, and Nathan had made notations on several of the papers where he had found an error or made a necessary revision. It was exciting to visualize the structure that would begin taking form soon. He heard the bells toll the noon hour and felt his stomach begin to growl.

Were it not for the tolling bells, I might never stop, Nathan thought. *My stomach would remain quiet and I would continue working until dark.*

Thirty minutes later, Nathan got up from his desk and grabbed his coat. He left the building and felt the force of the wind on his face. It was a cold overcast day in early November and most pedestrians were wearing hats and scarfs. Nathan walked to the corner of the street where his favorite street vendor was always parked. Dutch seemed to get busier every day, and Nathan waited patiently, shivering while the north wind continued to gust. When Nathan came to the front of the line, Dutch gave a friendly nod.

"Mr. Sinclair, wonderful weather we're having, right?"

Nathan buttoned his coat up tight. "Maybe for Holland, Dutch. But I could use a bit more sun."

Dutch was wearing no coat at all, and he thrust his large chest outward, taking a deep breath. "Feels like summer," he exhaled. The tarp on Dutch's stall flapped noisily in the wind. "The usual?"

Nathan nodded. "If you get any more customers, you're going to have to hire some help."

Dutch laughed. "That'll never happen. I tried it once. The scoundrel robbed me blind."

Dutch handed Nathan a cup of tea. The cup warmed his hands, and he took several sips of tea, relishing both the taste and the warmth it provided his throat. Dutch carved off several pieces of smoked ham and sliced a couple of pieces of fresh bread, then buttered the bread and inserted the ham and watercress. He added a small piece of currant cake and placed the food on a small tin tray as Nathan handed him the usual fare plus a shilling to spare.

Dutch grunted a "Much appreciated," and started assisting the next customer.

Nathan jostled between several other customers, holding the tray in one hand and his cup of tea in the other, until he found a spot a few feet into the street. He took a bite of his sandwich and savored its succulence, casually observing the bustling traffic.

A hundred and fifty yards down the street sat a motionless carriage with two neighing horses. The driver sat watching and waiting. He lowered the hat on his head and wrapped a scarf around his face, exposing just his eyes and nose; a long Chesterfield coat concealed his frame. He tucked his long hair inside the hat, ensuring that none was visible. Earlier that day, the driver had rented the carriage and horses near Vauxhall Bridge, a mile and a half away. He had arrived on King's Road thirty minutes earlier and was consuming a lunch of fish and chips to justify his stationary appearance on the side of the road.

Accompanying the driver had been a man of large stature whom he had employed several times in the past, when the performance of a special task was needed. The driver instructed the accomplice on his role and the two carefully rehearsed. The large man exited the carriage a block before entering King's Road, to prevent anyone from making a connection between the two. The large man had then walked down King's Road until he located one particular street vendor's stall. Inserting himself into the small crowd of Dutch's customers, he made eye contact with the carriage's driver, nodding his head.

Nathan was in the middle of consuming his lunch and his mind was elsewhere, as he reflected on his recent good fortune. His work was exhilarating. He reveled in his engagement to the most wonderful woman on the face of the earth, while enjoying the many benefits of his liaison with another remarkable woman. His new office in Chelsea projected the professional image he had always wanted to present. Living on the west side of London, north of the Thames, was also far more pleasant than Bermondsey had been;

with the north side aqueducts completed and the Thames's water flowing east, King's Road was largely exempt from foul sewage odor. Even Chelsea air was less ponderous, with far less trampling of livestock that in east London.

The street traffic remained heavy and the driver of the carriage nervously looked for a pause. It finally came. The time was now. The driver hastily threw his fish and chips to the side of the road and called out to the horses, whipping them in a frenzy. The carriage lurched forward with a sudden start. The driver felt a rush of adrenaline and frantically incited the horses, forcing them ahead in haste. The carriage gained speed and was soon hurtling forth at a great pace. The distance between the carriage and Dutch's stall contracted quickly and the driver's eyes fixated on Sinclair, who in midst of the street's cacophony was oblivious to the rapidly approaching conveyance.

The well-wrapped driver steered the carriage close to the right side of the road where Nathan was standing. Nathan's attention was diverted elsewhere, his left hand occupied with the tray and his right grasping the half-eaten sandwich. With the carriage closing the gap swiftly, the large man standing behind Nathan measured the distance and made a mental calculation. The driver suddenly veered the carriage hard to the right, toward the street vendor.

Now!

Standing directly behind Nathan, the large man bent down and suddenly shoved Nathan into the street with all of his might.

Nathan's tray, food, and cup flew into the air as he was propelled forward. He crashed onto the cobbled stones fully prone as the wheels of the carriage closed to within a few yards. Instead of deviating away from the fallen man, the wheels of the carriage thundered directly into the path of Nathan's outstretched hands. In a fraction of a second, the wheels would be grinding over flesh and bones, mangling them underneath. With precision, the driver aimed the right wheels for Nathan's hands and wrists. A nearby woman shrieked.

The carriage passed over and the driver thrust his head backward, with a triumphant howl, as his scarf came loose. He reached for the scarf, but the wind carried it away from him. The carriage continued down the road but the back of the driver's long golden hair came exposed before he turned off King's Road and disappeared.

Several blocks later, after navigating down several side streets, Roderick Charlesworth stopped. He was breathing heavily and his heart was racing, but there was a large grin on his face. He had done it! His plan had succeeded brilliantly. Nathan's days of musical mastery were in the past. He couldn't wait for the Duke to learn of his daring triumph. Yet, there was an uneasiness in the back of his mind. Everything had gone perfectly except for that bloody scarf!

Chapter 77

Nathan had just bitten into his sandwich when a powerful force from behind had thrust into his lower back and launched him forward. He went flying into the street, his hands extended outward. He crashed onto the cobblestone street, his hands, forearms, and knees hitting the hard surface just before his chin, softening somewhat the blow to his face. An instant later, he heard the grind of wheels and was aware of a carriage coming directly at him, just a few feet from ripping his hands and arms to shreds.

The impact was imminent.

There was no time to react.

Facing impending injury or death, Nathan abruptly felt his body dragged backward with a powerful grip on his ankles. The front wheels of the carriage missed his hands by mere inches, as Nathan was pulled from danger. Gasping, he rolled over on his side. Staring down at him was Dutch, who was kneeling, his hands still clamped onto Nathan's lower legs. Other bystanders came rushing over to aid.

Nathan had abrasions on his palms, elbows, knees, and chin.

"My God! You saved my life," Nathan exclaimed, after regaining his breath, realizing how close to death he had been.

Dutch smiled, releasing his grip. "A mighty close call, my friend."

Nathan sat up and brushed himself off. His extremities were painful and his chin was bleeding, his pants had been torn at the knee, and his coat had been scraped thin at his left elbow. As he took stock of himself, however, Nathan realized he had miraculously escaped serious injury. It should have been far worse.

"But, how did you...?" Nathan marveled at Dutch's quick reaction.

"A few minutes ago, I noticed a large man standing near you, studying you. He stared at the carriage as it approached and seemed to be anticipating its destination. I saw him lift his arms toward you and instantly knew what he was going to do. Although I couldn't stop him in time, I leaped forward and was nearly on top of you before you hit the ground."

"I'll be forever indebted to you," Nathan responded, visibly shaken by the narrow escape.

Dutch nodded. "The man who pushed you was a big man with a large frame, long black hair, anger in his eyes." Dutch extended his hand and helped Nathan up.

"Did anyone see where he went?" Nathan called out to the people standing nearby.

A bystander pointed down the road. Nathan strained for a look but could see no one running away. He continued scanning the crowd for several more seconds, hoping for a clue to the guilty party's identity, but there was no sign.

"Did anyone get a look at the driver?" another bystander shouted.

A middle-aged man dressed in a suit came forward holding a scarf in his hand. "I saw it all," he said. "It looked to me like the driver was hell-bent on running you over. Lost his scarf. Long blond hair. That's all I can say."

The man tendered the scarf to Nathan. Nathan examined the long silk burgundy scarf, and saw the initials "RC" sewn in the lower right corner. Of course. *Roderick Charlesworth.*

"You should call for a constable," the middle-aged man noted.

Nathan nodded, then reconsidered. It was unlikely the police would bring charges against a member of the Charlesworth family. Were the scarf and color of the driver's hair sufficient proof? Could Nathan *prove* it wasn't an accident? Without the accomplice, it wouldn't go far. Nor did Nathan want to complicate his life further. Nevertheless, he knew he needed to be extremely vigilant as the wedding approached. There might be other attempts on his life.

Chapter 78

It had been nearly three weeks since the public announcement of engagement between Nathan Sinclair and Jocelyn Charlesworth. The city of London was electrified by what promised to be a wedding of regal proportions at Westminster Abbey. The contrast in fortunes of Nathan Sinclair made intriguing reading for the gossiping public. Bystanders began congregating outside Nathan's new office, wanting to gain a glimpse of the man who had stolen the heart of the most desirable woman in the Empire, and hoping for a sighting of the beauty he was about to marry. An increasing number of street vendors set up shop nearby, trying to take advantage of the crowd and festive air. There were street sellers of toys, puzzles, songs, and ballads. A man played a fiddle while dancing a jig; another, in a loud voice, was selling a mysterious potion that could cure all ills; yet another was grinding an organ with an adorable monkey attached by a string. The attention brought more customers to Nathan's office, and he was soon interviewing for a second draftsman.

On today's agenda was a pre-wedding dinner arranged by the Charlesworths at their magnificent property in the country, Haightbury Castle, just ten miles outside of London. The weather had been compliant. It was surprisingly balmy for autumn, with only a light cool breeze. Invited were society's finest, including many of London's dignitaries and power brokers. The castle welcomed them with a bounteous carnival atmosphere. The vast grass meadows behind the castle were generously populated with jugglers, mimes, animal tamers, costumed actors, unicyclists, gymnasts, and men on stilts. Festive balloons, pennants, flowers, and imported gazebos dotted the grounds. Musicians were prevalent—both singers and instrumentalists. Tables full of fruit, vegetables, cold cuts, pastries, hors d'oeuvres, and decanters of champagne and other spirits vied for the guests' attention and appetites.

It was late afternoon when the coach arrived carrying Nathan up the long road to the castle's entrance. He still had scabs on his knees and elbow and his chin bore a red welt from the accident a few days before, but otherwise he felt fine. He debated whether to inform Jocelyn of his serious brush with death, but determined that he would spare her the embarrassment. Setting foot on the gravel at the castle's entrance, Nathan could hear the sounds of music and merriment coming from behind the castle. Rather than enter, he decided to walk around the side of the castle, through a labyrinth of tall hedges and bright flowers. Halfway around the castle he heard a rustling sound, and to his shock, saw the Duke of Wilmont fast approaching from behind a large bush. The Duke had a look of frenzied anger, with a maniacal madness in his eyes. In seconds his hands had seized Nathan's lapels, a heavy smell of alcohol on his breath.

"You vile, contemptible imposter! You have stolen my beautiful Jocelyn!"

Nathan stood speechless. The Duke's face was in contortion and he was trembling.

"What have you to say for yourself?!" he screamed at the top of his lungs.

In a composed voice, Nathan responded. "If she belonged to you, then I could never have stolen her."

"You have bewitched her with your music and your lies!" The Duke pleaded in a pained voice, "I demand that you release her from your engagement!" The Duke pulled out a thick wad of notes. "Ten thousand pounds!" He shoved the notes in Nathan's mid-section. "Tell her it is off and there will be ten thousand more!"

"I have no interest in your money."

"What more will you require? Land? Treasure? I must have her!" The Duke was panicking. Jocelyn had smitten him so that he was beyond redemption. The Duke pleaded, his face flexing in physical pain and mental anguish. "I cannot sleep, nor can I get a moment's peace! I cannot exist without her!"

At that moment, Nathan truly felt sorry for him. "You cannot force a woman to love you against her will."

"But she will *come* to love me. I shall make her a duchess. She will be the envy of every woman!" The Duke pleaded.

"I truly regret that I cannot help you."

The Duke raised his voice. "You dare defy me?!"

Nathan turned from him and started toward the back of the castle.

The Duke rushed from behind, grabbing Nathan's jacket.

"How dare you! You insult me again!" The Duke screamed at Nathan, as Nathan pushed the Duke's hand away.

Standing face to face, the Duke pulled the white glove off his left hand and struck Nathan in the face.

"I challenge you! A duel to the death! To the victor... Miss Charlesworth!"

Nathan shook his head and walked away.

What a desperate, pathetic man.

"You and I. *To the death!*" The Duke screamed from behind. This time, the Duke did not follow.

Nathan continued his trek to the back of the castle. The Duke had been drunk, but Nathan knew that he had not heard the last from him. He took a deep breath and gathered his thoughts. Another secret to keep from Jocelyn—there was no need to tell her about the encounter. When he arrived in the back, his confrontation with the Duke was soon effaced by the grandeur of the production his eyes beheld. It was a staggering sight! The vast grass meadow was teeming with an infinite variety of wedding decorations and flowers, alongside numerous performers and guests, with music and magic in the air.

I would never have imagined being a participant in such an event.

Nathan walked up the steps to the back terrace of the castle, which was filled with tables, many with seated guests. He accepted congratulations from several who recognized him as the groom-to-be. From the terrace's height above the ground, the magnificence of the production was even more impressive. Still looking for Jocelyn, he entered the castle. The castle's grandeur overwhelmed even the enormous Charlesworth estate in the London suburbs, although the interior was much less refined, suffering from lack of light and warmth. Nevertheless, the castle was sumptuously furnished. Nathan found Jocelyn in one of the large rooms of the castle, giving orders to the servants.

As he stared at her from afar, he could hardly breathe, she was so dazzling. She was dressed in medieval attire, fitting for the ambiance of the castle. She wore a light-pink taffeta dress, with gathered neckline, wide extended sleeves, and full skirt. Over-bodice laces streamed down the front, trimmed with lavender, rose, and soft orange. Jocelyn's hair was styled into two beautiful identical mounds, with braids extending down both sides of her head, ending in fastened gold balls. Across her forehead was a headband adorned with pink sapphires. Seeing her for the first time, even after a short absence, always took his breath away. But today was even more extraordinary than usual. How could there be a woman of such physical perfection? How could any woman's countenance provoke such a wonder of emotion and yearning? Nathan had studied the greatest works of art in the Louvre and other museums throughout Europe and the United Kingdom. Some of those works were astounding and breathtaking in their beauty and genius, but there was no man-made work that could compare to God's masterpiece that was manifest in the face and form of Jocelyn.

He remained stationary and continued to observe Jocelyn from a distance, marveling also how such a young woman could be so poised and in complete command. When her eyes descended upon Nathan, she gave a smile that showed great delight at his presence. She walked over to him.

"Lord Nathan, I've been waiting for you."

Nathan nodded and smiled.

Jocelyn noticed the abrasion on his chin and touched it lightly. She gave him a consoling look and asked, "How did you hurt yourself?"

"It's nothing, my dear. Nothing at all. I lost my balance and fell."

"You must pay close attention. My groom must appear on his wedding day without blemish." Jocelyn gave an impish grin.

Nathan stared at her, reflecting if there was a hidden meaning in her words. In her presence, Nathan could normally control his speech and suppress compliments of her beauty. Today, however, he was powerless in her radiance. "Jocelyn, your beauty outshines all of God's creations."

Jocelyn acknowledged the compliment with a smile, swiftly followed with a look of resignation. She caressed Nathan's chin tenderly again. "So very sweet of you. But I wonder if such a glowing compliment will ever be directed at me, shed of my outward appearance."

Nathan gave a perplexed look.

Jocelyn continued. "All day long, I am told how beautiful I look. Those compliments mean little to me and I tire of them. I was *born* with my face and my form. I have done nothing to merit praise for that—it is all God's blessing, and I am grateful for it. But, compliment me on my music, my conversation, my wit, my charm, my heart, my *French*, my personality. Something besides my beauty! *That* would mean something."

"You are extraordinarily blessed in those areas also," Nathan replied with feeling.

"If I were not so beautiful, men would pay me little attention, despite my other 'charms.'"

"You are wrong there! You have so much to offer. But, it is true, your beauty blinds many to your other attributes. If all you had were your handsome features, though, men would soon lose their fascination. No, there is much mystery and intrigue to you that keeps them on your path."

"And, Lord Nathan, *est-ce que tu trouve tant de mystère et d'intrigue en moi?*"[80]

"More than any woman I have ever met."

"Any? Are you sure?" Jocelyn gave Nathan a questioning look.

"I am quite sure."

"*Mais cela ne te suffit?*"[81]

"Quite enough." Understanding where Jocelyn was taking the conversation, Nathan elaborated. "You and she are so different. Like night and day."

"And she has her own charms, too, I am sure."

"Yes. But her eyes and heart are the windows to her soul. She has no deceit, no façade, no false airs. You instantly see her goodness and purity. She cannot withhold it." Nathan stopped himself short, not wishing the remark to be viewed as an aspersion on Jocelyn. "She has none of your mystery, your unpredictability, your spontaneity..."

"I cannot compete with that," Jocelyn said wistfully. "I would trade my physical appearance for such inner beauty, if I could."

"My dearest Jocelyn, you *underestimate* your inner beauty..."

It was time to change the subject. Jocelyn's glorious smile returned. "Wait until you see the gift my father has in store for you."

Nathan showed a look of surprise.

"*Tu sera étonné.*"[82] Jocelyn had a devilish look on her face.

"*Puis-je avoir un indice?*"[83] Nathan asked.

"*Et gâcher la surprise? Jamais.*"[84]

Smiling, Nathan put his fingers in the air and started playing an invisible piano. "Of course, I would expect nothing less than a Steinway."

Jocelyn looked crestfallen. "How did you know?"

Nathan believed her—for an instant—so skillful was her acting, and his facial expression evoked that belief.

"Not even close," Jocelyn flashed a sly smile.

"It must be *quelque choses de musical*[85]?"

80	Do you find such mystery and intrigue in me?
81	But that's not enough for you?
82	You shall be astonished.
83	May I have a clue?
84	And spoil the surprise? Never.
85	something musical

"Tu vas devoir attendre et voir."[86]

After she had finished instructing the servants, Jocelyn took Nathan by the arm. "Come with me, so we might mingle outside with our guests." She led him outdoors onto the terrace.

"Well, what do you think of Haightbury?"

"*Incroyable.*[87] Amazing what people could build three hundred years ago."

"You could do better. Maybe someday you shall build me a castle." Jocelyn looked up at him with intense eyes. Nathan laughed.

They walked down the steps to the vast meadow where the festival was in full force. Every few steps they acknowledged guests and received felicitations. With the attention paid to them, the actors, musicians, and circus performers quickly realized who the lucky couple was, and came closer to show off their skills. An animal tamer with a large lion approached, insisting that a petrified Jocelyn pet the lion's mane. Nathan and Jocelyn made their way the length of the production, expressing appreciation with their eyes and face.

I'll never experience another afternoon like this, Nathan thought. It was an unforgettable afternoon in his life; one he wished he could have shared with Regina.

Later that evening, in a massive room inside the castle where banquet tables seated nearly two hundred guests, it was time for Lord Charlesworth to be on stage once more. The day's events and evening's feast had nearly come to an end. Lord and Lady Charlesworth were seated at the head table, next to Nathan and Jocelyn. Lord Charlesworth stood up, quieting those nearby, and waited until the murmur in the room died down altogether.

"I have reserved something special for the finale," Lord Charlesworth's voice boomed. He waved his hand, and two servants entered carrying an object covered with a white sheet. "I have a gift to present to my future son-in-law."

Nathan looked at Jocelyn with curiosity. She returned a smile of delight.

Lord Charlesworth walked over to the covered object held aloft by the servants. He took hold of the white sheet and with a flourish unveiled a large painted canvas. Depicted thereon was a charming village.

---

86   You will just have to wait and see.
87   incredible

"Moret-sur-Loing," Lord Charlesworth announced. Nathan immediately recognized the name of the small French village where he had been born. *How extraordinarily thoughtful; a painting of my birthplace.* He recognized the ancient bridge he had walked over many times as a young boy, which led to the Burgundy Gate. He remembered the buildings with waterwheels erected on small islands in the stream.

Remarkable, thought Nathan. *This is precisely the same view I remember from my first attempt to paint on the banks of the Loing River.*

"Lord Saint Claire, if you please." Lord Charlesworth motioned Nathan over to the painting for a closer inspection. It was a beautiful and accurate rendition of the French village. The colors, the texture, the dimensions, and the shadings were lifelike in every way.

A superb artist, Nathan reflected.

Then, pointing to the lower right hand corner, Lord Charlesworth continued: "The name of the artist."

Nathan looked and beheld. He could scarcely believe his eyes. Written legibly in the corner was: *"de Saint Claire."*

"Your father's painting. We scoured the village and neighboring proximity and found one of his works."

Nathan was beside himself, speechless. He lustily shook Lord Charlesworth's hand in overwhelming gratitude. Jocelyn stood up and came by his side. *"Alors, tu t'attendais à ça?"*[88]

"Jamais de la vie."[89]

The crowd cheered and applauded.

I have something from my father. Something by which to remember him. He fought back the tears welling in his eyes. It was no coincidence that the perspectives were the same; his mother had intended to honor his father when she had chosen the location for Nathan's first painting. He studied the painting again. His father had been blessed with exceptional artistic talent, one that had been bounteously passed from father to son.

***

That evening, the Duke was in his London apartment when Roderick arrived. Roderick could tell that the Duke had been drinking heavily and was in foul mood.

Roderick could hardly wait to lift the Duke's spirits by informing him of the accident he had masterfully orchestrated. Yet, he was

---

88   Well, did you expect this?
89   Never in a thousand years.

mystified he had heard no report of Nathan's injury in the past few days.

Before Roderick could share the wonderful news, the Duke blurted out, "I challenged the bastard to a duel. You shall be my second."

Roderick was befuddled by the remark. "You challenged whom?"

"Sinclair, you imbecile!"

Roderick suddenly felt sick to his stomach. "When did you do that?"

"Earlier this afternoon. At Haightbury."

How was that possible? Roderick thought. *I saw the wheels all but strike him.*

"Are you sure it was him?" Roderick asked tentatively.

"Of course, it was him!" the Duke fired back.

"What condition was he in?"

"What condition was he in?" the Duke repeated Roderick's words with exasperation. "What the bloody hell kind of a question is that?"

Roderick kept his mouth shut.

How could he possibly have escaped injury? My God, this man has nine lives!

"I will kill him!" the Duke yelled. "He is a dead man!"

Time was running out.

Chapter 79

A few nights later, Jocelyn secreted away from the Charlesworth estate just after nightfall, meeting Nathan at the side gate. As she had done once before, she came wearing a brunette wig. She also wore a loose-fitting grey dress she had borrowed from her chambermaid, wanting to camouflage her appearance and wealth. Nathan smiled at the transformation, thinking she almost looked approachable now. Even understated, he was certain she would still turn heads if she walked down the street in the light of day. After she entered the cab, Jocelyn handed the driver a note containing an address on the southeast side of London.

The coach crossed the Waterloo Bridge in the dusk of the early evening. As they continued southeast on St. George's Road, Nathan was surprised by the much-improved air on the south side of the Thames. A couple of weeks earlier, amid much pomp and circumstance, a grand ceremony had taken place in Trafalgar Square, attended by such London dignitaries as Chief Engineer Joseph Bazalgette and Edward, Prince of Wales, announcing the completion of the south aqueduct, the final leg of the massive intercepting sewer network that had been in construction for more than a decade. Nathan found it ironic that he had endured the latter stages of the frantic construction while residing in Bermondsey, where the stagnation and horrid smells had been at their peak, as the workers dammed all of the neighboring brick sewers to complete the subterranean work. Now that the air was significantly cleansed with the sewage system working superbly, he was no longer a resident.

The coach continued to grind upon the cobbled road until it finally came to a rest deep in a maze of dark and dreary brick buildings. They were greeted at the front door by an older, slovenly dressed, bespectacled man with a sallow complexion. The grey-haired man inspected the cultured young couple, noticing a hint of wealth on Jocelyn, despite her having dressed down for the occasion. He invited them into his emporium. Jocelyn and Nathan observed with wonder the bottles of medicine, herbs, and other liquids on endless shelves in the large room.

"When you responded to my letter, you mentioned that you

can create a concoction that will cause sudden unconsciousness, lasting a day and night. How is that done?" Jocelyn inquired.

"It is a mixture of herbs called 'dwale.' It has been around for hundreds of years. I mix the right amount of laudanum, hemlock, henbane, mandrake, and ivy, and then add mulberry juice. Ingested in the right quantity, it will render a person unconscious in a few short minutes. It causes sleep for the better part of a day and night, without any adverse effects."

"Is it safe?" Nathan inquired.

"Good heavens yes. In the right quantities, there can be no danger."

"How do you know which quantity to administer?"

"It depends on the person's size and the desired effect," the apothecary responded. Then looking at Jocelyn, he remarked. "So, based upon your weight and the results you desire, I can create the proper dose."

Nathan asked: "Is there a way to test it beforehand?"

"Unfortunately, no. After receiving your first dose, the body will not react the same way on subsequent ingestion; it becomes much more difficult to predict and usually requires an enhancement in the laudanum, which is not advisable."

"How can we know it will work, then?"

"Perhaps I can find someone about your size," the apothecary reflected, "who would be willing to be a test case. For a price, of course."

"Do you have someone in mind?"

"I have a niece about your size. She trusts me implicitly and you must know that I would never offer such a concoction to a loved one, if I had any question about its efficacy. But she will require several guineas."

"Of course. Are you truly sure there is no risk?"

"None are dangerous when taken in small quantities."

"When can we see its effect on your niece?" Jocelyn inquired.

"I will talk to her tomorrow. If she is willing, I shall send you a post suggesting the date and time."

Reaching the Charlesworth estate, the cab deposited Jocelyn at the side gate, so that she could make an inconspicuous return home. Before leaving the cab, she spoke. "Nathan, since you are here already, you must come and perform for me. While I creep in, you may arrive at the front gate and descend to the music room." Looking forward to another opportunity to caress the ivory keys of the incomparable Steinway piano, Nathan was only too pleased to comply.

Once he reached the music room, he was surprised to see Jocelyn already waiting, no longer in disguise. Jocelyn greeted him as if she hadn't seen him in days. *It's all part of the act,* Nathan thought, *in case someone is watching.*

Nathan sat down at the keyboard, reflecting on what to play. He turned his head toward Jocelyn. "I have had the pleasure of playing for you many times, now. May I not hear your violin once more?"

Jocelyn smiled bashfully.

"*Tu as déjà rompu ta promesse, rapelles-toi?*"[90] Nathan reminded her.

"Perhaps you should try another random visit as before. You may find yourself rewarded."

"Which days would be best suited for such a 'random' visit?"

"*Les jours où mon âme aspire à la musique.*"[91]

"*Et quand est-ce que ton âme réclame ça?*"[92]

"*Tous les jours de ma vie.*"[93] Jocelyn continued her raillery.

"And what time of the day would a trespasser chance upon such music?"

"On sunny days—*a l'aube.*[94] On overcast and rainy days, *tard dans l'après-midi*,[95] when the sun has long forsaken the day."

"Would a thief look for this treasure in the library?"

"*Ou toute autre pièce.*"[96]

"Just how many rooms are there where the angel of music might perform?'

"*Pas plus d'une centaine.*"[97]

Nathan fenced sarcastically. "Just a hundred or so?... That shouldn't be too difficult."

Wanting to provide a hint, Jocelyn offered, "On Sunday mornings, a violin might be heard in the sunroom, but only if the sun is shining through. Of course, the violin must never know that a listener is near."

Nathan made a mental note, turned with a smile to the piano, and began playing Glinka's Nocturne in F Minor.

90	You've already broken your promise, remember?
91	On the days my soul yearns for music.
92	And how often does your soul so yearn?
93	Every day of my life.
94	at dawn
95	deep in the afternoon
96	Or any other room.
97	Certainly no more than a hundred.

Chapter 80

The wedding all of London was talking about was just two weeks distant. The Charlesworths had arranged for a Sunday pre-wedding lunch with close family members. With the wedding fast approaching, Nathan was getting increasingly nervous. The solution was yet to be finalized, since they had not yet heard back from the apothecary. If there was any question about the concoction's efficacy, then an alternative plan would need to be considered—and neither had come up with one. As each pre-wedding event, gala, dinner, or festival took place, Nathan felt another cord binding him to the Charlesworths. Lord Charlesworth was treating him as another son. Lady Charlesworth seemed ecstatic about Nathan joining the family, seemingly oblivious to her past knowledge of the *proposition*. The only impediment in her mind had been his lack of noble birth. Now that his nobility had been confirmed, she concluded that Nathan and Jocelyn had truly fallen in love, and the engagement party had convinced her of that—how could a man of noble birth, such as Nathan, possibly refuse a woman as beautiful and blessed as her daughter?

***

Standing in front of the crowd during the Sunday lunch, Lord Charlesworth began: "Honored guests and friends. This is the happiest of times for the Charlesworth family. My beautiful daughter, Jocelyn, has found her true love. She has found a most deserving man to marry. In my life, I have witnessed many a lord and baron, born to money and wealth, who wreak misery and mischief among all they meet. A child of noble birth, born with a spark of humanity, often finds that spark soon extinguished with all the pampering and boasting bestowed upon his elevated station. He becomes worshiped for his fine breeding and high rank, though deserving of neither. A bad child, spoiled all his young life, becomes the worst of men, convinced that he is exempt from consequence of corruption and debauchery. Consider a deserving young woman, a beautiful rose in the youthful bloom of her life, looking for a lifetime companion to share her life. A woman of humble station has a far better chance for a good marriage than does a woman of wealth. My sweet Jocelyn has defied the odds by finding an incorruptible man who prizes her not for her wealth or station, but for who she is. A young man with ambition and dreams. A man with immense talent and integrity.

"We are delighted to welcome such a new son into the family. We expect the happiest of marriages, soon overflowing with happy grandchildren." Jocelyn blushed and gave Nathan an embarrassed look.

"Rather than corrupting this couple with extravagant wealth from the Charlesworth fortune on their wedding day, I have bestowed upon them the priceless gift of land upon which I expect Lord Saint Claire to erect the grandest of estates one day, even more magnificent than this august property." Holding up documents in his hand, Lord Charlesworth continued. "Here are the papers transferring title of Ravensdale to my new son and daughter upon their wedding day."

The guests erupted in applause and cheers. Nathan knew not of what property Lord Charlesworth was speaking. Jocelyn did, however, and she had a look of utter shock.

Later that night, she confided to Nathan. "It is the most spectacular property you will ever see. The grounds are extensive, with forests, lakes, and meadows. There is a magnificent promontory, containing the remnants of an ancient castle. A palace built thereon could outshine any of the great chateaus of France. I never dreamed that my father would part with it, certainly not during his lifetime."

Nathan felt another Charlesworth tentacle slipping around him, perhaps the strongest cord yet. He would never own the property, but he felt the powerful attraction of the gift, all the same. He marveled that the face of Lord Charlesworth, who expressed such love and respect toward him now, had a short time ago wielded such fierce wrath and destruction. He had already bestowed upon Nathan a priceless treasure connecting Nathan to a father he had never known. Now this! Land that he could never hope to secure even if he became the most successful of architects. The temptations were great. But his love for Regina surpassed all.

Though all mortal men would lose their willpower to these charms and gifts, ever will I remain faithful to my beloved Regina.

Jocelyn saw Nathan's mind racing. "You have won him over — my father regards you as a son. He adores you. I never would have imagined it in my wildest fantasies a year ago, when I suggested our alliance. *C'est presque une honte que toi et moi ne sommes pas amoureux.*"[98]

Nathan felt tempted to respond, *It would be so easy to fall under your spell*, but said instead, "It has, indeed, been a remarkable transformation from my first encounter with him."

Later that evening, Nathan asked Jocelyn if she had heard back from the apothecary. She replied in the negative, but promised to send another letter on the morrow. Nathan's level of anxiety increased. *We are running out of time.*

---

[98] It's almost a shame that you and I are not in love.

Chapter 81

In Monday morning's mail, Nathan received a black-bordered letter with an extravagant black waxed seal. He did not recognize the writing, but sensed it was ominous. He quickly tore open the envelope:

Mr. Sinclair,

You have committed the most severe and unpardonable offenses against me. I demand satisfaction. You and your second are hereby summoned to Wilmont Castle, Wednesday morning at eight o'clock to duel.

The Duke of Wilmont

Nathan was not surprised by the missive. He had expected a follow-up episode to the encounter at Haightbury. The Duke would be disappointed. He had no intention of appearing. Jocelyn had warned him that the Duke was a powerful and devious man. After his nearly fatal experience with Roderick, he knew he would have to be exceedingly careful during the coming days. He could not rest until the wedding day's events unfolded and the marriage was put on hold. He hesitated to contemplate what diabolical plans were festering in the minds of the Duke and Jocelyn's brother. He had already had a close shave with death, and anticipated that his life was still at risk until the wedding day. Even afterwards, as the grieving fiancé, he would need to be vigilant. Not until the Duke and Roderick no longer saw him as a threat to Jocelyn's affections would his life be safe. Nathan cast the letter into the fire.

***

The following day, a party of three, accompanied by servants, began a short journey at the break of dawn. Clouds blanketed the sky and frost covered the ground when Nathan had arrived at the Charlesworth estate. Minutes later, he was shivering in an opulent, but bitingly cold, carriage with Jocelyn and her father. Servants seated above held boxes of meticulously prepared victuals for a lavish picnic planned later in the day. They were off to Ravensdale.

Who was this Lord Charlesworth with whom Nathan was slowly becoming acquainted? A man of brilliance and wealth beyond belief. A man of great power and prestige. A man of drama and spectacle. A man who thrived being on center stage, who enjoyed surprising and shocking his guests; Nathan could see where Jocelyn's passion for acting must have come from. A man, also, of unforgiving temperament and exactness. Now, a second father and friend to Nathan. Nathan recognized him not at all from their first encounter. Now, Lord Charlesworth was talking and confiding in Nathan as an equal.

On the trip over, Lord Charlesworth shared his dreams for Jocelyn. He had always wondered if there could ever be a man who could make her happy and give her the life she deserved. He was flowing in such praise toward Nathan.

"You and my daughter have much in common. You are destined to be the happiest of couples, to have the happiest of marriages. And you, my new son, are destined to be the 'most blessed of all God's creations.'" Nathan recognized a phrase he had used in the letter that he had written to Jocelyn, in reference to *her* future husband.

"Your letter sparked a glint of doubt in my mind. Nevertheless, I fully intended to bring you to your knees, for the impudence I *believed* you had shown. I must confess that I compelled your new clients to renege on their commissions, although I'm not sure I had sufficient control over Monsieur Lefontaine—there is a special bond there."

Lord Charlesworth paused and Nathan sensed he had something important to say. "I have never apologized to you before, for exacting my revenge. I rushed to judgment, which is uncharacteristic of me. In my desperation to protect my daughter from unscrupulous suitors, I had no tolerance for a man who I wrongfully assumed was an imposter. I couldn't have been more mistaken about you, and I offer my humblest apologies to you now and ask your forgiveness." Lord Charlesworth slowly bowed his head.

Nathan was flabbergasted. This man who intimidated kings and presidents was now seeking his humble pardon.

"Lord Charlesworth. There is nothing to forgive. If our roles had been reversed, under similar circumstances, I would hardly have been any less harsh than you."

That sentiment mollified Lord Charlesworth, and he continued where he had left off. "The two of you make a good match. Both of you are superb musicians, and we shall expect many duets from the two of you in the future. You both share lofty dreams and ambition. Best of all, Lord Nathan, you have not been corrupted by money; and, I trust, for my daughter's sake and yours, that you never will be. You are both artistic and creative. And, you will find in Jocelyn a woman of whom you will never tire. I suspect you will be a similar tonic to her."

Nathan was more a listener than a talker on the trip to Ravensdale, as Lord Charlesworth continued his discourse. He later asked the couple, "And where shall you go for your honeymoon?"

"We have talked of travel to the south of France, Italy, Austria, and even Greece," Jocelyn lied—there had never been any discussion of a honeymoon that would never take place, but she said it with such passion, Nathan assumed it was a dream of hers someday with her future husband. "But, there has been so little time to make any formal plans yet." That part, at least, was the truth.

"Leave all the arrangements to me," Lord Charlesworth volunteered. "I shall have my secretary get to work on the reservations first thing tomorrow. Will six weeks be a long enough honeymoon for you lovebirds?"

"That would be perfect," Jocelyn smiled and gave her father a kiss on the cheek. "You are so good to me... to us."

Never had Nathan seen land so beautiful. It staggered his senses. Ravensdale was a harvest of all earth's beauty in one breathtaking locale. A mild sea breeze greeted them as the sun finally broke through the clouds, warming the air. There were vast meadows, lakes, and forest. The property was immense, stretching several miles in all directions, yet it was merely two hours east of London by train and carriage. Lord Charlesworth had insisted on taking them there, wanting to see Nathan's first reaction to the paradise.

"You know that I will expect nothing less of you than a grand palace for my little princess," he said in earnest, imagining many a future visit there himself, with beautiful and talented grandchildren to come. "The Charlesworth fortune will finance the construction, of course. Even a successful architect has limits to his income. No design will be too expensive or too grand. I expect you to create a monument to my daughter that will surpass the wonders of the world."

Nathan swallowed a lump in his throat. *It shall never be erected.*

What will he do when Jocelyn awakens, forgetful, and recognizes me no more? — when his lofty plans are shattered?

"You haven't yet seen the site for her palace." Lord Charlesworth was eager to show it to Nathan. They rode on horseback over a rise, and before them was a magnificent lake, twenty times the size of Lefontaine's. On either side of the lake were dense forests, with the sun breaking through the tops of trees, highlighting the lush cover of growth below. Beyond the lake was a majestic promontory extending toward the heavens. The sun was glistening on the lake, reflecting nature's incomparable creations, and Nathan, for a moment, imagined a celestial palace of breathtaking splendor. Lord Charlesworth pointed with his riding crop. "There."

Before them, the land rose to an imposing height, a considerable elevation above the lake and surrounding forest. On one side were remnants of a moss-covered stone wall from an ancient chateau erected on the site during the eleventh century. Lord Charlesworth motioned for Jocelyn and Nathan to follow him up to the plateau. It was a panorama for which Nathan was totally unprepared. The North Sea was visible; Nathan had been unaware that the property extended all the way to the coast. From the height of the promontory, the sea provided spectacular views to the east. To the west was the beauty of the magnificent lake. Nathan imagined the breathtaking vistas that the height of his imagined structure would offer, if he were ever given the opportunity to build it.

Is it possible that I could surpass the eminence of Sir Rochester's design on this site? Nathan thought to himself.

Thoughts and concepts he had never considered illuminated his mind. The land ignited a surge of creativity that overwhelmed his senses.

Maybe Sir Rochester's design is not the culmination of my architectural prowess, but only the beginning.

Nathan imagined reaching levels of beauty and majesty never before contemplated by human genius. His entire frame was electrified.

Sensing Nathan's unsuppressed enthusiasm for the site, Lord Charlesworth asked, "Well, Lord Saint Claire. Have you ever seen such a property in your life?"

"My grace, surely there is no place under the heavens more beautiful." Nathan expressed his wonderment with his wide eyes and gaping mouth.

"Only the best for my daughter. Of course, if you build too beautiful a palace, you may expect frequent visits from your children's grandparents."

His mind now in free rein, Nathan envisioned a celestial palace that would soar to the heavens. He conceived of lush gardens and landscaping stepping up the slope that would accompany the spectacle of the structure. He memorized the topography of the building site, imagining the dimensions and layout. Nathan lavished unrestrained praise for the site and overwhelming gratitude to Lord Charlesworth for his generosity.

Imagine if Jocelyn and I were truly bound in love and destined to marry. What an amazing dream this would be.

Jocelyn rode over to her father. Gazing at her father with a brilliant smile of love and gratitude, she said quietly to him as she caressed his arm: "I love you, my dear father, with all my heart. You have made me so happy."

Nathan knew that Jocelyn was playing her part, but her sentiments were unabashedly true. Nathan had never heard a pronouncement of love from Jocelyn before, and it touched him to his very core.

What such an expression must feel like to a father. And how would it feel to truly be her future husband, and to be on the receiving end of such a tender declaration of love?

The servants had traveled ahead to the promontory, setting up the picnic on a beautifully embroidered carpet placed over the soft grass, a carpet large enough to drape several beds. It was adjacent to the remnants of one of the walls that remained from the ruins of the castle. Nathan smelled the kerosene from burners boiling kettles for tea. They feasted on lobster tails in freshly made mayonnaise, cold poached chicken in cream sauce, fresh fruit, and custard and cream. They quenched their thirst on lavender lemonade served in frosted glass tumblers accompanied by chilled champagne.

As they were lounging on the carpet, Lord Charlesworth spoke. "Tell me, Lord Nathan. What do you envision on this site? I have seen Sir Rochester's drawings, which I must say are breathtaking and inspiring. Can you exceed his grandiose design here?"

Nathan contemplated the site and surroundings. "There can be no other site to compare with the magnificence here, your grace. Thus, it must carry the most beautiful of all edifices. I would create a property of such majesty and beauty that people viewing it would wonder if it were an illusion or a dream. Viewed in the fog from the North Sea, sailors would believe they had pierced heaven's veil. From the opposite side, the palace would double in size from the lake's reflection..."

Jocelyn interrupted Nathan's reflections. "The music room must be exceptional."

"Oh yes. I can see it, in my mind's eye. From the bench of the piano, or from the bow of the violin, the floor will step down to long windows extending many feet downward... and upward... where the full view of the cliffs, sea, shore and sky will be in beautiful display for the performers."

Jocelyn leaned over to Nathan and whispered. "And will you build me a private theatre?"

Nathan paused to reflect. "Of course. We should have a full theatre and stage. We shall invite play-actors to our palace for private performances. And perhaps we may impose on a certain someone to play the leading role." Nathan winked at Jocelyn.

Jocelyn beamed at Nathan. "Oh, dear husband-to-be. You shall make me so happy." Lord Charlesworth beamed to see his daughter a partaker of such joy.

At that moment, it seemed no longer a deception. The dreams of Lord Charlesworth, Nathan, and Jocelyn intersected into a future of incalculable beauty and happiness.

After the picnic, on their return from the promontory, Jocelyn was soon riding at Nathan's side again, a good distance from Lord Charlesworth. Jocelyn leaned over, as if to whisper tender romantic thoughts to Nathan. Speaking softly, but with excitement in her voice, she said, "I received word from our 'mad pharmacist' yesterday. He is ready for us to test the elixir. He suggests we come by tomorrow. I'm dying to see if it works as he described."

Nathan nodded in return, instantly repenting of his fantasy of being the man upon whom all the riches of Ravensdale and Miss Charlesworth had been bestowed. Nathan felt a sharp twinge of regret that he would never enjoy the spoils of such a property as Ravensdale. Most men would forsake the love of a woman to gain such a paradise. Not without difficulty did Nathan remove the powerful Ravensdale tentacle that had enveloped his heart and mind during the magical journey. He breathed a sigh of relief, scolding himself for falling under the enchantment, however briefly. He reoriented himself to the task at hand—ending the engagement to Jocelyn. It was excellent news that they had finally heard back from the apothecary. Their time was short. The wedding would soon be upon them.

Chapter 82

The following evening, Nathan and Jocelyn returned to the apothecary. They were introduced to the niece, a girl two years younger than Jocelyn and shorter, but of similar weight. She was shy and soft-spoken and seemed reluctant to make eye contact. Her dark hair was gathered in a bun and she wore a plain grey dress with an embroidered hemline, and shoes that showed much wear.

"We must tidy up the financial transaction first," said the apothecary. "My niece's price is ten guineas."

"A bit steep, is it not?" responded Nathan, especially for an action without risk or effort.

"That is her price. She will accept nothing less." Nathan doubted that, based upon the girl's modest dress. One guinea would have been more than adequate.

Nevertheless, Nathan produced a ten-pound note and gave it to the girl. There was an instant gleam in her eye as she pocketed the note and placed it in her purse.

Thirty minutes later, the concoction had been prepared and placed in a small glass vial. The group went upstairs to one of the bedrooms in the upper floor apartment. The apothecary explained that he had asked his niece to lower her intake of liquids considerably during the preceding night and day, in order to reduce the distraction of a full bladder during the period following the consumption of the dose. The niece changed into her nightclothes and sat on the middle of the bed. She showed some last-minute hesitation when finally offered the vial, but the apothecary uncle prevailed upon her to finally take it.

At length, she put the vial to her mouth and drained its contents. Nathan looked at his timepiece; it was nearly half past eight. Seconds ticked by and the niece seemed her normal self.

"I feel a bit affected," she offered, making brief eye contact with her uncle. "I feel slightly dizzy."

"Completely normal."

Five minutes had passed and there was no appreciable change.

Two more minutes passed and the niece's head started leaning a bit to the left. She straightened it up again. Then suddenly, just past the eight-minute mark, she collapsed, falling to her side. She had completely lost consciousness. Attempts to revive her were of no avail. Her pulse was still at a natural rate. She was breathing easily.

"I cannot predict with certainty how long she will be unconscious, but if I have calculated correctly, she should recover consciousness about this time tomorrow. You may stay through the night and into tomorrow, to verify for yourself, should you like. There is an extra upstairs bedroom for the lady and you may sleep on a couch in the sitting room. I shall have Martha, my housemaid, stay in her room all night to make sure that there are no adverse consequences."

Knowing that staying all night was not possible, Nathan suggested, "I must return the lady to her home tonight, but I will be back tomorrow afternoon. Upon my return, twenty hours will have lapsed, so hopefully I can see your niece resuscitated."

The apothecary nodded. "That should work well."

"I wish to come with you tomorrow," Jocelyn asked.

"Can you be absent from the estate for such a length of time, without causing suspicion?" Nathan spoke to Jocelyn just loud enough for her to hear.

She whispered back. "I will pretend to not have slept at all the night before. I will lock my door and instruct my maid to not bother me, so that I can sleep through the night."

"Very well; I shall meet you tomorrow afternoon at the east gate."

***

The next day, they traveled for the third time to the same address on the far side of London, arriving before four o'clock in the afternoon. Jocelyn was excited as she contemplated the effect of the concoction on the young girl—her entire performance would hang on its efficacy. Upon arrival, Nathan and Jocelyn inquired impatiently about the condition of the niece.

They were ushered into the bedroom where the niece was sleeping. The housemaid had been keeping watch over the niece since the dose had been administered. The niece appeared to be sleeping quietly.

"She has not awakened since the dose was administered?" Nathan inquired.

"That is correct," replied the housemaid. "I have been at her side all night. I slumbered off and on during the evening, but I'm certain that I would have noticed if she had risen."

Nathan and Jocelyn kept quiet vigil in the bedroom, not wanting to awaken her by the sound of their voices. Time passed slowly as they sat next to the housemaid and observed the niece, the only sound her breathing as she lay in bed.

Six o'clock came and passed.

Just before seven o'clock, the niece started to stir, involuntarily moving her legs and arms. The housemaid sent for her employer, and the apothecary soon arrived in the room. More movement came from the niece, then she suddenly opened her eyes. She seemed disoriented and appeared agitated as she took in the presence of guests in the unfamiliar bedroom. Her uncle sat next to her, holding her hand, and she relaxed.

"Do you recognize me, Roxanne?"

"Of course, uncle. How long have I been asleep?"

"A full night and day. How do you feel?"

"I feel as though I have slept for a week. You'll excuse me please"—her bladder was nearly overflowing as she hurriedly left the room, without difficulty or in need of aid.

The niece returned soon after and the uncle inquired, "Do you feel any different from last night? How does your head feel?"

"I remember dreaming endlessly. But I feel fine."

The uncle turned to Nathan and Jocelyn. "You see, no ill effects. Simply a longer slumber than normal. Just as I said."

Nathan and Jocelyn looked at each other. Jocelyn appeared pleased. "It appears to have worked splendidly," she noted. "I would like a vial with exactly the same mixture as your niece."

The apothecary looked delighted. Soon after, he presented Jocelyn with a capped vial and demanded his price: "Fifty pounds." He had intended on charging a small fraction of that, but in noting the apparel of his customer and her anxiousness to purchase, had elevated the price five times in his mind, during the intervening hours.

Nathan was appalled by the price. Jocelyn waved off his reaction, showing no interest in negotiating. She produced payment from her purse. "It's expensive, but necessary," she said as she took the vial from the grateful uncle. "Thank you for your invaluable service."

As they returned to the side gate of the Charlesworth estate,

Jocelyn was energized. "This will allow us to act the final scene in grand fashion, just as I planned. It shall be the *performance of my lifetime!*"

With the wedding less than a week away, she bid farewell to Nathan. "Soon, you shall be free to marry your true love," Jocelyn smiled at Nathan. "I cannot help but feel a bit jealous. You shall make a fine husband. When and if I determine to marry, I hope to find half the man as you." She took his hand and kissed it gently.

"I'm sure you will find a man that dwarfs me in every respect," Nathan said modestly.

Jocelyn looked away, wistfully. "We have become such good friends. I shall miss your frequent visits to my home. I shall miss your lovely concerts. I shall miss our talks."

"As will I."

"We must remain friends, even after you marry."

"I expect we shall, after a brief passage of time."

Jocelyn's head remained turned away, as she looked out the window. Her eyes were moist. "I didn't expect to feel the way I do," she said quietly. "I do care for you, Nathan."

"As I do for you," he replied. Jocelyn squeezed his hand as she left the carriage.

"Until our wedding day!" She put on a brave smile and quickly disappeared behind the east gate.

Chapter 83

The following day, Regina was once again seated in her stunning burgundy gown. It would be the last time that Regina and Nathan would be together until after the Westminster Abbey wedding. Both were silent during the first hour, as Nathan focused on her portrait, a feeling of anxiety in the air about the coming days.

As he was painting, Nathan wondered how he could tell Regina everything that had happened to him during the last few days: his brush with death at the hands of Jocelyn's brother, the painting that Lord Charlesworth had presented to him at Haightbury Castle, the Duke's confrontation and letter, the incredible Ravensdale gift, followed by the day's journey and picnic there. Some things were better left unspoken. He did tell Regina of his father's painting; she was thrilled to hear that Nathan had something by which to remember his father. But he withheld the other matters, fearing that it would only create anxiety for Regina. He didn't want her to start having doubts about his commitment to her.

"It is nearly over. I cannot wait to start my life with you!" he exclaimed as he dipped his brush in the palette.

"You have been so often in *her* company. Have Miss Charlesworth's charms not worn you down?"

"Most men would succumb, I suppose. But then, they don't have the antidote."

"Which is?"

"The love of the most extraordinary woman on earth."

"You have met her?"

"I have."

"You must tell me of her."

"She is kind, generous, loving, even-tempered..."

"She sounds *very* boring."

"Never boring."

"I don't think I would have any interest in meeting her," said Regina shaking her head.

"That is just the beginning..."

"Please go on. What else makes her so extraordinary?"

"She has such grace and elegance..." Nathan looked for the right adjectives. "Her selfless service shines brighter than the noonday sun."

Regina blushed modestly, but recovered quickly and asked, "Those are certainly praiseworthy attributes. Is there nothing more?"

"She has an indefinable presence and depth of character. The most incredible eyes you have ever seen. And the sweetest, most tender voice you can imagine."

"Maybe I would like to meet her, after all. Are you certain that you would not tire of life with this *extraordinary* woman?" Regina pondered, tilting her head to the left.

Nathan laughed.

Regina continued. "No more mixing in such elevated social circles, no more box seats at the concerts? No more sumptuous feasts at the Charlesworth estate?"

"I'm sure it will be quite dull," Nathan feigned a look of utter boredom. "I will somehow manage."

"Will you ever wish you had married her, instead? This woman of whom you speak of could never hope to attain *her* beauty."

"There you are wrong on both counts. This woman 'of whom I speak' is far more beautiful to me than Miss Charlesworth could ever be." Nathan held out his thumb toward Regina, as if he were assaying a priceless work of art. "She is the one woman among all her sex on earth, who radiates brightly with purity and selflessness. No man could ever hope to be worthy of her, but I will devote my lifetime to trying."

"Oh, Nathan. I fear you set too high a standard for her. Like any other person, I'm sure she must have her faults, imperfections, and doubts. If you keep her on such a high pedestal, you shall surely become disillusioned with her. Besides, have you never considered that this woman may be the more blessed in the future union? She could never have entertained the possibility of experiencing the exquisite happiness of being joined to such a remarkable man as you. I don't think she can truly allow herself to believe in such a miracle until the marriage is solemnized. To love you and be your wife for the rest of her days would be to experience ten thousand lifetimes of pure bliss."

Nathan could no longer resist. He put down the brush, approached Regina, and took her in his arms. No words were spoken for several minutes as they shared each other's indescribable happiness at being so close.

Finally, Regina whispered in Nathan's ear, "Will it really be over? It hardly seems possible."

Nathan whispered back: "The next time I see you, the wedding will have been halted. And soon thereafter, it will be over. Forever."

"I keep expecting something horrible to happen."

Reassuring her, Nathan responded. "We saw the effect of the chemicals on a woman of similar size and weight as Miss Charlesworth. It will produce the desired effect. I will have to play the part of the grieving fiancé, who is desperate to recapture the love of his betrothed. But, in short order, she will insist that the engagement be broken off. Then, after the passage of a respectable amount of time, you and I shall marry."

"But, what if the vial doesn't have the desired effect? What then?"

"Then it shall be me who faints," Nathan said with a smile.

"But, I fear you are not the actor that Miss Charlesworth is."

Nathan looked intently into Regina's eyes. "Forget not my promise. Though I am before the priest, being asked to accept the woman kneeling at my side as my wife, I shall stand and forsake her."

"Your courage would not falter you? You would accept the dire consequences from the Charlesworth family of such a defying act?"

Nathan responded. "There would not be the slightest hesitation on my part."

"Let us embrace, one last time, until the wedding scene unfolds." Regina wrapped her arms tightly around Nathan, not wanting to let go. The embrace continued as they both sought refuge in each other's lips. Nathan experienced the full measure of Regina's love. It would be enough to carry him through the coming days.

He gathered his nearly completed canvas and his paint supplies, and left the Lancaster residence. He turned back for one last look at his true love, mouthing the words, "I love you." Regina's face showed a mixture of sorrow and fear at first glance, but she forced a brave smile and waved heartily to him, as he entered the pony chaise.

Chapter 84

When the morning dawned on the last Sunday before the wedding, the sun smiled on the city of London. An early riser, Nathan took note. It was the first Sunday with a promise of sun since Jocelyn had playfully hinted at an encore violin performance. With the glory of the sun's morning rays, a sudden impulse came upon Nathan to venture to the Charlesworth estate and listen to her play once more; he knew he would never get another chance. He would make certain that she did not see him and he would return as stealthily as he arrived.

He imagined the sound of the violin and the haunting performance of *"Nur wer die Sehnsucht kennt,"* the only melody he had ever heard her play. Nathan longed to hear her play one more time.

I can't believe that I am thinking of stopping by to see her again, when I should be thinking only of Regina.

It was merely about the music, he reassured himself. Nothing more. Nevertheless, his mind reflected on the angelic vision, the long tresses of gold, the unearthly music.

What harm could there be if I chance a visit? I will only observe her from a distance, not allowing her to know that I am present. Then I shall leave and no one shall be the wiser.

Nathan caught himself. *What madness is this? It is better that we don't meet again, until the final act.*

Nevertheless, he hurriedly dressed himself, shaved, and was soon outdoors basking in the sunlight. There were clouds in the sky, but they were scattered.

She must be playing even now. Can I truly be planning on going?

It was nine o'clock. Would the clouds overtake the sun on his journey over? He hailed a cab.

Why am I doing this? Then he answered his own question. *Because her music is so rare, so pure, so indescribably beautiful—one last time, if I am fortunate.*

With each passing minute, he became more obsessed to hear the violin again; there was no longer any internal debate. He looked out the window repeatedly whenever the sun's rays were shielded, praying that the sun had not again forsaken the city.

The cab arrived at the Charlesworth estate a little after half past nine, the sun still shining in the heavens. *I hope I am not too late.*

It took what seemed to be an eternity for the butler to answer the door. Once inside, Nathan walked in the direction of the sunroom. He had seen it from afar, but had never set foot in the room, which was located on the main level on the southern prospect, where it was designed to take advantage of a full day of sun during much of the year.

As he followed the curving hallway balcony, which hung above the ballroom below, he heard the soft refrain of a violin. His heart rejoiced.

I am not too late.

The music was as pure and as powerful as his first encounter. He recognized the piece: Mozart's *"Ruhe Sanft."* How was it possible that she was playing it? As a young child, he remembered his mother had often sung it to him as a lullaby when she was putting him to bed. He had never before heard the solo melody played by violin. Memories of his dear mother and the powerful love she had for him came flooding back. Jocelyn could never have known that—he had never told her of it.

Hearing the beautiful familiar melody compelled Nathan to steal a glance into the doorway of the sunroom, though he had not intended to venture so far. Jocelyn was turned away from him, on the far side of the room, facing the morning sun pouring in from the window as her bow moved gracefully upon the tight strings of the violin. He remembered her well from before, when she had been dressed in white, her hair down. Today, the sun radiated through the windows, causing her profile to be darkened from Nathan's view.

Not wanting to be seen, Nathan remained just outside the sunroom in the hallway, where he would not intrude on her privacy. After completing *"Ruhe Sanft,"* she continued with Mendelssohn's *Elias* Elijah soprano aria. *She is only performing soprano arias—in homage to my mother.* They were all melodies he had heard his mother sing. *She must know that I am here!*

Nathan silently walked over to the doorway again and stared at Jocelyn. He was shocked to see her face turned, looking his way contentedly as she played. She seemed to have been expecting him. Now exposed, he quietly entered the room and sat on a chair near the room's entrance. She continued the Mendelssohn aria, then started on Paisiello's *"Cavatina for Nina."*

When she finally lowered the bow, she walked toward Nathan

with a face glowing with delight. She was wearing a light green chiffon dress, her hair up in her customary fashion, with golden braids falling down her back.

"Lord Nathan, I didn't expect to see you until our wedding day. What a wonderful surprise. As I was playing, I felt your presence. It was not unpleasant having you for an audience. In fact, it was quite nice. I feared I might lose my nerve, but I felt strength instead. What made you come?"

"I needed to hear you play one last time. And what music! Those were all songs I heard my mother sing."

"I felt you deserved a special medley, having been so patient with me."

"It was extraordinary. Truly extraordinary! I'll never forget this morning."

"It was my pleasure to perform for you, one last time. Come. You must meet my brother Edward."

Nathan had heard talk of Edward, but had never met him before. Jocelyn had described Edward as a younger facsimile of her father. Edward lived near Manchester and managed the extensive Charlesworth land holdings in northern England.

"Edward, his lovely wife, and their three children arrived last night for the wedding," Jocelyn explained. Then speaking in a very subdued voice, she said: "They have no idea of the spectacle they are about to witness." Jocelyn took Nathan by the arm and walked down the corridor to the parlor. Sitting on the chair reading the *Times* was her brother. As they entered the room, Edward stood and came forward.

Edward was the same height as his brother Roderick, but endowed with far better looks. He had not Roderick's ruddy complexion, nor his high forehead, nor his blond hair. Edward's locks were black and wavy, like his father's. On this glorious Sunday morning, he was wearing casual attire for home consumption only, dressed in a beige shirt and matching trousers, with a pale blue sweater hanging over his shoulders.

"So, at last I meet the *extraordinary* Nathan Sinclair—the renaissance man," Edward smiled and offered his hand. Nathan bowed and took Edward's hand in a vigorous handshake.

"I have been most anxious to meet you," Nathan responded.

"More anxious to meet me than my brother, I'm sure," Edward made a snide remark directed toward his younger brother. "Sorry about Roderick. The black sheep. I suppose every family has one. His effort in life seems to be tearing down the Charlesworth image, while my father and I are forced to make constant repairs. I can tell that you will be a welcome addition."

Nathan smiled at the compliment.

"With the bequest of Ravensdale and your other assignments, I suspect that you will be busy for a while. But, I may also wish to engage your services in the north in the not-too-distant future."

"I shall be at your service." Nathan was flattered.

"I would introduce you to my wife Catherine and my children, but they are out on the grounds. I am sure we shall meet at the wedding, if not before."

"I very much look forward to becoming better acquainted." Nathan smiled and departed from the room with Jocelyn.

Jocelyn led Nathan back to the sunroom. To his surprise, breakfast had been delivered on a silver tray. They enjoyed tea with boiled eggs, meat, and sweet bread.

Reflecting on the memorable violin performance he had witnessed moments before, Nathan asked, "However did you become so accomplished?"

"Like you, I found the bow in my cradle. It has been my companion every day since."

"And during your years in Paris...?"

"I had the best musical instruction my father's money could buy. Do you know of Jean-Delphin Alard?"

"Yes, of course," Nathan recognized the name of one of the most prestigious professors of violin in Paris.

"He was my private tutor during my years there."

"What a great privilege for you."

"And, before leaving for Paris, my father bought me this," Jocelyn pointed to her violin. "A Stradivarius. It almost plays itself."

Jocelyn stood up and led Nathan over to the table where she had placed the beautiful seventeenth-century wooden masterpiece. "Rumor has it God showed him the design. The bridge position of the violin, where the string vibrations coalesce into sound, is patterned after the human body—located in the same proportion in the violin as the navel is to the human form." Nathan had never heard the engineering genius of the violin explained so simply and elegantly.

Jocelyn continued: "Music and acting were my passions. I kept my musical talent to myself, as you know. But play-acting was another matter altogether, because I was able to lose myself in the role of someone else. I adored the occasions when we performed plays."

"So I have seen firsthand. And you are the consummate play-actor as well."

"And, in a few days' time, I shall be back *on stage*," Jocelyn smiled.

"Are you prepared for it?"

"Oh, yes. I am nervous, feeling the same way I always do before a performance. But I am looking so forward to it. Unless, of course, you convince me not to take the vial."

Nathan showed bewilderment. "You would actually go through with the wedding?"

"No—but it was delightful to see your reaction. Tell me, Lord Nathan, how is it that you, of all men, do not fall under my spell?" Jocelyn batted her tantalizing azure-blue eyes playfully, making the most beautiful face imaginable as she curved her lips upward in a sly smile.

"Because I alone know your quest for freedom. You need to be allowed to sail free, to soar without restriction, like an eagle in flight. Marriage would be so restrictive."

"With most men, I suppose you are right. But with you, what would it be like?"

Nathan looked up. "I don't honestly know. I have never truly reflected upon it."

"Have you not daydreamed about married life with your true love?" Jocelyn said with a faraway look in her eyes.

"I have."

"So, how will the two of you spend your days together once you are *enchaînés* as man and wife? Will you keep her in your sight every minute of every day?"

"I hardly think so. I shall want to devote time to the piano."

"But surely she will not want to miss a minute of your music."

"Now and again, she *surely* will."

"I never would. No matter what task or pleasure was at hand, *je laisserais tout tomber pour t'entendre jouer*."[99]

"And I *must* take time to do my work."

"So, if we were married, I would be liberated from you while you work." Looking away, she breathed more to herself. "That would provide me enough freedom." Meeting Nathan's eyes again, she spoke louder. "A gentleman, who has nothing of consequence to do, might never let me out of his sight. How suffocating that would be. I think I might enjoy being married to you."

"Now, you truly are talking in jest."

"Perhaps I should amplify my charms. You know if I do that,

---

99   I would drop everything to hear you play.

tu seras incapable de me résister."[100] There was a seductive, irresistible look on Jocelyn's face.

"My dearest Jocelyn, perhaps more than any man alive, I know you speak the truth. There is a limit to the will of even the strongest of men."

"It would be so delicious for me to test them on you." Jocelyn, who had been standing five feet from Nathan during the colloquy, took two short steps forward, swaying her hips lusciously as she cut the distance between them in half.

"And what charms would you try?" Nathan asked lightheartedly, without thinking, instantly regretting his recklessness.

"You've forgotten already—when you were vying to usurp my performance by taking the concoction yourself? I know exactly where to start." Jocelyn spoke with supreme confidence, primed to magnify her powers.

Nathan thought better than to pursue the inquiry. He was treading on ground far too dangerous. But it was too late. He had already uncaged the tigress.

"Daily sessions at the violin. Would *that* wear you down? You experienced a small sampling today."

"Yes, that would be my undoing, if I had a daily dose."

"*Et je te contemplerais avec une telle intensité d'amour et de dévotion que ta volonté s'écroulerait.*"[101] Her gaze intensified and Nathan felt the power of her regard, as he had many times before. Her cadenced use of French, in her most seductive voice, was intoxicating.

Nathan looked away, trying to gain control over his thoughts. "I know of that power, having experienced it firsthand. Fortunately, it has been dispensed only in small doses, allowing me days to recover in between."

I am confessing too much.

She took a step closer, barely caressing his cheek with her right hand, forcing his eyes back to hers. "*Tu sais, bien sûr, que si je t'avais pour une longueur de temps, tu succomberais.*"[102]

Nathan nodded involuntarily, drawn into her lair, unable to lower his eyes.

"*Une étreinte, peut-être?*"[103] The gap closed between them, so that her face was less than twelve inches away. Nathan looked into

---

100   You will be unable to resist me.
101   Not at all. I would gaze at you with such intensity of love and devotion that your willpower would crumble.
102   You know, of course, that if I had you for any length of time, you would succumb.
103   A tight embrace, perhaps?

her dilated pupils, feeling his soul being drawn in by her inviting eyes, as Jocelyn continued. "*Ne pas te lâcher jusqu'à ce que je sache que je t'ai.*"[104]

"I have experienced that for a flicker of time." Nathan felt an arousal in his loins, knowing he must look away, but powerless to do so. "I must admit, I could not survive that for any length of time," he confessed, under his breath, as his willpower began to crumble.

"*Un baiser de mes lèvres? Que, tu n'as jamais osé.*"[105] Jocelyn moved so close to Nathan that he could smell her sweet breath. He lowered his face and she raised hers, until just an inch separated them. She was daring him to try. Nathan felt below a burning sensation of intense pleasure, unlike anything he had ever experienced before.

"Nor do I dare. Touching them, even once, might transport me to a place of no return." Nathan imagined the passion a deep kiss with Jocelyn would ignite.

I must turn away from her.

Exerting the full power of her sorcery, Jocelyn placed her hands on the front of his shoulders, then moved them slowly around to the back of his neck in an embrace. As she did so, she opened her mouth ever so slightly, moving the tip of her tongue slowly upon the top, then bottom of her full lips, in a sensuous, longing hunger, while magnifying her radiating rapturous regard. Nathan felt flushed, all remnants of his willpower vanishing. His lips were trembling, so close, he felt the moistness of her passing tongue.

Suddenly, her lips were Regina's and Nathan broke from the embrace, turning away at the last instant before contact was made.

Jocelyn laughed. "No. I would have little trouble placing you under my spell." Her voice carried a flicker of triumph mixed with melancholy. Then she retreated, breaking the trance. "You have your charms, too, Lord Nathan. I fear you know not your own power."

Nathan was still recovering his equilibrium.

"Because I can't have you, it makes you all the more desirable. It would be a delectable challenge to turn you from her." She paused. "What a horrid woman I am, to even consider such a thing."

"And, if ever I did succumb, would you not soon discard me like a wilted flower?"

"You would have to *tempt me* to find out," Jocelyn retorted, a mischievous grin on her face.

---

104   Not letting go of you until I knew I had you.
105   A kiss of my lips? That, you have never dared.

"I pity the flood of poor men who will fall under your spell, only to be cast aside. They shall never recover, for as long as they shall live." Nathan thought of the poor Duke, who had been bewitched for the rest of his life.

"But, Lord *Sainte Claire*. You seem to have recovered quickly enough."

"Not without the greatest of effort."

"If you can resist me so, then you must be deserving of her love."

"I hope to be."

"Is her soul truly so pure and divine?"

Nathan nodded respectfully.

"However did she gain such inner beauty? Tell me, that I may learn," Jocelyn gave an earnest look.

"I believe God must have blessed her with it at birth. But life dealt her the greatest of sorrows, which she has borne with transcendent grace. Have I never told you her story?"

Jocelyn shook her head. Nathan led Jocelyn to the wicker couch nearby, where they sat. Taking Jocelyn by the hand, Nathan slowly related the story of the fire that had robbed Regina of her parents and siblings, and the aftermath of her glorious work. By the time he had finished, tears were streaming down Jocelyn's face.

Between sobs, she uttered: "I shall never trifle you again with my charms. Ever. I am so sorry. You should go." Nathan hesitated, but Jocelyn repeated. "Go. Now. Please." Nathan quietly departed without further objection.

Chapter 85

The next two days were spent in anxious contemplation of the enormity of the events soon to unfold. In his office on Tuesday morning, Nathan distracted himself with sketches of the palace at Ravensdale that *would never be built*. He had created a formidable design for Sir Rochester, but the building site in Ravensdale trumped even that in its beauty and majesty. What height, what size, what immensity of beauty could be constructed there! Nathan sketched beautiful paths around the oval-shaped lake, in the shade of tall trees, that would provide ingress and egress to the palace. He contemplated long windows overlooking the North Sea that would bring nature's beauty into the interior. He envisioned a palace on such a colossal scale that Lord Charlesworth might even demur. It didn't really matter. Nothing would ever be built upon it, at least nothing in which Nathan would ever partake.

The fantasy of Jocelyn was so alluring: her beauty, her wealth, her music, her playfulness, the royal spoils of marriage surpassing any rational dream. Could any man withstand the onslaught of affection, love, excitement, and wealth that would be so abundantly bestowed by a woman of such ineffable beauty? Even the most faithful of all would surely succumb under such an unrelenting attack of female sorcery.

How have I been able to remain loyal to my Regina under siege from such an enchantress? Because Regina is worth all of it and more. Through it all, I have remained faithful to her still. I have been weakened, bewitched, vulnerable, and on the verge of submission, but my love for her has conquered all. Thank God, my time with Jocelyn has been limited. Surely, she would have had me under her dominion long ago, if I were in her presence daily. One last adventure together—our wedding day—and then I shall be free from her power.

Will I have no regrets then?

***

Later that evening, Nathan had a quiet dinner at the local tavern, a short walk from his new residence. In two days' time, he would be dressed in an immaculate black wedding suit with tails, in front of a thousand members of the London elite, for marriage to the most beautiful woman on the face of the earth. He imagined Jocelyn in her wedding dress. With her golden hair, her spectacular frame, her entrancing features, bedecked with jewels worth countless fortunes. She would radiate beauty beyond belief. However, had the *proposition* come to this? He reminisced about that evening, so many months before, when she had first offered a seemingly innocuous bargain intended to benefit them both. Neither would have imagined what the following year would bring, culminating in an event that had the city of London electrified.

The tavern's waitress came over to take Nathan's order. She smiled at him. He had seen her before. She had started a conversation several nights before, while serving him.

What would it be like to be an invisible member of the London masses? She is pretty and sweet. If I were not madly in love, where would her flirting ultimately lead?

"You come here often. Do you live nearby?" She spoke the Queen's tongue with nary a trace of a working-class accent. She had dark blonde hair, a nice form, and pleasant features. *Many would find her more desirable than Regina at first glance*, Nathan thought. He was surprised to find her working here.

"I have a place a short distance away."

She smiled. "Then, I expect I shall see you from time to time."

He ate his dinner of roast beef, roast potatoes, and Yorkshire pudding, but his mind was a million miles away. He felt anxious that his future would be dependent on the effects of an elixir containing a few herbs and laudanum. So much was riding on something so small. A thousand alternatives rushed through his mind, including a surprise appearance from the Duke, hoping to halt the wedding. He sipped the tavern's swill. Never much of a drinker, tonight was different. The spirits seemed to exert more power than normal, calming his anxiety. He should be leaving soon. The waitress came over with his tab.

"My brother walks me home at night, but he is not well tonight. I could use a gentleman for an escort," the waitress said to Nathan in a soft voice. "If it is not too far out of your way. Would you mind terribly?"

Nathan looked at her pleasant smile and nodded. "It would be my pleasure."

Minutes later, in the cold of the late autumn evening, the waitress had her arm in Nathan's. "It is an enchanting night, is it not?"

"Most beautiful."

"You are very well dressed. So you are a gentleman?"

"Not exactly. I am an architect."

"Oh, you design beautiful homes?"

Nathan smiled and nodded.

"I would love to see one of them someday."

She looked up at Nathan. "My name's Sarah McLaughlin."

"Nathan." He replied, hesitating to mention his last name, fearing she would recognize it from newspaper reports.

So what would another man in my shoes do tonight? Would he tempt a kiss? Would he hope to be invited into her apartment? It's amazing how decorum and propriety are dispensed with among the commoners. A lady would never imagine walking alone with a stranger... certainly not at night...

Her home was quite a bit farther than she had represented *and* in the opposite direction as his. Twenty minutes later, she pointed down a dark street. "Over there."

Nathan heard footsteps in the shadows. The last words he heard came from the waitress. "I'm so sorry."

Chapter 86

He woke with a start, but could see nothing. His eyes were covered with a cloth tightly wound around his head. He lay prostrate in a wooden cart, his full body covered by a large tarp. His arms and legs were bound. He tried to wriggle free without success, while being jerked violently from side to side in the cart, pulled by panting horses. The wind was gusting, causing the tarp to dance above him. His head ached.

It all came flooding back. The strong drink at the tavern. Walking the waitress home. Being attacked in the dark of night by unrecognizable men. Ambushed and beaten. His ribs hurt, his eyes were swollen, and he could tell that his face had been battered.

At length, the horses and cart came to a stop. Nathan was forcibly removed from the cart and felt immediately the strong current of the wind. Still blindfolded, he felt one of the men releasing the bonds on his feet, and Nathan searched for stable ground while the other abductor held his arms in a vice-like grip. In the fierce wind, he was compelled by both men to walk blindfolded on uneven terrain, struggling mightily to maintain his balance. They brought him to a stop and the cloth covering his eyes was lifted. The gusting wind continued to howl and Nathan strained to focus his eyes. It was early morning, the sun just breaking over the hillside. Despite a swollen right eye nearly closed shut, Nathan could see the men who had abducted and ambushed him—neither man was recognizable.

Looking to his right, Nathan saw two other men, both well-dressed with black top hats and capes; Nathan instantly recognized the Duke and Roderick Charlesworth. They hardly seemed to notice Nathan and were occupied priming two pistols, adding gunpowder and then pressing steel balls deep into the barrels. Completing their task, the Duke and Roderick approached Nathan as the wind currents slapped against Nathan's swollen face. Nathan could almost feel their fury and knew they were looking for blood. He felt a tremor in his frame as he became conscious of the scene unfolding.

With venomous eyes, the Duke offered Nathan a pistol with

each hand. "Select your pistol," he commanded in a loud and trembling voice.

Nathan's hands were still bound in front of him, and he made no effort to grab the pistol.

"For God's sake, release his hands!" the Duke said in a loud voice to the two strangers standing next to Nathan.

One of the men pulled out a knife and carefully cut the twine that bound Nathan's wrists.

Nathan flexed his hands and massaged the redness on his wrists left from the tight cord.

The Duke tendered the pistol again. "Mr. Sinclair, if you please."

Nathan's hands remained at his side.

"What are you waiting for?" the Duke cried out.

Nathan glared back at the Duke, weighing his options.

"Imbecile. I am giving you a fair chance." The Duke's face betrayed nervousness and anxiety.

"I choose not to duel!" Nathan raised his voice over the howling wind.

"Coward! Then you deserve to die."

"And my blood shall be upon your head," Nathan replied defiantly through clenched teeth.

Roderick stepped forward, grabbed one of the two pistols, and thrust it into Nathan's midsection. Nathan staggered back from the force, but remained standing. Knowing any explanation regarding his "relationship" with Jocelyn would be useless, Nathan held his tongue. Roderick grabbed at Nathan's belt and shoved the pistol inside it. "There! You are now properly armed."

"Jocelyn will despise you for this!"

Roderick smirked in response. She already despised him. He had nothing to expect from his father or his sister, for that matter. His only allegiance now lay with the Duke.

The Duke insisted once more. "Defend your honor!"

"My honor needs no defending."

"I demand satisfaction. You are an imposter, and a pathetic one at that. You have no right to Jocelyn's affections." The Duke's trembling increased.

"She detests you."

The Duke struck Nathan in the face, causing Nathan to nearly lose his balance. "If I can't have her, you surely shall not."

Raising his pistol to Nathan's head, the Duke screamed menacingly, "I should kill you now!"

The wind gusted fiercely and Nathan stood intrepidly, staring into the barrel of the pistol without flinching.

The Duke lowered his pistol. "You don't deserve it, but you have been given an equal chance. There will be no blood on my conscience when the ball strikes your head."

"I refuse to duel."

"Then you shall die a coward's death!"

Roderick hurriedly walked over to a carriage nearby. He opened the door and a distinguished-looking man, wearing a wig, stepped out. The wind continued to blow mercilessly as the man made his way toward Nathan and the Duke, a hand securing his wig from the gale, with Roderick by his side.

The wigged man looked both men over, as the Duke removed his gloves and hat, handing them to Roderick. The wigged man addressed them in a strong baritone voice: "Gentlemen. Take ten paces, then turn facing each other. On the count of three, fire."

The Duke turned and started pacing. Nathan remained stationery. His two abductors came over and pushed him in the direction opposite the Duke. After a distance of roughly ten paces, the men forcibly turned Nathan around. Nathan now faced the Duke from a distance of just twenty yards.

"Gentlemen. Aim your pistols!" the man yelled over the howling wind.

The Duke cocked his pistol and with trembling hand aimed it at Nathan. Nathan's pistol remained secure in his belt. He felt a deep ache in his stomach, but showed no fear.

So this is how my life is to end. Over a woman whom I do not love. A woman I would denounce now, if I could, to save my life. The most beautiful woman on earth, whose manifold charms I have been able to resist.

The referee raised his voice again, louder this time. "Gentlemen! Take aim!"

"I refuse to fire!" Nathan yelled back at the wigged man.

"You cannot refuse to fire!" the referee cried back, over the wail of the wind.

Roderick shouted to the wigged man. "Count!"

The referee demurred. "I cannot begin to count until both men have taken aim."

Roderick shoved the wigged man to the side, taking his place. "One... two..."

Yelling at the top of his voice, Roderick bellowed, "Three!"

Nathan waited for the explosion inside his head from the Duke's pistol.

It was now the Duke's turn to scream. "Take your gun, you imbecile!"

Nathan stared defiantly at the Duke, the wind biting his face.

"Shoot him!" Roderick screamed.

Nathan trembled, but stood silent.

"I said, shoot him!" Roderick repeated.

The Duke's pistol remained aimed at Nathan.

"*Put him down!*" Roderick yelled maniacally at the top of his lungs.

Seconds passed. Nathan stood silently waiting for the sound of fire.

"He is not a man! He has relinquished his right to live! He is excrement under your feet! Shoot him! Shoot him now!" Roderick charged toward the Duke.

The gunpowder ignited with a flash of light and smoke as the invisible steel ball approached Nathan. As contact was made, Nathan spun to his left and collapsed, laying on the ground motionless.

"Bravo!" yelled Roderick, seeing that the steel ball had hit its mark. The Duke looked stunned, then triumphant.

"You killed a defenseless man in cold blood!" the wigged man shouted.

"Absurd. He had a gun. He chose not to fire," the Duke responded angrily.

Roderick yanked on the Duke's arm sharply. "We need to get out of here, now!"

The Duke and Roderick fled back to the carriage, hoisting the protesting referee between them. "You breathe a word of this to anyone and you and your family shall live to regret it," the Duke threatened. The wigged man turned white and cast his eyes down, nodding subtly his assent. The Duke noticed that his trembling was gone; he felt invigorated. At last, he had defeated his rival! The men entered the carriage and drove off in the wind, with the cart and two ruffians close behind. Nathan lie motionless on the ground. His consciousness sensed his life seeping away with the smell and sensation of blood oozing down his chest underneath his shirt and jacket.

I'm dying.

Chapter 87

Lying on the ground, Nathan tried to maintain consciousness, attempting to pinpoint the place of impact from the projectile.

He was vaguely aware of the sound of horses, carriage, and cart departing. Suddenly, a searing pain emanating from the top of his left shoulder overpowered him. He tried to wriggle his arms and legs and was amazed to be able to do so. He took breath after breath, without difficulty. Hope swelled within him.

I'm alive.

He was fast gaining control of his faculties.

It's a miracle I wasn't killed from that distance. It must have been the wind and the Duke's trembling hand. The steel ball had deflected off the top of his shoulder. The skin had been broken and his shoulder was bleeding, but not profusely. Slowly and with care, Nathan rose to his feet. Although exquisitely painful, he applied pressure on the wound with his other hand.

I must end this madness!

He had a hazy sense where he was and walked slowly to the east in the face of the rising sun, until he found a country road that led him to a small farm village. There, he received the friendly assistance of a farmer and his wife, who wrapped his shoulder with bandages and escorted him to a larger town, where he was able to purchase passage on a London-bound train. It was the day before his planned marriage to Jocelyn.

Upon arriving home, Nathan's shoulder was still numb. He slumbered all afternoon. Upon awaking, his whole left upper torso was aching. He looked at himself in the mirror. His right eye was swollen. His face was bruised.

What a sight I will make tomorrow, he thought. *Perhaps I should call the wedding off altogether.*

The more he reflected, the more he wanted to end the charade now, not put it off to some time in the future. He would go forward and play his part in the wedding scene. It would soon be over, and he could get on with his life.

***

Tonight, I shall choose little Molly to commemorate. She is the first child I ever placed and she will forever have a cherished place in my heart. She was three years old when I first met her; she had been living in the London Orphan Asylum for two years. Her parents had been stricken with typhoid and she was orphaned before her first birthday. So withdrawn and incredibly shy—she rarely received attention from the staff because she was so quiet and never complained.

Regina kneeled at her bedside and prayed. She poured her heart out to God, but asked nothing for herself, as was customary. After praying for Molly, she prayed that no harm would befall Jocelyn. She prayed that only peaceful sleep would come upon her after the drug was taken, and that she would be revived without injury or harm. She asked that Nathan would have the courage to do what was right. She prayed that all would go according to His will. Her petition requested that no matter what the coming days would bring, she would have the strength and courage to go on living with grace, humility, gratitude, and service.

When her prayer was finished, she walked over to a nearby chest of drawers upon which her jewelry box was located. She opened the box and picked up the silver locket necklace that Nathan had given her nearly a year ago, on Christmas Eve. She placed the necklace around her neck. Tonight, for the first time, she would wear it as she slept.

Chapter 88

It was midday. Nathan's head was still aching from the beating. There was throbbing pain at the spot where the top of his left shoulder was grazed by the projectile, but most of the neighboring area was numb. He wondered how the wedding guests would react to his appearance. Wearing a tightly tailored suit, the latest London fashion for a groom, Nathan imagined that he must have cut a striking presence with a swollen eye and purple bruisings on his face. Yet, he was standing on two legs without assistance. He wanted not to delay the final act of the play.

There was a fragrance of orchids and orange blossoms in the air as Nathan made his way, alone, into the back of Westminster Abbey. He could see Jocelyn exiting a vestiary of the church into the back foyer, resplendent in her white wedding gown. On her head was a tiara of orange blossoms, with a veil attached, pulled back to reveal her face. She was carrying a gorgeous bouquet of flowers wrapped in Belgian lace and tied with a ribbon. Never had heaven shined on one as it shined on her that day. Jocelyn's entry was yet shielded from the massive crowd. Nathan stood opposite from her in the back, separated by forty feet. He was to walk down the aisle with Jocelyn, because she wanted to ensure she was caught when she lost consciousness.

Their eyes met and Jocelyn saw, for the first time, the wounds Nathan had suffered. She had a quizzical look, wondering what had happened to him. Nathan shrugged his shoulders and conveyed that it was nothing important.

Jocelyn looked tentative and fearful. Nathan could see, even from his distance, that she was trembling. He realized that she was nervous about the gravity of the role she had chosen to play. He saw her clutching the small glass vial, the key to this final scene between them; she seemed intensely insecure about consuming its contents. It was now time for her to empty the concoction into her mouth, before together they joined arms and began the slow and lengthy procession to the altar. In a few minutes, she would fall unconscious and create a scene that no one would have ever imagined. Nathan saw a look of fear in her eyes that he had never seen there before. The music of the processional march began from the powerful organ beyond, signaling the time to begin the promenade forward. She was poised to make her grand entrance. Yet still she hesitated, holding the vial in her hands. Her regard seemed to inquire if there was any other way. Nathan looked away for a moment, not knowing what alternative he could offer—he merely wanted the deception to come to an end. Nathan pictured Regina in her wedding dress and imagined the outpouring of love that he would shower upon her on their wedding day; he visualized a look of rapture upon her face and in her being, not the trepidation and anxiety that was so plainly visible on the face of Jocelyn.

Looking back toward Jocelyn, Nathan saw her take the vial in both hands, uncork the top, and with a trembling hand raise it to her lips—hesitating for an instant—then draining the contents. She carelessly threw the empty vial into the corner of the foyer. The glass vial shattered against the stone wall, causing the sound to echo. It was done!

Jocelyn turned her eyes toward Nathan; as they approached one another, she nervously lowered her lace veil and took Nathan by the arm. Not a word was spoken by either, as they entered the massive cathedral with its heaven-bound arches, ribbed vaulting, and flying buttresses. The bright light of the sun through the enormous ruby and sapphire stained-glass windows blinded them temporarily as they began their long processional march toward the altar, Jocelyn on Nathan's left. There were rose petals and orange blossoms in the aisle, obscuring the checkerboard floor. The solemnity of the occasion struck Nathan like a thunderbolt. As he glanced at the woman at his side, he no longer sensed her fear. Nathan could discern, through the nearly transparent veil, a dazzling smile as only she could do. It made him shiver. She could turn on her powerful charms and display her magnetic gaze at will, even in distress. She was the consummate actress and did not want to disappoint the huge gallery gathered to watch her every move. It would be the biggest performance of her life.

Guests in the back rows of the abbey suddenly became aware that the bride and groom were making their entrance. The awareness spread, like the ripple in a stream, until all guests had turned their heads to follow the processional march. An audible rush came over the crowd as they gazed at the dazzling beauty walking arm in arm with every man's envy, one step at a time and stopping, then continuing again, up the aisle. There were also shock and murmuring from the crowd, in wonderment at the groom's battered and beaten face. Nathan made eye contact with Jocelyn's brother, Roderick, who stared through him as if he had seen a ghost; believing that Nathan had been shot and killed in the duel with the Duke, the blood drained from his face and there was a look of utter panic. It mattered little to Nathan. Nathan was waiting for the climactic event of the wedding; he was waiting for his bride to swoon mid-step in her march.

Nathan felt like a spectator in a play. The woman walking next to him was no more his bride-to-be than any other woman in the cathedral. He had never proposed to her and she had never accepted, yet here they were walking together toward the altar for the purpose of being joined as man and wife. As they reached the quire, Nathan sensed that several minutes had elapsed since the vial had been emptied. It dawned on him that Jocelyn had planned her collapse to coincide with her approach to the high altar, for dramatic flair, ever the actress. Her radiant smile remained, but Nathan felt her grip on his arm tremble as they entered the spacious area between the quire and the high altar.

Nathan was barely aware of the guests, so focused on catching her when she fell, wanting to ensure that she suffer no injury. As they completed the lengthy trek to the foot of the steps which led to the altar, Nathan felt her lose her balance. The drug had finally had its effect and she was falling.

Before Nathan could react, she caught herself. She had only tripped on her gown, ever so slightly. It was hardly noticeable to the crowd. She hesitated at the foot of the steps and looked toward Nathan. He could see, through her veil, a worried expression on her face. Instantly, Nathan felt the same concern. Was it possible that the apothecary was a charlatan, that he had orchestrated the entire scene with his niece? After all, they had only remained a short time after she had succumbed, returning twenty hours later, when she had been revived. Could it have all been an act, an effort to take advantage of a young desperate couple with obvious wealth?

The priest signaled for the couple to ascend the steps. The noise from the crowd had vanished, and anyone could have heard a pin drop in the cavernous cathedral. The guests were breathless to hear each word of the ceremony. Both Nathan and Jocelyn hesitated and the priest motioned again. Sensing the crowd's penetrating look from behind, they slowly walked up the steps to the high altar. There, the priest motioned for them to kneel. Jocelyn discreetly lifted her veil and looked at Nathan with an expression of confusion, as if to say: *Why hasn't the drug produced its effect? Help me!*

her eyes were pleading. Panic hit Nathan and he prayed that she would momentarily faint and the wedding ceremony would come to a climactic halt.

Nathan heard none of the prefatory words the priest said, merely a monotone drone of meaningless sounds that seemed in a foreign tongue. He hoped the priest would go on forever, or at least long enough to prevent the vows from coming. Jocelyn looked at Nathan. Replacing the expression of exquisite delight that had been present moments earlier on their processional march was a look of intense sadness and apology. Her eyes were welling up as she looked toward Nathan, as if to say: *I'm sorry. This wasn't supposed to happen.*

At length, the priest turned to Jocelyn. "Miss Jocelyn Charlesworth, wilt thou have this man, Lord Nathan Saint Claire, to be thy wedded husband, to live after God's ordinance in the holy state of matrimony? Wilt thou love, honor and keep him, in sickness and in health, and forsaking all others, keep thee only unto him for so long as ye both shall live?"

Jocelyn looked at Nathan. He read her thoughts. *What am I supposed to do now, Lord Nathan? Tell me what to say.* Nathan's face was frozen, and he knew not what to suggest. Jocelyn hesitated. The crowd murmured at the uncomfortable delay. With tears streaming down her face, she said quietly but audibly, "I will."

Time came to a halt for Nathan, when she spoke those two words. There was still time. The drug could take effect momentarily. If he waited long enough, she would yet faint and lose consciousness. Nathan heard the monotone voice of the priest again, this time directed toward him. He paid no heed to the words, but knew their meaning. There was still time. Nathan had promised Regina that he would flee the altar, if necessary, to prevent this union—and he had assured her he would do so without hesitation. Now, he hesitated and looked inside himself for a reservoir of courage. Could he stand up in front of all of London's elite, could he humiliate Jocelyn by rejecting her at the altar? Could he ruin any chance for the future he wished for himself and his beloved Regina by turning away from the ceremony at this final moment? Yet, Nathan had made a promise—he had never gone back on his word and never imagined to breach such a promise! Nathan imagined getting up, running from the altar to the back of the abbey, hailing a cab and gathering Regina, leaving on the next train for Portsmouth and gaining passage to the Americas. That could be their only desperate hope for a life together.

Nathan looked back at Jocelyn. She was staring straight ahead, her face now full of tears, falling like rain onto her wedding dress. She looked so helpless, yet unimaginably beautiful. The priest finished his inquiry of Nathan and stared at him with a stern look that conveyed: *What is wrong with you, man? Speak!* Would Jocelyn now faint? There was still time before Nathan could be compelled to speak. The crowd murmured again as Nathan froze and debated what to do.

Nathan willed the drug to take its effect on Jocelyn. It was useless. He put pressure on his knee and willed himself to propel away from the altar. Where was his strength to move? The temptation of fame and fortune, a palatial estate, mattered not to Nathan—he could easily forsake it all. But, could he forever shame Jocelyn's name with the stigma of rejection at the altar, after she had spoken her consent? How cruel that would be to one who meant so much to him. And what of Regina? What kind of life would she have with him, if he was on the run, penniless and shamed? There was no more time. Now was his last chance to honor his promise to the woman he loved. Nathan couldn't move. He felt bewitched by the beautiful sorceress kneeling next to him. He had given Regina his word! He must honor his promise, or he would be no man at all.

There was a flood of emotions and thoughts; the priest was demanding a response with his eyes, the gallery was beginning to buzz. Nathan was paralyzed, not knowing what to do. This *was* the precise moment he had promised Regina to leave the altar, if it ever went this far. Now! With every ounce of strength he had, he slid his right knee forward until the heel of his boot was on the floor, getting ready to stand. He had found the courage. It had finally come to him. Regina!

He glanced to his left to bid farewell to Jocelyn forever. He knew he would never see her again, despite her wishes that they remain friends. His desperate act would ensure that. She continued facing forward though her eyes were shut, her face covered in tears. Sensing his stare, she turned toward him and opened her eyes. Their eyes met and new tears emerged.

She held his stare through her flowing tears. How beautiful she appeared to Nathan now. More fragile than a fallen bird. He remembered the many clues to her vulnerable heart, and recalled her fear at ever revealing her inner self, even to her future husband. He remembered her mother telling him of Jocelyn's fragile heart, that once broken, would never open to love again. He recalled the wondrous kindness she had shown him, in bringing a surprise symphony for his accompaniment, the violin homage to his mother. He felt the full force of her power, her sorcery, and more. Now, from deep within the windows of her soul, Jocelyn could no longer disguise from Nathan the love she felt for him, a love he had never recognized before.

Could he abandon her now?

Nathan saw her lips move and Jocelyn mouthed the word: *Go*. She turned away, releasing him from her sorcery.

In that instant, Nathan felt the majesty of her sacrifice. He knew her heart was breaking. He watched her a few moments longer, and observed the involuntary heaving of her breast and head as she sobbed.

Where was his courage now! Where had his strength gone? The buzzing from the crowd intensified. Nathan turned his face back to the priest, who was now remonstrating him with an angry look.

From Nathan's throat, exhaled two words, which would chart the course of the rest of his life: "I will."

Jocelyn looked over at Nathan in shock, as she heard the words leave his mouth. But, their eyes did not meet as Nathan continued his forward stare.

The rest of the ceremony was a blur. A ring that had never been intended for use, but which had been part of the preparation for the event, was placed on the third finger of Jocelyn's left hand.

Nathan had passed the point of no return. He repeated the words of the priest: "With this ring I thee wed, and with my worldly goods I thee endow, in the name of the Father, and the Son, and the Holy Ghost. Amen." With each betraying word, Nathan inflicted mortal wounds upon his beloved Regina.

The priest joined their hands and droned on: "...I pronounce that they are husband and wife together... Those whom God hath joined together, let no man put asunder. Amen."

They were married. Nathan Sinclair had married Jocelyn Charlesworth. She was his wife, and he, her husband. Nathan was in shock. The look in Jocelyn's eyes showed that the feeling was mutual.

"I present to you Lord and Lady Sinclair."

The crowd cheered lustily. Through her tears, Jocelyn put on her actress-face, and smiled to the crowd.

Walking back down the aisle, people cheered, saluted and pressed to touch them. It was all as in a dream. Within a short time, they were in their elegant carriage, the horses leading them away from the abbey, in a parade-like celebratory atmosphere. Neither spoke for several minutes. Jocelyn had hold of Nathan's hand and was pressing it in a vice-like grip.

"Nathan. I am so sorry. I wanted to stop the ceremony, but I didn't know how. I kept waiting, praying for the drug to take effect. I felt a tingle, but nothing happened."

Nathan looked back at her and mustered a forced smile. "We were both deceived by the apothecary. He undoubtedly gave you a benign concoction. For the price of fifty pounds, we have been married."

Jocelyn looked at Nathan, her finger tenderly touching the bruise on his face and caressing lightly his swollen eye. She wanted to know what had happened, but she had more pressing comments to make: "Our children must never know of our deception." Nathan couldn't answer her and turned away.

After a long silence, she tried again with a forlorn smile. "But they shall be blessed with great musical ability, will they not?" Nathan held his peace and continued to look out the window, refusing to look back at the face of his bride.

For the first time, the gravity of the event sunk in. Nathan was actually married to the woman seated next to him. He was bound to her as partner for the rest of his life. He was destined to have children with her, to become the father of the children she bore. How could this have happened? What would happen to the woman he loved? Regina would be devastated beyond all hope, beyond all reason, once she learned what happened. She would hate him forever for breaking his promise.

Oh, Regina! What have I done? How did I forsake you? How can I go on now, without you?

The carriage was directed toward Nathan's new residence. Arrangements had been made by Lord Charlesworth for a honeymoon in Europe, an event that was never supposed to happen; their departure had been reserved for two days hence. It had all been part of the plan, to make all outward appearances and plans conform to the nuptials and tradition.

As they continued silently on their journey, neither spoke again. Suddenly, Nathan noticed Jocelyn's grip on his hand relax and he saw her head fall forward. Nathan caught her before she struck the opposite side. Jocelyn had fainted. Or, was she dead? She appeared lifeless. Yet, Nathan felt her warmth. He checked her pulse; her heart was still beating. She was still breathing.

The concoction had finally taken effect—a full thirty minutes beyond the time intended.

When the carriage arrived at his home, Nathan lifted Jocelyn in his arms and explained to the coachman that she had fainted. He carried her across the threshold as his manservant opened the door. He carried her up the stairs to one of the bedrooms—no bedchamber had been appointed for her, because this day had never been planned for—where he lay her on the bed.

Chapter 89

Nathan instructed the maid to remove Jocelyn's wedding dress and place her in a nightgown once he left the room, and then to keep watch over her, never to let her out of her sight. He explained to the maid how the wedding ceremony and crowd had overwhelmed his bride and that she had fainted from the exhaustion and excitement. Nathan thought briefly about calling a doctor, but was convinced that Jocelyn was in no danger and would be soon revived. If there was any delay in her resuscitation, there would be no hesitation to place the call.

Nathan then retreated to his library downstairs, his mind in a daze. As he entered the library, he was confronted by the nearly finished portrait of Regina. In the furor and commotion of the wedding day, he had forgotten about the painting, which lay perched on an easel in the middle of the room, along with palette, paint, and brushes. Overwhelming sorrow descended upon him, as he was exquisitely reminded of his unpardonable betrayal.

Her resplendent burgundy dress was beautifully depicted, but it was Regina's eyes, which pierced his heart.

"Why didn't I have the courage to flee the altar, as I promised you I would?" Nathan said in a whisper. He hated himself for breaking his promise. Would she ever forgive him? Could any woman, even one so pure and virtuous as Regina, ever forgive such a betrayal?

Nathan couldn't turn away from her lifelike gaze. He hadn't touched the painting since seeing Regina last; the paint was now dry. He doubted that she yet knew of his betrayal. In agony, he realized that she loved him still, never wavering in her faith in him, though that would soon change when news of the wedding came her way. Nathan wondered how she would learn of his broken promise? Would she first hear a rumor? Would she read it in the morning newspaper? Would she disbelieve it, at first? He then imagined her collapsing in sorrow and tears, when the truth was confirmed. Would she hate him? No, she would never hate him. But she would be forever disappointed in him, she would think him less a man. That was far worse.

He opened his eyes and stared at her image again, speaking softly: "How did I forsake thee, my love?" He reflected on a life without his beloved Regina, knowing he would never see her again. Nathan fell to his knees in front of the painting, clutching the sides. He looked up at her eyes but could not hold her stare, and with his head down, tried to justify his actions, relating in a soft and pained whisper the delayed concoction, Jocelyn's acceptance of vows, and his inability to rise from the altar. With tears in his eyes, he explained they could never have had a life together, what with the Charlesworth power, if he had humiliated Jocelyn and her family by leaving her alone at the altar. Finally, he begged her forgiveness and spoke a tearful farewell to the only woman who had ever received and accepted his proposal of marriage.

Nathan rose and walked to the nearby couch, where he sat with his head buried in his hands. Gradually, he began to ponder his future. He slowly opened his mind to a life with Jocelyn—his future now lay with her as his wife and companion. Had he not promised to love and honor her? Had he not promised, in his vows, to forsake all others, even Regina? Had he not promised to keep unto her only, for as long as he should live? Nathan solemnly promised himself to become a loving husband. He would love, honor and cherish Jocelyn, as his wife, for all the days of his life. Together, they would build a new life together.

During the ensuing hours, Nathan left his study periodically to check on Jocelyn, making inquiries of the maid as to her well-being. Jocelyn's breathing and pulse remained regular. She appeared to be in no danger, and Nathan resisted the temptation of bringing in a needless physician to check on her, remembering how the niece had awakened without incident. He studied her face and features. Was this truly his wife at whom he was now looking? It hardly seemed possible. How could matters have changed so dramatically in the span of a few short hours? As he gazed at her, he felt empathy for her, knowing she had also been a victim of the failed concoction. He repeated his vow of fidelity to her; he promised to cling to her, to devote the rest of his life to loving her, and hoped she would love him in return. Nathan stayed up all night, looking in on Jocelyn on the hour. Not until early morning did he finally find slumber on the couch of his library.

Nathan was awakened by the butler. The maid had dispatched him to inform Nathan that Jocelyn was stirring. Nathan immediately rose and ran up the stairs to the bedroom where Jocelyn lay. Jocelyn was moving, stretching, her eyes momentarily fluttering open, then shutting again. Several minutes passed. Then her eyes opened wide.

Jocelyn's first perception was lying in bed in a small bedroom with a Spartan interior. The walls were white and the lone window had no drapes. There were no paintings or tapestries on the wall and the only other furnishing was a chest of drawers opposite the bed. The room was wholly unfamiliar; she felt disoriented and wondered if she were still sleeping. She glanced at Nathan, but without recognition.

"How are you feeling?" Nathan gently inquired.

"Who are you?" she asked with a quizzical look. She was disoriented, but coherent enough to remember to play her part with others present.

Nathan motioned for the maid to leave, leaving Jocelyn alone in the room with Nathan. Slowly and sadly, Nathan shook his head.

"I feel as though I have been asleep for weeks. What day is it?" Jocelyn asked quietly.

"Friday morning."

"Nathan, this doesn't look like one of the upper rooms in the abbey. Where am I?" She had never been to Nathan's home before. Then in a state of agitation, she cried, "I dreamed that we married! Tell me that didn't happen!"

Nathan paused before speaking. "It did, my dear."

"Oh my God!" And the vivid memories of the day before came flooding back into her mind.

After she had bathed and dressed, Jocelyn remained in the bedroom pondering. She took her purse and opened it. There was the envelope, still showing the burn marks from the fire before her father had retrieved it, containing the letter her father had given her after the wedding ceremony, as he had promised—the letter Nathan had written, breaking off their engagement.

I should destroy this, she thought. *There should never be any evidence of our 'false relationship.'* Nevertheless, she opened the letter, intending only to read the first few words:

My dearest Jocelyn,

My hand trembles as I begin to write this letter, knowing that the time has come to say good-bye. After all you have done for me, how do I bid you adieu? How can I describe the void that will follow our parting? Life will never be the same. In your presence, the sun shines even at night. Your laughter is intoxicating, as is your personality. You claim to be immature, petulant, and spoiled. I have seen none of those traits. I have only witnessed your zest for life and freedom and your incredible condescension toward me.

Your father raised you to be the consort of kings and presidents. Years from now, when you are fulfilling your destiny, people will scarcely believe that I was the man upon whom, for a brief flicker in time, you showered your attentions and generosity. I have no membership with the London elite. I wish that I could claim right to the noble birthright that you so generously bestowed upon me, despite your knowledge of my lowly station.

I have always known this day would come. I have always known that each second with you was a precious and temporary gift. I shall cherish the memories of our mutual passion for music. I shall never forget your extraordinary gift of a full orchestra to my humble piano accompaniment of the Schumann concerto—how profoundly thoughtful and such an exhilarating surprise, one which I shall relive for the rest of my life. Nor shall I forget the afternoon soon after, when I came upon you quietly (and unexpectedly) and learned that you possessed an exceptional gift for music. When I heard your bow upon the strings of the violin, my ears heard the most divine and sublime sound which has ever graced my ears, though my eyes believed it not. There you were, your golden hair dangling to your waist, dressed in white like an angel, bow in hand, creating music I expected never to be worthy of in my lifetime. I could hardly breathe when I heard you play. I was astonished at your mastery of the instrument. I shall never forget the haunting melody you played; I was so obsessed with it, that I memorized it, wanting to play it for you someday, in my own way. Since I shall never see you again, I can tell you of that glorious unforgettable afternoon. Your secret is safe with me.

I marvel at your courage and character for having continued to be my dearest friend, even in the face of strong opposition from your brother and, certainly, although you have never expressed it, other family members and relatives. I would never want to be the cause of any loss of affection among your family. I knew that, even if my dreams ever took flight, it would be unforgivable for me to cause you or your family pain or embarrassment.

When the time is right, you deserve and shall find a lifetime partner who shall be loved and revered by your family with the same passion you feel for him. The man in your life will cherish you first for your beautiful heart, your sunny disposition, your playfulness, your passion for life, and then for your beauty. He will worship you every day of his life, as you deserve to be worshiped. He will never let you forget how much he loves you. He will never take you for granted. Though your outward beauty is unsurpassed, he will love your inner soul far more passionately. Such a man will be the most blessed of all God's creations. Despite my lowly birth, I have fantasized in quiet times about being such a man; wondering what it would be like to spend a lifetime being the beneficiary of your infinite love and amazing regard. I knew that one day I would be compelled to release you. That day has come and I thank you for every moment we have shared. I will forever be in your debt; you have had an incalculable effect on my life and career. You will always hold a most precious place in my heart.

Should our paths cross someday, I pray that God will have blessed you with a life of such happiness that you cannot express it, a happiness that will shine so brightly in your face that you will not be able to contain your exquisite joy. You deserve that, and much more. I end now. I must deliver this letter to you tonight. I whisper to you and whisper softly now: Farewell.

With the most ardent devotion and affection, I remain yours truly

Nathaniel Sinclair

After reading the letter, Jocelyn needed time to compose herself.

How could he write such a letter to me when he is in love with another woman?

At length, she left her bedchamber and walked thoughtfully downstairs, finding a somber Nathan in the parlor.

"Nathan, tell me about the woman you love. How did you meet? What was there about her that made you fall in love with her? Describe her to me. Your heart must be breaking."

Nathan got up slowly with a pained expression on his face. "I'll show you her portrait."

Jocelyn's face showed anguish. "Oh, my Lord. You painted a portrait of her? You never told me that. How can you ever forgive me?"

"Come with me," Nathan said and led her into the library.

Entering the library, Jocelyn observed large curtains hanging on a wall where no light shone from a window.

"The portrait is behind the curtains. Are you sure you want me to show it to you... or shall I destroy it?"

Jocelyn was crying softly. *It would be better if I never see it.*

"I must see it. I must see the woman whose heart I have broken with my foolish, selfish acts. I must see the woman you love."

Nathan raised the horizontal curtains slowly, from the bottom upward. A beautiful burgundy gown was revealed from the breast upward. As the curtains rose, the neck appeared, then the chin, nose and eyes, the paint still fresh.

Jocelyn began crying uncontrollably as the full canvas was revealed. It was a portrait of a woman with breathtaking beauty. A woman with golden hair like her own.

It was a portrait of Jocelyn.

Unable to control her emotions, she turned to Nathan and through her tears, showered him with the most glorious regard that Nathan had ever received, filled with devotion, admiration, and overflowing in a boundless supply of beautiful, resplendent and pure love.

Staring intently into her eyes, Nathan took her hands in his and asked quietly and intensely: "Are you acting now, my love?"

So overcome with emotion, Jocelyn could only shake her head. When her tongue was finally loosed, she said softly: "Did I not tell you I loved you... with my eyes, *le soir de mon anniversaire, quand je suis venu à toi?*"[106]

---

106   When I came to you the night of my birthday?

With tears covering her face and glistening eyes, Jocelyn rewarded Nathan with a radiant smile that would stay with him all the days of his life.

Epilogue

No messenger brought the news. It was the faraway tolling of bells.

Following breakfast, Regina had retired to her bedroom, wanting to be alone. She sat on her bed marking each minute of the wedding's progression in her mind. She envisioned Westminster Abbey teeming with London's elite and agonized that she was not a witness to the spectacle; at the same time, she felt relieved to be so far removed. She closed her eyes, took a deep breath, and imagined the sound of the powerful organ playing the processional march. She pictured Nathan and Jocelyn slowly walking up the interminable aisle.

It has happened by now, she thought. In her mind, she could see the hysteria converging among the crowd, as Jocelyn swooned on her way to the altar. She envisioned Nathan on his knees administering to his fiancée, as others pressed to render aid to the bride-to-be. She imagined shrieks from the multitude calling for a doctor, and viewed Jocelyn being lifted up and carried to one of the upper rooms of the abbey. The masses were buzzing, wondering if the woman in white was dead or alive.

Regina stood up from the bed and walked over to the open window, willing her eyes to see beyond the rooftops and trees to the abbey miles away. Suddenly, a heavy wind came gusting through and she thought she heard the sound of bells tolling from afar.

It is only my imagination, she surmised—until another gust of wind convinced her otherwise. Nor was it the sound of just one cathedral's bells; it was the sound of many.

She walked away from the window and rested upon her bed, trying to make sense of the reverberation of so many bells.

All of London is celebrating the culmination of a great wedding.

Then she knew.

***

The second day after the wedding, Nathan and Jocelyn departed on their honeymoon to begin their tour of European capitals. They had been booked passage on a luxury liner operated by the Peninsular and Oriental Steam Navigation Company. Lord Charlesworth had arranged an elaborate suite for them with a large private deck.

They spent their first morning together on the private deck facing the coast of France as the liner slowly migrated south. It was a sunny day, but cool and breezy. Nathan and Jocelyn sat on matching deep-cushion lounge chairs, separated only by a few inches. Nathan was deeply immersed in *The Moonstone*, by Wilkie Collins. Jocelyn was in a contemplative mood; she reached for Nathan's right hand and began inspecting it.

"So, these are the long elegant fingers that were nearly crushed by my brother Roderick?"

"The very same." Nathan continued reading, holding the book in his left hand. The day before, he had shared with Jocelyn, for the first time, Roderick's desperate attempt to run him over with the carriage.

"They are so much longer than mine." Jocelyn compared her left hand to his right.

"A decided advantage for a pianist."

"You have paid a dear price to have me in your life, Lord Nathan." Jocelyn raised her cheekbones as she spoke, wincing slightly at what might have been. "You gave up a woman of great virtue and inner beauty, whom you dearly loved. The Duke of Wilmont nearly took your life. You might never have played the piano again, or for that matter painted my beautiful portrait—which would *truly* have been a tragedy!"

Nathan smiled back at Jocelyn. He dared never breathe a word about the transformation of Regina's nearly finished portrait. Soon after Jocelyn succumbed to the elixir, Nathan had been hard at work in his library, replacing Regina's features with Jocelyn's eyes, nose, chin, and particularly her luminous hair. His regular visits to her room that evening were not just to check on her status, but to ensure the perfection of her features in oils. There was no reason that Jocelyn should ever know; Nathan would carry the secret to his grave.

After a pause, Jocelyn stated in a melancholy tone, "*J'espère que je le mérite tout à toi.*"[107]

Nathan's smile remained, but inwardly, he still felt remorse for Regina and couldn't keep his mind off the pain and betrayal that she must be feeling. Nevertheless, Jocelyn was proving to be a delightful, entertaining, and stimulating companion. And their first

---

107   I hope I am worth it all to you.

intimate evening together had been a revelation.

"Just a few more inches to the right and downward, and you would have been rid of me and still enjoying your freedom," Nathan moved his hand from where the projectile had grazed his left shoulder to his heart.

"Don't you jest about that," Jocelyn retorted. "It would have ruined my life!"

"Well, I hope you always feel that way."

"I just feel, at times, that I ruined yours." Jocelyn said softly. She returned Nathan's hand and stared at the open sea.

Jocelyn rose up from the chair and walked to the railing, looking far across the ocean to the barely visible French coastline. She tried to calculate how far south they had traveled and wondered if they had passed La Rochelle.

"Perhaps I should jump. Then *you* shall be rid of *me* forever," Jocelyn said wistfully and leaned over the deck's railing.

"Not until the deed to Ravensdale has been recorded, *please*," Nathan's eyes remained fastened on his book. "We don't want your father to renege on that."

Jocelyn came storming over to Nathan with a look of anger in her eyes. "How dare you!" She grabbed the book out of his hands and tossed it away, then pulled Nathan from his chair and yanked him over to the railing. "I shall push you off for that remark!"

Jocelyn did push Nathan, shoving him hard against the railing.

"But you said my death would ruin your life," Nathan protested.

"Not any more. Jump!"

"All right, then." Nathan grabbed hold of the railing and raised one leg up.

"Stop!" Jocelyn screamed.

"Well, make up your mind. Do you want your freedom back or do you want to be shackled with a husband for the next fifty years?"

"That long?"

"Maybe sixty!"

"That's too long. Jump now! Please." Jocelyn smugly turned away.

"Not today," Nathan said as he pulled Jocelyn back and stared into her lovely eyes. "I shall stay in your life for at least one more day." He moved his hands up to the back of her head and brought it next to his, then lowered his lips to hers, kissing her passionately.

Breakfast was soon served on their deck. As he sat across from

Jocelyn drinking tea, Nathan could scarcely believe he was a married man. Nor did it seem possible that he was married to the celebrity beauty who had enchanted all of London.

Here she is. Adoring me. Loving me. Why am I not the happiest of men?

***

Since the tolling of bells, Regina had been inconsolable, unable to sleep or eat. She had drowned her bed with tears, refusing to see anyone despite knocks on her door from her maidservant and family members. At length, she took out a pen and paper and began composing a letter.

> *Dear Nathan,*
>
> *How do I begin this letter? You, whom I loved with all my heart, with whom I shared everything? Why did you promise me your heart? Why did you promise me that you would love me forever? When the world was crushing down upon you, I never doubted your honor and integrity. Now you have forsaken me. Where is your honor and integrity now? Didn't you promise me that you would 'flee the altar' if it ever came to that?*
>
> *How could you have declared your love so passionately for me and then recited your vows to another? Were you so bewitched by her beauty that you could no longer bear to look at me or to touch me? I opened my soul to you. I trusted you*

A large tear fell onto the letter. Soon her tears were falling like a summer's storm, and Regina dropped the quill.

***

The newlyweds soon reached their first port: Lisbon, Portugal. In midmorning they left the ship and by the afternoon were touring the city. On their visit to the Lisbon Cathedral cloisters, they viewed the display of Phoenician artifacts, which dated back three thousand years.

"I wonder what life was like in those primitive times," Jocelyn whispered to Nathan as the tour guide droned on in Portuguese.

"Probably much better than today," Nathan whispered back.

"Oh, how is that?" Jocelyn looked curiously into Nathan's eyes.

"Well, in Phoenician days, the men ruled with an iron fist. The women were their slaves."

"I heard otherwise, that women had considerable freedom for the times... that there were even queens in ancient Phoenicia."

"So, that's what they taught in Paris? No wonder you are so progressive in your thinking."

"*Mais, je ne suis pas ton esclave?*"[108] Jocelyn gave Nathan a quick wink.

"*Non, en fais, j'étais ton esclave heir soir.*"[109]

"Yes, you were. And a good slave, too, I might add." Jocelyn showed a look of pleasure. Then in a voice and look dripping with seduction, she said, "And you shall be my slave again *ce soir.*"[110]

"The subjugation I must endure to be your husband."

Nathan was in awe not just of Jocelyn's beautiful face and hair, but also her form and figure. He caught himself wondering what his evenings would have been like with Regina. Would she have been as ravenous as Jocelyn? As uninhibited? He doubted it. He had only seen her damaged left arm and felt sorrow that he would never be able to worship her other scars, as he had promised he would. He felt guilty that his choice left him with perfection, when he had embraced Regina's soul and body, though damaged.

Will I never get over this guilt? he thought to himself. *God, please comfort her and let her know that I did what I thought was best for her.*

Yet, as he made that silent prayer, he wondered if it were true.

***

In late afternoon, Regina arrived at the orphanage on the south side of London. With a melancholy smile, she remembered Christmas Eve nearly a year ago, when she had visited the same orphanage with Nathan and her uncle and aunt, dispensing Christmas gifts to the children. She had made a promise that evening.

As Regina entered the orphanage, she looked at the vacant stares of young children, searching the building for one in particular. Not finding her, Regina anxiously walked down the hallway to the back of the structure. She opened the door and looked into the yard, but not a soul was present. Suddenly, fear seized her breast, and she wondered if the child had become ill or worse; sometimes

---

108 But, am I not your slave?
109 No, actually I was your slave last night.
110 tonight

things happened so quickly at orphanages... dreadful things.

Where was she? Regina had seen her just a fortnight before and there had been no indication of illness then.

I promised you, dear Marta. I promised you I would come back for you. I promised you a mother and a father—a family. Dear God, please...

Regina felt tears welling in her eyes. It had happened before. A child passing on before the adoption was completed.

She's not here! My Lord, they will be arriving any minute.

Regina walked to the front of the orphanage again, peering again into each room as she passed down the hallway. No sign of Marta anywhere. Her heart beating madly, she ran down the hallway to the backyard once more.

"Marta! Marta!" Regina shrieked in panic.

Suddenly a small face emerged from behind an oak tree in a corner of the yard--the face of a small girl with long dark braided hair. The young girl shouted with delight and came running toward her. Regina breathed a sigh of relief and rejoiced.

She lifted little Marta in her arms.

"Why are you crying?" Marta asked.

"Because I am so happy," Regina responded.

"Then you shouldn't be crying." Marta's small dirt-covered hands wiped the tears from Regina's face, leaving dirty smudges on her cheeks. Regina began to laugh and twirled Marta around and around, the laughter turning into an ecstatic chorus of two.

"I have a surprise for you," Regina said softly as the twirling slowed. In the corner of her eye, she saw a familiar man and woman approaching.

She placed a hand over Marta's eyes. "Don't peek.

"Marta, I have some very special people I want you to meet..."

***

Six months had passed since the celebrity marriage. Nathan sat at the edge of the park bench enjoying a late spring breeze in the early afternoon of a cloudy day. On random days, he would venture down familiar roads to the park that held bittersweet memories from a time long-since passed. Despite his growing love and devotion to Jocelyn, Nathan occasionally pondered the life he would have led, if he had married Regina instead.

The wind agitated the leaves and branches of the willow trees, which extended above the rippled-water. A mother and daughter picnicked on the grass nearby. A young couple held hands as they leisurely strolled along the border of the lake. Nathan felt a rush of wind caress his face and watched as nearby leaves took flight. He needed to get back to his office and complete the intricate detail of the Rochester mansion's exterior; they would begin clearing the site next week. But today, he took his time reflecting on the past. Nathan considered himself the luckiest man alive, married to a bewitching woman and busily engaged in projects that most architects could never imagine. Yet, there remained a melancholy sadness which occasionally disturbed his calm when his thoughts turned to Regina.

He sat idly for several minutes, listening to the sound of the wind. He heard footsteps and watched an elderly man pass by with a dog in tow. A few minutes later there were more footsteps and the sound of laughter from young children.

Everyone has a life to lead. I'm privy to a few seconds of those who pass by, glimpsing just a blink in their long journey of life. Do any of them truly know what future lies ahead? Nathan thought, as he reflected on his own tempestuous past.

He closed his eyes and listened to the medley of birds chirping, branches swaying, and children laughing. The sound of approaching footsteps added a percussive accompaniment to the symphony, while a gust of wind brought a sweet familiar fragrance. He felt the bench move ever so slightly and heard the creak of wood, informing Nathan that he was no longer seated alone. In an expression of politeness, he leaned to the right, opening his eyes.

He blinked wide in astonishment.

It was the last face he had expected to see.

"My *Needle Nate*. Sitting on the same bench." Regina offered a gentle smile, but her large brown eyes burrowed deep into Nathan's soul.

Nathan fumbled for something to say.

"Still at a loss for words, like so many years ago?"

Nathan nodded with half a smile. "Regina, what a lovely surprise. So nice to see you again."

"So you returned to our park. How long has it been?"

"I come here often. It's not far from my office."

"I know."

An awkward lull passed, as they both stared at the lake.

Regina's soft voice broke the silence, "When I heard the sound of bells, I couldn't believe it, at first."

Nathan looked down, feeling ashamed.

"I felt as though a part of me died that day. I wondered how I could go on."

Nathan lifted his eyes to meet Regina's stare. "When it mattered most, I failed you."

Regina closed her eyes, reliving the moment. "I couldn't understand how... after you had pledged your undying love... after you had asked for my hand in marriage..."

So many emotions flooded Nathan's mind as he struggled to find the words to say, wanting to bare his soul. Avoiding her eyes, he looked again at the lake as he began. "Jocelyn took the concoction just before we began our long march down the aisle. We were both nervous. The plan had seemed so simple before, but now it had to be executed--and flawlessly. I tightly held her arm, expecting her to lose consciousness with every step. As we approached the quire, I began to feel anxious; it should have happened by now. We continued toward the steps that led to the altar. Surely, now she would faint. We mounted the final steps. I saw panic in her face. The priest motioned for us to kneel. Jocelyn was in tears, powerless to act. She paused an eternity when the priest asked for her consent to marry. She looked at me helplessly; I turned away, unable to guide her. Finally, she uttered the only words she could. The priest turned to me and began repeating the same refrain. I prayed mightily that the elixir might finally produce the desired effect. There was still time. The crowd began to murmur. I lifted my knee from the altar, ready to forsake Jocelyn... ready to flee. I turned to her to say 'good-bye' and her lips released me... she told me to go..."

As Nathan looked back at Regina, he saw tears falling from her eyes.

"I was paralyzed. I couldn't move. In that instant, I knew she would suffer disgrace... humiliation... if I left her there alone..."

"What about me?" Regina interrupted in a pained voice. "Did you even think of me? Did I matter at all?"

Nathan stared intently into Regina's eyes. "Don't you understand? The Charlesworth revenge would have been relentless and would have followed us wherever we went, no matter where we sought refuge. You would have had to abandon your family. You would never have seen again all the dear children whose lives you saved. I couldn't do that to you..."

Regina touched the top of Nathan's right hand, sobbing as she absorbed the gravity of his predicament. He had spoken the words she needed to hear--Nathan *had* valued her. He had acted out of love for her, wishing to spare her a lifetime of grief and regret. Regina's fingers engulfed his hand and she lifted it to her lips. Speaking softly in her soothing voice, she asked, "Didn't you know that I would have forsaken everything for you?"

The depth of Regina's love pierced Nathan's heart and he bowed his head.

"Why didn't you write?" Regina asked, her voice effusing pain. "It would have eased my heartbreak."

"I tried to… but I couldn't find the words…"

Regina recalled her own feeble attempt to write, grateful her hurtful letter had never been sent.

"I saw you sitting here a few weeks ago, from afar, but I wasn't ready to come to you yet," Regina said. "I felt you had come here to honor me."

Nathan nodded.

"I have something for you." Regina reached into her purse and pulled out the silver locket necklace that had belonged to Nathan's mother. "This belongs to your …." She couldn't bring herself to say the word *wife*. "… to her."

Nathan accepted the necklace, struggling to maintain his composure.

"Neither you nor I can have any regrets, or we will cripple our future and those we love. I will always cherish our time together. You left me with a gift, Nathan. You allowed me to taste romantic love and accepted me despite my scars. If a man as fine as you can accept them, then surely shall another. I shall love again."

"I'm certain you will," Nathan responded kindly.

The clouds had darkened and the wind increased in force. Both felt the first light drop of rain.

"Are you happy, Nathan?"

"I am," Nathan said without reservation. "Jocelyn has been a very loving and attentive wife. And you, Regina?"

Regina smiled. "My work has been my tonic. I am at peace."

"I'm pleased."

More sprinkles of rain fell.

"We first met in this park many years ago," Regina spoke wistfully. "It is only fitting that *here* we should bid farewell."

Regina stood up and Nathan followed her lead, only inches separating them. The rain began to drizzle. In an impulse, Nathan reached out and embraced Regina and felt her arms enfold him. They clung together, neither wanting to let go.

Regina raised her lips to Nathan's ear and whispered. "I forgive you."

Those were words that Nathan yearned for, but had never expected to hear. Choked with emotion, he whispered back, "God bless you, my love."

Nathan felt Regina's arms release him and both looked away, neither wishing their last remembrance to be one of sorrow.

Regina turned in the light rain and began walking down the path.

As he followed her graceful carriage, Nathan felt a pang of renewed regret and heartbreak at having lost a woman of such inestimable virtue, and wondered if he could have ever been worthy of a lifetime of Regina's love.

Before disappearing from view, Regina turned back for a final glimpse of Nathan. She sent him a pleasant smile. Nathan nodded and smiled back.

Regina turned the corner and disappeared as the rain began to fall with intensity.

A sweet peace descended upon Nathan following the reunion in the park. The guilt that he had been carrying began to recede. Nathan began to slowly unfold the layers of his heart to his bride, and she reciprocated in kind. As the days turned into weeks and the weeks into months, no longer did Nathan second-guess his decision at the altar; no longer did he punish himself by wondering how Regina was coping and if she would ever forgive him.

***

After an evening of passion and pleasure, Jocelyn lay intertwined in her husband's arms, as the morning's sun filtered through their bedroom window.

"Did you ever wonder how it was that we took possession of the Steinway pianoforte shortly before my nineteenth birthday?" Jocelyn inquired dreamily. To their mutual delight, Lord Charlesworth had transported the grand instrument to their sitting room months before, while they were on their honeymoon.

"Well, it isn't surprising, with your love of music. Of course, a piano is the ultimate musical instrument of all creation, as I am sure you will agree."

Jocelyn looked into Nathan's eyes. "On par with the violin perhaps."

"But a pianoforte provides the ability, *through strings*, to play many notes simultaneously and produce sounds with such versatility and range," Nathan raised his eyebrow, believing he had swiftly brought the debate to a close.

The look on Jocelyn's face showed that she was not about to concede, and she responded in a mischievous tone. "You told me yourself, when you first heard me play, that you believed you were hearing *la voix des anges*.[111] Has your music ever been compared to that?"

"You have me there, my love," Nathan kissed Jocelyn's cheek. "So what inspired you to persuade your father to purchase the magnificent Steinway?" Nathan was, indeed, curious.

Jocelyn paused, suddenly hesitating if she should reveal the truth.

"I did it for you."

Nathan sat up in bed and looked at Jocelyn. "Truly?"

"I am surprised you didn't know that. I needed to entice you to participate in my *proposition*. Without the Steinway, you may never have accepted."

"But with your vast legion of male admirers, why did you select such a humble candidate as I to participate in your *proposition*?"

"I told you before, I conducted my own inquiries," Jocelyn laughed. "And that Chopin ballade; I will never forget it. You must play it for me again, now that we are married."

"So, you did truly purchase the Steinway for me?" Nathan still wasn't convinced.

"I swear on the life of our first child…" Jocelyn offered with a solemn look, "who incidentally will be a girl… but with *my* hair, not yours."

"And a good thing, too. But, how do you know our firstborn will not be a son?"

"We women know these things."

"You are not telling me…"

"When the time is right," she answered. Jocelyn wasn't sure yet, but she *was* several days late. She couldn't wait to see his reaction, when there was no longer any doubt.

"So, shall she be a pianist or violinist?"

"*Les deux, peut-être*,"[112] Jocelyn responded with a shrug of her shoulders.

"You didn't believe your beauty and charm were enough to entice me?"

"I had to be sure."

"Did you ever wonder whether I would come?"

"My spies assured me you were on your way."

---

111   the voice of angels
112   Maybe both.

Nathan had a mock look of fright at the invasion of his privacy.

Jocelyn laughed. "If you hadn't come then, I would have forced my way upon you at some other gathering, where I *knew* you would be in attendance."

The comment gave Nathan a pleasant feeling inside which produced a confident smile.

"But, don't become too sure of yourself," Jocelyn chided her husband. "If you *ever* take me for granted…"

"And… was your *proposition* merely to keep your suitors at bay, or did you have a more *calculated* design?" Nathan had never before asked the question, but had always wanted to know.

Jocelyn looked at Nathan with a sly smile. "If I tell you my dream was always to marry you, you shall see me as a designing woman and instantly leave me. Or, if I tell you that our marriage was an accident, then you will always question my love for you."

"Most assuredly," Nathan responded with one eyebrow lowered. "Thus, you must reveal your deepest thoughts to your husband, so he may decide what to do with you."

Jocelyn turned away from Nathan and rose from the bed. Nathan playfully reached to stop her, but it was too late. Standing, Jocelyn looked down at her husband. "My lips are forever sealed. You must form your own conclusion. Someday, you will surely know, but not from my lips."

Nathan wasn't prepared to let the topic drop yet. "Just a small clue, my love."

"Oh, I have left ample clues already. Surely, you need no more."

With that, Jocelyn left the room.

Nathan reflected on their time together and felt warm inside. His knew his life with Jocelyn would always be something of a mystery.

***

Mr. Travers stood at the window of his office and looked outside. It was raining heavily and he promised himself that for his 80th birthday he would take a cruise to the Mediterranean and enjoy the sun that seemed so rarely to shine in London. During the last couple of years, he visited the office just twice a week, but never stayed for more than a few hours. Most of his days were spent at his country estate, just two hours' train ride from his London apartment. It rained there too, but the air was much fresher and the scenery sublime.

The pitter-patter of rain seemed an old familiar friend, a sound he had often heard inside his office for more than fifty years. He glanced at the mahogany clock on the wall. It was ten minutes to eleven. He was anxious to meet his eleven o'clock guest. Occasionally lawyers actually contributed to the public good and today was one of those occasions.

From all accounts, she was a remarkable woman. After all, she had helped the London aristocracy develop a conscience. He looked at the clock again and watched the minute hand's barely perceptible movement upward. Just five more minutes. His clients' generosity had motivated him to contribute as well, a far better use of the inheritance that would otherwise rain upon his indolent descendants when his time came.

The soft chime announced the new hour, soon followed by a knock on the door; Mr. Travers' secretary indicated his guest had arrived.

Seconds later, a dark-haired woman entered, wearing a nondescript black coat, partially soaked in rain.

"Randolph Travers, at your service."

The young lady extended her hand. "Miss Regina Lancaster."

"Please be seated," Mr. Travers gave his warmest smile.

He returned to his chair. The wind caused the rain to pelt against the window pane. "I have been looking forward to making your acquaintance ever since meeting with my clients last week."

Regina smiled back. "I responded to your letter, sir, but I have no idea why I have been summoned."

"Your work has gained the attention of the English gentry. No small task, I might add. It seems to have inspired some of them to lend support to your work with orphans."

Regina was delighted to hear the news. There had been several recent articles in the *Times* about the plight of London orphans and the "Good Samaritan" who had helped place hundreds of such children in homes during the past several years. Regina had been interviewed in a recent post, sharing her dream of establishing an orphanage devoted to the loving care of homeless children--one that that might serve as model for others. Since the article had appeared, she had received nearly a thousand pounds in donations, but was still far short of her goal. When Mr. Travers' letter had arrived, she had hoped it might pertain to her work; she was so pleased to hear her hopes confirmed.

Mr. Travers studied the woman seated across from him. She couldn't yet be thirty, he thought. When he had learned of her story and accomplishments, he had been astonished. She had a gentle face, but her intense dark eyes conveyed a noble purpose and a maturity far beyond her earthly years.

"What is your goal, Miss Lancaster? For the building you wish to erect?"

Regina smiled shyly. "It is quite ambitious, sir. I have received estimates that it may cost as much as forty thousand pounds."

"That is a lofty goal, indeed. How much have you received thus far, if I may inquire?" Mr. Travers leaned forward.

"I have yet so very far to go. Not quite a thousand pounds, but I'm pleased to say that many have contributed. Even if it takes another ten or twenty years, I will never rest until it is done."

Mr. Travers took a deep breath, admiring her dedication. "Well, I am delighted to be the intermediary in providing you with some additional financial assistance." Mr. Travers opened the desk drawer to his right and took out an envelope. "The check has been drawn on my firm's trust account, inasmuch as the donors wish to remain anonymous."

Mr. Travers held the envelope in his hand for an instant, savoring in advance, the reaction that its contents would soon have on the recipient. He then extended it across the desk to Regina.

"Thank you, sir."

Regina opened her purse to place the envelope inside.

"Go ahead. Open it," Mr. Travers wanted to be a witness to the moment.

Regina nodded politely and opened the sealed envelope, removing the check. Her mouth opened wide in astonishment and she stared at Mr. Travers, speechless.

"Will that do?" Mr. Travers asked modestly.

Regina's joy knew no bounds. She couldn't believe the amount. *Fifty thousand pounds!*

"Mr. Travers ... I don't know what to say ... I can't believe this ..." Tears filled her eyes. "You have no idea what this means. We can begin immediately."

"My clients are glad to be of service."

"Please tell me who they are, that I might personally thank them. The edifice must be dedicated in their names."

Though he was mightily tempted to divulge their identity, Mr. Travers was duty-bound to honor a client's confidence. "It would give me great pleasure to inform you of their identity, but I must abide by their wishes to remain anonymous."

Two weeks earlier, he had finally met the client who had retained his services some six years before. He had long since given up hope of ever meeting her, after his disappointment in delivering the confidential Sinclair file. But soon after, he had been delighted to read in the London newspapers of her romance and eventual marriage to the man he had investigated. What an extraordinary beauty and charming woman! And what an extraordinarily lucky man Lord Sinclair was to be married to her. During their meeting, Lady Sinclair had filled in many details, telling him the story of the "other woman"—a story the London tabloids knew nothing about. Was it from feelings of guilt, or from a desire to contribute to such a worthy cause, that the bequest had been made? he wondered. It must have been the latter, since Lady Sinclair's happiness in life and marriage shone so brightly in her face. Lady Sinclair would never know that he had *added* a matching amount to her donation. It would have been nice to have seen the *Travers-Sinclair* names engraved above the entrance, but if anonymity suited Lady Sinclair, then it would certainly suit him as well.

Regina Lancaster refused to let go of Mr. Travers' hand as she stood by the door, ready to depart. "This must be a dream. I am so happy."

"I think we are all entitled, sometime during our life, to see our dreams fulfilled," Mr. Travers spoke. "Good luck to you. May God hasten your work."

Mr. Travers returned to his desk with a warm feeling inside. Though he was a lawyer, maybe, just maybe, his contribution would serve him well in the world to come. Hopefully, the rain was less frequent there.

***

A young girl, with golden hair, looked at the newly-erected puppet stage, brimming with excitement. She couldn't wait for the opening scene. Her younger brother sat quietly at her side, with no expectation of what his eyes and ears would soon behold.

The curtain was pulled up by the unseen hand of the children's mother. The backdrop for Act I was a painted forest full of trees. The children's father held the control rod from which the strings descended, manipulating the marionette of a young girl, also with golden hair.

"Is that me, Mummy?" the girl cried with joy.

"Sh-sh-sh," came a gentle scolding from behind the stage.

Act I concluded and Act II's backdrop displayed the interior of a cabin in the woods. The two children squealed with delight, as they watched the story unfold. First a baby bear appeared, then a mother bear and finally a daddy bear. The finale featured the three bears and the girl, Golden Hair, dancing together on the stage accompanied by the singing of the concealed parents.

Later that night, mother and father played a duet on the violin and piano, a lullaby to their children before bedtime, performed in the light of the hearth's fire. It was the same melody the father had first heard years before, when he had discovered his wife's exceptional talent.

***

Their mutual compatibility was never more evident than in their love of music, and Nathan was amazed by Jocelyn's depth of knowledge and understanding of composers and compositions, which in many respects surpassed his own. In Nathan, Jocelyn came to know a man of exceptional talent, modesty, ambition, gentility, devotion and integrity—to her a *'forever gentleman'* in every way. In Jocelyn, Nathan came to discover a woman of many shades and hues: unpredictable, witty, impossible, spontaneous, demanding, affectionate, temperamental, generous, beguiling, adventurous, and *always* the most of beautiful of women.

When they had married, neither knew for sure what their marriage would become, but both put their hearts and soul into it.

As the years passed and children blessed their lives, both knew what their marriage *had become* and they rejoiced.

Le Fin

Author's Note

The opening musical composition in my novel is Chopin's Quatrième Ballade. It is one of my favorite pieces from the piano repertoire, a feeling shared by the late John Ogden, a consummate pianist, who gave it high praise: "[It is] the most exalted, intense and sublimely powerful of all Chopin's compositions... It is unbelievable that it lasts only twelve minutes, for it contains the experience of a lifetime." While many of the compositions referenced in the book are well known, sadly, other beautiful works have all but disappeared from the concert stage. It would give me great pleasure if *Forever Gentleman* inspires readers to search and discover some of these abandoned compositions.

As the story began taking form, I searched for the ideal time period to cast the characters and events. I ultimately settled on 1869–70, because I wanted Nathan to first discover Jocelyn's sublime musical talent by hearing the Tchaikovsky composition *"Nur wer die Sehnsucht kennt."* It needed to be music he had not yet heard, but one to which Jocelyn could have gained access. The song premiered in Moscow in 1870 by Russian mezzo-soprano Yelizaveta Lavrovskaya, but was first published as one of six *Romances* in 1869 by P. Jurgensen, a relatively obscure Russian publisher. As you will see, the selection of these years proved fortuitous, as it affected other important events in the story.

Much research goes into historical novels, as an author attempts to provide a realistic backdrop for the drama unfolding. Mine was no exception, as I endeavored to portray London as it was from June of 1869 to December 1870. My objective was to immerse the reader in the actual sights, smells, and sounds of Victorian London, including authentic references to concerts, plays, and other venues referred to in the book. In this regard, I am deeply indebted to *The Athenæum, Journal of Literature, Science, The Fine Arts, Music and The Drama*, which was published on a weekly basis back in 1870, and *The Musical Word: a Weekly Record of Musical Science, Literature and Intelligence*, also published weekly, considered by many the preeminent nineteenth-century journal on British music. Both publications were invaluable in providing the actual performed plays, concerts, concert programs, names of performers, venues, and even critic reviews. By way of illustration, when Regina and Nathan attend *Il Barbiere* at the Drury Lane Theatre in Westminster (Chapter 28), it is on the precise date (Tuesday, April 19, 1870) that the performance actually took place, with mezzo-soprano Madame Monbelli in the lead role. Later Jocelyn and Nathan attend the final performance of the fifty-eighth season of the Philharmonic Society at St. James Hall on Piccadilly Street (Chapter 45). This performance actually took place on July 11, 1870, consistent with the story's chronology. As noted in the story, Charles Hallé had just completed an exhausting Beethoven series of concerts spanning many evenings and was replaced by Madame Goddard. The program recited at the beginning of that chapter is one actually performed that day—a significantly longer concert (estimated at nearly four hours) than what is customary today. The actual review of the performance from *The Athenæum* several days later is also excerpted in the story.

One delightful coincidence occurred with respect to the Schumann piano concerto, which Nathan performs for Jocelyn in Chapter 46, not realizing that she has arranged for a surprise orchestral accompaniment with the Philharmonic Society. In an early draft, I had chosen Schumann's concerto because of its seamless beauty and lower level of technical difficulty, so that Nathan would not require as much advance preparation to perform it. For that sequence to make logical sense, it needed to be a composition recently performed by the orchestra, so that they could polish it up rather quickly for the impromptu performance. With the discovery of the above-referenced journals, I became committed to historical accuracy and began poring through the publications, expecting to have to substitute Schumann's concerto with another that had been recently performed. You may imagine my shock when I discovered that the Philharmonic Society had, in fact, performed the Schumann piano concerto on May 9, 1870, just two months before Nathan's private rendition at the Charlesworth estate (*The Athenæum*, May 14, 1870, p. 653). Consequently, no substitution was necessary.

The same realism was achieved with the plays referenced in the book. Nathan and Jocelyn attend the play *The Two Roses* at the Vaudeville theatre (Chapter 50), with Henry Irving in the lead role (an up-and-coming actor and later to become perhaps the most popular of British actors of his day). The play was performed shortly after the Vaudeville opened on April 16, 1870, and was so popular that it ran the rest of the year and into 1871, playing for three hundred nights. Happily, I was able to locate a script, which enabled me to briefly weave the play's plot into the story. Later, when Jocelyn wishes to give an audition in disguise to test her acting skill, I learned that H.J. Byron's *The Lancashire Lass* was holding auditions during the summer of 1870. With so many nineteenth-century plays having disappeared from modern society, I had little hope of finding a copy of the actual script. Providence smiled again and an extant publication of the play was located, in order to demonstrate Jocelyn's superb acting ability in Chapter 52.

Verrey's on Regent Street, where Nathan takes Regina and her aunt to dine (in Chapter 14) was considered one of the finest restaurants in London (serving French cuisine, of course), one of the few deserving of the aristocracy. École Spéciale of Lausanne, where Nathan received his education in architecture, was considered one of the top European universities for technical education during the latter part of the nineteenth century. It exists today, much larger than in Nathan's day, and the name has been changed to L'École Polytechnique Fédérale de Lausanne.

The piano that Nathan sees from afar the evening of Jocelyn's birthday on May 25, 1870 (Chapter 32), is the same piano that Steinway & Sons showcased at the International Exposition of 1867 in Paris, winning three medals, including the gold medal, prevailing over Chickering and Sons. It made the story more compelling that Jocelyn had a revolutionary new piano that any pianist of the era would have coveted playing.

The visit to Kensington Gardens depicted in Chapter 26 is another excursion that is intended to describe the gardens as they were a century and a half ago. Similarly, Nathan's and Regina's visit to the South Kensington Museum depicts the museum as it was in 1870, along with the paintings and sculptures that were present at that time.

Street vendors were a big part of Victorian London's commerce. The convenience, low cost, and generally fresh quality of street vendor food allowed even the lower class to be "regular customers." Young street sweepers also thrived during this era because of the frequent mire and filth that covered the streets.

The Asylum for Fatherless Children, affectionately known as the "House on the Hill," was one of the better-run orphanages in London. The book describes its true appearance and history in Chapter 20. Orphans were a blight on the city of London, with many thousands housed often in poor and dirty conditions (as also noted in Chapter 20, a typhoid epidemic caused the death of many orphans at the London Orphan Asylum a couple of years before), and many more thousands of homeless children lived on the streets.

Another important resource I used was Claude Booth's Descriptive Map of London Property 1889, which graphically portrays, by color, the London streets according to their economic status, from the lowest class to the upper class. In addition, I had access to Edward Weller's Map of London 1868. These maps were instrumental in identifying the economic status of boroughs and in helping to navigate Nathan through London streets.

In 1858, the year of the "Great Stink" in London, Parliament passed an act, at enormous expense, to completely revolutionize London's sewer system. This was a massive undertaking, which as noted in Chapter V involved eighty-two miles of brick intercepting sewers built beneath London's streets, all flowing by gravity eastward. The intercepting sewers were then connected to over 450 miles of main sewers, themselves receiving the contents of 13,000 miles of small local sewers, dealing daily with half a million gallons of waste. Chief Engineer William Bazalgette was in charge of the project, which took more than ten years to complete. By the time of the events in the story, much of the work had been completed, but as noted in the story, Londoners had to suffer through enormous inconvenience and discomfort as construction work often blocked other sewer outlets, creating cesspools of filth. In the end, it was all worth the long wait and disruption to life, as not only did the sewage epidemic get contained, but cholera and other dread diseases were virtually eliminated.

Coldbath Fields was a vast prison complex (which Nathan experiences ever so briefly in Chapters 15-17), as depicted in the book. During its early years, the prison developed a reputation for severity and horrendous living circumstances. Rhapsodized by the great English poet, Shelley described the horrors of Coldbath Fields in *The Devil's Walk*, where he claimed the conditions exceeded hell itself:

> *As he went through Coldbath Fields he saw*
> *A solitary cell;*
> *And the Devil was pleased, for it gave him a hint*
> *For improving his prisons in hell.*

Providence, it seems, also smiled on Nathan's imprisonment, providing an early escape from indefinite incarceration at Coldbath Fields. Readers may assume that I picked the week, month, and year of his incarceration in order to keep his time there at a minimum. In reality, that was not the case. I was vaguely aware that imprisonment of debtors in England had ended long ago (although I thought it was some years later), and my research of it was to merely ensure that imprisonment of debtors was still legal in 1869. No sooner had Nathan been imprisoned in an early draft of the story (during the first week of August 1869), than I was literally forced to free him (or else change the chronology of the entire plot), after obtaining a copy of the Debtors Act of 1869. There were undoubtedly a handful of other "lucky" debtors who reaped the same fortuitous benefit as Nathan from the passage of the Act on August 9, 1869. The language of the Debtors Act is quoted verbatim in the story, including the rather bizarre proviso that imprisonment for fraudulent debtors was restricted to debts of fifty pounds or less.

I am also deeply indebted to *The Victorian Web*, an internet website of particular value, and a resource I highly recommend to anyone wishing to gain further insight into life during the Victorian era. Another source provided Jocelyn's description of a violin in Chapter 84: "The bridge position of the violin, where the string vibrations coalesce into sound, is patterned after the human bodylocated in the same proportion in the violin as the navel is to the human form." It was so beautifully worded that I brought the excerpt intact into the story.[113]

While writing this book, I immersed myself in books written by contemporary authors of the day, including Charles Dickens, Jane Austen, Wilkie Collins, the Brontë sisters, Elizabeth Gaskell, and others, hoping to develop a voice and tone that would not be too distant from those celebrated writers. While I make no pretense to even scratch the surface of their genius, I hope the language and detail will cause the reader to hearken back to the Victorian era.

Writing this book has been a love affair for me, intersecting my passions for music, architecture, and the French language. In this day of Internet access, I encourage readers to listen to the music identified in various scenes throughout the book, especially if it is unfamiliar to them, because I believe the music will enhance the story in the same way a soundtrack does a movie. In the electronic version, we hope to provide aids for the reader to easily do precisely that.

---

113   See www.krutzstrings.com/the-divinity-of-the-violin/; *Huntley, H.E., The Divine Proportion: A Study in Mathematical Beauty*; Pedoe, Dan, *Geometry and the Visual Arts*.

OTHER ANAPHORA LITERARY PRESS TITLES

Film Theory and Modern Art
Editor: Anna Faktorovich

Interview with Larry Niven
Editor: Anna Faktorovich

Dragonflies in the Cowburbs
Donelle Dreese

Domestic Subversive
Roberta Salper

Radical Agrarian Economics
Anna Faktorovich

Fajitas and Beer Convention
Roger Rodriguez

Spirit of Tabasco
Richard Diedrichs

Skating in Concord
Jean LeBlanc

CPSIA information can be obtained
at www.ICGtesting.com
Printed in the USA
FSOW01n0529060716
22315FS